Στον !
με την αγάπη τα

HAUNTING VOICES

VIVIAN AVRAAMIDOU PLOUMBIS

HAUNTING VOICES

The Mediterranean Jewel Speaks

PALMETTO
PUBLISHING
Charleston, SC
www.PalmettoPublishing.com

Copyright © 2024 by Vivian Avraamidou Ploumbis

All rights reserved.

No portion of this book may be reproduced, stored in a retrieval system, or transmitted in any form by any means–electronic, mechanical, photocopy, recording, or other–except for brief quotations in printed reviews, without prior permission of the author.
For rights and permissions send written requests to vivavrp@gmail.com.

Paperback ISBN: 979-8-8229-4079-6

Front cover photo by Alexis Hadjisoteriou, used with permission.
Originally titled *Shame*. This English edition edited by Rodney Richards was translated from the Greek by Achilleas Antoniades

Disclaimer
All other images owned or licensed by the author, in the public domain, or used with permission. Sentiments expressed remain those of the author, including opinions. Details and remembrances are to the best of the author's or other recollections.

Table of Contents

Preface ix
Introduction by the translator xi
Acknowledgments xiv

1. Where They Nestle 1
2. Forty-five Years of Dust 3
3. The Turkish Coffee 5
4. A Note to a Friend 7
5. The Savior 9
6. Mister Savvas 11
7. On Dimokratias Street 13
8. Birthday Gift 15
9. Flouris's Shish Kebab Stand 17
10. Those Unsuspecting Wild Cats 19
11. Shame 21
12. To a New Life 23
13. Events of July 1974 25
14. No Sound 27
15. I Saw It in the Coffee Cup 29
16. Rape 31
17. The First Up Front 33
18. Thus Spoke... 35
19. Edelweiss 37

20. The Yiangoudi · 39
21. Old Man Arestis' Bakery · 41
22. Welcome · 43
23. All About the Name · 45
24. Mujde or Pelin? · 47
25. A Pack of Cigarettes · 49
26. Parades · 51
27. Visitors · 53
28. Mr. Oulis · 55
29. At the stop for Varosha · 57
30. The Groom's Suit · 59
31. At Hadjihambis Cinema · 61
32. Number 23 · 63
33. The Name of Our Street · 65
34. The Trap · 67
35. The Letter · 70
36. Behind the Doors · 72
37. The Slippers · 74
38. Who Knows About Such Things · · · · · · · · · · · · · · · 76
39. Smoke and Bad Smells · 78
40. Eros · 80
41. The Crane · 82
42. Rust · 84
43. The Waste · 86
44. Fairytales · 88
45. Lentils · 90
46. How Can You? · 92
47. Messed up · 94
48. Barclays · 96
49. The Photo · 98
50. Directions · 100
51. Mr. Socrates · 102
52. My Beloved Evangelia · 104

53. The Perfume Bearing Ladies Showered Your Tomb ······ 107
54. Christina from Myloneika ································ 109
55. Fiddler on the Roof ·· 111
56. Under the Light of the Late Afternoon ················ 113
57. The Cats of Varosha ·· 115
58. The Sour Man ·· 117
59. The Night the Trees Fell ······································ 119
60. The Light at the Front Door ································ 121
61. Stringed Moments ·· 123
62. The Blindness of People ······································ 125
63. For a Peach Juice ·· 127
64. At Famagusta Lyceum for Greek Female Students ········ 129
65. About the Future ·· 131
66. We Have Already Burned Ourselves ···················· 133
67. The Palm Trees ·· 137
68. Parking Rights ·· 139
69. Interpreting Dreams ··· 141
70. Melody in Three-and-a-half Measures ················ 143
71. Knits ·· 145
72. Va, Pensiero ··· 147
73. Holidays Betrayed ·· 150
Appendix A Brief History ·· 153

About the Author ··· 159

Preface

Varosha.

Ammohostos is the official name. Ammohostos in Greek, meaning a place buried in the sand.

Varosha, my birth town. The city with the most beautiful sandy beaches on the island. First to welcome the rise of the sun, by the ancient town of Salamis, which was erected by the distinguished hero of Trojan war, Tefcros (Teucer).

Varosha. The Turkish invaders in 1974 stripped the beautiful city, raped her, put a crown of thorns around her and left her chained up, so that no human eye could see her. Forty-nine years wizened. Kissless and hugless. Only in October 2020 did the occupying Turkish army lay a thin layer of asphalt on two central streets of the city, like a black carpet, a shroud. With red ribbons, it strictly defined our steps, the steps of a false return.

We, its ex-residents, routed and scattered.

During the days of the invasion, we were forced to leave with only a blanket and a pail of water. Upon return, we could only cross two streets. We crossed them again and again among the carcasses of our houses, desperately in search of some fragment of our youth.

Friends' pictures uploaded on the internet reveal the theft of the lustiness for life the city had suffered. It was precisely these images that awakened emotions, some sweet, others of unbearable pain.

My tears fill these pages with words and sounds of silent cries.

I wrote this collection of short stories between October 2020 and March 2022 under the title "Shame".

Shame on the merciless Turkish occupation of Cyprus.

Shame on the unpunished treason that preceded it.

Shame on the unresolved problem, solutions which for so many years we have repeatedly rejected.

Shame our country continues to be split in two, leaving the northern half of the island under foreign occupation and open wounds to fester.

Shame.
Prague, 2023

Introduction by the translator

I first visited Famagusta (Varosha) as a young boy on a school day trip. The impressive St. Nicholas Cathedral and the famous Othello Tower remain ingrained in my memory.

I visited again in May 1974, two months before the Turkish invasion and capture of the city. With my then wife and her parents, we stayed at the Constantia Hotel and enjoyed the golden sandy beach.

It is now a derelict structure.

At some point, we visited the old city within the walls. The city was under absolute Turkish control. At the gated arch, we stopped. Should I go with them or not? The recent murder of two Greek officers who had ventured into the city was still too fresh. At the urging of my wife, I did not go.

They did. The disappointment still sits in my throat.

The city within the walls was off limits to Greek Cypriots since the capture of Famagusta from the Venetians in 1571. The Greeks who were displaced established a new city called Varosi or Varosha, a Turkish word for suburb, taking advantage of its extensive golden sandy beaches. After the Republic was established, it became a renowned tourist resort in the Eastern Mediterranean.

When I read Vivian's stories, emotion overwhelmed me. The injustice of a captured gem of a city lying in ruins for almost fifty years raised my anger and my determination to do something about it. By independent accounts, the city was not in the strategic objectives of Turkey.

In the wake of the Turkish forces' advancement, its inhabitants fled to save their lives, many with the shirt on their backs, expecting to return soon. The international Community, recognizing this as a matter of justice, passed mandatory resolutions at the United Nations Security Council demanding that the city not be settled by anyone other than its lawful inhabitants.

Yet it has remained since that time under Turkish military authority and is cordoned off as a military zone. No settlement was allowed by the Turkish military.

Recently, Turkey's increasingly authoritarian leadership began demanding the recognition of a separate state in the area of the Republic of Cyprus it has occupied since 1974. This is expected to include the occupied part of Famagusta, Varosha. Using salami tactics, recently it allowed some settlement and commercial activities in the area still under its military authority. More is expected to follow.

Turkish soldiers are not the lawful inhabitants of Varosha.

Vivian's book is an emotional book. I praise it for expressing emotion to support a just cause.

I recently watched the Greek tragedy "Trojan Women" by Euripides. I left the theater better educated about the effects of war. For me, the central message of the play is: "In war there is no real winner. Both losers (mostly) and winners have lots to wail about."

Vivian and all Greek Cypriots have wailed fruitlessly for fifty years. Like another refugee Trojan woman, Vivian does it with sensitivity, dignity, justified anger and bitter disappointment. All who read her book, I am sure, will share her outrage at the continuing injustice.

Shame is the title of the book in Greek. Shame is what all of us should feel for not doing our part to ensure our leaders and the international community apportion justice to Varosha and Famagusta. It is the law. It should be respected. Greedy pillaging and crass blackmailing for political gain should not be allowed.

I consider it my privilege to translate this book so people in the English-speaking world can enjoy Vivian's unique voice and become more aware of this just cause.

Achilleas Antoniades
Summer, 2023

Acknowledgments

Thank you, Chloe Akrithakis, Andreas Anastasiou, Pavlos Attalidis, Andri Epifaniou, Pavlos Iakovou, Eirini Klokkari, Costas Konstantis, Dimitris Ploumpis, Konstantinos Stavris, Avghi Frangopoulou, Alexis Hadzisoteriou, and Katia Christodoulou.
    Thank you all.
    In your pictures I found a warm place to perch my memories, the space to comfort my soul.
    Special acknowledgement and thanks from deep in my heart to Achilleas, a dear, dear friend who believed in my work and devoted all his experience together with a passion to translate these short stories and the George Seferis poem from Greek to English. I cannot possibly thank him enough.
    Special thanks also to dear Rodney for his amazingly thorough care and editing of the text. Without his efforts, this book would not possibly meet the high standards necessary for the requirements of thoughtful readers.

The Voices

1. Where They Nestle

She approached Dimokratias Street and threw a last glance behind her. She had forgotten the door half-open.

She shrugged.

She thought of yiayia[1] Theodora; only yiayia would have the freedom to go in and out as she pleased. Until, of course, the new ones came. She wouldn't have the heart to walk among her own things anymore.

She thought of yiayia more than anyone. Where would she find comfort now?

Those alive get used to changes. They may even forget the hurts and laughs, bumps and hurdles, beginnings, in-betweens, and endings.

Others are like cats. They like the place they are used to, places where they first kissed and were kissed, where they heard the first cries of their child, the smells absorbed by the walls of their kitchen, hushed conversations hovering behind closed bedroom doors, good words or bitter ones. All dance in our heads like nightmares because we miss it so terribly much.

That's where they nestle. Together with laughter around Sunday's dinner table, the heartbeats from life's wrong turns, the stressful thoughts, and the honey-sweet taste of success. Beside the jasmine plant

---

1 Yiayia literally means grandmother. In Greek, however, it is very common to address close old women or old ladies as yiayia.

that grew and grew to engulf the entire house and drove the neighborhood wild with its aroma.
    How desolate they look
        houses
            homes
                empty of souls.....

2. Forty-five Years of Dust

She sat cross-legged in the kitchen of their apartment in Pagrati. A cigarette burned between her fingers.

Once in a while, she extended her hand over the ashtray in front of her and tapped without looking where ashes would fall. Nor did she care. Her gaze turned to the stove pot where carrots, celery and potatoes were boiling to make a soup.

Her thoughts were traveling again, somewhere far away.

Turbulent seas and endless uncultivated fields with the color of yellow daisies and crimson poppies flowed underneath. Lines of heavy, rusted barbed wire, barrels and bags filled with sand, prickly pear trees sprung up next to dilapidated houses. And over rivers, dry, mostly dried out like her own eyes.

She found herself in another kitchen over a different pot, where she had left her fig jam boiling. She had just poured in half a small glass of ouzo, her big secret. This was the fig jam the whole of Varosha talked about.

Did I turn off the stove? She wondered. She could not remember. When her husband was pulling her by the sleeve to leave, when the bombers were above their heads screaming, did she turn off the stove? She could not remember.

When city sirens started howling repeatedly, when the entire neighborhood was running to start their cars and get away, did she turn the stove off?

The vegetables boiled slowly in the pot and from time to time she turned to Tasoula sitting beside her, bent over the knit sweater she was working on, and repeated with a sigh the same phrase.

"That's how it goes, Tasoula dear...."

If ashes from her cigarette fell to the floor... it didn't matter.'

3. The Turkish Coffee

To Yiayia Theodora

"Because she lets me dip my biscuit in her coffee," you used to say when asked why you loved yiayia Theodora so much.

Yes, because of this. And more because your little head fit exactly in the hollow between her shoulder and her breast. The fake breast. A little cushion. The one you saw her stick under her bra one morning, that made you rush and hide behind the big walnut cupboard lest she see you. To avoid putting her in a difficult position, and yourself try explaining the unexplainable in your mind.

They didn't give you her imperial name, but she was your own beloved yiayia. Even though she used to hide bananas on the highest shelf of the cupboard. Even though she told you to get off for smudging her clean clothes drying on the line on the roof of your house.

She left this world early. From another cause. As if God was angry with her for beating the terrible disease.

And you hated the door of her house, which allowed her to leave. You hated the kitchen, which insisted on existing without the scents of her smelly pots. You hated the big walnut cupboard; you couldn't hide behind it anymore.

And now, having reached her age, when you look at yourself in the mirror, she is there, in your eyes. Reflected in your eyes, staring. And every time you dip a biscuit in your coffee, it is still the coffee that belongs to her.

And you gain courage.

And continue to live.

4. A Note to a Friend

You used to talk to me about Tashkent in that peculiar Greek of yours.

Occasionally, your speech seemed funny to me, the way you pronounced words, but they were perfectly correct. I had to admit, your language, if you will, was richer than our Greek Cypriot dialect.

Yes. The way you said things in that thin, thin little voice of yours. It suited so well your delicate features, and your pure blue eyes, pure blue and deep. Different.

You looked like a child in everything, except your gaze.

Deep. So deep an entire world fit inside it, a harsh world totally unknown to me. A world you kept stubbornly to yourself, as if you were afraid that wasting it here and there will leave you an orphan.

It is possible to become an orphan of your homeland.

It can happen. I know.

How exotic your city seemed! And those words of yours that filled my mind with successive images, one springing up incessantly from inside the other. If I put them to color, I would paint your bustling city pure white. If I dressed it in music, it would be Stravinsky's "The Rite of Spring."

I used to talk to you about my city.

During the five months we shared that desk in the Pagrati Gymnasium, before we went our own ways, I managed to tell you about the tiny white lilies that grew in the golden sand of our own sea. I spoke to you about the magenta colors of sunrise and about our aromatic jasmine.

After all, aren't these what a city is all about?

We lost each other, Eleni. But, from time to time, you know, some evenings, some difficult ones, I turn my mind back to those years.

I wonder if the "chosen one," the celestial virgin, managed, with her dance, to appease your own gods of Spring.

5. The Savior

In my bathing suit and a white t-shirt, in the middle of the day, I sat on the deserted beach and read *Ariagni*, by Tsirka.

I remember it because I was making parallels with the *Scorch of Africa*. Sand burned the bare bottoms of my feet, but I insisted on sitting motionless, absorbed by the story.

At some point, a nebulous nudge made me turn to look high over my head. There were no clouds above, but a whirring sound twirled in my head. Something like sirens, like the buzzing noise of airplanes. How many were there? Five? Seven? They swooped down over me and dove in front like breaking waves of the sea.

I looked behind my back. High-rise buildings transformed into a long, lifeless concrete reptile, with tens of mouths gaping open to the full. Terrified, the sea opened in front of me, my only refuge.

Endless, shallow, calm between her and me. The hot sand burned, singeing everything.

It was impossible to move.

Suddenly, my feet absorbed the color of the sand, my skin lost its moisture, dried out, transformed. My body filled with scales. Terrified, I threw the book away. Everything around me became enormous, and the sea was moving far away.

I felt a strong tightness under my chest and my breath cut short. Gills took the place of lungs; I couldn't breathe. I had been transformed again, into a fish.

Wriggling on the sand, I suddenly felt a drop of freshness wet my face. An enormous giant in bare feet bent over my head, lifted a green bucket full of sea water and emptied it beside me. With a robust push of my tail, I dove into the sea, relieved. Merging with the water, I recognized my savior was none other than myself, when still a boy.

It was the olden days...the city was still bathed in the aroma of orange blossoms....

6. Mister Savvas

We never took him for a small ride. Or a trip.

Yet he was the most frequent visitor to our office. He never went inside, and it wasn't because of its size.

The taxi office was just big enough to fit the afternoon light, our boss with his desk, and a second chair. It was the straw chair, the one we used to take out on the sidewalk for him the moment we saw him coming down Dimokratias St.. He wanted it to be under the doctor's balcony, whose back wall rested next to our office wall.

That's where he'd finish his day after work was done.

When men of the city congregated in the coffee shops and gambling clubs, it was his pleasure to mingle among us, the drivers. He came for us and our enjoyment of his company. He came to listen to the stories of the day, our troubles, our fights which were never absent from soccer talk to stormy events happening in our country.

He spoke hardly at all, but his few sentences were sensible, imparting wisdom. I always gave him a refreshing lemonade. He was a strange man. Attractive. I thought of him as a teacher, so educated, so wise.

"He is a real estate agent," our boss said finally. This sounded like a big deal to me, too. A big deal, since it had to do with land.

We never learned where the road to a refugee's life took him. I tried to find him many times. Why did I look for him? What more have we to say, now that we have seen everything, everything?

Nothing....

But the moment he says he wants that ride; I will take Mr. Savvas myself. I will bring him back to our lands.

In our minds, that is.

This time he will give me a lemonade to douse the fire burning inside me.

7. On Dimokratias Street

I stroll up Dimokratias St. hastily, dancing and skipping happily.

I am almost eight. I hurry to catch my beloved Pappou[1], in the coffee shop at the Ermou Arcade. He always waits for me with his back turned against the glass wall.

I sit close to him, longing to hear his stories, about a voyage, a boat, a story long enough to last until I finish my Turkish delight treat.

And then I dance. My version of the dance of the Dervishes.

Twirl non-stop with my arms opened wide to the height of my shoulders until becoming dizzy. He scolds, "Such a wild little goat," laughing under his breath.

As I head up Dimokratias St. I notice the khaki tapes in the shape of an X stuck in the shop windows. Everywhere large X's. "Wrong means wrong...."

We made a mistake. Somehow, we deserve blame. We gave an excuse; we caused the approaching terror.

I run to Pappou to nestle close. Our side street is dug up from one end to the other. Tr-en-ch-es is the new word in our children's vocabulary. "These are not good times to play hide and seek," we are told.

---

1 pappou literally means grandfather

I linger under the arches of Hadjihambis Cinema and stick my head in the enormous hall. The lights are dimmed. Absolute silence. I wait, but the movie does not start. There is no one in the hall.

I run to Pappou. I catch my figure reflected in the Georgiades shop window across the street. I am alone. Not a soul in the street. The wind picks up. Something creaks. The same creaky sound made by the swings on the beach.

But this is not the neighborhood of the Golden Beach, and I am no longer a little child. I raise my head. The signs of the deserted shops squeak at the push of the wind. Photo Christi, Alpha Lemonade, Memory Shop.

I close my ears, shout, "Enough! I can't take more!"

I run to Pappou.

Dimokratias St. is dead.

Colorful ribbons fly in the wind through the broken windows of Yiangoudi like tongues of fire. Like poisonous snakes. Like the hair of Medousa. I turn my head away, lest I too turn to stone.

In the shop window of the newspaper, time died.

Tuesday August 13, 1974

BREAKDOWN AT THE
PEACE TALKS IN GENEVA

I run to Pappou. Where did everybody go?

I run to Pappou.

I keep wondering, was the dance of the Dervishes to blame?

8. Birthday Gift

Six pounds. That's how much they cost. I remember, no matter how many years have passed. They were made of fine brown suede, wrapped around the calf, reaching just two fingers below the knee.

"I can't keep them for you for more than two days," the saleslady at the Bata shoe store said. "They are in great demand, and we have brought only a few pairs."

Why wouldn't they be in great demand? The way she placed those suede boots at the center of the window, they captured everybody's gaze and overshadowed all the other shoes.

"Terribly expensive," my mother said, "and on your feet they won't even last the season."

She was right; she was always right. However, I thought I had the right to choose for my birthday gift whatever my heart desired. I was just fifteen.

I went past the shop many times in the next few days, looking in agony lest I didn't see them in the window. I don't remember how I brought Mama around to letting me buy them, but I managed.

Oh, so happy that day! The happiest kid on Earth in six-pound boots.

The thing I remember well is the shame I felt after.

Returning from a school trip to the Troodos mountains, we discovered that snow had penetrated the suede and destroyed it. The boots were a sorry sight, only ten days from the day I bought them.

Forty years have passed since.

Of course, I will not buy suede boots for my birthday this year or any other. I wouldn't think of doing so. Not after that.

But if I still had the right to choose for a birthday gift whatever my heart desired, I'd wish that we could take everything right back from the beginning.

I'd wish to see my city not only through sad photos, taken on the sly, in photos that remind me of stories about places we lost. Or photos of loved ones who left us early, before we had a chance to enjoy them, relish them, hug them again.

Like boots of fine suede, all soaked by the snow.

9. Flouris's Shish Kebab Stand

Yes, it's true my dear good friend. They say everything is ready.

In two weeks, our side will enter Varosha with pen and paper. They will be well-educated, those who enter, not simple Turkish soldiers like me.

They will not be just anyone.

They will be engineers and inspectors to see if the houses are still sound, to determine what needs to be done.

Sure, things must be neat. Let's get it over, the joke about this city. That's what our side says.

And me? What can I say? Even if I say something, who will listen to the son of Ahmet the baker? Fortunately, I will soon be released from the draft, my dear, dear friend. When all these important things are happening, I will be with my father and mother kilometers away. I will take off this somber uniform and put on the white apron of my old man.

Don't ask me more questions, my dear friend. Don't ask me to hide in these places to take photos of its ghost there in secret. Let someone else do it. Let those important ones go. Those with big diplomas and degrees go.

Here, take this photo of your shish kebab stand you asked me for but know this is the last one. No more photos. The few evenings I have left in this city, I want to spend peacefully.

It's the truth, my dear friend. We will never return Varosha to you. It is to you, the living, that I say this, because those who, well... look here, look at this photo, here by the window. Do you see the shadow he left behind?

Those others from the mainland will never leave us alone.

10. Those Unsuspecting Wild Cats

A deserted house behind barbed wire.

I look at the color photo and feel my irregular heart thumps, like every time my mind searches to recall memories of our life in Varosha.

No, it's not my house in the photo. I don't remember walking into those rooms. I mustn't have played as a little girl in this yard. The productive orange tree by the entrance did not treat me to its delicious fruit. I don't know the owners of this house.

Nevertheless, my heart beats irregularly. Observing the photo awakes images in me.

Five children run around the yard in a never-ending hunt, their voices fill the entire neighborhood with joy. They are the four children of my Godmother and myself. She stood by the kitchen door watching us with a smile, our faces still smothered with marmalade and the remains of bread slices she had prepared for us.

I see my Godfather too, austere like the numbers he teaches in the schools, lest his golden feelings are exposed. At some point, he starts his little Volkswagen Beetle and heads for the center of town.

Looking at this photo, I craft a short story. But I will not tell you right now. It would be like smudging the colors of the picture; like cutting off the oxygen which, even to this day, the orange tree is breathing, insisting against all odds, to be loaded with fruit. It would be like tarnishing the memories of the people who lived through happy and sad moments in this house, like I stole something that belonged to them. As if anything remained to be stolen....

It would be like I filtered the light, the only thing left to enter the rooms freely—the light and the wild, free unsuspecting cats. They do whatever they want. Happy in their ignorance.

Yes, THEY can. Not us.

11. Shame

"A holiday? You don't say. You are looking for excuses to be lazy!"

"The end of the war, Pappou! You, of all people, should know. It's a big holiday all over Europe. It's the same holiday we celebrate here in England."

"Which war are you talking about?"

"The Second World War! May 8, when everything went silent."

The aged man shook his head at the young man. With no condescension in his look, he approached the screen.

"Didn't I tell you not to believe whatever you see in books, my boy?" he murmured, as if confiding a big secret. "That war did not end when they say it did. The fires it lit burned until 1989, when half the world fell over."

"That's when the wall of shame fell, eh? Yes... the same thing will happen to our wall in Cyprus one day. Because walls can't stand the pressure and one day, they must fall."

The grandson, a student in London, Cypriot on both sides but born in Athens after 1974, had grown up hoping one day he would live in the land of his parents. It was a hope which, even though not fulfilled, was still alive.

The eyes of the old grandpa lit up like they did every time he spoke to his grandson on Skype. That always happened, but especially when he talked about those faded pages of history he lived through himself.

"The wall of shame ... it may have fallen because of this..." he continued his monologue, lowering his head, then turned to the screen, he repeated it to his grandson with a strange coarseness in his voice.

"It fell because they called it the wall of shame. For our wall, the one dividing the north from the south, nobody feels shame. That's why they left it without a name. Our wall has grown roots, my boy."

The grandson tried to speak, but the picture on the screen suddenly became fuzzy, as if filled with water. He stayed there, shaking his head and tightening his teeth until more water and then more water and more, until he had nothing to say.

12. To a New Life

The cabin below had a little window that did not open to the outside world. You could not even get a whiff of fresh air. Truth is, I would choke and the liquids in my stomach would gush into my mouth. Every five minutes I would rush to the bathroom, which was not bigger than two square meters.

Despite this, I preferred to spend my time there, instead of the grand salon of the ocean liner, where our four families—friends and us—sat in an imaginary circle with six small tables between us, eyes red, swollen from crying, and the hands, oh, those hands. We didn't know what to do with them....

In a few hours, we would arrive at our destination. A little after the noon hour, the three of us waited in the four-bed cabin, Mother, myself, and Dora, my sister. Our father stayed in Cyprus, trying to find a job in the free areas.

Quiet. Each one of us in our berth, each with her thoughts, with anxieties and worry. Each with her own images in her mind of what we had left behind-our whole life: that other, previous, older life. In front of us lay the unknown, the foreign. The enormous Russian ship, making the first trip after the invasion, starting from Limassol, was going to drop us off in our new, unfamiliar world.

A light knock made me jump right up. A tall, beautiful Russian young woman stood at the door. A heavy blond braid fell on her shoulder.

"Gointu piri orantiessa?" she asked, and I stood there unable to decipher what she said. "Gointu piri orantiessa?" she said again.

I turned my head to the cabin, and saw two more pairs of eyes, perplexed like I was.

"Gointu piri orantiessa?" the young lady repeated for a third time, more slowly, pointing to the one and only suitcase, half-full of the few clothes the Red Cross had given us.

"Piraeus!" I shouted then. "To Piraeus!"

The Russian woman shook her head happily, as if she had heard the password she expected, and made a note in her notebooks. "Going to Piraeus or Odessa," I explained with all seriousness to my mother and sister, and shut the door behind me.

"Tou Piri or Antiessa."

Those three words, which suddenly increased to four, became clear, magically emptied our minds of anxious thoughts. We started laughing, the first laughter that came to our lips. In the bosom of that new sea that glistened at the porthole, the first breaths in this strange life dawned at the edge of the water.

13. Events of July 1974

I called him Costas although he was my uncle.

He was 28 years old, and I had just turned eight. I liked him for being the tallest and strongest of all his brothers, Uncle Andreas and Uncle Varnavas, and even my father, his brother-in-law.

I enjoyed listening to him speak so eloquently around the Sunday lunch table when the whole family gathered. My father rarely entered the conversation. The other two, however, created a ruckus.

Grandpa scolded them.

"In my home," he said, "I don't want any talk of politics."

Grandma smiled shyly. She was proud of Costas, her youngest. He was her weakness, and everyone knew it.

Until that damn Monday came in the middle of July. Schools were closed. It was too early in the morning, but I awoke to Yiayia's screaming from the next room.

"My God, where did you get this, Costas? Costas! Who gave this to you?" she screamed. "Costas, where are you going? Didn't you hear it on the radio? They killed President Makarios![1] Where are you going? Don't get tangled up in anything."

I jumped outside.

---

[1] Makarios III, a Greek Cypriot Archbishop, was elected President of Cyprus in 1960 through 1977.

He was dressed in khaki head to toe, wore a military beret with "EOKA B" on the front, the initials of the Greek Cypriot para-political organization that dared the coup against the lawful President of Cyprus. A gun wrapped itself around his shoulder.

I just managed to see him giving a quick kiss to Yiayia, his mother, and he winked at me as he was leaving.

She continued to scream. Pappou veered his head out of the bathroom window, one of his cheeks shaven, the other still covered in lather foam, just missing him. Costas had jumped on his motorcycle and disappeared at the end of the road.

We did not see him again for five days, except one evening when he came like a thief to pick up some underwear.

Then the conscription came.

I don't remember his features very well. So many years have gone by. But I remember Yiayia never smiled again after that time. She was not proud anymore. Secretly, away from everybody else, and for years, she had her little talks with Holy Mary.

Until she left us, too.

Even though, Holy Mary was already gone by then.

14. No Sound

Dafni sat at the computer so she could work on the photos she had taken while on the beach. Only one month was left before the exhibition.

She continued to work "down to the last stroke."

That's what she said to the gallerist, who asked persistently for the photo she was meant to choose for the invitation.

"The last stroke," she kept saying, but she had in mind something much more important than a simple detail. She was looking for something that reminded her of the last talk she had with Yiayia before she died.

On that last day, Yiayia sat on the edge of the sofa with a blanket covering her bony legs. Dafni was showing her a video she found on the internet, a video from their city, the enslaved Varosha. The camera moved slowly street by street among the deserted, looted houses. Asphalt roads were overgrown, and derelict shop signs could not even remember to themselves what they advertised. Light music accompanied the video.

Yiayia, speechless, gobbled the pictures up as deep agony reflected itself on her wrinkled face.

As the last turn of the road was shown, the screen filled with the sea.

Yiayia grabbed her arm. "The music!" she said in a hoarse voice. Dafni turned up the voice, perplexed.

"Turn off the music," Yiayia hurried to explain, and Dafni did as she commanded. The eyes of the old woman, hiding in their hollows, colorless from the years, were filled with tears and stayed fixed on the sea.

Since the time they lost their lands, the more hungrily she looked at photos, and the stronger her determination was to not cross over the barbed wire. In the summers at their holiday home, as the sun descended, they placed a recliner on the beach, where the waves broke, and she sat there until the moon appeared.

Everybody knew she was reminiscing about her city.

But whenever her son offered to take her to see it up close, she replied with certainty, "I see everything in photos. I will go when the time comes. The sea will whisper to me."

The next day, Yiayia left us.

Only then did Dafni realize why Yiayia had asked her to turn off the sound when she was looking at the sea in the video. Feeling that the end was coming, she hoped that even at that moment, the sea would call her to return to her city....

Suddenly, an older photo jumped onto Dafni's screen: an empty recliner in front of the waves. Yes, without a doubt, the sea had whispered it to Yiayia.

Yes, without a doubt, this would have to be that last stroke.

15. I Saw It in the Coffee Cup

"Life has ups and downs, my sweetie," she said, biting hedonistically into the chocolate biscuit.

She continued, "Things may look difficult, my good friend. But you will forget everything and better days will come.

"Everything will go back to the way it was.

"Here. I see it in the coffee cup."

She had chosen the green armchair and slipped off her high heels, as if she was in her own living room, and sat on her folded legs. Every so often she threw a flirting glance at a group of men sitting at a nearby table, and continually fixed her hair to catch any strands trying to escape.

She was the one who invited me to meet.

"Tell me everything," she told me. "Take it off your chest."

My heart was indeed heavy, like lead, after yesterday's visit to Varosha. I showed her the tens of photos on my cell phone, telling her about streets and homes unknown to her, and she shook her head. Occasionally she sighed.

She sighed out of boredom. Now I know it. Her eyes kept escaping to the next table, but I, stupidly, tried hard to bring her attention back to my cell phone, broke out in more sobbing.

I finally said, "It is not fair, what is happening, Anna, and..."

"You are sniveling," she interrupted. "At some point, every refugee gets over it and remakes their life. You are constantly sniveling and dragging the solution backwards. So many years have passed. Why keep returning to the past?"

Going back to the past, she called it. I was silent. I had gotten to know Anna ten years after the invasion, during the time of our beautiful youth. We were colleagues in the same company. Those years we had the stamina to work non-stop like Santa's elves at Christmas in pursuit of the dream. We shared a common goal: to build our lives. To become a somebody.

I don't know at what exact moment things changed, but I found myself light years away from Anna. At any rate, it was too late by then. It was too late when I realized I had adopted the wrong dream. The more I "go back to the past," as she calls it, the more I see the distance that grows between us.

When for the fifth time she smiled at the nearby group, I jumped to my feet, incensed.

"Calm down, girl," she said. "Relax! Nothing bad is going to happen. Nothing will change."

"Nothing will change!" I felt... stupid.

I grabbed my purse and as I turned to go, my eyes fell on her half-full coffee cup.

Cappuccino!

Obviously.

A correct cup, a Greek coffee cup, would never lie.

16. Rape

At the beginning, you can only see wooden fragments and broken, beaten, red-faded bricks. One shop is next to the other, but to your eyes, they all seem nondescript.

Gradually, your gaze gets trained. You distinguish insignificant items: a shoe heel, the thick cover of a book, a dresser drawer. At the same time, you spot traces of a certain color, different from the dull colors of destruction and abandonment.

That's what I thought as I photographed what was left of a broken pen I found hidden in a small trough, between the door and the shop window. As I bent to scrutinize it, my eyes became magnetized by a bluish object which had fallen under the only wooden shelf at the center of the shop. I came closer and pushed the shelf slightly.

On the floor lay a small blue plastic shoe, the shoe of Amanda Jane, my favorite doll I played with as a child. I wiped its dust off on my blouse. I washed the little shoe with tears, and it shone in my hands like a precious gem. I squeezed it, hard, and my nails tore into my palm.

My wails filled the entire shop. They hit the walls, came back, went up to the loft and found the owner, bending over his documents and his orders. He looked up at me with a sad gaze. As my wailing got stronger, it awoke the little souls of tens of other Amanda Janes. Those raped savagely by the invader, abducted, and lost in foreign lands.

Their own wailing rattled the boys with the Sabbuteo shorts. All together now, girls and boys from our youth, let our groaning be heard all over the shop, all over Dimokratias St., all over the city, all of Cyprus, the whole world.

My heart beat crazily. I opened my palm. Blood had dyed the plastic blue color of the shoe and turned it purple. The Amanda Jane little shoe had taken the color of grief and my heart was broken into pieces, lying down on the floor of my beloved toy shop.

Coming out, I turned my head and looked up above the shop windows. A big sign insisted, in defiance of the invader, to single out ownerships.

It said clearly in big letters: Panos E. Panayiotopoulos.

17. The First Up Front

Now you have seen everything, Mrs. Tasoula. You will be the first, right up at the front.

Isn't that what you said?

"I will be the first one to go, the first among the rest, when they open Varosha."

Who could imagine that this is the way it would turn out?

Who could have predicted that they would lie out for us a black carpet and sad greenery without flowers in the pots?

First among the rest. The house, at the center, the heart of the city, was your dowry. You know, Mrs. Tasoula, I don't remember what a beautiful front door you had. Perhaps because it was always open, a stopover for the friends with their shopping for a coffee on your little balcony. For a dash of bitter orange preserve, made by Yiayia Kleio.

On the same little balcony, you watched the bustling city pass by on noisy mornings.

Later in the early afternoons, after school, you watched nonchalantly as the group of youth strolled to their sweet rendezvous in the cafeterias.

The same youth stood erect in front of you on days of national celebrations, under flags and banners flying in what we thought was our free skies. Alas, it was from this same post you saw them become fanatical at demonstrations which ended under the cinema marquee, just a few meters down the street.

As dusk came, a new picture appeared before you as the steaming lights of the city came on, and you saw lovers in couples enthralled by the big movie signs, sliding under their arches of "Hadjihambis" cinema for a few hours of a voyage into fantasy.

Your home was the center of the city, Mrs. Tasoula. An epicenter for us too, the friends of your children, always full of life, joyful voices, and songs.

But also, the crying of little Kleio from time to time. She woke up disturbed by the same nightmare, because as she told us, all night she was haunted by verbs. Creatures she did not understand well in the classroom.

Now you have seen everything, Mrs. Tasoula. Now I have seen too, together with everybody else, the two most beautiful green doors of your house. Boarded up, though, faded. If someone puts his ear against them, he will hear neither laughter nor joyful voices. Not even the crying of little Kleio.

Because... Do you know Mrs. Tasoula? Do you know little Kleio? Everything has changed, even the verbs. They all took the form of a big noun.

It is called TREASON.

18. Thus Spoke...

It is your rollicking laughter I remember from that day, Auntie Elenitsa.

It was Sunday noon, and we came for lunch to your new apartment on the first floor at Serenissima, right on the beach. I stand on your balcony with my back on the avenue. In my hands I have a beautiful conch shell, one of those you had spread among your flowerpots. You had told me that if I brought it to my ear, I'd hear the sea sing to me.

But I would rather listen to you, Jimmy cracking jokes and teasing you and you laughing.

I stand with my back to the street, and observe your beautiful apartment, with the living room turned to the outside. Next is Jimmy's office with the extensive library. I find a wooden music box there. I wind it up nonstop, watch it, mesmerized as the copper blades, like piano keys, climb over the little spindles on the barrel, filling the room with metallic music.

Everything in this house was magic, Auntie: the one step separating the living room from the dining room, the large mirror further back, which showed everything double and enormous. Everything was magical, full of color and light.

It was on that same day that Jimmy had a gift for Grandma Theodora.

"A small bat bone to help you win in your card games," he said. She wrapped it in a piece of paper and put it in her wallet. It was her turn now to laugh and be happy at the jokes of her eldest son.

But more magical than everything that happened that day was the first ninety seconds when you welcomed us into your home. Next to the entrance, Jimmy had put on the turntable the introduction to Strauss's *Dawn* from *Also sprach Zarathustra*. Uncle Jimmy raised the sound to the maximum, and you kept pushed him and laughed. Oh, how you laughed!

Everything is lost, Auntie Elenitsa.

Now our friends pass underneath your apartment, look up to the open porch, shake their heads, and listen to the silence. They sit on the sidewalk to rest a bit, but they don't expect sounds. We all know it well now. The music is lost, magic has been lost with it.

I keep wondering: What is it we did not understand well, from what Zarathustra had said then? How did we stay like that, so tiny and minute, without God?

19. Edelweiss

A milkshake for three shillings and three piastres, and a slice of cake for 22 piastres. That's for the girls only. The boys had no qualms just asking for tap water and nothing else.

Stavros, the waiter, was in the loop too, offering us refreshing water to our heart's content.

We jammed inside, summer and winter, always inside. No, not because we were worried our mother would spot us. She knew. She knew everything. She sensed, she understood, everything. There was infinite tolerance towards the fiery blood of youth. It was something else we were most worried about. That we would be caught by the eye of some aunt with a rusty mind, and she would make our mother feel embarrassed.

Boys and girls mixed, as if we were in the salon of some mansion, mingling around the tables, changing constantly from group to group, as if we were dancing the ballos dance. As if we were flirting with our very own lives.

Among us are the tender student couples, those in love. They were happy to nest on couches, side by side, his thigh touching hers, sharing slowly, slowly, the same milkshake, until darkness fell. Some stole a few minutes for a quick stroll on the beach, making sure they returned in time to secure the alibi of the large group.

Outside, on the sidewalk, a pile of steel carcasses, our bicycles, waited until dusk to carry twice the weight back home that they had brought. That's how much our joy and good cheer weighed.

Who said that the edelweiss had no fragrance? Our Edelweiss, the hangout that witnessed our first thrills, had the aroma of our first budding youth, the same as that of freshly picked jasmine.

Three shillings and three piastres for a milkshake. The three piastres were for the tax. Another tax, one which should be owed to us, is the tax paid by our lost lives.

Now that we are reaching the end, we realize no one will ever pay it to us.

20. The Yiangoudi

It looked like a light rain at the beginning.

Localized, it fell exactly on the fifteen square meters of the shop. It was tiny, small, like its owner, Mr. Yiangos. I don't know for which of the two apparent reasons we called the shop "The Yiangoudi or Little Yiangos."

It was not wet drops; it was a rain of plaster particles and dust. It fell like rapid gunfire, as though from a machine gun, but no sound came from anywhere. Just the image, a hazy picture, as I looked through the dust covered window of the newsstand.

I stuck my nose to the glass. The dust and particles got thicker like a dense cloud and soon I saw bricks and stones start to break and fall.

I feared Mr. Yiangos' shop would not withstand the severe attack. The earth shook, and a deafening blast came out of the guts of it. It sounded like the groaning of a wild beast.

Instantly, glass and wooden window panels flew into the air, as if the little place threw them away because they were choking it. Through its now toothless openings, I could see the beautiful ribbons flying in the air like flames of licking fire. They were the ribbons that hung on spools from the metal beam above the counter, cotton, silk, and satin. Those same satin ribbons my mother chose to make bows that tied our braids.

Now each of them tossed and wiggled and flew in the air like poisonous snakes, like the hair of Medusa, and I had to turn my head away before she turned me into stone.

When it quieted, I tiptoed out onto the street and proceeded carefully in that direction. Nothing remained to remind me of my beloved ribbon shop. Empty of merchandise, no counter or shelves could be seen. On the beam where long colorful ribbons hung before, a spontaneous plant had now climbed, with flowers the color of sunshine, those flowers that bees adore.

I turned back and walked down Dimokratias Street. Reaching the newsstand once again, I turned with surprise. There was no more glass on the front window and its metal rolling doors were closed. I bent to look inside and saw an abandoned newspaper.

The headline and major article read:

The Turks are ready to inhabit Varosha

On the upper right corner of the paper the date printed was one month after today's date.

21. Old Man Arestis' Bakery

He pulled his chair and sat outside his bakery, with his back to the wall. Those who were there to buy their daily bread had already done so, and the pans with the lunch roasts were all delivered.

Now, he was about to close up and head home, however; he had a need for this last cigarette, while sitting facing the sun. He figured these were the first days of October and the sun was still hot. Calculations were essential. No newspapers come out, neither does the priest come for Sunday services at the nearby St. Nicholas' church.

He has to figure out everything by himself.

He was thinking of Mrs. Theodora, who had just dropped by to pick up her pan of a mere half chicken and five potatoes. Long gone are the days when she would come down with Eleni, her housemaid, and fill two pans. And she was no longer dragging along her little granddaughter, the talkative one with the unending string of questions.

For years now, Mrs. Theodora has come alone.

"You count on the fingers of one hand those of us who have stayed," old man Arestis was thinking. "So few around the table. How much can they eat? How much to drink?"

He lit the cigarette, inhaled deep and let his imagination run. Across the street, where their short street joins Dimokratias St. he noticed a young man stop beside the red ribbon. The young man held his camera in front of his face and looked towards the old man who signaled him, but he did not respond. He only lowered his camera, put his backpack down, and placed it between his legs.

He bent down, took a bottle of water out, and guzzled.

"Hey, boy. Come here, let me sell you a bagel or a tahini pie! It is lunchtime. You must be hungry," he heard himself saying.

Nothing. The young man, slim, fit-looking with a short haircut, kept looked towards the old man without talking.

"Hey! Whose son are you?"

Again, nothing.

The young man focused his camera on the windows of the church and the pediment above the door and click, click, clicked snapshots non-stop. The old man raised his shoulders indifferently.

"What do we need such visitors for if they are to come with their backpacks full?"

Mrs. Theodora came to his mind. When he had mentioned it to her, she replied, "Let it go, Arestis. They are all well-fed, full. Can't you see them? Nobody cares about the liberation of our city anymore."

Old man Arestis got up, put the chair inside and closed the rolling doors. If there weren't a few more like Mrs. Theodora, he would have shut down the bakery for good.

Enough. He was tired.

"Besides, with those who are now in control, we don't know what to expect," he thought, and shook his head, disappointed.

22. Welcome

The Florentines by Michelangelo was the first art book I possessed, and in English at that. It was my Christmas gift from Aunt Sandra, my teacher of English.

This book may have been my introduction to the world of Renaissance art, but its wrapping was the key to the temple that housed the book.

The temple of Pavlos Kyriacou.

Only two or three years had passed since his bookstore appeared on Dimokratias St. giving a new prestige to the commercial neighborhood. At thirteen I was in awe, such that I did not dare go past its entrance alone.

The day after the Epiphany, clutching Pappou's pocket money in Michelangelo's wrapping paper, I dragged my bicycle out and rode down Dimokratia's St.

Suddenly I felt Auntie's gift give me new rights of entry to the Kyriacou temple.

I knew exactly what I wanted because I flirted with it in the shop window throughout the holidays. It captivated me just by looking at the cover. It was a paperback art book with sketches by Da Vinci.

I stood for a moment at the entrance of the shop, hesitant. I still have that problem. I feel I can't touch a piece of merchandise in a shop and leave without buying something, however small. This shop, with its rich wooden paneling and the big staircase in the middle, seemed too expensive.

I was still standing at the entrance when the eyes of the big boss, the very pleasant and plump Mr. Pavlos, fell on me as he wiped his glasses beside the tall counter.

"Welcome!" he said in a loud voice, and I turned to see who he was talking to.

Wow! This whole, rich invitation was all for me, that first time and every time since then, when I courageously visited the shop. His welcome greeting became something like my private membership card.

I bought the book right then. I blushed when everyone laughed on my comment that "I too, later in life, will open a "Pavlos Kyriacou.""

Those were my thoughts yesterday when you called me from Varosha.

"It's empty," you said and your voice broke.

"Only the sign remains and even that is only half.... Not a book or a piece of paper. Not even Mr. Pavlos was there to whisper, *Welcome* to me."

Under different circumstances, I would be jealous realizing that I didn't have the exclusive welcoming, Theodora. But I know by now that the "Pavlos Kyriacou" bookshop, apart from myself, has inspired an entire generation in art and literature.

The last surviving generation that will remember Varosha.

23. All About the Name

If you looked back at her, as she looked at you with her big, deep black eyes, withdrawn into her own skin ever since she lost her husband, you might detect nonplussed resignation in her gaze.

No, you did not understand correctly. Mrs. Kika calculated everything very carefully in her mind. She studied and arranged everything in perfect order. The only detail that concerned her was to detect the right moment to take the next step. At that specific moment, after having everything well organized inside her mind, she would turn to her children.

She was a proud woman, Mrs. Kika. She always dealt with everything on her own. She didn't burden another; she did not bother anyone. But the decision as to the name she was going to give to the new shop was of a different significance. She had an unshakable belief that this new beginning was going to give a new air of importance to the family.

It concerned everyone.

Therefore, the name had to be decided by all of them together.

The shop was on the most central street of the city. The market in recent years started expanding further down, to where hangouts appeared for all ages, where sunburned tourists took their afternoon strolls. Her merchandise would be intended for these tourists but also for anyone looking for something elegant, handmade by our compatriots.

Sitting around the lunch table, they all squeezed their brains that Sunday, including Grandpa Sotiris. He didn't talk at all. He had turned his chair towards the window, looked at the neighbor's fig tree and practiced his songs while softly caressing his mandolin's cords.

Many suggestions were touted about. Some matched syllables from their own names, some jumped out of the history of the city and others were just nice-sounding words so they could be pronounced easily by the tribes of Israel that paraded in hospitable Varosha.

It would not have crossed her mind that the name would never become necessary for anybody to remember her shop.

Today its smart black and white sign is gone, leaving the shop looking barren, but no one forgets that in that corner, attached to Christy's photo store, next to the giant hotel Esperia, Mrs. Kika, a thoroughly agreeable lady, had her shop.

A lady who, together with her love, shared memories with everybody, memories that dripped with honey like every sweet preserve.

I don't know who, that Sunday around the table, gave the baptismal name to the shop.

For the sake of history though, and to spite those who think we'd forget, they called it "The Memory Shop."

24. Mujde or Pelin?

It was close to the exit from the cordoned off area within Varosha, on the border. The city split in two.¹ I was about to pass into the deserted area when I saw you.

Until the beginning of October, whenever I reached that point by the barbed wires just off the dead city, I thought my heart was reaching its limits. I felt one more dose of pain would finish me.

I held my camera chest-high, ready to capture in its guts one last remembrance, one more breeze of our youth. You appeared then, in front of me, two steps away. You heard my steps on the freshly paved asphalt, took half a turn and looked at me.

Your gaze confused me.

Perhaps that's why I pressed the camera button.

Were you nonplussed? Or angry?

Were you angry because I caught you in the act, trespassing on my lands? Because I bothered you in your walk with your husband and son? Because I would not return to my world, leaving you to return to yours? You got angry, eh? Pelin?

Is that even your name?

---

1 After the invasion of 1974, the city of Varosha was split into two by the Turkish army. The smaller sector was immediately settled by Turks. The rest, after it was looted, remained closed and in their hands behind barbed wire, and remains deserted to this date (2023).

Pelin, with foreboding dark news for us with your bitter fragrance, more bitter than bitter?

Or were you just nonplussed, my dear? Is it possible that you are called Mujde and you feel ashamed? Is it because your name—I was told it means good news—will not be realized even this time around? Not for me, not for you. Did you feel shame, as much as I did, for the wasted years of betrayal without solutions?

That's what the carcasses of our empty houses whisper to me today. And yes, I feel myself ashamed.

I look at your face in the photo again and again and wonder what your gaze tells me. Mujde or Pelin?

If you are Pelin, you should look down at the ground. We are doubly fed up with the wretchedness and lawlessness of the world. Our blood is saturated with poison.

But if you are Mujde, then relax. Only stoop so that you can meet in my gaze the fatigue of our generation.

Yours, as well as ours.

Whoever you are, I have nothing more to tell.

Only that, here between Varosha that was once home, and this desolate Varosha that is home no longer, we must admit it exists whether or not we like it, whether or not we want to.

For we are all the losers.

25. A Pack of Cigarettes

A strong pain ran down his spine as he stooped to raise the heavy rolling doors of his kiosk.

"Ohh," he cried and stayed bent in two.

"Just wait, old Nick! Let me help you," Yiannis yelled from across the street as he straightened his uniform carefully, ready to cross.

Recently, old Nick was increasingly late to open his sidewalk newsstand, and Yiannis, without a smoke all night, nursed his anxiety by killing time, gaping idly again and again at the photos of the movies "Coming soon" to Hadjihambis cinema.

Upon hearing Yiannis, old Nick quickly pushed open the rolling doors with a forceful motion, causing them to emit a grumbling and screeching noise.

"I can do it myself," old Nick whispered dryly, as Yiannis proceeded sternly across Dimokratias Street.

"Why did you come to me again? How many times do I need to tell you? You are not getting any cigarettes from me," he said as he turned swiftly towards Yiannis.

Yiannis stood outside old Nick's kiosk, lifted one eyebrow in a mock and straightened the front of his uniform with his fingers. The diameter of the hole that reached back to the spine was seven point sixty-five millimeters. So worn and dog-eared was his uniform you could not miss it.

Stubborn old Nick wouldn't ever find another customer, yet he would never serve an enlisted military man who, together with a bunch of others of his kind, was to blame for making his universe collapse.

Yiannis took from his pocket the keychain with the bird, which kept getting burned without ever turning to ashes[1], and ran it along the rolling windows which were still closed. The irritating "racka-racka" noise from the contact of metal to metal made old Nick shudder.

Once enraged, the uniformed man looked at him a few moments and laughed.

"You, Ha, the boss of chewing gum and candy," he said, "keep it well in your mind. No one is ever going to touch us."

Old Nick turned his back on him and kept stacking newspapers.

Day after day old Nick pretends he is selling and Yiannis pretends he wants to buy. They exchange words, the same dialogue, but a transaction never takes place. After the ritual, each goes his separate way, each into his own corner.

It has been a few years since old Nick's soul returned to Varosha, hoping to find justice in this peculiar world.

But what he found was Yiannis, the uniformed soldier, with a badly shaped wound high on his chest, insisting on haunting the city since 1974 and circulating through the streets free, the unrepentant and unpunished, writing slogans on semi-demolished walls.

When old Nick returned to the city, he thought he had seen it all, but this....

In the meantime, large, faded posters outside Hadjihambis cinema kept promising "Coming soon," some movie which would never be shown.

---

1 An Eagle was the emblem of junta in Greece between 1967-1973

26. Parades

I always found the little soldiers that move when you wind them pitiful.

Fifi and Konstantinos had a sizeable collection of them. They were made of zinc. They were British in distinctive red uniforms and wore ridiculously tall black hats. Some carried cymbals. When you wound them, the piercing sounds they made raised the hairs on your head.

That's exactly what I felt about parades, the ones we watched from Auntie Eleni's balcony. I was always there.

Sometimes I sat in Fifi's lap, sometimes under her armpits, which had the rich aroma of talc and flowering gardens. Yes, I always found them pitiful, and I don't know what made this feeling so strong. Was it the stiff and ungraceful walking of the students, in such discord with their youth, that it reminded me of lined up strutting geese?

Was it their solemn faces, without one smile, giving my heart such an irregular beat? Was it the kerfuffle of all those flags flying and undulating here and there, celebrating?

Celebrating what, really? A lame compromise that no one wanted?

No, never. I never loved these parades. Wild excitement in the faces of the young, the drums and the trumpets arousing their souls for something destructive.

These parades were for the sake of war.

If we were to celebrate its end, if we were to jump with joy for peace and democracy that comes with its end, things would be different. Joy, laughter, and flowers go with peace, like they go with other celebrations, the flower festival, and the orange festival. Those are the parades worthy of peace and joy.

Those are the only ones I love.

I never loved parades. Now I hate them.

Here, where I find myself, leaning on an old, dilapidated small table in the front yard outside of Nico's and Antoni's house, I am forced to see tens of strange faces passing in front of me every day. I don't know them, but they have curious gazes, the gazes of merchants who count, weigh, and calculate.

I hate these parades which pass in front of me.

I find myself alone as a war-disabled veteran on the platform for all the dignitaries to see.

And now I miss the aroma of talc like never before.

27. Visitors

I witnessed their rage go on a few days now.

I stand here at my window and watch them.

First, machinery mowed the weeds. Then they laid asphalt and painted the faint lines. Anyone must admit, everything was done properly.

The other day a truck brought a whole nursery here. Palm trees and other trees, even cacti. Beautiful.

"It is the perfect season," I turned to my Andreas, "neither too hot nor too cold."

But he didn't say a word. He sat behind me, sad, not a sound.

I wanted to talk about the others, those who set out to spruce up the city. Yesterday I saw them carrying some wooden benches. I thought they were taking them down to the sea for us to have somewhere to sit, to sip our orange juice, munch a donut or a bit of Tahini-pie. Kids are always hungry when they come out of the water.

The truck, however, stopped outside Tasos and Olympias's place, there, by Faliron's restaurant, by the seaside. What on earth? I asked myself. Are they possibly coming back? I haven't seen them for years.

But then workers placed the benches outside their restaurant. They put down the first, the second, fifth, the sixth…. There must have been ten. All on the side of the road. They are loco, I thought. Who will sit with their backs to the sea?

I couldn't hold back. I went down and heard them say, "Some big shots will be arriving to have a picnic."

Picnic!

Visitors! I ran back into the house to tell Andreas the news. But he looked at me with a sad face, without talking. My mother, that woman from Smyrna, used to call him the mute dumb. I stood at the window for a while longer and then weighed what I would do.

Some bigshots are coming for a picnic. How could I stay idle? At once I decided, since Olympia is not here, I will make the meatballs myself.

As my grandmother used to say, "No sooner said than done." The recipe comes from her too. My Andreas likes them so much, he licks his fingers every time I make them.

So, today as people gathered, I brought them down hot off the fire. When I came close to the benches, I did not recognize their faces. So what? They are visitors, I thought, and shrugged.

I had hardly put the sauce on the table when the tall one with the mustache reached out, grabbed a meatball with his pudgy hand and put it whole in his mouth.

Suddenly, he opened his eyes wide, threw me an aggressive look, and spit the meatball on the ground with disgust.

My meatball, Yiayia Theodora's meatball!

"Garlic. Disgusting," he yelled and stood up.

He turned me into a wild beast, an untamed animal. How dare he spit my meatball on the ground, the ill-bred pervert?

It was my turn.

Still holding the plate with the sauce, I hurled it in his face. The others around me mustn't have seen. The living are like that. Only those with big sins can see us. Others don't.

He, the one with the mustache, kept swearing, while the others wondered what happened, not knowing what to do.

I grabbed the bowl with the meatballs and turned to go.

That's the end of treating them. I will make more sauce and give all the meatballs to my Andreas.

He may not say much, but he is a compassionate man.

28. Mr. Oulis

He looked like he was dancing as he walked, trying to find his balance on his too thin legs. With one hand, he raised the big metal funnel to yell out "The movies" and his balance was thrown off even more.

Even so, after working for hours as a parking attendant at the open field across from our house, he had enough strength left to traverse twice the length of the long marketplace and advertise movies that were showing at the cinemas that evening.

His only protection: a straw hat.

"Are you going to the kiosk?"

It was the first time he ever spoke to me.

He took me by surprise. I couldn't stand him. I considered him responsible because one morning bulldozers came and leveled everything in the building plot and covered it with gravel. It was not just any plot; it was across from our house. It was my beloved playground, my joy.

I hated him, this abuser of my kingdom, the way he came into it victorious.

He pushed a white umbrella deep into the ground, stretched out a lounge chair under it, and sat permanently.

"Will you get me a packet of Craven A?" he continued, holding a five-shilling note in his extended arm.

I was perplexed; I felt I had no choice. I took it and a few minutes later returned with the cigarettes and the change.
"Are you Theodora?" he said, lighting up a cigarette.
"You confused me with my grandma Theodora."
He started laughing.
"What? They did not give you her beautiful name? What is your name?"

I was angry that he laughed, but I was angrier because he reminded me of the injustice done against me, that they gave the name of my beloved Grandma to my sister.
I shrugged my shoulders and walked away.

Next morning, I left the house.
He signaled me to come over to him. I pretended I didn't see him.
He picked up a metal funnel, brought it to his mouth, and called my name. I couldn't ignore him, besides the whole thing seemed so funny. As I came close, he extended his arm and gave me something incredibly important: The photo of a shining actress with the writing on the strip: "Gone with the Wind."
"She is the best actress," he said. "And she has your name."
That's how I came to accept my name. I was proud too, that I had a photo of the "best actress."
After that, whenever I passed by him, I asked if he wanted me to get him cigarettes. Sometimes I treated him to a candy, one of those English ones that Grandma Theodora didn't like, because, she said, they stuck to the teeth.
But my friend Mr. Oulis was all-accepting.
He never made me feel bad.

29. At the stop for Varosha

I sat alone at the stop, waiting for the tram to appear, when I heard a strange noise come from behind me. I turned and looked.

Nobody. Only the black night, staring at me, choking my senses.

I felt my head turn. I looked at my watch. With my right hand, I felt my forehead. If I had a fever, I wouldn't have felt it in this freezing temperature. The little bench may have been protected, but I felt the cold draining the blood from my feet. The snow had ceased falling from the day before, but it covered the streets with a dirty messed up sheet.

I heard the tram coming from around the corner and tried to get up. Before I could manage, the strange noise suddenly became louder and a dense black mass passed by me, something like a ghost. When it reached the wharf, the black mass halted and broke into separate shadows.

Human shadows, if one can say that, since almost all were headless. Only one, the one who had thrown on its shoulders a cloak buttoned down to the last button, wore an empty helmet in the place of a head.

As the tram approached the stop, it reduced speed, but as soon as the driver saw the shadows, he sped up, causing a thunderous groan.

And yet, something held it motionless. I froze in my seat too, looking once at the tram which wanted to escape and then at the shades dragging themselves a few centimeters above the dirty snow.

I feared my heart would break into a thousand pieces.

Suddenly, the shapes separated like rays, one after the other, bursting through the windows of the tram. Under the powerful lights of the cabin, I saw them become colorful, taking on flesh and bone. They all wore brown military attire and, holding onto the handlebars, swung back and forth against the movements of the tram.

But the tram did not move.

Then the empty helmets turned towards me, and even without heads, the shadows, I swear, looked at me with disdain, laughing at me.

As the tram continued to groan, remaining in the same place, the shadow theater came close to the windows and, always looking at me, made indecent gestures.

I turned my gaze away.

Giddiness grew inside my head like a huge abscess.

Suddenly I slid slowly off the bench until I lay dead on the much stepped on snow.

30. The Groom's Suit

He kept repeating, "It's the right length, Mr. Costas. It's not that I am lazy to shorten it, but... I am afraid it will look strange to you."

I insisted. I had seen this suit in the movies. That's how Steve McQueen wore it in a movie I watched last winter in Athens. In all his suits, the sleeves were short, well above the wrist, and the shirt was visible, well below the waist.

That's why I insisted.

But... that's how it always is. By the time the new fashion comes to us, six months have gone by. If you are the first one to wear it, everyone thinks you are eccentric.

But I insisted. Besides, the delay suited me too. I had not yet received my monthly salary; I couldn't pay the new suit off. The wedding at St. Nicholas was not to take place until the Sunday after next, anyway.

In the end, Father Kyriacos married us at the Evangelistria church, just outside Xylophagou village. We kept the date. Maro insisted on the extreme.

"How are we going to get married, homeless in the tents?" I told her, but she wanted to hear nothing of it.

"I am not going to stay alone and unmarried again," she replied, referring to the few days of the resistance, when she went here and there asking after me and somehow was too shy to say that I was hers.

How quickly the wind blew everything away....
We did not stay under military outfits for longer than a month before we found ourselves naked on the street.

In Xylophagou of course, I did not wear the suit. I did not wear any costume. Neither short nor long sleeves.
I have to admit, I never paid off that groom's suit. Not that it matters in any way. Either he would be the loser or me. As it turned out, after the down payment I gave him, the loss was evenly split.

You may say, why am I thinking about these things half a century later? Even so, now that I see the looted city, I think that whether I had picked up the costume in the way we left, abandoning everything, some despicable man would have found it, no matter where it was hanging.
Why do I think of these things now? Well, I think of Andreas, the tailor, who went to the trouble to shorten the sleeves.
I'm sure a looter found it and wore it, showing off.

31. At Hadjihambis Cinema

I had no interest in cinemas and movies. We knew nothing about these things in the village. Heaven forbids I should go sit in the dark the few times I got leave for the city.

That's what I kept telling Costas. We were drafted now, and every time we could get away for a few hours' relaxation, I'd hear "chup, chup," and he would disappear under the arches of Hadjihambis Cinema. I didn't have a bad time myself. While he watched the movies, I spread out my legs at Rodon cafeteria and watched the passersby.

Time and again I watched him go and then I thought, let me see why the cinema is such a winner for him.

I just wanted to see. I wasn't going to spend any money.

On the way there, he says, "They won't let you in without a ticket."

"What do you mean, I just want to see."

"What do you want to see, chum?" he says undeterred, as if the cinema belonged to him.

"What if I don't like it? The other day I went to a tavern by the sea. Enormous fish kept coming out of the kitchen. I inspected the rich patrons. Enough," I thought, "I don't need this. This shop is like bitter medicine."

He laughed. "At the cinema, there is only one price wherever you sit."

We were still chit-chatting when we arrived. Costas went straight to the cashier's window. I stood by the motorized cart of Patsalos, selling roast beef sandwiches, and leaned over to look inside the cashier's window.

I was shocked.

By my mother's soul, I swore I had never seen such bright green eyes. I approached.

"Why did they imprison you behind these bars, my doll? Who committed such a crime?" I asked her.

Costas began laughing.

The teller didn't betray the slightest move on her little lips.

"What are you looking at, mister? The movie is playing inside. Do you want a ticket or not?" she said with insolence.

I felt hurt.

Sure, she was beautiful. But she was not to play the smart aleck with all the people around us listening.

"What do you think?" I said, slurping back the honey in my mouth. "You think I came here just to look at your beautiful eyes?"

Long story short, not only did I pay for the ticket, but I also stretched out on the red seats and had a KEAN orange juice during intermission. It helped push down the sandwich Costas treated me to.

As for the movie, I went crazy watching how the bad guy always remains unscathed amidst all the gun action.

I went to the movies for the first time out of a hurt ego. Just like that, smiling, I went back every time we were out on leave.

Let's say at first it was for her emerald eyes. But from some point on, afterward I got my fill from the beauties in the movies.

They, at least, did not cause the slightest wound.

32. Number 23

He passed by our house every day on his little motorcycle, about the same time, a few minutes before the municipal siren sounded lunchtime.

That's when the girls who worked for Vourkas, seamstresses sewing readymade garments on the ground floor of our house, took their break.

I don't remember how I noticed him the first time, nor do I remember how, in such a short time, I learned to identify the sound of the exhaust pipe of his motorcycle. I recognized him immediately. He was the football player with the number 23. It was natural. I had all the cards with the photos of the players of my team. Some I even had doubles, and I was looking to exchange them.

As soon as I heard his motorcycle, I hung out the window. I did not fall in love with him right away, not right away. He did not play in the First Division, and that seemed below my standards.

But you know how these things go. A tight siege for an entire summer softens the hardest heart.

He would come along Dimokratias Street, pass under my window and disappear around the bend, leaving the ruckus he created behind. I returned to my collection of cards, happy to the nth degree.

Sometimes he greeted me with a nod of his head. Not always, mind you, and I attributed it to the traffic in the street.

Yesterday I went down to the entrance where Theoris waited with his bicycle and the fresh milk. Usually, Yiayia Theodora picked it up but, I offered.

In the middle of the transaction with Theoris, my beloved arrived. I heard his motorcycle zooming from far away and the ground gave way under my feet. I must have turned red like a poppy because Theoris asked me if I was sure I could carry the milk upstairs without spilling it.

My love passed by me at low speed without turning to look at me and... and... he stopped. Completely.

My hands started to sweat. I turned my head slowly... and then I saw Stella.

Stella! The one I loved the most among Vourkas's girls. The one who kept for me the most beautiful remnants so I could make dress suits for my dolls.

With breath suspended, I saw her slip among the other girls and approach my beloved. And then he grabbed her hands and gave her a quick kiss on the lips before starting his engine and disappearing.

That's when a groan fell out of my insides, together with the zinc pot. Milk doused the sidewalk, wetting the trousers and the shoes of Theoris.

33. The Name of Our Street

Costis thinks he knows everything but is no better student than I am. He is simply the son of the headmaster. I am positive his father tells him everything Mrs. Aliki is going to ask us tomorrow.

No wonder he comes to school well prepared and behaves like a smart ass.

Last Friday she distributed the papers, the type we use for writing an essay on one half and for drawing a picture appropriate to the subject on the other half. She told us we were to write the essay at home, to take our time, study the subject, and get well prepared. The subject was "The name of our street."

Costis and I live on the same street, one block from each other. When he turned around in class to look at me, I detected a great terror and a bit of jealousy deep in his green eyes. I smiled triumphantly. This subject was all mine.

On Monday, during Reading, the teacher asked us to read aloud the essays we wrote, one at a time. First, we heard about the Parthenon, then about a man called Shiller, a German, who was, among other things, a poet.

Then it was Costis' turn. When he started reading, I lifted my head and smiled, waiting for his star to fall and roll onto the floor. No one could know the story of our street better than I. No one!

As soon as he began, I realized something was wrong. The name of our street was "16th of June." Costis said, On the same day in 1943, the day Hitler and the Italians occupied Greece, AKEL, the communist party, aroused its followers to enlist and go fight."

He was halfway through before I regained my senses. I got up and slipped outside into the empty yard. There, over the garbage can, I shredded my essay to pieces, together with my photo as a baby in the stroller, which I had stuck in the place of the drawing.

I have to admit my biggest distress had nothing to do with Costis. It was that, all these years, I was sure that my parents wrote my birthdate on the corner post of our street, while that of my sister's was written only on the back of our cupboard door.

34. The Trap

Partly because of the torment in the airports, partly because of the heat, we arrived exhausted at the hotel.

"NO signing of autographs today," I reminded the young female receptionist when we saw the crowd gathered at the entrance. Behind us, through a double door, calm murmurs and the smells of thousands of spices snuck toward us. The sign hanging on the wall said Dining Room, but my stomach guessed it too when it rumbled.

"Andreas, let's take the suitcases up to the room and come back down for lunch." He was still signing us in at the reception desk.

"The dining room is waiting for you," the desk clerk answered on his behalf, showering him with a honey-smile. He returned the compliment.

As we waited for the elevator, Andreas stretched his muscled arm around my shoulders and gave me a wet kiss. I cringed. I tried to recoil, but he pointed with his eyes to the crowd, which was not about to disperse.

Villagers, I thought. We had instructions from our producer to pretend we were in love.

"It sells much better in the countryside," he explained.

I stayed motionless, pretending to admire the truly impressive sculpture above the elevator door, and complained only after the door closed.

"But Zoitsa... " he tried to excuse himself. I cut him off.

"Andrikko, I am the one who calls the shots." He shrugged his shoulders with the face of a punished child.

We found our rooms, placed our luggage down, and headed back down.

We finished the shrimp cocktail and awaited the main dish when I heard a faint voice from the opposite table directed at us. She sat there all alone, elbows on the table, face hidden in her palms.

"Does this mean you are a married couple?"

She mustn't have been over eight years old. She wore a pair of striped shorts with suspenders. We looked at each other.

"No, we are not married," Andreas answered, which she took as encouragement to continue.

"Why did you kiss her, then?"

"Because we are actors and it's allowed."

"I know. You are playing in a funny movie called *The Trap*. Are you still joking around with her now?"

Andreas laughed, but I got impatient.

"What are you doing here, running around in the hotel?" I asked tersely.

"The Palace belongs to my sister's godfather, and you sign right here," she continued audaciously. She approached and took out of her back pocket two crunched up photos, one of mine and one of Andreas.

"The Palace!!!" I laughed sarcastically, but she did not budge.

"Famagusta Palace Hotel, and don't you speak English," she replied, pushing the two photos towards us.

I grabbed mine. Let's get it over with, I thought.

"What's your name?" I asked nervously.

"Write 'To Areti.' It's for my friend. I only collect photos of soccer players."

We sighed and signed with a smile as the little one grabbed the photos and ran to the reception. We then heard her scream.

"Come closer, everyone! The actors are signing autographs!"

Andreas barely managed to caress my hand when a crowd gathered around us. The little girl was now shouting,
"Ah! And about the kisses, they are just a trap!"

35. The Letter

I wanted to be alone. I wanted to be there before the foreigners came for their walks. I wanted to walk along the route we used to take together on the way to school one year ago, before I left for my studies and you, for your National Guard service.

As soon as I walked past the barbed wire, I felt the new asphalt burn the soles of my feet. The houses were deserted....

A red and white ribbon encircling them could not hide their nakedness. Silence. Only the sound of my own footsteps, hitting the ruins and echoing back in multiple intensity.

I approached the bank, where the avenue crosses our street, your house across from ours. Suddenly I heard a cry, which became voices, many voices entangled like strings. They came from inside the letterbox and became increasingly louder.

I can distinguish words now.

"I am waiting for you," "Give my regards to...." "I send you my kisses."

The words intertwined. Youthful voices overlapped others, men's voices over those of women.

Suddenly I heard you, you Vasili. Your voice was so distinct, I couldn't confuse it with anybody else's. Calm like a whisper, but rough, like it came from your soul. It covered all the other voices, and I could hear only you. The timbre of your voice made it sound richer, heavier.

This time, you found nothing to say to hide from reality. No new blunders, not like the ones you used to always send me in your letters. Those you thought were hiding your anger. You thought by describing funny stories from your everyday life in the army, you would hide how enraged you were with this nonsensical—you used to call it nonsensical—service you were forced into.

You thought you would hide from me how much you hated the military uniform, how much terror you felt with the gun they put in your hands, the idea that you must turn it against someone else.

You thought you would fool me when you wrote to me it was the two bags of onions they had you peel that brought myriads of tears to your eyes. You thought through funny stories you could hide what your soul really wanted to say.

You thought I wouldn't discern it. But... this time I was hearing different things. I heard terror, chaos, machine guns, blood, retreat... Treason.

I never received your last letter, the one you are now reading to me out loud. I can't imagine when you could have mailed it, since the mailman did not manage to pick it up. The mailbox is empty.

The hurricane of the looters took everything with it, our letters, our words, our love, our pain, our life.

That was your last letter, Vasili.

Even if you didn't write it, what does it matter? One way or another since then, I hear your voice read it to me every night as I close my eyes to sleep and reminisce as I dream.

36. Behind the Doors

I never went inside your house, Constantia, a big, two-story house at the corner, touching the two streets on both sides. No garden, no trees, nor flowers, nor a single centimeter of space for a playground.

Whenever we arrived there after school, when you disappeared behind the large door with the semicircle skylight, a thousand bad images soared through my mind, and I felt an unbearable tightness in my child's chest.

You always sat at the front desk. You were the shortest in the class, Constantia, and I the tallest. The only sure thing, beyond all those things only a child's mind can imagine, was that six desks separated our age. I always strived anxiously to make you laugh. I don't know what distressed me more.

Was it your very few words during recess at school? Was it that your little round face, very much like a little moon, rarely shone with the smile of your innocent child's soul? Or rather, was it that when I saw your house, with its thick walls, its few windows almost always closed, I imagined something dark? Was it that the moment you closed the door behind you, deep darkness engulfed you, and those various apparitions hovering around you filled you with infinite sadness?

When I thought of friends, you were always there, Constantia. And forty-six years later, as my body and mind stroll in the streets of our deserted city, the tall walls of your house appear mysterious and proud as I walk past them. I pause just in case I might catch a glimpse of you.

I have lost your traces, but I remember your voice, low like a whisper.

I remember your gaze, full of wonder.

I don't know what decisions you made in your life. I don't know where you are or how you are.

However, today I have something important to tell you. Something about me. I want to tell you how, looking at the ruins of your house in the photo, after so many years, I realize how wrong I was then. How misled I was by unsettling conclusions.

Because now, Constantia, after the Turks emptied our houses and left the doors of our lives wide open to public view, I see with great relief that hidden at the back of your house is a garden bathed in light. A garden all to yourself, without darkness and apparitions, free for you to rule over as you wished, as the beats of your own heart desired.

That's how, I hope, they rule over your life, always.

37. The Slippers

Sometimes news flew over our helmets like hungry squawking birds.

This time everyone held the good news to himself, as if we did not have in front of us a whole city with properties galore. As if we should only deal with five neighborhoods.

So, my brother-in-law Ahmet and I spent days scouring poor neighborhoods. Everything, of course, looked so abundant in this city. By the time we got wind of the fact that the rich houses were on the seaside road, it was the last day. Next day we were to board the ship for our homeland.

Very early in the morning of that last day, the two of us took the seaside road. On both sides of the street, we saw a huge X in the entrances of apartment blocks, a sign that others had gotten there before us. Forced to walk much farther, we did not exchange a single word. A strange, unsettling feeling lodged in the hearts of both of us.

What was that feeling? Were we not leaving victorious, loaded with trophies?

We were already in September, but as hours went by, the heat became unbearable.

At last, at some corner, a wide-open door of an apartment block stood waiting for us. I tried to get into the first apartment, pointing at the one next door to Ahmet, but he chose to follow me. He wanted to share the spoils.

The apartment held all the blessings of Abraham and Isaac. We picked up everything from each room that seemed special and laid it near the front door. As I started loading our bags, he became stubborn. He wanted to divvy it up right there.

I shrugged.

Everything was going great until we came to a brand-new pair of slippers. I smiled.

"These are for my Fingen" I said to him.

He became angry.

"I saw them first," he nearly shouted.

I don't know how the fight started or escalated, or how we descended into hell. Nor do I know how guns were drawn and how my gun went off. Everything happened so quickly.

Before I set out on the road to return to my military unit, I threw the two slippers as far as I could. I saw one pulled by the waves. The second sunk among the reeds.

Those days, many stories circulated in our unit about haunted houses and cursed objects. But I never imagined that the curse that befell my head would come in the form of a pair of slippers.

Ahmet would never walk home in them.

38. Who Knows About Such Things

At the age of fifteen Andriani lost her mother.

She was the eldest of the four siblings and the only girl in the family. Without argument, she left school to look after her brothers until they graduated and learned a trade. Her father asked her opinion, of course, and she answered without hesitation: "I don't know about such things."

When Pavlos her eldest brother was done with the army, he apprenticed with Mr. Costas, the architect, to learn the trade. He was good with numbers, and it turned out he was good at drawing, too. Mr. Costas was pleased and gave him more work. In the evenings, Pavlos continued to work at home and Andriani, as soon as she finished cleaning up the kitchen, hovered over him.

She too was good with numbers and lines but, sort of, well... she didn't know about such things.

As time went by, she was enticed by it all and slowly, slowly, became the one to draw the first lines with a pencil and ruler. Only after she finished her housework.

"You have done that perfectly," Pavlos would say, and she always answered, "Well... what do I know about such things?"

The time came for Pavlos to get married, and soon the other boys followed too, and Andriani stood by all her sisters-in-law like a real sister. All the boys set up their homes and the old homestead emptied.

Andriani was left alone with her elderly father. Every so often, her brothers sent marriage proposals from prospective candidates, but Andriani had no time to spare.

"I must look after Father," she said. The only thing she asked them to do was to watch after the homestead and make repairs, as dampness rose from the floor and stained the walls half a meter high.

With time, Pavlos grew to be a big name. He was preferred by everyone. He had taken over the office of Costas, the architect. One afternoon, he went to the homestead with a bunch of drawings under his arm.

"I am going to fix the house," he said. "The walls will fall down if we do nothing."

"I have the plans for the tiles," Andriani answered shyly. She was excited, as if this was the day she had been waiting for all her life.

I passed by the house the other day, at least what remained standing of the house. The door was open.

The perfect design of the floor tiles was Andriani's, of course. It is completely intact and the way I remember it as a little girl. Geometrical design and pale warm colors which matched nicely together... magical.

Even though Andriani... knew nothing about such things.

39. Smoke and Bad Smells

A garbage truck?

No. Not a garbage truck passing by our house.

To the contrary, I remember very well they burdened me as the youngest in the family with the task of emptying the garbage into the big metal barrel at the side of our garden. One by one, I took the trash cans from every room and went down to it.

There sat the barrel. Normal, as the name implies. A cylindrical shape and was, by my estimates, huge. The color of zinc which coated it was suffering terrible hardships.

How could it not? This barrel, beyond the fact that in the garden it was exposed to wind, sun, and rain, beyond the fact we forced it to digest into its enormous belly all the dirt of our house. Besides the fact that every Saturday, Pappou went down and threw a lit match inside to burn the garbage of the week into ashes.

As years went by, the fires singed the metal at the lips of its perimeter and left it crippled.

Pappou didn't let me watch up close the sacred rite of the burning. It wasn't because he didn't trust the fire, or he was afraid the flames would jump out of the limits he had set.

"Stay away from the smoke and the smells!" he called out to me, while just a little further away he watered the lemon tree, the two orange trees, the medlar tree, and the pomegranate tree. He remained a faithful guard of the fire until it devoured all the useless, harmful things. Nothing was left.

"Away from the smoke and the unpleasant smells."

What I imagined was that these two together, smoke and awful smell, was a dirty liquid. Those years, I often heard adults talking about how the walls of the city had now become dirty, covered with offensive or provocative graffiti.

As I looked at the wall behind the barrel of changed colors with time, I kept saying to myself that the dirty liquid was sprinkling our wall too.

Years passed. Now people have different ways to get rid of garbage.

But dirt remains sprinkled on the walls of our houses.

The dirt that soiled our beautiful years, the dirt that harmed our world and our lives. Surely, a thin layer of white paint was not enough to erase its traces.

So, like the oblivion that always comes like rain, I am afraid, eventually, the white paint will wash away.

And then the dirt, free now, will threaten our lives again.

40. Eros

They did not want us in the playing fields of the hotel. That is... at the "good" times, when the sun went down, and the city cooled itself off.

During the rest of the day, both tennis courts under a green rubber cover were open to the youth. They tolerated even us, the younger ones, despite the noises we made, and the balls flew towards the swimming pool as if a magnet attracted them.

I was ten and Lelia, my Godsister, thirteen. While we whisked through the courts, my mother and my Godmother, two inseparable friends, swam in the sea and drank their lemonades on the front veranda of the hotel until midday.

On that day, we found ourselves in the tennis courts together with three other kids Leila's age. The game cannot be played with five. I was the youngest. Downcast, I picked up my racket and passed by the hotel bar to tell my sad story to Mom and Godmother.

I never got there.

I saw the young couple not at the bar but in the empty salon further down. She was beautiful like a doll, wearing a tiny yellow bikini and sitting on the chair with her legs pulled up. It was a beautiful, revolving, modern seat, which looked like half an eggshell open alongside.

He was a big man, two meters tall, with an athletic, brass-like body, standing over her and hovering. She was dying out loud with laughter.

I stood there, admiring the beautiful couple, so well-matched, like cinema actors, I thought.

I kept looking at them non-stop.

Then, he stopped circling around, glued his body to hers, kissed her passionately and fondled her, his hands traveling all over her body. With my eyes wide open, I saw for the first time what they call "eros."

Years passed. I never forgot the beautiful couple or the shiver that went through my little body like an electric current.

Nor did I forget the shape of the revolving chair.

When, at our first meeting in your office, you showed me a similar chair to sit on; I knew things were on the right path. A little while later, I tried to tell you something about the meaning of the seat, but you jumped ahead and told me your own story.

You had paid a lot of money for those two seats, and they were designed by the famous Philippe Starck.

"This seat..." you told me, "Starck called EROS."

41. The Crane

Certain professions excite the imaginations of the very young, and those who work at them become their heroes. That's how my children, Evie and Pericles, saw me.

I operated a crane on construction sites of dozens of super-high-rise buildings going up at extremely fast paces at the beginning of the 1970s. The company I did this for was much sought after, and I was too, as a technical person with specialized knowledge and experience.

That summer, which from the beginning came upon us like a roaring lion, and which burned us to death before it even reached midday, both my children turned six. Two beautiful twin little souls.

One day, I was working at a site one street up from our house.

They pulled on their mother's skirt without pause, demanding that she take them to see Daddy, as if going for a stroll in the park. Then they pestered me all afternoon for a promise to take them with me up into the sky.

Pericles held the banner, while Evie stood beside him, looking more at her brother than me, from time to time agreeing with him in a big "YES" and her little fist raised up high.

In vain, I tried to explain to them that this was not a Ferris Wheel and that Dad's work was not a place for games.

But the boy was the first one to be disappointed and turned his back on me without another word. Evie followed, but in two minutes she came back and handed me a little plastic monkey-like doll with orange hair.

"Daddy, at least take Troll doll for a ride, so he can tell us what he sees from high above."

Pericles looked suspiciously from far in a corner without saying a word.

The next afternoon, I brought Evie's little doll back and told them stories about what he saw from up high. Pericles came forward shyly and gave me Snoopy, dressed as an astronaut, a gift of his godmother from Seattle.

Next day we worked only till 10:00 in the morning. It was August 13, our last sad day in Varosha. Snoopy the astronaut never came down from "space." He stayed forever there, in the crane cabin, stuck between metal and metal, memory and memory, bitterness and bitterness. Between silence and silence.

Since that time, my Pericles has been afraid of heights. Afraid of cranes, airplanes, and anything that can separate one from the earth that gave him birth.

42. Rust

He woke up, his tranquility disturbed by an annoying nudge which interfered with his dream.

In front of him, mother was raising the rolling windows. He sat up in bed and stayed there, eyes half closed, looking outside at the cracks of dawn.

She turned and looked at him. "You agreed to take me to Varosha today. If I didn't wake you up, it will be midday before you move."

The day before, his mother had gone to see the city with a childhood friend of hers for the first time. It was dark before she got home. As soon as she arrived home and saw her son at the computer, before she even took the key off the door, she addressed him.

"Tomorrow, you take me." She did not expect him to object. She didn't ask for favors often. Especially for Varosha. She almost never talked to him about it.

"You were born in Nicosia," she used to tell him, "like your father. Lucky you. Leave all the pain to me about the city I lost."

On their way to Varosha, the two did not utter a word. She concentrated on the road, as if she was driving. Her son, sitting beside her, was trying to decipher the dream he had just before he woke up. In it, he and his mother sat at the edge of a well. Under the hot sun, his mother, with lips dry and cracked, repeated and repeated just one word "Water!"

He tried in vain to draw from the well. The pulley was completely rusted.

They parked the car and proceeded on foot. He remained speechless as he looked at the things she showed him. He listened to her describe her life in just this one stroll, all those things she hadn't told him all these years. Along the seaside road, the freshly laid asphalt turned right. They walked a few meters on the parallel road and stopped. Further down, the cordoned off area stopped all movements.

"Here, behind this building, one street over, was our homestead," she said, out of breath.

Where she showed him, the son saw a huge, semi-finished building rising. A crane, half a century old, stood tall above the building, with time having left its indelible mark. Up high, you could see a rusty pulley. The same as he saw in his dream.

He lifted his cellphone to take a photo and then heard his mother say: "My lips are dry, my son. Did we bring water?"

He turned and looked at her. Two big tears licked her cheeks. Salty tears. Like the ones that rust our dreams.

Because, yes, dreams rust when you don't share them. Like pulleys that no longer work.

43. The Waste

One hundred thirty-two point three tons of asphalt.

That's how much it took. One hundred and thirty-two, together with that 10% extra, to be on the safe side, which eventually was also poured and layed. It was the first time I miscalculated. What does it matter if I am off by 300 kilos among all those tons?

Well, it did. It had. That's how the last few meters, the most important ones, were left unpaved. Exactly where the asphalt was to meet the kiosk, where the Big Chief was to sit. They impressed it upon me from the beginning; under no circumstances should the slippers of his wife get dusty.

"After all, your reputation is on the line. You are the famous quantity surveyor who estimates everything precisely, who never makes a mistake."

I was informed of the problem at the last minute. Tomorrow was the day of the Big Chief's visit.

I panicked.

I arrived on the scene midday, and asked to be taken to the point which remained bare of asphalt. It was as they had told me on the phone.

"From the seaside road to the kiosk, people will sink in the sand."

In this terrible Varosha sand, so thin, like flour, which at every step sucks your feet in, as if it wants to take you with it to the depths of the earth. Sand that singes your feet and burns your soles.

There was no time for another solution. The only thing we could do was lay down a wooden platform, which we would cover with a red carpet. That's the only way we would hide the mistake.

But how was the mistake made?

I couldn't stomach it. I left my colleagues to worry about ordering the lumber and carpet and I walked the road backwards. It wasn't long before I discovered the reason for the mistake. The missing quantity of asphalt was poured down the sewer!

The supervisor of the project sat on the sidewalk, just down from where I was, smoking, looking at me like a beat-up dog.

I approached.

I had to take an oath on our holy Quran before I convinced him to talk.

"I thought I could cement the beast in, isolate it. Make sure it stopped groaning, haunting us every night," he said in his course, raspy voice.

"In vain..." he said sternly, throwing his cigarette butt on the side of the road.

"It's too late. The ghost of this city dwells in our souls."

44. Fairytales

"Is it true Grandma?" I asked after the end of every single story. "Is this story true?"

I don't' know what got into me. Had Grandma told me it wasn't true; I would have lived a great drama. I identified with every story of hers. I lived every moment of it, its heroes, its kings and village boys, bakers and magicians, chimney sweepers and fairies, beautiful swans and ugly ducklings.

I saw everything unfold in front of my eyes, in beautiful palaces, endless forests and green pastures, poor huts and noisy streets, beside burning fireplaces, murmuring rivers and snowy scenes.

Yet everything ended under the thick cover of the trees in our yard, with Grandma sitting on the front steps of our house and me going around and around on my little yellow bicycle.

"Is it true, Grandma?" I would say as she tried to push in my mouth the last mouthful of egg white, which I hated so much.

"Last one, last one," she would stress, as I kept asking and turning my mouth away from the spoon.

"Is the story true, Grandma?"

"Absolutely," she answered, wiping my mouth with the white kitchen towel.

"And did they all live happily ever after?" I insisted.

She then looked at me, exhausted, partly from never-ending hardships, partly from the fatigue of years, and partly from hopes now faded.

With longing in her eyes, with absolute certainty about our own future, she answered, "It is true, my little angel!"

I believed her.

45. Lentils

"Even this time, he won't succeed," Yiayia said, bent over the tin plate of lentils piled up in a little mound.

Mother did not raise her head from the embroidery she was stitching, but I noticed creases gather around her lips, as they always did when angry.

Here we go again, I thought and sat quietly beside Yiayia. I started counting the hrut-hrut of the lentils as Yiayia pushed a few at a time from one side of the colorful tin plate to the other and waited for the outburst.

"Did you light a candle, as I told you?" Yiayia continued.

Occasionally she threw an onerous glance at her daughter, over thick black eyeglasses perched on the edge of her nose that made her look like a spider.

Mother did not respond.

"Did you at least tell him not to expect anything more from me?"

"Mother, don't start again. The little girl can hear you."

I crossed my gaze with that of Yiayia's.

"What are you doing here? Why don't you go play on the veranda?" she said to me.

I withdrew deeper into my chair and declared, "I'm not going anywhere."

That's how it always happens. No matter what father does, Yiayia finds it isn't enough.

She is not fair to him! She does not dare say the slightest thing to him! She just grumbles to Mother about him being an atheist and a leftist.

That's why, she says, "He will never become anything."

I don't know how, but Yiayia performs magic on him. Mother is afraid of her and says nothing. Therefore, it is left up to me to break the magic spell on him.

"Hey, why do you sit here with that malicious look on your face?" she said to me again. She keeps repeating that my face has an identical roughness to his.

"Hrut-hrut," said the lentils every so often, and then she pinched a little stone or a hollow lentil and threw it on a little coffee saucer.

"You'll see. He will be fired after the first month," she started again.

"Hrut-hrut."

"Of course, he will resort to drinking again. The useless man."

"That's enough, Mother!" My mother said in a low, tired voice. "With your nagging, you bring bad luck to our home..."

"Hrut-hrut,"

"My nagging, eh? It wasn't me who turned my back on God!" shaking her head disapprovingly.

At the next hrut-hrut I put my slippers on, now spread under the table. I winked at my mother and went out into the yard, pleased with myself. Father was going to keep his job and bring lots of money home. I was certain.

Before the twentieth hrut-hrut was heard on the tin plate, my lucky sign was revealed:

A flying saucer in the color of an orange.

It appeared on the plate before I reached the count of twenty.

Thus, the magic spell was broken, nullifying the injustices of this world.

46. How Can You?

It reached my ears like a whisper. It came out of the door. The open door.

I stopped. I looked left and right. Nobody saw me. No, I did not recognize this house. I did not know anybody in this neighborhood. There was no one to know, not now.

Alert, I stepped watchfully over the red and white cordon strip and listened carefully.

I heard voices, singing of our younger days, with lives worth living. They sang of everything wanted, everything hoped for, everything possible, just waiting for their accomplishment.

But they could never see tomorrow, and I realized, neither could I.

I thought of sorrows past, and sorrows to come,

But I was determined to carry on.

My head buzzed. It had to be this song.[1] The same song that oppressed my soul just a summer earlier. It oppressed my soul, but for four summers before this moment, it had laughed and kissed me.

I did not have a broken heart, not yet.

But I did not know how to stop the rain from falling, or storms from blowing, or armies from invading.

---

1 The Bee Gees *How Can You Mend a Broken Heart*, released 1971.

I looked inside the house from the doorway. Empty. Like all the houses in my beloved city. Yet, I could hear the song clearly. I held onto the door handle so I wouldn't lose my balance.

A light breeze rose and stroked my neck.

I was in a dream. A faded, yellow-tinted image. An old photo filled the space behind the door.

I was here, me and my girl. We rocked slowly to the sound of the music.

And I recalled misty memories of times gone by with her in my arms. How I kissed her gently on her fine neck, and she laughed. She always laughed.

But we couldn't see what tomorrow would bring, and no one could have guessed the sorrows.

I passed my fingers through the thinning hair left on my head and leaned on a wall that wasn't mine. Everything twirled around me at a speed I could not take.

In a dance, joyful images from the past broke into pieces, little pieces like mosaic tiles in misty colors, the yellow color of the dream dominating everything. I was carried away, floating by and with them, by this powerful wind, which now blew freely across our past, our once alive homes, our once alive lives.

I realized I am broken, like thousands of others, and how do you mend a broken heart if you're a broken man?

I ask you, how does the loser win?

My eyes filled. Water coursed into my clothes. I had never shed so many tears, not even in front of the open door of my own house. Completely weak, I was empty, a shell. I slipped my back against the unfamiliar blank wall and screamed.

"Please help me mend my broken heart and live again!"

I don't know to whom I addressed myself.

No one could hear.

47. Messed up

Sometimes, big trouble starts from insignificant causes. Someone important said it, but I don't remember who.

In our case, that's exactly how it happened. Am I to blame? What can I say... I am confused myself.

When Maro showed me the material for her dress, immediately I said to her, "Your cousin Maria bought exactly the same one." In fact, I showed it to her, because I still had it in the shop. Maria had done only one fitting.

Maro did not appear to be surprised, and that's what confused me the most.

"What a coincidence!" she said and kept looking at Maria's dress on the hanger, laughing. Laughing! I swear. What could I do, refuse to make it? I gave her the fashion sketch magazine to choose the dress design.

"Whatever I choose, in your hands it will turn out just perfect," she said playfully as she turned the pages of the magazine, staring at the dress on the hanger with a smile. That's when I could interpret the smile.

Maria, her cousin, was well stocked in kilos. Creases here, creases there. How much can a piece of cloth hide? I am a talented seamstress, one of the best in town, but I cannot perform miracles.

Maro, though, had the figure of a model. Thin waist, beautiful legs, above all, a chiseled out bust which we had to show off.

When Maria came for the second fitting, I did not show her what I was preparing for Maro. Deliberately, I have to say. I didn't want to hurt her. I know how such things hurt.

Two weeks later she came again and threw it in my face as if it were a dishrag.

"You and her, and your cunning ways!" she screamed. "You let a vain woman engage you in her whims! Just for ten piastres."

That's what she screamed at me.

The second person to be accused, I thought, would be Marcos, the draper. As if he was supposed to remember which lady bought what?

At any rate, when I dropped by his shop, he did not let me explain I was on his side. He screamed he got into trouble because I schemed to ridicule his clients, that Mrs. Maria had told him everything.

"In the future," he said, "I will not utter a single good word for you."

I lost Maria as a client. I lost Marco and his recommendations as well!

Of course, I was left with Maro, but ... really... she is so skinny.

For Maria, I was quite justified in charging more if you consider the extra thread and twice as much time to sew her gown.

48. Barclays

I could only walk through the city where allowed by white and red cordon strips. They wrapped around buildings like ribbons without gift packages.

Without no recipients.

Sometimes I walked a bit further, where the gaze of Big Brother does not reach. I snuck onto the side streets whenever the guards looked the other way. Some were aware the things they guarded belonged to us. Others were tired of bullying stubborn people who could not accept that they lost their city.

I observed every single building with eagerness. My eyes reached deep into their hearts through wide-open or missing doors. I saw Pavlina's kitchen, where her mother taught us how to make beautiful, colorful butterflies from paper cuttings. I saw, in Loukia's hall, beside the living room door, Renoir's "Spring" seducing the butterflies. As if drunk, they flew around her.

I saw Mr. Michalas in the schoolyard of the elementary school, keeping the rhythm to the group's gymnastic exercises with his whistle, while tens of butterflies flew over the flowers in Mr. Constantinides' garden. Sometimes they entered the classrooms through the open windows, where the little ones who attended quietly studied their lessons.

I kept looking and searching insatiably until my eyes, tired from the years and desperation, began seeing the images, now naked. Repeatedly my eyes only saw wide open, destroyed, dead doors. Everything else had vanished. Everything except for the colorful butterflies. Rusted wide-open doors and butterflies!

Everything looked so surrealistic now.

At some point, my gaze hooked on an image that didn't fit. Different from anything observed before. It was an austere door[1], metal, painted purple and grey, the colors of coldness, of power, and wealth. And isolation!

Is that why it was left closed shut, the insides untouched? Is that why the butterflies here became solid metal, and fixed forever, like guards, threatened to keep even the enemy away?

I wonder. Is the owner of this building the unquestionable king of the city?

---

1 The reference is for the main door of the English Barclays Bank, which remains shut, keeping the interior unlooted.
The sealed metal lock has the form of a butterfly.

49. The Photo

I had explained to her our houses were empty. After the looting following the invasion, the looters didn't even leave a needle behind. She insisted she wanted to see the photos I took.

Honestly, I did not know what to do.

"There is nothing to see, Mother!" Sophia, standing next to me, said to her, clearly irritated. "You want to see nothing? Forget it all!"

The shock we had experienced, Sophia and I, upon entering the house, was enormous. We didn't want to communicate to her how disturbed we were, but Mother insisted. She had been confined to bed in the last months, so taking her with us was out of the question. She wanted, at least, to see the photos. Sophia stroked her forehead, looked her deeply in the eyes and repeated herself, slowly, with less anxiety.

"They didn't leave a single thing. Not a single photo. Not a picture frame on the wall, not one of those hand embroideries of yours. Not one book, a piece of furniture, or your flowerpots! Nothing was left. Do you understand? Not-a-thing."

Mother shook her head.

"What you are doing to me now is even worse for me," she said to us.

I put the tablet in front of her and started showing her the photos, one by one. In every room, in every corner, she remembered every detail.

"Here, we had the brown armchair. On the wall behind, Grandpa's framed photo was hanging. Here was the small table for the telephone. And right there, on the wall...."

She went on like that, insisting on commenting on every photo for the longest time. Sophia stood up and looked out the window, turning her back to us. I could see her shoulders shaking.

She had just turned five when we left. What could she possibly remember of all those things Mother was describing? Yet, Mother was calm. You would think she could touch everything in front of her. As if she walked from room to room, in our house, the house where she, too, was born.

Until we came to this one. I took this photo by mistake. I pushed the button accidentally. A rickety switch and cut wires. That's all.

Mother fell silent. She took the tablet in her hands and kept looking without making a sound.

Sophia, perplexed, turned to see. Tears began falling from Mother's wrinkled face. They ran down her cheeks, onto her blouse.

"They killed it. They cut its veins. Our house is dead."

She dropped the tablet and leaned her head on the pillow.

These were the last words she uttered to us about the house. The last words she ever wanted to say about our city. As if these, the wires, were what was connecting her with our past. It was like a story that came to its end.

For Mother, the house was a living organism. A huge uterus out of which all of us came to life.

Now the umbilical cord has been severed.

We are all orphans.

50. Directions

"You don't remember well, Georgia, but Dimokratias Street is a two-way street," she said calmly and inquisitively.

"I am certain, a thousand percent," her sister used to say to her in the past. It was always in a terse tone, almost angry. And her sister laid the bets. Five pounds the first years, ten pounds even when reduced to five shillings, then a hundred euros after entering the European Union and currency changed.

But Martha was almost always lost. And then she got angry. She blamed herself. She didn't remember her city.

What a crime! As if forgetting a detail would forgo any chance of return.

Now she avoided these contests.

"Leave me alone, you and your bets," she said to her sister every time a disagreement arose, as if it was Geogia who laid the bets. Money never changed hands, anyway. The talk about what they could remember from Varosha always ended up with such bitterness that they did not have the courage to even say "Good night," when they went their way at night.

Always at night.

Those hours when the little ones in the neighborhood withdrew to their homes, when the only noise you could hear was the voice of the female TV news anchor spreading the news through the open windows, when the only light that bathed the two sisters was the streetlight. It was at those times that the two of them were tickled by memories, together with the fragrant flower that separated their two houses in the refugee camp.

"Let it go, Martha. I don't remember either, when the change exactly happened, but it did. The upper part of the street is one way down. Here! Look at the pictures Maria sent me."

Martha bent over her sister's cell phone looking at the pictures of their city, perfectly complimenting the myriad bits of memories that singed her mind. Georgia stopped at an ungracious picture that showed a vandalized traffic light, exactly at the crossing they were discussing.

"Here. Look," she said.

Martha peered closer. Two white arrows over the faded blue on the sign right under the traffic light showed a mandatory turn either to the right or to the left.

A bitter smile hung from Martha's lips. Raising her gaze from the rickety bare lights, she looked at her sister, eyes filled.

"What are we arguing about Georgia... What on earth are we arguing about? It is so obvious. We both are terribly wrong. We both lost the bet.

"Nothing goes anywhere."

51. Mr. Socrates

"I never expected to see this. Ever! The gates of the Varosha stadium closed!"

This is not possible, I thought, and went closer to push them open. My feet sank into a huge pile of eucalyptus leaves that covered the sidewalk.

Then I heard, "Swish swish."

I hid my head in the foliage and saw him sweeping the leaves with a broom in the narrow passage along the changing rooms behind the stands. He lifted his head and smiled at me.

This is the angel of our stadium. Mr. Socrates.

He wore khaki pants, turned up on both legs, and a straw hat to protect his head from the sun. It's the same hat Erato stole from him at every opportunity, laughing loudly and teasing him.

I passed by him and coming out from the long walk under the stands, I found myself in the stadium. Absolutely soundless. There was nobody else beside me.

On the left, at the starting point of the 100-meter run, the ground was freshly evened. Socrates always starts his work from there. I looked towards the finish line. Hurdles were already in place, in proper order.

When I reached the long jump pit, I picked up the rake to even the sand. I didn't get a chance.

He was already walking toward me, in his hurried, strange stepping fashion, as if he balanced his weight on one leg before bringing the other one to the front. He approached with his characteristic movement, first gathering his arms in front of his chest, then stretching them left and right, as if trying to keep a crowd of people at bay.

It was a gesture meant to say: "Leave it. I will do it."

Then I remembered. He adopted this gesture once he lost his voice.

I did not see the accident on that fateful, horrible day. In that dark moment, late in the afternoon, the stadium had almost emptied. I did not see the horrible event unfold with my own eyes. I did not see the metal shotput ball or its seven kilos, tossed high, fly long, and fall with enormous force on his neck.

But even such a blow as that could not sideline him.

He lost his voice, but never his smile. Not ever.

Those eyes, always wet, communicated all messages his voice cords could not tell us anymore. His messages were always good, kind, and sweet.

The same as his soul.

52. My Beloved Evangelia

25 March 1975

We spoke earlier on the phone, to convey, naturally, my wishes for your name day.

But what can one say on the phone, with one end at the telephone company office at Patisia, and the other in a small hall of a strange home? I have not yet seen the house you have found in Larnaka, and I don't have an impression of it when I speak to you. For some reason, though, I imagine a bunch of strange people standing over you trying to listen to what I say to you.

You may think your sister has gone crazy.

"What! 1975? And what telephone company office?" you'd say, softly followed by, "How many years have gone by since then, my beloved?"

You know... sometimes I think that however many times we quarreled in our younger years; we became that much closer in later ones, holding no grudges against each other.

Two sisters in different camps. You with the cops and I with the robbers.

Why? Because I was the more conservative thinker, I did not believe in overturning anything. You used to call me "undaring, timid."

And you, our little one, a reed in the wind. A wick ready to light up at any flicker. An uncompromising, intense kid, fighting for the union of Cyprus with Greece.

When I hang up the phone today, my mind turns back to 1975; my first year at university. I left you searching for a home in Larnaka. My mind turns back, and I hit the roads.

It is raining non-stop, getting dark, and I have arrived at Syntagma Square, wanting to see Greece in celebration. But you, over there, what do you have to celebrate?

Are we still discussing for the nth time what we should say at the Five-party Conference, when we are still searching for an identity?[1]

What am I trying to tell you, you will be wondering.

Just this...

It is something from the past. Something I never said to anyone, but now I want you to know it...

During that evening in 1975, during the first national celebration I attended since setting foot on Greek land, it was raining again; I found myself at Syntagma Square after our phone conversation. I don't remember how, but one thing I did not forget is that suddenly my heart fluttered. And tightened.

My breath was cut off. I started crying. I became the reed in the wind. I became you.

That's what I want you to know.

Many years have gone by since then, years infertile for us, one after the other. Yet, it's been a while, and I have been overwhelmed by the stench of a strange rot....

I extend to you, my dear sister, my good wishes to all those who celebrate today. As for us... no good wish applies to us.

With my love, your sister, Aphrodite.

---

[1] The formal UN-sponsored Five party Conference was to discuss the Cyprus Problem. It included Greek Cypriots, Turkish Cypriots, Greece, Turkey, and Great Britain.

PS. The name Evangelia comes from Evangelismos, the celebration of the Annunciation of the Virgin Mary, which is celebrated on March 25, and which happens to be Greece's national holiday.

53. The Perfume Bearing Ladies Showered Your Tomb

On Good Fridays we'd rush to catch a place on the steps of Dr. Chilimintris clinic on Dimokratias St., from where Christ's funeral procession, the Epitaph, originating at St. Nickolas church, passed.

Despite the sad spectacle of the dead Christ figure, I was not sad at all.

Perhaps because I knew the story, perhaps because I knew the Resurrection would follow the next day. Perhaps because I thought God was not serious about killing His Son, He just wanted to chastise us.

Then, again, I may not have felt sad because… I knew little about graves. I did not have a special relationship with them.

I knew about rose water though and loved it's scent and touch.

On the evening of the Epitaph the "myroforoi," the perfume-bearing ladies, who followed the procession in the streets, showered the dead Christ with it from their bottles, also singing sweet hymns. I knew about rose water because Aunt Loulla sprinkled it on our palms each time we visited with her, to get rid of the dust of the road.

I also knew that apricot preserve would follow, in a ball with silver spoons hanging on its sides, such a tasty, sweet treat from the hands of auntie.

I did not know about graves. That's why the strange shadows thrown on the walls by the candles of the faithful did not scare me.

I did not know about graves. That's why the Epitaph was like a richly decorated flower float, like the ones we used to make at the flower festivals. It was most beautiful, even though it was not original, since the subject never changed.

I did not know about graves even though Yiayia Theodora often talked to me about those who had left us. She often complained when I did not pay enough attention: "Who knows... Will anyone light a candle at my grave?"

Eventually, in our last happy year, a little before we lost our city, we lost Yiayia Theodora.

She was gone so unexpectedly; I did not have a chance to say goodbye, or hold her still warm hand. Not even to say that I will light her candle myself.

That evening, on the dining room table, half covering it, I saw for the first time the yellow-gray color of death on one of my closest and dearest heart's loves.

The following Easter we celebrated without Yiayia Theodora's flaounes, her traditional egg and cheese pies. Nor did our kitchen fill with the fragrance of freshly baked bread in sesame-covered round rings.

On this Good Friday on Dr. Chilimintris' steps, the ladies held open perfume bottles and showered everyone with smells like the dozens of tiny white jasmine flowers from the bush Yiayia had planted which grew tall and wide beside our door.

Our candles barely lit our faces, and it was cloudy all over. It was as if we knew that from that year on, even though the Resurrection would keep coming, we would not stand on the Doctor's steps to welcome it.

No one would anymore ever be in Varosha to light Yiayia Theodora's candle.

54. Christina from Myloneika

We met at the long jump trench during a track and field meet in Athens. Taking part in Pan-Hellenic competitions was the greatest dream of every young athlete, hers too.

She was from Patra, I from Varosha. I smiled at her, and she came back with a smile full of light. By the time we took part and the event was over, we were fast friends. From that moment on, the letters we exchanged were full of our girlish anxieties and "magical" exercises, which were going to make us better athletes. Some poetic verses as well, venturing timidly into poetry-writing by both of us.

The postman became my best and most anticipated friend.

I don't remember how she spotted us in the apartment we rented in Pangrati, right after we arrived in Athens as refugees. Perhaps it was me who wrote to her. But I remember her first unexpected visit.

I remember how surprised I was, how moved, when I saw her in front of me the moment I opened the door: Christina from Myloneika.

The smile I knew was absent. During the two hours she stayed with us in the small apartment on Frynis St., Christina cried non-stop. She slurped up every word of mine, and was shaken by my every anguish. She wrapped her arms around my shoulders and brought her head close to mine as if to say, "Relax. Everything will be fine."

One minute after we embraced for our last goodbye, and she put on her coat on the way out, the doorbell rang again. When I opened the door I was faced with a huge bundle of bedding and blankets, and behind it, hidden, the doorman, Mr. Thanasis. Christina had left the bundle with him to bring up to us after she finished her visit.

I have nothing more to add. Except that every morning, when I take my gift-blanket out to shake it clean, the total story repeats itself.

From those first smiles to our last cries.

55. Fiddler on the Roof

I never looked down at the orchestra before the first part was over. I didn't think it would be good luck. The sale of the tickets didn't interest me either, but... the cinema was in my heart and blood, even though I was king only of the eight square meters of the projection room.

Here, in the half-lit room, I attached the reel to the machine and withdrew to the corner with a book, until intermission time.

Then I started a music tape on the loudspeakers, turned on the lights, and changed the reel, making it ready for the next half. I lit a cigarette and went outside onto the small balcony.

From this vantage point, I observed the attendees of the evening: young couples, shoulders touching, whispering their secrets; the young soldier, sitting on one of the front rows, pondering his wasted years in the army; the young boys who, after separating from their girls since they had to return home before nine o'clock, came back to catch glimpses, yelling words with mannerisms like the handsome brave men on the screen.

I saw the seller of small items with the peculiar wooden box hanging from his neck passing among the rows of seats announcing "Pepsi, KEAN, Coca-Cola!" I looked behind, too, at the neighborhood balconies with the impostor spectators. After intermission, when the foot traffic died down and lights went dark for good, they watched the show undisturbed.

I found myself again tonight at our cinema after many, many years. But everything looked so different....

The reel on the machine had reached the end and turned around aimlessly, the vinyl tip of the film hitting the table "flap-flap-flap."

I reached to press the light switch but was stopped by a noise from the orchestra. I put my face to the hole where the image passes through, and clearly heard the dialogue from "Fiddler on the Roof."

Then it hit me. That was the last film we showed before the great disaster struck.

I went out onto the small balcony, and saw the deserted orchestra: no spectators, deserted seats. However, on the top of the screen I saw our boss, with a violin in his hands, swaying from left to right. I couldn't believe it. He wore a blinding white suit, so unfitting to the dirty, torn-up screen, where nothing was being shown.

From up there, with his violin playing the gypsy numbers of the film, he looked at me with a certain meaning in his eyes, reminding me how uncertain is our very future in this part of the world.

Very uncertain.

For like the gypsies, no one knows when they will be displaced.

56. Under the Light of the Late Afternoon

She sat at the window, head turned outwards, looking at the city in the late afternoon light. The paper in front of her is still blank.

This view suits her. She doesn't dip her gaze into the deep green forest on the hill close by, nor do her eyes travel to the river's cooling waters.

She just looks at the city.

People going back and forth, this way, that, the noise of the cars in the streets at the time they return home and the shadows of the buildings stuck together, growing bigger and covering...the monotony of daily life.

She just looks at the city, the last fever of the day. That's how she stays alert. She manages to resist.

Her mind flies like a needle on a tapestry. One time to the right side, one time to the opposite.

The paper in front of her remains blank. She knows full well what her heart is asking her to write. She has constructed the story in her mind. Everything fits together now. There is a beginning, a middle, and an end.

In the colors of another city, bathed in the strong sun of the East and the fragrance of orange blossoms, it even has a sound, a fast tempo of the vigorous lute of her homeland.

She knows what to write, but she manages not to put a single word on paper. She insists on looking at the pale light of the late afternoon, which makes the city look even more foreign.

She keeps looking and resisting. A distressing feeling fills her chest. It oppresses her; it crushes her. And her hand—the good hand that knows how to write—shakes like a reed in the wind.

No, no.

Not a single word on paper. None. She knows what she wants to write. What she desires to say. But she knows even better, that if she puts down those words as she planned them in her mind, if she writes this story which will be painted with the light of the East, which will have the aroma of orange blossoms and the deep sound of the lute, a story with a beginning, middle and an end, a good end like the "Opa" of the graceful dance, she knows that after the last full stop, all her courage will run out.

After this ending, she will be unable to stand reality. And nothing more will be left to write.

If this story falls on paper, she knows it will be her last one.

Her soul will have dried out.

57. The Cats of Varosha

My world has been filled with photos and videos of Varosha.

Just a few days before my visit, I look with an insatiable appetite at the pictures my friends have captured, as if I am trying to sketch out my route.

As if I have forgotten....

I play the video back and forth. Then again. And again. I try to discern the images, to connect them. To marry them with my memories.

Thousands of kilometers away from my city, I have already started the descent from dream to reality.

I indulge in the photos of other people. On the street I look at, I remember being... in this building, then... in this school, in the stadium.... I keep looking and recollecting. I keep looking and decoding. In this corner... in the other....

My black cat always followed me to this corner by the kiosk of Dimos every time I left home. He looked at me with sadness, even though he didn't have the eyes of Salome.

His name was Jinx.

He was coming to the kiosk and back to the house, disappointed I wasn't taking him with me. I search the corners of the other buildings. Did he grow too bold? Did he go on to other neighborhoods?

I proceed to the next street. Another ten steps. Another thirty, fifty. I look with surprise at the bougainvillea that insists on blooming. What a miracle! What a miracle! Forty-seven years....

How many years do cats live? Less than a bougainvillea? Less than jasmine? And the palm trees? There were not so many palm trees in the city. I read somewhere about an indigenous variety. That's our variety, for sure.

And the cats? Where did the cats go? I search again in the corners, under the ruins, inside the toothless entrances of houses. Where did the cats go? The eyes, those eyes that are not like Salome's, come alive in front of me, and I feel sad.

I whisper the words:

> "What can they do, poor cats
> fighting and drinking day and night
> the poisonous blood of snakes?
> Aeons of poison, generations of poison."*
> I remember and suffocate! I wail!

I repeat Seferis' verses, especially the last one: "Keep a steady line, the captain responded, indifferent."

I am despair.

---

* Excerpt from George Seferis poem "The Cats of St. Nicholas." Translated into English by Achilleas Antoniades.

58. The Sour Man

The worn sign above the front door showed this was a taxi office. Other soldiers had already looted the place. Only a blackboard hung on the wall. That's what caught his eye as he traversed the wide avenue.

The teacher. The strange man. The sour man.

That's what the entire platoon called him, how they made fun of him. He doesn't care. The only thing he cares about is getting rid of this nightmare. To return to their homes.

He stood in front of the blackboard, obviously touched. Car license plates were written in blue chalk and the names of the drivers next to them. He wiped the Greek names with his sleeve, chose a white chalk and started to write: "Allah…"

From shops around the area, sounds could be heard from broken windows, mixed with the wild clamoring of his frenzied buddies, busy emptying the properties of Greek Cypriots of anything that could be removed.

He closed his eyes for a minute, tried to isolate himself from the disgusting fanfare, and then continued inscribing his prayer: "…grant me health, help me live in a world without the need for doctors."

He had heartburn all morning but said nothing. He wanted to see this wealthy city for himself. The day before, the other platoons had pillaged the seaside road and spoke of nothing else. He wanted to see this wealthy city, but not enter other people's houses, nor dip his fingers into the honeypot.

Let's get it over with. This nightmare, he thought. He turned to the blackboard and continued to write.

"Let my military service end without more evil." And underneath, "Open the schools!"

From the shop next door came laughter and loud voices rousing the street. He looked outside. Two soldiers of his own platoon were loading clothing onto a truck. The rest had formed a circle around Mehmet, who, wearing a gaudy shirt over his uniform and, with lewd provocative motions, shouted out an obscenity.

The rest screamed and laughed hysterically.

He was beside himself now. He rushed back into the shop. "That's enough!!!" he shouted. "That's enough, for fuck's sake!"

He howled it out with as much air as he could master in his lungs.

Taking the chalk into his hand again, he scribbled on the blackboard what Mehmet had uttered earlier.

"Let me thrust my dick in your dark blue asshole."

Then he threw the chalk away and bent his body down in two. Heartburn had spread to his insides, reached his head, burned his eyes, painted black his soul.

Like theirs.

"Enough!!!" he screamed for the last time and sobbed, falling to the floor.

Outside, his buddies continued to enjoy the looting.

59. The Night the Trees Fell

I ran, head down, wall to wall, among the ruins. Wind blew furiously. The moon, hiding behind dense clouds, made the way difficult.

Nothing other than my steps disturbed the quiet of the night.

Night in the abandoned, wounded city.

When I reached the kiosk, I stopped to catch my breath, leaned on the rolled down shutters and looked left, where I knew my home was. Only a shadow was visible in the deep darkness.

Suddenly, a tremendous storm broke out and I found myself exposed to its savage blows. I ran with all my strength, stepping over little hills and dry weeds among fig trees loaded with fruit, their branches lying on the ground, breaking under my feet. My shirt is stuck, becoming one with my wrinkled, tender skin, both soaked.

The more I ran, the more the mass of my house, which was visible behind the dense foliage, stayed at the same distance.

The rain stopped as quickly as it came.

I found myself in front of two huge eucalyptus trunks which had sprung out of the cement tarmac, and which now hid the entrance to my house. I passed carefully between them and discovered with great surprise that our jasmine plant had grown to a gigantic size, reaching up to the roof and engulfing the whole house.

I dragged myself up the big staircase and climbed the stairs two at a time, continuing blindly to my room. Very courageous; in the darkness of our hallway there was no ghost to scare me. I pushed the shutters open, exactly when the rain started coming down heavily again.

Looking out to the empty lot across the street, I barely caught sight of a tank going up and down little hills at the same place where half a century before we had dug childhood trenches. It turned the thick barrel of its gun to our front entrance. I watched in slow motion; a puff of smoke emanate from its mouth.

The explosion was deafening.

Before I managed to bend down under the window, the eucalyptus trees bent their branches like an arrow, sending the fire back, hurling the tank into the air, then falling to the tarmac.

The house remained unguarded. I felt naked.

I awoke to the alarm radio, frightened and drenched in sweat. My sheet was thoroughly wet. The rain outside fell "slap, slap" on the windows. I pulled the curtain wide and saw the trees surrounding the church lying on the ground, uprooted.

The news anchor was announcing the decision of the Sultan to lift the militarized zone status of part of Famagusta, known as Varosha.

60. The Light at the Front Door

"You must change the bulb at the front door, Apostolis."

She repeated this every evening when she returned home.

It was getting on her nerves. She was older now and her eyesight was worse and worse. She couldn't even get the key into the keyhole, despite fumbling with her other hand.

"Yes, yes, in the morning." But, like a myriad other replies, it was a promise sent to the postponement file.

The two siblings, Stavroulla and Apostolis, were twins.

Always together and always whining. Years went by, but they stayed together, just the two of them. Neither married, nor let anyone get between them. Together in business too, they ran the shoe store.

He opened it in the morning; she closed it in the evening.

"Everything shared equally," Apostolis would say, but Stavroulla had a different opinion, and she was right. All morning, when he was taking care of the shop, his sister worked hard to do all the cooking and housework, arriving at the shop to replace him dead tired.

The week before, as Stavroulla closed the shop shutters, she felt a strange, strong pain pierce her back. She fell to her knees and remained rolled up on the cement tarmac, short of breath. She did not stay there long, though. In seconds, Apostolis was bent over her head. He found himself there by chance; he said later. It was by chance that he was led to the shop at that specific moment.

They beat back the heart attack that evening.

After five days in the clinic, Stavroulla returned home. Accompanied by whom? Her brother Apostolis. He held her with his left arm, and with the right, he struggled to put the key in the hole. He turned, looked at the dark light on the ceiling, and then at her. Stavroulla smiled.

He tried to say something to her, but she stopped him.

"Come, don't go silly over a bulb. It is too high for us. When Andreas comes to look after the garden, I will ask him to replace it."

She took the keys from his hands.

The door of the house where the twins were born slid open sweetly.

A warm light spread from inside, engulfing the two siblings.

Even though the bulb on the front door was burned out.

61. Stringed Moments

We sold fresh kefir.

My father did, that is.

I went with him only in the afternoons.

At 13 in 1974, I had just finished school and my parents and I concluded there was no point in me continuing to trouble the teachers. So, in the mornings, I apprenticed as a shoemaker at my uncle Ahmet's, and in the afternoons, I pushed my father's cart outside the walls up to the upper neighborhoods. There, people jostled at the bus stops to catch a bus to their villages.

One day I heard her music. Notes glided off her violin strings like swirling autumn leaves in the wind, traveled through the open window and mingled in my head, making my heart thump strongly.

I was overcome with magic.

After that, I rushed to park the cart so I could return to her house and nestle under her open window. I let my mind travel as I rode the wind along with her notes, desiring with all my soul to see the face of this magic person. I stood on my toes and tried to look, stretching, and leaning left to right to the sidewalk across the street, hoping to catch a glimpse inside the room.

Until, one day, she saw me first, and came to the window frame in a fury.

"Eh, you little hobo! Why are you looking into other people's windows?" she screamed.

I was upset. And shamed.

Not because she scolded me. I felt shame at my audacity, to stand outside the window of a fairy with an angelic face and red cheeks and mouth, with fine chestnut curly hair flowing down her shoulders.

She pulled the curtains hard.

The next day, my country's soldiers overwhelmed the city before the war.

Today I returned for the first time since then, into the city, together with my son. When we came to the window of the fairy, I stopped.

"Why are you looking into other people's windows?" my son said, perplexed.

I smiled and raised my shoulders.

What could I tell him? That I was looking to see the angel of the house? It is years now that I wanted to tell her I, the little hobo, have an angel of my own, a son, who plays the violin in the best orchestras in Europe.

I stayed there, looking at the window frame, even though I knew that if by some miracle I could see her again, I would feel ashamed to talk to her.

Only... I would be happy we could be together again in this city of golden sand, grown now like a mother with wide arms.

Great enough arms to take us all in.

62. The Blindness of People

Mr. Takis's jewelry shop was inside the old arcade beside my optical shop.

He was probably the first to open a shop in this part of the city. At almost twice my age, he could have been my father. He treated me that way with the care he always showed me, the advice or admonitions, even scolding's as well. It depended on what he thought was appropriate under the circumstance.

His shop was old-fashioned. At first, I took it negatively that such a shop stood next to mine, renowned for its carefully chosen style. Windows and shelves of stainless steel and glass in mine, poor quality plywood boards for the jewelry of Mr. Takis, which... let's face it, were the same settings and gems as those my grandmother wore.

Gradually, though, I lowered my objections. After all, Mr. Takis had clients from all the surrounding villages. I took advantage of this opportunity, provided, of course, I supplemented the variety of frames with less expensive ones and more conservative designs.

Whenever Mr. Takis was not busy, he pulled a straw chair outside, beside the door, unbuttoned the first button of his shirt, and pushed the two legs of the chair backwards. This allowed him to lean his head on the wall. He half-closed his eyes, but nothing escaped his attention. He observed people going by and had comments on everyone as soon as they moved on.

I laughed and enjoyed looking at him. He rubbed me the wrong way only when he picked up the newspaper to read. How did he pick only the bad news reports? He attracted them like a magnet. He always turned to me and said, "What do you think you can achieve? Can you straighten out people?"

When I protested, he turned the newspaper towards me and showed me the huge headlines.

"Here," he continued. "Look! They don't see where this whole thing is going. Everybody insists on remaining blind in their ignorance."

The papers talked about bombs, terrorist attacks, and deaths. In black ink, of course, how else? Thick and black, like the malice of people.

Years went by. I don't know where Mr. Takis ended up. If he is still alive, I think he too will remember our talks. Every time he puts his glasses on to read his newspapers, he will shake his head and think that the world will never see clearly.

The same way I think.

Even though I am an optician.

63. For a Peach Juice

"Sheftali![1]"

These kinds of things you used to tell me, and it made me mad.

Not at you, but at Mr. Christakis, who chose you to be his second worker. As if there are no workers available from among our own people.

I used to get mad also when you searched for words to finish a sentence. Your Greek was poor. You could hardly cope. And you faltered and hesitated. Mr. Christakis said that you were afraid you might choose the wrong word, and a misunderstanding might arise between us.

"Never fear. The Turks are not known to have such sensitivities," I would answer.

I used to get madder when customers got us mixed up. "You two look alike," they said.

Nonsense! It was our green overalls and the sawdust that made our hair white and made us look alike. Everyone laughed around us. I pretended to laugh and pointed at you with my finger. Then I used to say, "All is fine."

I felt I had the upper hand. Yes, indeed, all was fine.

---

[1] Sheftali in Greek is a small sausage made of ground meat and spices wrapped in lamb's gut membrane. It is particular to Cyprus.

I get even madder when at Marios's home cooking shop, where the two of us used to have lunch at noon, we were forced to share a table. Half the seaport personnel came down there, and no vacant table could be found.

That's where you engaged me in your nonsensical talk, at the same time wiping oil from your lips with the hard edge of your bread. If your words came out confused.

You ended up saying, "At any rate, we will not go hungry, koumbare."[2] You said this because, however confused you were in your words, regarding food, we were very much alike, with one exception.

Peach.

In your language, you call it sheftali. It didn't sound at all funny to me. I didn't feel sympathy for anything concerning you and your world. Even when we chose the kind of juice to drink to quench the thirst from our common labors.

You used to call me koumbare, as if it would have ever been possible for us two to become "koumbaroi." You, with your crooked faith, which fortunately did not in any way relate to mine. We were not even friends. Apart from meeting at Marios's shop, we never even shared a cup of coffee together elsewhere.

As it happened, we both remained hungry. I don't know what went wrong, nor do I want to.

Now... of course... if that coffee we never had together would make the difference, if it would take me back to my home, eh, it is then well deserved!

Well, my deserved Ahmet. May we return home and make it a rule to go out together for a walk in the afternoon, nice and tidy. We'd sip coffee or even a sheftali juice, and chat.

You never know.

I may get to like you.

I may even call you koumbaros.

---

[2] Koumbaros in Greek is the Best Man, a position of friendship and honor.

64. At Famagusta Lyceum for Greek Female Students[1]

It was the first piece, next to the entrance, on its own easel. The fine script read, *Portrait of Dorian Gray,* on the little white plaque under the painting.

Above, a stunningly beautiful youthful face with a slight smile painted his red lips.

I stopped, perplexed. The title of the exhibition was "The Forest," and I did not expect this.

The crowds pressing to get into the exhibition forced me to cut through and move deeper to the back. I pushed my way through the throngs, trying to get close enough to the paintings to read and recognize the artists' names, all my friends.

Self-absorbed, I found myself walking under the thick foliage of really tall trees, in an endless dense forest.

And... I was alone!

The thick foliage blocked the light. I shuddered.

I started running, looking for a clearing.

Fortunately, it didn't take me long to locate the exit, but just then, I saw the last visitor coming close to the exit.

I followed.

He turns abruptly towards the portrait, takes a sharp painting spatula, and drives it deep under the cheek of Dorian Gray.

A drawn-out wail pierces the cloaked silence. I spin around, terrorized. The forest has disappeared, together with the panels and the exhibits. In their place, hundreds of bright gay dresses lay on the floor like rugs.[2]

I bend down, pick up a few, but as soon as my fingers touch their hems, they lose all hues and tints and instantly take on the color of my now pale skin. Frightened, I pitch them back to the floor and as they touch the rest, all become the same color as my drained skin, and they look like human bodies crawling intertwined over each other.

Suddenly, the sleeves raised high in a begging posture, the wailing from the portrait becomes a rattle and my wits escape me. As I pass by it, I see copious blood flowing from his eyes down his cheek, reddening his white, straight collar. The stunningly beautiful face is now ugly, repulsive, with a malicious look and lips so thin, they allow two lines of rotten teeth to show.

I run outside the Lyceum and stop to catch my breath, looking across to the Municipal Garden. Erdogan's bulldozers are hard at work, moving towards the Gymnasium.

I want to jump out of this nightmare. I cannot take it anymore.

But I do not manage.

Because what I see before me now, and taste in my dry cotton mouth, is bitter reality.

65. About the Future

I am not in the mood to fight.

Not today.

I had sworn that as soon as I got to our shop, and before he started gnawing at me and sucking my blood with his nagging, I would go upstairs to the Accounts Department and close the door so I couldn't hear him. It's my sole refuge from his unending nagging.

He's my father. Over forty and I just reached half his age.

How could he understand me? How could he understand that young blood boils? What drives me crazy is that he never takes a position on events that happen in our days. He is indifferent. He argues not because he has the opposite view from mine, just because.

He just DOESN'T HAVE an opinion. He doesn't give a damn about our country. Money. That's all he cares about. He fights with me because when I am away at demonstrations, he thinks I cheat on the hours I work for him.

I enter the shop decisively and find him looking at me... eyes filled. I am dumbfounded. I forget the oaths and start explaining, but he turns his head the other way, as if to ignore me.

I get angry; *he can't ignore me.* Nor can those of his generation. They are given over to money and profits. Can't they see that if we leave the initiative to the others, the country will go to the rocks? Can they not understand that this new struggle is more sacred than any other? It is not a matter of different points of view. It's a matter of direction, of our future.

"Father," I say, and he turns his head towards me, always looking at me with the same wet eyes.

I try to continue, but he stops me with a sudden movement of his hand, which feels like a powerful blow on my face. It upsets me more. I turn towards the end of the shop, to go upstairs, to close the door behind me, to stop looking at him.

Then... then I see clearly around me.

The staircase that led to the loft has disappeared. I proceed in great surprise and touch my hand on the wall where it had left its marks. I have no refuge.

I turn towards father, but in the place where I left him, there is a huge vacuum. The shop is deserted. Without furniture, without merchandise, without the presence of my father; without history, without Makarios and Grivas.[1]

Robbed of the past... but also of the future.

---

1 Makarios and Grivas were the two legendary leaders of the anti-colonial struggle of 1955-1960. Later, differences arose between them that led to clashes between their supporters. The rift eventually led to the coup by the Greek Junta that led to the Turkish invasion of 1974.

66. We Have Already Burned Ourselves

I was in a hurry to go upstairs—it was already almost noon. I saw her coming down our big staircase furiously.

Furiously!

Arms at right angles and fists resting on the waist, she looked like a koukoumara.[1] Like she always did when she was about to undertake a mission, when she wanted to impose herself on things.

I moved to the side. I know what to do when Yiayia Theodora had her sleeves rolled up, when nothing in this world could stop her. She shuffled in her slippers past me, went out onto the landing and started untying the apron hanging in front of her dress.

I smiled as I remembered grandpa Savvas who scolds her every time she goes out the house with her flowery apron on, open to the wind. Not that this happens very often. But when she is out collecting the groceries, Uncle Tasos sends her from his grocery store, then she doesn't untie it, just for one breath's worth of work.

---

1 A double-handle pitcher. Ceramic art used to be a tradition for Varosha, especially the making of koukoumara, where people used to keep fresh, cool water.

Yes, Grandpa wants her to look smart, stylish, inside and outside the home. He wants her to be beautiful, well-dressed, with beautiful jewelry. He wants her to look like an empress.

After all, she has the name Yiayia Theodora.[2]

I was telling you about the other day, the beginning of October, when I saw her rushing out of the house in a fury. She didn't even stop to smell her jasmine. The fragrance of its flowers pierces your nostrils, even now. She didn't stop to say good morning to Aunt Olga next door, sweeping her yard. She just went down the three steps, dragging her slippers in the street.

She stopped for a moment, looked at her feet, but immediately shrugged her shoulders indifferently. She crossed the street diagonally and passed by the empty glass showcases, where in the summer the "future shows" are posted outside Hadjihambis' open-air cinema.

I rushed after her.

I yelled, "Eh, Yiayia, where are you going?" But she continued towards the Avenue without turning around to listen.

I caught up with her at the corner by the kiosk of Dimos. I tried to tell her something but at that moment two steamrollers going up the Avenue blocked our ears.

She signaled them to stop. She was waiting for them. That's why she came out of the house in a storm. She raised her arms, signaling them to follow her.

"Here," she yelled. "Come this way. It is the turn of our street. My husband's name-day is coming soon."

The drivers burst out laughing. They pointed their fingers at her, looked at each other, and laughed, as if Yiayia had just told them the most outrageous joke.

I looked on in a fright. I had seen these two people before somewhere else. I could swear I knew them from somewhere.

---

2 Reference to the Byzantine empress Theodora, who was thought to be born in Cyprus.

Yes! In clean, shiny, tidy suits. I saw their pictures in those huge banners waving to the crowds. One in the south, the other in the north.

I have seen them before.

They ignored Yiayia Theodora's screaming and continued their march on the big Avenue, riding on their two beasts, paying no attention to her.

Yiayia broke out sobbing and beat her chest furiously. She screamed like a wild animal.

"Not another year! No more years!"

I had never seen her in such desperation. She was always so optimistic. She always had her way of facing difficulties, and a smile never left her lips. But this time, she rolled over on the sidewalk like a cat and started lamenting.

I went insane. I couldn't bear Yiayia in this state. I got angry, riled up, and started running after the two beasts as if I could ever win a fight with them.

Me, a ten-year-old child.

I chased after them up to the bend for Ermou St. and there, seeing that they were moving away, still laughing, I stopped exhausted. I was out of breath.

With my head low, I slowly turned back down the Avenue towards Yiayia. When I arrived at the kiosk, I couldn't see her anywhere. No one knew where she went, nobody saw her. I thought she might have returned home, but suddenly the evening started falling, hiding like a vast screen the once beautiful city.

And I, one more time, found myself outside the city, lost.

I woke up the next morning talking to myself, saying I will never go back to my city. I don't want to see Varosha wounded anymore.

But how can I get around the fact that I am dying to live there for just a little while, just one moment, sunning and smiling in our once beautiful years together?

I am dying to get into my house again.

There, however funny it may sound, I want to catch Yiayia in her fragrant kitchen around noon on Sunday.

She will open the door of the oven to turn the roast over, and like a co-conspirator, will take out a semi-cooked potato just for me, and place it on a coffee saucer.

More than anything, though, I am dying to hear her, my adorable Yiayia.

She whispers, "Take it easy, my angel. You will burn yourself."

67. The Palm Trees

Palm trees are sly.

I never liked them.

However, I am in love with the sweet taste of their fruit. The only palm tree I accepted was the one in Yiayia Loukia's garden, and only because of the date pies and date cookies Yiayia made for us from its pleasurable gifts.

Other trees I despised. Those were to blame for everything, those behind the Venetian walls of the old city. They were uncountable. They were provocative. They raised their tall, long heads proudly above the stone walls, above the medieval buildings, above the three hundred and sixty-five churches people swore sat behind the Walls.

They moved their heads slowly left to right like giraffes, and they made fun of me, drove me wild. They goaded me like malevolent monsters because the heavy doors below the vast arches remained closed forever for us.[1]

Palm trees, those palm trees with the great privilege of looking from high above and enjoying our now forbidden city.

I despised them the most.

---

[1] In 1964, after a widespread intercommunal fighting the Turkish Cypriots ceased their participation in the central government and the populations of the two communities were forced to split. Since then, the Greek Cypriots were not allowed to enter in the old city of Famagusta within the Venetian walls.

I found myself at the barbed wire[2] at nine in the morning; the first time after so many years.

Nine o'clock in the morning, as early as I could, so I would get to see it. Not the whole city, but this little bit, just the two streets the Sultan allowed. Before the sun goes down, I must get back through the checkpoint.

I walk and look everywhere, insatiable.

My gaze gets hooked on the places we grew up, our houses, our schools and our gardens, our very life, broken into pieces. Everything is familiar, beloved. Images, memories wake up and jostle in my mind, travel my feelings to the past.

Until... in the horizon, I observe something that doesn't fit, something foreign. It invades my mind with audacity, insisting on changing my memories.

I found it!

It's the tens of palm trees that grew all these years in empty lots, in the yards of our houses; beside those few older ones, planted with love and care by the homeowners. These new ones rose from the ground on their own, with no plan or design, without order, without permission from anyone or anything.

They grew in the encircled city and shot up tall as rockets. They move and assume coquettish airs like giraffes, and they are provocative.

They mock me. They goad me malevolently because we can't go beyond the cordons, which are light plastic, but for us they are inviolable stone and steel walls. We can't step beyond them.

Cordons of red and white that hide our forbidden city, from ourselves, from the world.

These newer palm trees, with double privileges, I don't just despise. I hate them.

---

2 High barbed wire fencing around the Varosha ghost town within the larger city, Famagusta. After the Turkish invasion in 1974, the Turkish Army prohibited Greek Cypriots from entering. From 2020, only two streets allowed access to visit Varosha for just a few hours per day.

68. Parking Rights

She parked on the main market street and took out her wallet to count her change. Eight half-shillings.

They were enough for lots of parking rights.

She went to the meter and began inserting coins one by one in the slot. "Ca-ching, ca-ching." She wondered in what order she would spend her four hours of "parking rights,"[1] in city center.

She would leave the vegetables last for Yiayia Theodora, so she wouldn't have to haul them everywhere. She would start from the supermarket of Paralimnitis for two Jinxy's cat-food cans, and immediately after, head for threads and other sewing materials from Yiangoudis. She would stop at the newspaper stand for a Greek newspaper and...

The machine wouldn't take her fifth coin. She quickly tried another.

She would stop by her koumbara's[2] house to copy the new recipe she brought from London for apple tart. Certainly, also for coffee and a relaxed chat.

---

1 The author is playing with the word "tariff" which was shown on the parking meters in Greek. It was referred to as δικαιώματα, meaning "rights".

2 Maid of Honor.

She wouldn't, of course, forget grandpa's medications, and to chat with Uncle Michalakis about the news of the family. She hadn't seen Auntie Pipitsa and Yiayia Maria for some time.

Her metal coin gurgled again in the insides of the machine and jumped out. She tried a third time.

She would also stop by Florenzos to choose the color of her material for her skirt suit, then by Uncle Christos and Aunt Fotini's patisserie for fresh galaktopourekko[3] and... and... what else?

What else?

The parking meter continued to throw up the fifth coin.

She pushed her far-sighted glasses onto the base of her nose and bent down to read the instructions again.

"Maximum Period Two Hours."

She panicked.

How much can you do in two hours?

She passed her fingers through her pure white hair and looked away, at the playful waters of the fountain, outside Hereon cinema. Her heart jumped, together with the colorful waters.

She smiled. She would manage everything in two hours, she must. Even twice as much. Because this heart does not grow old. This heart will continue to beat at the rhythms of the city, which buzzes around her like a beehive. The city before canned food came to food banks, before they put on the charity collection dresses, before the noon announcements on the radio by the Red Cross.[4] All and more, when the dreams changed schedule; when they jumped into the space between 6:30 am and 6:30 pm.

Those other dreams, which once claimed rights to happiness, cost two shillings at a time.

---

3 A Greek dessert made of phyllo dough and custard.
4 That is, before the Turkish invasion.

69. Interpreting Dreams

Petros thinks we see fairies when Alena, Katerina, Niki, and I talk about our dreams.

He even thinks we live in them!

It's not that we remember our dreams clearly, nor that we enjoy searching for interpretations or explanations, or anything except for one extraordinary thing.

What enlivens our discussions is that the four of us systematically manifest the same dream—each one her own—like the reruns of a soap opera on TV.

Alena describes herself falling into a dark, bottomless hole, with endless swirling, which goes on continuously until the moment she shoots up from bed drenched in sweat and riled up.

Katerina talks to us about the noiseless fights she has, sometimes with her father, often with her physics teacher twenty years ago, in the last year of Lyceum. In these violent fights, they grab her by the hair and while she struggles to slap them, her hand freezes just a few centimeters from their cheek.

Niki is the lucky one who spends her nights flying over people, listening to them talking, absorbing their secrets undetected. Despite all her efforts to convey how disturbed she is, I envy her. I envy her terribly.

As for me... I always see the same unexplainable, monotonous, repeated dream. I see only the door of our house. Not any house. I see the door of the house where I was born. Where I spent my childhood, where I played, where I laughed, where I cried. The house I enjoyed until it was destroyed by the Turks.

Niki insists on reading for me excerpts from a book interpreting dreams, which says, "Good days wait for you, full of prosperity and happiness." And I believed her until the day before yesterday.

Two days ago, I passed the crossing point to the occupied area, and managed, for the first time, to reach our house in Varosha. Our rusted door hung off its hinges, resting on the wall, as if waiting for something or someone, leaving our house exposed to the mercy of time.

Then I remembered Alena's words to me when I first mentioned this insistent dream.

"In our lands, front doors, beyond being guardians of the house, have a second function. Dead masters are laid on them until it is time for the funeral."

And the thought passed through my mind: we are lucky.

At least our doors still wait for us.

70. Melody in Three-and-a-half Measures

"What you are doing makes absolutely no sense," she said to me in a calm tone without lifting her eyes from the knitting needles.

"It's best you mind your own business," I said calmly, even though boiling inside, as I listened to the sound on the other end of the line ringing endlessly and no one answering.

Many of us gave into the temptation to try. Maybe all of us. At any rate... I don't believe my sister didn't stand, not even once, in front of the black phone set. It seems impossible to me she didn't put her finger in the dial holes. She didn't caress the numbers—first number six, then the other four digits.

They appeared to fit so well with the prefix and the whole number sounded like music in my ear.

Six, twenty-six, twenty-seven. A melody written in three-and-a half measures.

At the beginning, I used to call only our number. I used to let it ring five times, a full half-minute, enough for someone to pick it up from one of our bedrooms.

Afterwards I let it ring ten times, in case the Turkish settler was in the kitchen, then ten more, giving enough time for anyone out on the terrace. In front of my eyes I saw the image of our house, its rooms, the furniture-like obstacles one would need to jump over. I counted the steps, sometimes of a grown-up, sometimes the happy jumping of a small child.

Yes, a small child would not resist the temptation to answer it.

Then, swearing, I slammed the handset back on the phone set, certain that someone was indeed in our house and was laughing maliciously, suspecting the drama we were living.

As time passed, I tried to dial my Godmother's number.

Later, I dialed Father's work. I thought they would see the storage rooms full of merchandise as a goldmine.

The day I heard a female voice on the other end of the line talking deep from her diaphragm, slowly, deeply, and clearly in a stable rhythm, taking short pauses, when I heard her say in great self-confidence, "The subscriber number dialed doesn't exist," on that day, the very umbilical cord of my life was cut.

What hurt even more is what I suspected.

At some point, doing her job well, the well-trained telephone operator even smiled.

71. Knits

We wanted the shop to be on the central street. To be in clear sight of everybody in the market. Knitted goods—woolen for winter, cool threads for summer.

The two cousins, me and Nina.

"Don't make this mistake," my mother kept saying. "For four years, you couldn't get along as roommates. Now you agree to open a shop together?"

"Stop making your bad luck predictions, Mother," I yelled back. "Everything will go well. Each one in her role. I will be responsible for sales and she for accounts."

We had our inaugural opening at the beginning of November. We treated people to red wine from a dozen bottles in exchange for promises that the next day they would come shopping.

By Christmas, we had sold just four pieces.

"You were late," people told us. "Shopping for the winter season happened long ago."

But our treats numbered in the dozens. Our location was ideal.

As May rolled in, with fresh sweet fragrances, the woolen pieces were moved to the loft and the shop window was adorned with the summer collection. Coffees were replaced with cool lemonades.

But they told us the blouses were too short, or two wide, or the wrong color. Nina grumbled behind the books, as if I couldn't see the empty coffer.

Mid-July, when we were supposed to put in the order for the winter lot, Nina put her foot down.

"We don't have any money," she said. "We must sell the old stock first."

Our waterloo came one day before the coup, when technicians came to install the awning. That's the awning she ordered by herself through her husband's brother, having spent our last savings that were meant to pay for the new merchandise.

From that day on and up to the second phase of the Turkish invasion, we did not exchange a single word, even though the entire city passed by our shop lamenting the great disaster that befell the people of Kyrenia.[1] Our gaze and souls were empty, as was the till.

Everything was empty except for the shelves, loaded with unsold merchandise.

Until the Turkish army came and emptied even that.

As refugees now, we found ourselves in different areas. Fortunately, our paths didn't cross except for a few times.

Yesterday, however, as I stood in front of our devastated shop, spontaneously I picked up my cellphone and called her.

"Shall I send you pictures?" I asked.

"I was there myself yesterday," she said in a sad voice and, after so many years, I felt sorry for her!

Five minutes later, she called back.

She asked. "Did you notice the awning has stood the test of time?"

---

1 The northern city in Cyprus, which was the first to be captured in the 1974 Turkish invasion.

72. Va, Pensiero

"Fascinating!" she said to her mother with excitement.

Red cheeks and bright wide-open eyes carried the images she had just experienced in the great theater of First Gymnasium, Christmas 1972. For the first time, all gymnasiums were celebrating it together.

In the morning, the audience was students, in the evening their parents. Claire had no role to play in the celebrations then, as, of course, she had no role to play in the celebrations of today.

Today, the conquerors were celebrating the establishment of the "Turkish Cypriot state"[1] at our most provocative location: in front of the First Greek Gymnasium of Famagusta.

How wrong it proved to be to pick this specific day to visit her betrayed city....

She turned to go back when her eye stopped at the imposing modern building of the theater.

As she gazed into her mind, it all returned to life as it had been.

She sat in the middle of the room when the lights went out without warning. Whispers came out of the mouths of the students like waves and then, absolute silence.

---

1 After the Turkish invasion, Turkey declared the occupied part of Cyprus as the independent "Turkish Republic of Northern Cyprus." However, no other country recognized it. In international law, it is still an occupied part of the Republic of Cyprus.

Then two rows of girls dressed in white, holding a light that reflected on their faces, walked down from the balcony singing a cappella a superb hymn. One after the other, they glided in the two corridors of the theater like a stream of light, and their thin voices filled the space with sweetness.

But also, with something like, something like... overwhelming stress.

"Fly, fly golden-winged thought," the girls of the Gymnasium for Female Students sang, and Claire, speechless, felt she was flying with them in other worlds, in places without animosities and frictions. Without Grivas or Makarios supporters,[2] without reds and blues, without oranges flying over the heads of protesters. Without explosions at police stations, without people on the Most Wanted lists.

Without deaths.

She felt overwhelming stress that morning without ever being able to decode it.

Until today.

Looking at the grand theater now, she realized that the superb hymn their music director had chosen in this year of civil clashes, leading to an apogee of insanities, was in the end prophetic. Because in this hymn "Va pensiero..." from Verdi's opera *Nabucco*, the Hebrews longed for their homeland.

The homeland they were forced to abandon.

Exactly like the homeland we were forced to abandon.

Verdi, with the Choral of the Hebrew Slaves, who "Hasten thoughts on golden wings," is sending a message of freedom for his own homeland, Italy, then enslaved, calling for liberation and unification.

O, my homeland, so beautiful and lost!
O memories, so dear and yet so deadly!

---

[2] Georgios Grivas and Archbishop Makarios (later President), the two leaders of opposite factions among the Greek Cypriots who were fighting each other.

A prophecy; a tragedy; one more homeland betrayed.
Waiting for us to wake up.

73. Holidays Betrayed

Yiayia Theodora left us in 1973.

The empress of our home, she was the joy of the family. Her heart betrayed her, and we were together with her during her last fleeting moments.

That's why those holidays seemed dry.

They seemed tasteless, dark, dull, empty.

The big buffet table remained bare for the first time. No big plate with date cookies, no sweet thin dough sheets, not even ladies' fingers.[1] In the hallway, beside the everyday teak couch, the corner remained bare, without the traditional Christmas tree. Without blinking little lights, without impressive glass ornaments that our mother enriched each year with the brightness of two or three more, bought from the most unimaginable places during the year.

For the first time, those celebrations had no sound. They were not filled with joyful laughter and the familiar voices of the family. No one went out on the balcony to replace Yiayia Theodora, to throw down the full earthen water pot, our beloved koukoumara, so that every evil spirit would be frightened away.

How strange... even the horns of the ships did not manage to be heard through the walls of our house.

---
[1] A special Cypriot pastry filled with nuts and honey.

The holidays of 1973 were the first time we had this awful experience. Equally dull and dry holidays followed for forty-seven years.

Only those holidays were not betrayed by the heart of a Yiayia Theodora. They were betrayed by the hearts of our people, those unable to reunite and return.

People who do not know how to throw koukoumara from the balcony so that every evil departs forever.

Appendix A Brief History

10th century AD. The founding of Ammohostos, the original name of the city foreigners called Famagusta. Great Cyprian cities had flourished and declined in even earlier years. One was ancient Engomi, the kingdom of Salamis in the years immediately after the Trojan War. Arsinoe later came under the rule of the Ptolemies. Then the Byzantines renamed it Nea Justiniani until it too was lost under furies of Saracen raiders.

Cyprus, with its position at the crossroads between West and East, has always been at the mercy of the appetites of the great powers.

Ammohostos, therefore, was founded during the Byzantine years on the ruins of Arsinoe and Nea Justiniani. A city that will grow through the beautiful sandy beaches of eastern Cyprus, hence its name, *buried in sand*.

> 1191: On his way through Cyprus during the Crusades, Richard the Lionheart, then king of England, envies the island's strategic position and conquers it. Thus, the island passes from the Byzantines to the Crusaders.
>
> 1192: The French Lusignan Dynasty buys the island of Cyprus and Famagusta experiences unprecedented

prosperity. It is fortified with thick, strong walls. Its port is the most important port of the Eastern Mediterranean Sea, and trade flourishes, making Famagusta one of the richest cities of Christendom. Magnificent buildings and churches adorn the city, and Lusignans crown their kings in the Cathedral of Saint Nicholas.

1373: The Genoese occupy the city, but it retains its glory and wealth.

1489: With various intrigues, the city passes into the hands of the Venetians, and Famagusta becomes the new administrative center for the entire island and general headquarters for the Eastern Mediterranean.

1571: After a legendary siege where the city walls, reinforced by the Venetians, hold out for 11 months, the indigenous Greek population ends up under Ottoman rule and is exiled outside the walls. They establish a suburb of the city, where the citizens had their orchards. They call it **"Varosha."** In Turkish it means *suburb*.

1878: The British lease the island from the Ottomans, and Famagusta administratively consists of both the old walled city and Varosha.

1960: After a bloody armed struggle of the Greek Cypriots under the organization EOKA aiming for their self-determination and union with Greece (1955-1959), the island becomes independent from British rule and the Republic of Cyprus is established. The two largest national communities are Greek Cypriot (76 .6%) and Turkish Cypriot (18.1%). Both communities take part in the country's governance. Britain, Greece, and Turkey gain the status of guarantor powers for the smooth functioning of the new, yet very complex and cumbersome, Constitution.

1963-1964: Nationalist expressions from both sides prevent smooth governance from early on, and the first armed conflicts break out. Turkish Cypriots abandon the Government and retreat into enclaves. In Famagusta, Turkish Cypriots close the gates of the old city, allowing only foreign tourists to enter. At that time, Turkish Cypriots make up 16.1% of the population, while Greek Cypriots outside the walls (Varosha) make up 82.4%.

1971: While the conflict between the two communities is ongoing, a new nationalist armed paramilitary organization is founded among the Greek Cypriots in cooperation with the junta government in Greece, It pushes for the dissolution of the Republic of Cyprus and the union of the island with Greece. This organization, EOKA B, operates illegally throughout Cyprus, and their first aim is to remove the President of the Republic, Archbishop Makarios, assassinating him if necessary.

1974:
July 15: EOKA B, with the support of the Greek junta, stages a successful coup against the legitimate government. President Makarios manages to flee to London.

July 20: Turkey, in the guarantor's guise of power, invades the island with massive military force and easily occupies the city of Kyrenia first, followed by a large part of the northern region of the island. The hostilities are named Attila I. Armistice agreements are made as early as the second day of the invasion, but the Turkish army continues to advance throughout talks begun at the United Nations. Varosha during this time is attacked only by air.

August 13: Negotiations officially break off and the second round of the invasion, named Attila II, begins. The Turkish army, outside the city of Varosha, advances on it almost without a fight, and the Greek Cypriot population flees to the south to escape the conquerors.

Today:

Negotiations for the solution to the Cyprus problem have led nowhere. In occupied areas, Turkey expelled all legal residents and populate the cities and villages with Turks brought from its Eastern regions, also changing all names from Greek to Turkish.

This did not happen with Varosha. Turkey only populated the small part of the city just outside the Walls and left the rest of Varosha abandoned after being systematically looted, so that it may be used as a bargaining chip in the talks. They keep it closed behind barbed wire.

There are two resolutions from the UN Security Council, calling for the transfer of Varosha to UN administration, saying that any attempts to settle any part of Varosha "by people other than its inhabitants" is "inadmissible." Turkey systematically ignores both mandatory resolutions.

In 2020, the Turkish army cleaned and re-paved just two main streets of Varosha. Since then, it is possible for anyone, even tourists, to visit under strict controls during certain daily hours.

Today, almost five decades after the Turkish invasion in 1974, the relevant resolutions of the UN Security Council remain unenforced, and the legal residents of the city still cannot return to their houses and properties, which remain looted and ruined.

About the Author

Vivian Avraamidou Ploumbis is an awarded author and a passionate fighter for the rights of the weak, individual freedom, and freedom of speech. Born in 1958 in Famagusta, Cyprus, the center of Varosha was her neighborhood. The Turkish invasion in 1974 and the occupation of her hometown by the Turkish army forced inhabitants to evacuate. Her family emigrated to Athens, Greece.

She studied Economics at the National and Kapodistrian University of Athens and continued with post-graduate studies in Statistics at the University of Washington in Seattle, USA

Returning to Athens, she was first employed as a statistician at Urban Transport Organization and was then appointed as the General Manager by a large multinational company, a leader in market research. In 1997, she was promoted to head their business in the former Eastern European countries, based in Prague, Czech Republic. Since 2001 and until today she works in a private company which she maintains with her husband, still in the city of Prague.

Literature has always been her great love, and she entered the field as a novelist in 2004. Twelve of her works have been published in Greek; eight novels, and four collections of short stories. Her first novel was honored with the National Prize award by the Republic of Cyprus.

Two others were awarded by the Panhellenic Association of Writers. Most of her works were shortlisted for the National Prize in Cyprus.

Some of her books are translated into Romanian, Czech and Turkish.

Her Facebook page is Vivian Avraamidou Ploumbis
You can write via email to vivavrp@gmail.com
If any part of *Haunting Voices* touched you, please leave a review.

Thank you for reading.

'What a delight it is to read *Heart to Heart with Rosie Boom* and feel like we're having a conversation together in which she's encouraging, guiding and affirming me all at once! Her stories are a delightful mix of real and hope-filled words that point us to the One who holds us and our children in His care. Rosie has compiled such a heart-warming and practical collection here that I know will be read and re-read by mamas who are ready to soak up the wisdom between the pages.'

—Homeschooling mother

'I was so excited when I heard Rosie was writing this book! I have loved listening to her speak over the years and this book is like being able to listen to her any time you want! It is so refreshing to have someone share on loving life, their husband, their children and homeschooling. I needed to read this. Rosie inspires me and gives so many practical tips and encouragement. I recommend this book to anyone new to homeschooling or thinking about it, or even my fellow homeschoolers still on the journey who need some fresh inspiration. I love it, love it, love it!'

—Dot

'In this busy world we desperately need reminders to slow down and soak in the ordinary, beautiful moments with our families, and that's exactly what this book offers. From tips to create your own gezellige home that exudes warmth and joy, to finding patience when you're at a loss, to selah moments and permission to be a cracked vessel that allows God's light to shine through... there is something here for everyone. Whether you're just starting out or have been at it a while, Rosie's reassurance will bring you joy and inspiration for your journey even if it's feeling hard. So, grab yourself a cuppa, curl up in a comfy spot and dive in!'

—Kristy

Heart to Heart with Rosie Boom
ISBN 978-0-9951123-7-7
Copyright © 2023 by Rosie Boom
Published by Boom Tree Publishing
Whangarei, New Zealand

Rosie Boom contact details:
Email: rosie@rosieboom.com
Rosie's website: www.rosieboom.com

All rights reserved. No part of this book may be reproduced or transmitted in any form or by any means, electronic or mechanical, without prior written permission.

Cover, content design and creative layout by Corto Champroux, JOP, Whangarei.
Edited by Marja Stack, Clearlingo.

Printed and bound by KHL Printing Co Pte Ltd

A catalogue record for this book is available from the National Library of New Zealand

Unless otherwise noted, Scripture quotations are taken from The Holy Bible, New International Version®, NIV® Copyright © 1973, 1978, 1984, 2011 by Biblica, Inc.® Used by permission. All rights reserved worldwide.

Scripture quotations taken from the New American Standard Bible®, (NASB) Copyright © 1960, 1962, 1963, 1968, 1971, 1972, 1973, 1975, 1977, 1995 by The Lockman Foundation. Used by permission. (www.Lockman.org)

Scripture taken from the New King James Version (NKJV).
Copyright © 1982 by Thomas Nelson, Inc. Used by permission. All rights reserved.
Scripture quotations marked (GNT) are from the Good News Translation in Today's English Version- Second Edition Copyright © 1992 by American Bible Society. Used by Permission.
Scripture taken from THE MESSAGE. Copyright © 1993, 1994, 1995, 1996, 2000, 2001, 2002. Used by permission of NavPress Publishing Group.
Scripture taken from the Holy Bible: Easy-to-Read Version (ERV), International Edition © 2013, 2016 by Bible League International and used by permission.
All Scripture marked with the designation "GW" is taken from GOD'S WORD®.
© 1995, 2003, 2013, 2014, 2019, 2020 by God's Word to the Nations Mission Society.
Used by permission.

Dedicated with love to the next generation
of homeschooling mamas

Foreword

Daring to be different by teaching our children at home is no easy task. It takes courage, endurance and patience, all of which don't necessarily come naturally to us. If you are struggling from swimming against the current, then here is a treat for you! If ever there was an encourager to come alongside you and champion you in your homeschooling journey, it's Rosie Boom. Her inspiration and enthusiasm are contagious.

Steeped in God's Word, Rosie has a way of gently sharing the powerful truths that have the ability to change hearts and lives – not just of the mums, but also of the children whom they are teaching. The tips she shares in *Heart to Heart with Rosie Boom* restore the joy of digging deep into Scripture for life's answers.

I have had the immense privilege of listening to these wise teachings by Rosie every year for over twenty years at our annual H.E.A.R.T. conference (Home Educators' Annual RetreaT). I have gleaned so many nuggets of gold that have had the power to transform my vision for homeschooling and my attitude towards teaching my children on the 'not so smooth' days. I will be forever grateful for the encouragement and wisdom I have gleaned from Rosie, which have made the *world* of difference to teaching my own children at home.

Whether you are a new-to-homeschooling mama with doubts about whether you can do this, or a seasoned 'pro' at homeschooling, this resource will be a treasure trove for all, full of gems that are sure to bring delight and wonder to your journey. You will be enabled to stand on the shoulders of giants, as you learn from those who have gone before, and be inspired to teach your children with creativity, wisdom and fun, just as Rosie has done.

Enjoy a wonderful journey!

Preface

After 23 years of homeschooling, the day finally dawned when I marked the last test and dismissed my last 'class' (of which Jacob was the sole student). Close to a quarter of a century. I shed a few tears that day, sad to say goodbye to such a huge, blessed part of my life. But there are new things beckoning me, and my heart is overflowing with creativity and books I want to write. And now I have the time.

The idea for this book germinated some years ago at a mothers' and daughters' camp where I was speaking. I shared the lunch table with two women who were excited to have some one-on-one time with me to talk about homeschooling. One of them asked me to explain to her friend the meaning of *gezellig*, saying that she'd heard me share about it at a H.E.A.R.T. (Home Educators Annual RetreaT) workshop a few years earlier. Then she gripped my hand and said, 'Rosie, you should write your homeschooling talks into a book so we can all "listen" to you again and again and so we can share your message with others.'

That's all it took. After lunch I sat in my cabin, opened a new word document, and wrote *Heart to Heart with Rosie Boom*.

The title has a double meaning. I want to share with you, my readers, some messages I have given over 23 years of speaking at the H.E.A.R.T. conferences. And in doing so, I want to share my heart with yours.

In the last two years there has been an unprecedented surge in the popularity of homeschooling worldwide. This has been in a large part due to the pandemic, frequent lockdowns and mask mandates. Parents have felt an urgent need to provide something better for their children, and some have embarked on this journey with very little time to prepare and no prior exposure to the concept. If that is you, I really hope this book will help you as you settle into a new way of life.

It thrills my heart to see a second generation of homeschooling mamas beginning their own journey. Some of my own children will be starting in just a few years. My nieces, my friends' children, my own children – I'm writing this for you! I pray that the things I share will help you find joy in the journey.

Some of you have already been years on the road and need some encouragement to finish the last few years well. I'm writing this book for you also.

I love the word 'pilgrim'. When I was a young girl, my heart was captivated by an old hymn that we used to sing at school assembly – 'To Be a Pilgrim' by John Bunyan. My homeschooling journey has been like a pilgrimage – a sacred journey.

Psalm 84:5 says, 'Blessed are those whose strength is in you, whose hearts are set on pilgrimage.' Mamas, when we decide to homeschool our children, we are setting our hearts on a pilgrimage. And we become sisters on the road. That's a lovely thought.

Beatrix Potter once wrote, 'There is something delicious about writing the first words of a story. You never know quite where it will take you.'[1] Well said, Beatrix! I know exactly what you mean. I felt a thrill of joy as I wrote the first words of this book, and I'm excited to see where the story will take me. I hope I can persuade you, my fellow pilgrims, to come on the journey with me, and enjoy sweet companionship and encouragement along the way.

This book is by no means a complete guide, and I'm very aware of all the things I could have said, and should have said, but, nevertheless, I offer it to you as nourishment for your journey, from my heart to yours.

Rosie

Table of Contents

Chapter One - I'm Thinking About Homeschooling…   1
Chapter Two - Gezellig   9
Chapter Three - Building a Gezellige Home   15
Chapter Four - Starting Out on the Homeschooling Journey   33
Chapter Five - Till the Stars Come Out at Night   39
Chapter Six - Creating a Family Mission Statement   49
Chapter Seven - A Student of Love – Marriage   57
Chapter Eight - Joy on Our Homeschooling Journey   71
Chapter Nine - Don't Wreck Your Engine   77
Chapter Ten - Hand in Glove – Structure and Creativity   89
Chapter Eleven - Susanna Wesley's Apron   97
Chapter Twelve - Help! I'm a Cracked Vessel   109
Chapter Thirteen - Selah Moments   119
Chapter Fourteen - Starry, Starry Night   127
Chapter Fifteen - The God of Hope   137
Chapter Sixteen - Homeschooling up a Tree   145
Chapter Seventeen - The Gift of Music   151
Chapter Eighteen - Terrific Teens   161
Chapter Nineteen - Life Skills   177
Chapter Twenty - I Can   185
Chapter Twenty One - Family Traditions   195
Chapter Twenty Two - Peace in Our Homeschooling   207
Chapter Twenty Three - The Strong-willed Child   217
Chapter Twenty Four -Hiding in the Shadows   229
Chapter Twenty Five - Love is Spoken Here   235
Chapter Twenty Six - The Fear of God – A Treasure Key   243
Chapter Twenty Seven - The Way of Wisdom   253
Chapter Twenty Eight - Homeschooling with Patience   269
Chapter Twenty Nine - Dealing with Squabbles   277

Chapter Thirty - The Burdened Donkey	285
Chapter Thirty One - Refreshing at the Brook of Cherith	291
Chapter Thirty Two - Finding Your Second Wind	299
Chapter Thirty Three - I Can Plod	305
Chapter Thirty Four - Favourite Family Read-Aloud Books	311
Chapter Thirty Five - A Fence Around the Cuckoo	317
Postscript	323
Acknowledgements	324
About the Author	326
Other books by Rosie Boom	328
References	335
Index	342

The Shema

Hear, O Israel! The LORD is our God, the LORD is one! You shall love the LORD your God with all your heart and with all your soul and with all your might. These words, which I am commanding you today, shall be on your heart. You shall teach them diligently to your sons and shall talk of them when you sit in your house and when you walk by the way and when you lie down and when you rise up. You shall bind them as a sign on your hand and they shall be as frontals on your forehead. You shall write them on the doorposts of your house and on your gates.

—Deuteronomy 6:4–9

S.D.G

CHAPTER ONE

I'm Thinking About Homeschooling...

All that I am or hope to be, I owe to my angel mother.
Blessings on her memory! I remember my mother's prayers,
and they have always followed me. They have clung to me all my life.
The greatest lessons I ever learned were at my mother's knees.

—Abraham Lincoln[2]

In April 1994, I wrote in my diary, 'I am absolutely in love with my children! Feel sad at the thought of Josiah going to school. Am thinking about homeschooling...'

Little did I know what those three little dots would hold for us as a family.

Josiah was an active boy, and at four-years-old still enjoyed an afternoon nap. As 'D-Day' loomed nearer, Chris and I began to look seriously at the local school and other schooling options. We lived in the country, twenty minutes out of Hamilton, New Zealand. The local school was ten minutes' drive away, but we had reason to feel unsure about its suitability. The more I thought and prayed about it, the clearer one thing became to me. I didn't want to hand Josiah over to a teacher for the biggest part of his day, only to have him for a few tired hours at the end.

I also realised his teacher probably wouldn't hold the same values and beliefs that Chris and I wanted to share with our children. And then we read Deuteronomy 6:5–7. Those verses became the mandate we had from the Lord to begin homeschooling.

> These commandments that I give you today are to be upon your hearts. Impress them on your children. Talk about them when you sit at home and when you walk along the road, when you lie down and when you get up (Deuteronomy 6:5–7).

So, I began. Four-year-old Katie was very keen to begin homeschooling with her big brother. What fun we had in those early days! The three of us spent many happy hours reading together, doing art, and making simple projects about lions and elephants and insects. We sat outside at night and learned about the stars. Learning became a natural part of our days.

As we welcomed more children into our family, we marvelled at how each child was unique, with different personalities and giftings. This became obvious in our homeschooling too. Some took to reading like bees to flowers, becoming fluent readers at five, while two of the children found reading a struggle until they were eight and ten. Several of the children showed a natural aptitude to mathematics, revelling in difficult problem-solving, while some of their siblings got stuck on basic concepts. But because I could take them at their own pace and encourage them in their different areas of gifting, they have never struggled with low self-esteem. I will always be thankful for the way homeschooling saved my son from the hurtful embarrassment and frustration endured by so many children who struggle with reading at school. At age eight, Samuel was diagnosed as having dyslexia. The woman who assessed him took me aside afterwards and commented on what a lovely, confident boy he was.

Then she told me that, in her opinion, the best thing I could ever have done for Samuel was to homeschool him. Hearing her say that was like tonic to my mother's heart.

She told me to just carry on doing what I was doing with him each day and promised me that the day would come when things would fall into place for him. Sure enough, when Samuel was ten, he turned a corner with his reading. He began devouring the Redwall series by Brian Jacques. I still remember the day his younger brother Jacob came to me and complained, 'Mum, all Sam ever does now is read, read, read!' When I clapped my hands with joy, he put his hands on his hips and said with a frown, 'It was not meant as a compliment!'

I revelled in those early years. Homeschooling had given me the gift of time. Time to enjoy my children. Time to nurture and teach them. And most importantly, time to share my Christian faith with them. It wasn't something I had to squeeze in at the end of the day. It was all day, every day, as natural as can be.

But as wonderful as those early days can be, this is also a time when so many new homeschooling mothers lose their way.

If you're new on the journey, may I give you some advice? Start small and simple. My dear friend Celia gave me this sage advice and I'm so very glad I heeded it. I had caught the vision of homeschooling my precious children and my enthusiasm knew no bounds. I wanted to do the very best I could. But that passion and enthusiasm had the potential to derail me. I was keen, diligent and well-intentioned – the perfect candidate for burnout.

When beginning homeschooling, the temptation is to see all the wonderful curricula available and buy, buy, buy. Our bookcases begin to groan with the weight of all the books, and within a short time, the books themselves seem to chide and reproach us for not having used them yet.

We can very quickly lose our way in the maze of possibilities and become overwhelmed with all that we think we should or could be doing.

We began with just a few textbooks. Something for English. A simple maths book. A journal that they could write short stories in and then draw a picture. In our early years, the children used a double-lined journal which had a blank space at the top of each page. They would tell me what they wanted to write, and I would print it for them on the top line. 'Today Daddy came home with a lamb for me.' Then they would copy the words below. In the beginning I helped them with this, making sure they held their pencil correctly and formed the letters the right way. Then they would have fun drawing a picture of their story.

As the years went by, I accumulated many wonderful resources and used a variety of curriculums. But those early years were simple – nothing complicated or high-pressured. My main aim was to foster a love of learning.

One of the best purchases I made in that first year was a stack of old National Geographic magazines from the local second-hand shop. I bought the children two large scrapbooks each, which they named *God's Creation – Animals,* and *God's Creation – People.* They spent hours looking through the magazines and cutting out stunning world-class photographs of animals or people. (A simple word of caution here: have a look through the magazine before you give it to your children just to make sure there's nothing dubious.) I would read parts of the article out to them as they worked with scissors and glue, and then I'd write a few notes for them beneath each picture: 'The diver is swimming with the killer whale. It is 24 feet long. It eats squid, fish, birds, seals, dolphins and penguins. One killer whale had thirty-two fully grown seals inside its stomach! Another had thirteen dolphins and fourteen seals!'

Their scrapbooks soon filled with an eclectic mix of interesting, funny, amazing photos – an old man with a long grey beard resting in a wheelbarrow, a beautiful African woman with countless rings around her neck, a massive bull elephant roaring at a camera on a tripod. I wrote simple questions beside some of them: 'Does God love old people?' And Josiah wrote 'Yes!' beside it. They learnt about different countries and cultures. They discovered the wonder of the Amazon jungle and the Great Barrier Reef. We covered science and history and geography in those early years, courtesy of those National Geographic magazines.

The scrapbooks also became favourites for my younger children to look at with me, and the facts I'd added made for interesting reading.

Throughout our homeschooling, we continued to do project studies. These were based on the personal interests of each child, or something connected to other subjects we were exploring. For example, when we began reading the aerogram letters I had sent to my parents while living in Kuching, we did a project on Borneo. When we read *The Hiding Place,* we did one on Corrie ten Boom's life. One thing I've learned (by trial and error) is that these projects don't have to be exhaustive. I wanted them to know *everything* about the Nile and Florence Nightingale and where I grew up in New Guinea. I needed to keep reminding myself that we could revisit these subjects in stages – layers of learning. I didn't need to cram everything into their initial discovery of Papua New Guinea ad nauseum.

I love watching the start of an Olympic running race, with the lean, muscular runners from different countries ready in the starting blocks, waiting for the gun. The thrill and excitement of the race washes over me as they explode from the starting blocks. I've met mothers who explode into their homeschooling with the same intensity and drive.

But I know from experience that homeschooling is not a 100-metre sprint. More like a marathon – a triple marathon! Learning to pace yourself is essential if you want to finish your race. Mamas, set yourself an achievable pace. Too many mothers, in their eagerness and determination to do a good job, set themselves up for failure. If you have a five-year-old, you don't need to be doing bookwork with him through into the afternoon. Far from it! The afternoons can be free to explore, do art, make huts, have an afternoon nap... whatever! If little Annie or Liam wants to help you do some baking, wonderful! Never forget that helping Mama with the household chores is a huge learning curve. Your little ones will be learning, learning, learning. Include them in the tending of your garden. Go for a walk in the park and enjoy the outdoors. More of that in other chapters.

Our mornings, months and years flew past in a noisy jumble of learning and teasing and daydreaming. Some days, it seemed like everything fitted together so easily and I felt quite smug at the end of it. But often, we muddled through our day, and when I finally collapsed into bed at night, I would lie staring up at the ceiling, wondering what on earth we'd actually achieved. I remember feeling so tired that my eyes would droop and my speech slur as I read to the children in the morning. I remember the ghastly feeling that maybe I wasn't doing enough, the regret that I couldn't offer all the diverse courses the local high school offered, the days that seemed a write-off and a blur of noise with endless distractions, the time when I felt a complete failure and that if things didn't improve, I'd have to send my strong-willed daughter to school. Often, I would write in my diary on those difficult days, 'Oh Lord, help me do my very, very best!' And I would try to encourage myself with the thought that school is fraught with the same challenges I faced— fast learners mixed in with slower learners, other children causing distractions, keen students alongside reluctant ones, a morning muddle of teaching and unsuccessful lessons, a tired, overworked and underpaid teacher...

I'm Thinking About Homeschooling...

Now, with the blessing of hindsight, I can look back on the worst of days and smile to myself, knowing that, in fact, none of those chaotic crazy days were complete write-offs. So often we're tempted to dwell on our areas of lack and the things we haven't done well. But, mamas, let's not forget all the blessings of homeschooling. Yes, my children squabbled and argued at times, but on the whole, they enjoyed each other's company. I loved watching them play board games together, laughing loudly. I treasure the closeness we have as a family, and I know we owe much of it to our years of homeschooling.

Mamas, you will make mistakes in the journey ahead. You will have times of exhaustion and despair. You will second-guess yourself and doubt your initial decision to homeschool. Your inabilities and weaknesses will loom large, and you may lose sight of the goal at times. But be encouraged! It's amazing how God gives us strength for the journey and makes up our areas of lack.

Blessings will follow you through every season – babies, toddlers, the teenage years, adulthood. Each season laden with both challenges and blessings.

Are you thinking about homeschooling? I hope so! When I wrote 'am thinking about homeschooling…' in my diary, I had no idea what the future would hold for us as a homeschooling family. Now, I think the three small dots in the ellipsis could accurately represent hard work, challenges and blessings.

CHAPTER TWO

Gezellig

*My mother was the source from which I derived
the guiding principles of my life.*

—John Wesley[3]

In 2015, I had the joy of accompanying my friend on a trip to China. We planned to meet with homeschooling parents and encourage them on their journey. I provided a long list of different topics I could cover and asked each group I'd be addressing to choose what interested them most. It was amazing to discover that in every city the parents chose the same topic as their number one choice: How to create a close, loving family home. For me, it was a real thrill because I have long felt that this is vital to successful homeschooling. For that reason, I have made it the first thing I write about in this book.

Much of the world knows the story of Dutch woman Corrie ten Boom through the book and film *The Hiding Place*. I have been greatly impacted by Corrie's life story and want to share just a small bit of it here because it highlights what I want to share in this chapter.

Corrie was born in Amsterdam, The Netherlands, in 1892, the youngest daughter of Casper and Cornelia ten Boom, both devout Christians. She worked alongside her father in his jewellery and watch-making shop in Haarlem.

Their home was a place of music and laughter, faith and love. Fifty years earlier, in 1844, Corrie's grandfather, Willem ten Boom, had started a weekly prayer meeting to pray for the Jewish people and the peace of Jerusalem (Psalm 122:6). That prayer meeting would continue for a hundred years! Casper continued his father's tradition of prayer with his own family.

Corrie said that her father's example inspired her to help the Jews of The Netherlands. Every night, he would read Psalm 91 to the family before they joined in prayer.

In *The Hiding Place* she writes about the time she asked a visiting pastor to help them hide a Jewish mother and newborn infant. The pastor's face paled, and he replied, 'No, definitely not. We could lose our lives for that Jewish child.'

Corrie writes, 'Unseen by either of us, Father had appeared in the doorway. "Give the child to me, Corrie," he said. Father held the baby close, his white beard brushing its cheek, looking into the little face with eyes as blue and innocent as the baby's. "You say we could lose our lives for this child. I would consider that the greatest honour that could come to my family."'[4]

What amazing courage! What an example to his family.

Throughout their childhood, Casper ten Boom would tuck his girls into bed each night and pray for them, telling them he loved them. He would lay his hand on their heads and bless them. Many years later, on the night of their arrest by the Gestapo, Corrie and her sister Betsie heard him speak his final blessing: 'God go with you, my daughters.'

Corrie's mother also had a deep faith and great compassion for people. When she had a stroke later in life, she lost the ability to say anything other than three words – no, yes and Corrie. Corrie writes of how they used to sit her in a chair beside the window overlooking the street in Haarlem and her mother would gaze out, watching the people go by. When her mother called out to her, Corrie would go to her side, and they would play the '20 questions' game.

'Did you see someone you know, Mother?'
'Yes!'
'Was it a woman?'
'No.'
'Was it a man?'
'Yes!'
'Is there something you know about that man?'
'Yes!'
'Is it his birthday?'
'Yes!'

And so, as soon as Corrie had deciphered what her mother was feeling, she would write to that person and tell them that Cornelia ten Boom had seen them from her window and was thinking about them and praying for them. Then she would give her mother the letter and put a pen in her hand. With a shaky hand, her mother would sign the letter with a cross. And that cross became the most loved signature in Haarlem. Corrie writes:

> It was astonishing, really, the quality of life she was able to lead in that crippled body. And watching her during the three years of her paralysis, I made another discovery about love. Mama's love had always been the kind that acted itself out with soup pot and sewing basket. But now that these things were taken away, the love seemed as whole as before. She sat in her chair at the window and loved us. She loved the people she saw in the street and beyond. Her love took in the city, the land of Holland, the world. And so, I learned that love is larger than the walls which shut it in.[5]

When the maelstrom of World War Two engulfed the ten Boom family, they made the courageous commitment to do whatever they could to save the lives of Jews who were being arrested and sent to concentration camps across Germany. They sheltered some in their home, hiding them in a small secret room they'd constructed behind a bedroom wall. In February 1944, the Gestapo arrested Corrie and her family and sent them to the Scheveningen prison. They later transferred Corrie and her sister Betsie to the Ravensbrück concentration camp. The story of their ordeal and ministry within the camp is both challenging and inspiring. The courage and faith that sustained them during that dark time had been nurtured in their joyful, devout family home.

Later in her life, a reporter asked Corrie to describe her home. She thought for a while, and then said, 'There is no single word for it in English. It is hard to translate into English. The Dutch word is *gezellig*. It means cosy, homely, a place of warmth and togetherness; a sense of belonging.'

How beautiful! That is exactly what I want for our home. When we cuddle on the sofa and read a good book together – gezellig. When we listen to the rain on the tin roof – gezellig. When we sit around the fire and talk about the day – gezellig. When we watch a good movie together – gezellig. When we play board games in front of the fire – gezellig. When we listen to music together – gezellig. When I sit around the table and help the children with their maths – gezellig. When we sit in the evening and have a hot chocolate together, listening to Katie play the piano – gezellig. When we linger with friends around the table after a good meal – gezellig. When we talk about Jesus and pray together – gezellig.

When Samuel was first diagnosed as having dyslexia, I was allocated the supervision of a wonderful Christian friend who worked with children with learning difficulties. During one of our phone calls, I mentioned to him the question Sam had asked me just that morning:

'Mummy, how is it I can read quite well when I'm cuddled up beside you on the sofa, but it's so hard when I'm by myself in my room?'

My friend gave a warm chuckle and said, 'Gezellig.'

It was a wonderful moment for me. He had no idea that I had only recently discovered the word. Or that Sam had carved me a sign with 'gezellig' on it to hang in our kitchen.

Mamas, don't ever underestimate the power of creating a gezellige home. It helps our children know they belong, that they have a safe place where they know they are loved. It can even help them with their reading! This is the place where we teach our children about God. Not in a cold, stern, impersonal way, but with warmth and togetherness.

My parents gave me with this type of home, and I have tried to build the same for my children. But for those of you who never experienced the warmth of a gezellige home, let me finish this chapter with a wonderful truth – you may not have a godly heritage like Corrie ten Boom, but you can start building one now in your generation. Mamas, you can build a gezellige home.

CHAPTER THREE

Building a Gezellige Home

Stories first heard at a mother's knee are never wholly forgotten – a little spring that never quite dries up in our journey through the scorching years.

—Giovanni Ruffini[6]

So, with the beautiful example of Corrie ten Boom's gezellige home warming our hearts, let's look at the all-important question. How do we build a gezellige home?

The essence of gezellig lies in the warmth of relationships and the shared companionship of a cosy atmosphere. Togetherness. A place of belonging. A shared sense of joy. The origin of the word is a derivation from the medieval Dutch word *gezel,* meaning 'friend' or 'companion'. So, mamas, anything we do to create that family warmth and togetherness is helping to build a gezellige home.

Building warm and loving relationships takes time and intentionality. For those of you who are married, this marriage relationship becomes central to the atmosphere of your home. When we fall in love and marry, we cherish the thought that this special person will be our constant friend, our chosen lifelong companion. Gezellig. But that dream is only realised by hard work and commitment. Joyful companionship and peaceful contentment in our marriage become possible as we commit to working on our relationship and building it together.

Proverbs 14:1 says, 'A wise woman builds her house, but a foolish woman tears it down with her own hands.' Mamas, we need to be building our house, not tearing it down. Too often we pull down the beautiful gezellig work that we've been trying to build in our homes. Much of that destruction comes from our mouth, the words we speak. We need to constantly ask ourselves, 'What am I speaking into my marriage? A blessing or a curse? Are my words gezellige words?'

Mamas, we need to learn to speak gezellige words. Words that create a sense of belonging. You might say to your child, 'Let's read a book by the fire, darling. It's the perfect night for it. Listen to that heavy rain outside!' Those are gezellige words. An invitation to companionship, to closeness. Togetherness. Or to your husband when he walks in the door after a day at work: 'Welcome home, darling. You're just in time for dinner.' Belonging words.

I remember seeing an amusing caricature of a famous man. His nose was ludicrously big, and his eyebrows long and bushy, but I could still recognise him. He was, in fact, a handsome man, but the caricature had robbed him of that while still revealing his identity. As I studied the drawing, I realised how easy it is for us to create a caricature of our husband. Focusing on one aspect of his character, or one thing he doesn't do so well, can blow it right out of proportion. Perhaps he is slow to respond to our pleas for a dripping tap to be fixed. Or maybe he leaves his clothes on the floor no matter how often we remind him to put them away. These failings can become bigger and bigger in our mind until we end up with an unbalanced, disproportionate view – a caricature. When we catch ourselves doing this, we need to take the focus off that failing and turn it instead on some of his good points. The tap might still drip, but he spent a quality hour with our teenage son who is struggling with his studies. His clothes are still on the floor, but he cut the kindling and lit the fire for us before we even had to ask.

It's amazing how powerful small intentional changes can be. If we choose not to allow ourselves to paint a caricature, our marriage will thrive instead of dying by degrees.

History tells us that the captain of the *Titanic* was warned six times to slow down, change course and take the southern route because icebergs had been sighted. But he ignored these warnings because he thought his ship was unsinkable. What are the warning signs, the icebergs in our marriage? Perhaps one or the other of us has begun snapping, criticising or withdrawing. We need to be aware of these signs and take heed of them. All the captain of the *Titanic* needed to do to avert disaster was slow down and make a slight adjustment to his course. So too with us. Even a tiny, seemingly insignificant change can have enormous positive effects on our marriage and help build a gezellige home. More of that in the marriage chapter!

I love the verse in Psalm 113:9: 'He makes the barren woman abide in the house as a joyful mother of children.' A gezellige home. A shared sense of joy.

This verse prompts an important question. Am I a joyful mother? If the answer is yes, great! But if there's a hesitation in offering a truthful answer, we need to look deeper. What is robbing me of my joy? Is it my frantic, busy life? Perhaps the culprit is chronic tiredness? Am I losing my joy when I compare my life or situation with others? There are countless 'joy-stealers', and we must learn to identify them and then make the necessary changes. Again, it comes down to choices. It may be as simple as choosing to go to bed earlier. (Not so jolly easy!) As homeschooling mamas, we're often guilty of burning the candle at both ends because we have so many things we want to do once the children are in bed. I'm guilty of that.

One simple way to increase our joy is by becoming more intentional in recognising the joys of motherhood. We need to be on the lookout for them daily, especially on the days we're tired after a sleepless night with a baby or stressed with a sick child.

I love the quote by Van Dyke: 'Opportunities swarm around us every day, thicker than gnats at sundown. Every day we walk through a cloud of them.'[7] How true! And I think we could accurately interchange the word 'opportunity' with 'joys of motherhood'. Every day we walk through a cloud of them. The problem is that all too often, the mess on the kitchen table or the chaos of a bedroom distracts us. And in doing so, we walk past the joy of seeing one child put aside their Lego creation to comfort a younger sibling who's just fallen off the tramp. Or we fail to appreciate the tiny bunch of wilted dandelions that a daughter has placed on our pillowslip. (So many examples of gezellig are as simple as a steaming cup of tea by a crackling fire. Simple pleasures.) Yes, there are the tremendous joys that no one can miss, such as a baby's first smile or the first time a toddler says, 'I love you, Mummy!' But so much of the joy of motherhood is made up of small things scattered throughout each day. They are everywhere. But we must train ourselves to see them. To *look* for them. In her book *Gold by Moonlight*, Amy Carmichael, a missionary in India, wrote of little joys strewn beside the rough paths like tiny edelweiss flowers on the mountains. She points out that these tiny flowers often go unnoticed except by those who are looking for them.[8]

Much has been written of late about the importance of gratitude and how it has the power to transform our lives. Practising gratitude. Intentionally noticing our blessings and giving thanks. This habit is life-changing. Let's ask God to give us the ability to see the good things and find the edelweiss every day. As we do this, our homes will be filled with joy. Gezellig.

Psalm 127:3 reminds us that 'children are a blessing from the Lord.' I know how hard it can be to remember that when you're drowning in a sea of washing and dishes and sleepless nights. But we must try to focus on this wonderful truth. Children are a blessing from God. And they grow up so fast. As the mother of six adult children, I can attest to that! Where did my babies go? Where are my chubby toddlers?

Those early years flew past. So, mamas, enjoy your children while you have them. Remember that, as mothers, we have the power to create a loving, joyful atmosphere in the home. If we are grumpy, we'll soon discover that grumpiness is extremely contagious. But more often than not, if we are happy, our little ones will be too. Gezellig.

During my travels, I've had the privilege of meeting many mothers, and it didn't take me long to discover a secret. The most joyful mothers I met were the ones who had fully embraced motherhood. They had willingly let go of many of the other things that can vie for our time and attention. Conversely, I discovered that the unhappy mums I met were often desperately trying to hold onto their 'before children' lives, and in doing so had become resentful about the demands of motherhood. Let's give ourselves fully, whole-heartedly, to the huge but fulfilling calling of motherhood. Let's gather the edelweiss. Let's find the joy.

Unfortunately, there's no magical potion we can drink that will create a gezellige home. But if there was, I think it would bear the label – TIME. This is one of the greatest blessings that homeschooling offers us. Time with our children. Seven extra glorious hours a day that we can share with our children. For those of us whose 'love language' is quality time, this is heaven. But whatever your love language is, or your child's, time spent with family holds a miraculous power. However, to lay hold of these miracles and create a gezellige home, we need to be proactive about how we utilise this precious gift of time. I'd like to list a few simple ways that we can build a joyful, gezellige home, and I'm sure that as you read them, you will think of countless others.

Read together

Even if your child is a great reader, there is nothing like having Mum or Dad read to the whole family. Mamas, invest in good books.

Sharing the thrill of the adventures, the laughs, or the tension as you read together is an incredibly powerful and bonding experience. It also provides us with the opportunity for much-needed physical touch as we cuddle together on the sofa or on the bed to read. One of the fondest memories of my childhood is the hours we spent in New Guinea snuggled up beside Mum and Dad in their bed, under the mosquito net, while Dad read to us by Tilley lantern. Gezellig.

Have fun together

As family life gets busier and busier, it's easy to let this slide. We must make time for this to happen and intentionally plan fun times together. Why not have a family brainstorming session and write down all the ideas your children have about fun things to do? I'm sure they'll dream up some you would never have thought of. (Hmmm… is that a good thing or a bad thing?) On that note, it's important we don't just do things *we* think are fun. Our young son won't consider op-shopping fun. And perhaps not all our children will love climbing mountains. Having said that, when we plan the family fun times, it's good to encourage the whole family out of their comfort zone at times. And yes, mamas, that means us too!

Work on individual relationships

A family unit is only as close as its individual closeness. This means we need to spend one-on-one time with each child. Date nights are wonderful for this. Those of you with large families might be thinking that you could never fit regular dates with each of your children into your already busy schedule. I know that feeling, but I also know it's possible.

When my children were little and days were busy, I decided to create a system that ensured each child had a regular scheduled date with either Mum or Dad. After talking with Chris, we decided it was a realistic goal to take one child out on a special date once a fortnight. Looking back, I think we made a wise decision. Once a week would have been too often and would have set us up for failure.

I still remember the excitement of the children on the morning when we set up the first 'date roster'. I asked each child to write their name on a piece of paper and then put them all in a hat. With one child providing a loud drum roll, I pulled out the first name for the two January dates. Emily! She squealed with delight and danced around the room. Then I got her to pull out the next January date name. Josiah!

It was such an exciting morning. Katie and Jacob in February. Ellie and Samuel in March. It didn't matter that some of them had to wait two months before their special date. They sellotaped their piece of paper on their mirror and looked forward to the special time with great anticipation.

With six children, it meant that each child was going on a special date with either Chris or me once every three months. I know that doesn't sound like much, but it was achievable, and the weeks passed quickly for the eager children. The anticipation was part of the joy. Every now and then we did have to take a rain check, but on the whole, it worked.

Our dates weren't expensive. Lunch or an ice-cream at McDonald's, shopping adventures at the Hamilton Dump shop with a few dollars to spend, a trip to the library, a visit to the local park to play on the swings, music evenings at the beautiful Hamilton English Garden, movies, work trips away with Daddy, overnight camps at the back of the farm... The important thing is that your child has your undivided attention. Of course, I should add here that sometimes it can be elaborate or exciting! Why not? My friend's husband took each of his daughters on a daddy/daughter date.

They had to get all dressed up, and throughout the evening he showed them how a gentleman treats a lady. He opened the car door for them and pulled back their chair at the restaurant. I bet his girls never forgot that night!

These dates are the perfect opportunity to create a gezellige time with your child. Togetherness, music, fun, food, closeness, laughter… all gezellig.

Work together

This is possibly one area of great potential blessing that many families miss. Somehow we've become reticent about asking our children to do hard work. I'm afraid that our current culture is producing entitled children who don't know the meaning of hard work. For various reasons, we shy away from expecting our children to pull their weight in the family chores, or to help on a big project. Yet this is such an important part of their homeschooling and growing up. Teenagers can be quite vocal when it comes to expressing the unfairness of our demands on their time or effort. I'm sure many parents have been labelled slavedrivers by disgruntled children. However, those same children will later take great pride in the fact that they have helped build the family home, or paint the fence, or stack the shed with firewood. (Is there such a thing as looking back on a time and realising that, in hindsight, it was gezellig? I think so!) Despite their complaints, when we work together, a bonding takes place, and the family becomes a team.

Serve others together

I love the story Steven Covey shares in his book *The 7 Habits of Highly Effective Families* of the time when his family decided to reach out to their neighbourhood in a novel way. They created what they called the 'Phantom Family'.

For about three months, at family night, they made a special treat – biscuits, popcorn, cupcakes – and then chose a different family in their neighbourhood to bless each week. Secretly depositing the basket of goodies on the unsuspecting family's porch, they'd ring the doorbell and bolt for cover among the garden bushes. Each basket contained a note that said, 'The Phantom Family strikes again!' What fun! Pretty soon, the whole neighbourhood was a-buzz about the mysterious Phantom Family. And then, one night, their own doorbell rang. There on their doorstep was a basket of treats with a note that said, 'To the Phantom Family – from your suspicious neighbours.'[9]

What a wonderful way of teaching your children the joy of blessing others. I found it hugely inspiring. I imagined the fun it would be to go all out and dress up in black, complete with masks – wouldn't our boys love that? But whatever way we choose to do it, we must try and capture our children's hearts and get them excited about helping people. Remember, mamas, having fun together is gezellig.

Practise hospitality

Simple hospitality is a powerful influence in creating a gezellig home. Sadly, too many women shy away from this, thinking their homes need to be like something you'd see in a House and Garden magazine, and that the meal needs to be gourmet. They couldn't be more wrong! Invite people for a simple lunch of soup and bread after church. Share your evening meal, whatever it is, with a lonely person. Let an old person have the joy of being surrounded by the noisy chatter of youngsters again. They won't care about the toys scattered across the floor. I bet they won't even notice the dust on your bookshelf or the soap scum ring in your bathtub. They'll be too caught up basking in the warm vibe (gezellig!) of your home to even notice.

Create family memories together

There's that important 'gezellig' word again – together. Of course, some family memories are created spontaneously. But there's a whole world of exciting possibilities waiting for us once we decide to create family memories intentionally. Explore. Go on a family bike ride. Travel. Go camping. I remember one disastrous camping trip we had with our two small children. The heavens opened just before midnight and a small river started flowing through our tent. We spent a long night trying to sleep in the car. But I took heart because just a few weeks earlier I had heard Dr James Dobson talking on 'Focus on the Family' about family camping trips. He commented that, in his opinion, the things that bound his family together the most were in fact shared trials and disasters.

Be creative about what you can do together as a family. Keep your eyes open for special deals on adventure packages. Follow your leads. Some may eventuate in a dead-end, but others may lead you on a grand adventure.

A few years ago, I noticed a special deal being offered for a guided canoe trip down the Whanganui River. The thought excited me, but despite being on a special, the cost was still prohibitive for our family of eight. However, it didn't take long to realise we could actually do the same thing a lot cheaper without a guide. I rang all the children, as well as some of the extended family, and they were all keen. So, I booked our Canadian canoes. That trip created some standout family memories. It's just as well we didn't have a guide. He may not have approved of the shenanigans we got up to along the way. We dressed as Indians, complete with war paint, and enjoyed many a skirmish. Huckleberry Finn also made an appearance.

Another wonderful memory we share as a family is walking the Tongariro Crossing. Again, we went without a guide. What fantastic memories we have of that time!

Katie was in her fifth year of going barefoot to raise money for her charity Shoeless and did the whole 19.4 kilometre tramp in bare feet. We made a large sign out of rocks saying 'THE BOOMS' and took a family photo. I grimaced my way through the long descent, walking backwards down the countless flights of stairs in an attempt to lessen the pain in my knee. Gruelling, but I did it.

Of course, family memories aren't just created by sharing big adventures. Family traditions, simple shared activities and spontaneous outings also form them. One family decided that every full moon they would all take a moment to head outside and gaze at it together. I love that idea.

Eat meals together

There is nothing like sharing food to create a gezellige moment. Especially when it's mixed with music, good conversation and a cosy atmosphere (candles!). Mamas, we need to catch (and keep) a vision for this simple ritual. Psychologists talk about the incalculable benefits of the often-under-valued family meal table. This simple ritual is a known key to creating and maintaining a close family, a gezellige family. Google it! The importance of the family meal. Here are just a few benefits I found:

- Better academic performance
- Higher self-esteem
- Greater sense of resilience
- Lower risk of substance abuse
- Lower risk of teen pregnancy
- Lower risk of depression
- Lower likelihood of developing eating disorders

To quote Kathleen Ferrigno, the National Center on Addiction and Substance Abuse's Director of Marketing, who directs the Family Day – A-Day to Eat Dinner with Your Children: 'The message for parents couldn't be any clearer. With the recent rise in the number of Americans aged 12 and older who are using drugs, it is more important than ever to sit down to dinner and engage your children in conversation about their lives, their friends, school – just talk. Ask questions and really listen to their answers. The magic that happens over family dinners isn't the food on the table, but the communication and conversations around it. Of course, there is no iron-clad guarantee that your kids will grow up drug-free, but knowledge is power, and the more you know, the better the odds are that you will raise a healthy kid.'[10]

We can do this, mamas! Let's plan a healthy meal each day, set the table with flowers and a candle (small but important touches for creating a gezellige atmosphere), and encourage our children to linger at the dinner table.

Face challenges together

Don't be afraid to do something exciting, scary or challenging as a family. It might be doing a mission's trip together, living overseas for a time, renovating an old building… the possibilities are endless. For our family, the challenge of living in a hundred-year-old barn for four years while we built the family home was invaluable in binding us together as a gezellig family. Oh, the cosiness of crowding around the Homewood fire as the rain clattered on the tin roof!

Laugh together

Mamas, we need to learn to laugh. A chuckle or guffaw of laughter has the power to release joy into our hearts and homes. Let's not take ourselves too seriously. Practise laughter.

It was a given in our home that if we shared a good laugh during our devotional time together in the morning, it would turn out to be a good day.

For some, laughter is easy, but for others, it can present a serious challenge. But I am convinced that we can all learn to laugh. Watch old family videos together. Choose some funny books to read aloud or watch a funny movie. Come on, mamas, let the children hear you laugh. Fill your home with laughter.

Share the Christian faith together

The mandate from Deuteronomy written at the very front of this book says it all!

> These commandments that I give you today are to be upon your hearts. Impress them on your children. Talk about them when you sit at home and when you walk along the road, when you lie down and when you get up. (Deuteronomy 6:4-9)

As parents, we need to make the time to talk about our faith and teach our children the word of God. It can happen as we drive the car, go for a walk or sit at home. Anywhere. Everywhere. And while it's ideal that this happens spontaneously throughout the day, having a set time for this will always prove to be a blessing. Call it what you may, the main thing is that you have a regular time together to talk about spiritual things. Don't be paralysed by thinking you can't do a perfect job. Just start.

For our family, the best time for devotions was at the start of each day, before we began our schoolwork. When the children were little, it simply consisted of singing a fun song together, reading a Bible story (which we often had fun acting out in a totally impromptu manner), and then praying.

We had a prayer box, which I filled with bits of paper with different names on them. We'd each draw one out and then pray for Nana, or Daddy at work, or Grandpa or some friend. Simple heartfelt prayers for people they loved. We also enjoyed memorising Bible verses together. I bought each child a blank hard cover art book, and they would write the verse and draw pictures. Jacob's first entry as a four-year-old was from Psalm 56:3: 'When I am afraid, I will trust in you.'

There are so many wonderful resources available to help you in your devotional time – beautiful books that will introduce your young child to Bible characters and basic spiritual principles. What a great way to spend a bit of your homeschooling allowance! Just remember to choose age-appropriate books or Bibles. As your children grow, they can begin taking turns reading from the Bible, several verses each. For older children, there are countless inspirational biographies and Bible study books.

But the best thing you can do is come to devotions with something fresh and alive that you yourself have just read or heard. We want to offer our children cool fresh water to drink – not stale water.

Perhaps you had an interesting dream and woke with a verse going round in your mind. Share it! I once had a weird dream about a mouse family who lived in a stone church in the south of France. I woke and wrote the dream into a wee story that I then read to the children at devotions. It was all about the beautiful truth of Philippians 4:8 – thinking on whatever is true and noble and lovely. It was a quirky fable, but it provided fresh water and the opportunity for great discussion.

But most importantly, share your own walk of faith with them. Tell them about how you first came to love Jesus. Share your trials, your failures, your dreams and prayers…

One term, we had a very special time reading aloud a stack of aerograms that I had written to my parents while I was a single missionary in Borneo. What fun that was!

The children squealed with excitement at the first mention of a certain Chris Boom who was coming to visit me. When I wrote those letters, I never would have dreamed that one day they would help me share my faith journey with my own precious children.

In the introduction to *The Gift of Values – Volume One*, I share some pointers on how to have a meaningful, enjoyable devotional time. Let me share it with you here:

> The fact that you are reading this book shows you have a desire to instil in your children a love for God, a thirst for truth, and a solid foundation of true values. We all long to see our children develop a strong character – a character which will help them navigate their way through this ungodly world, not just by the skin of their teeth, but as shining examples to others. We have the awesome responsibility of planting the seed of God's word in the hearts of our children. Within the seed of strong, clear moral values lies the fruit of joy and personal fulfilment. Our children will lead happier and more fulfilling lives if they have a strong foundation of Christian values. It is never too early (or too late) to start. Some of you reading this may be thinking, 'How can I possibly teach my children the values of honesty and forgiveness when my own life has been such a mess? Aren't I being hypocritical trying to teach my children something that I am still struggling with myself?' Absolutely not! You can teach your children not only from the things you've done well, but also from the things that you wished you'd done differently.
>
> Richard Eyre writes in his book *Teaching Your Children Values*, 'We all want to teach better than we ourselves have learned. We all want our children to surpass us.'[11] Amen to that! Ideally, we want to make devotions a time which all the children enjoy. This can be a challenge, but I believe it can be done.

I have included stories that will appeal to the younger ones, and that the older ones can listen in to as well.

Always be thinking of age-appropriate questions you can ask each of the children. I have included thought-provoking quotes for the older children.

The words 'Once upon a time' never fail to thrill me. A story can move you, challenge you, open your eyes. There is nothing like a good story to get a truth across. Jesus knew that. He was a master storyteller. In each chapter, I have included stories you can share with your children, and suggestions for further reading as well. But don't forget – your own life is a book full of wonderful stories you can share with your children. You may never become a children's writer, but you can learn to tell your own stories. Your children will love to hear you share about your own life. As you read a new chapter, ask God to remind you of anything in your life that will help apply the truth. It may be just a small incident that happened when you were a child, but as you share it, it will have a real impact. And once you start looking for these 'stories', you'll find them everywhere. Encourage your children to tell their own stories as well. You'll be amazed how even the youngest can tell something so pertinent to the value that you're talking about. It only takes one of them to say, 'I remember when…' and the others will be bursting to have their say.

Jesus asked a lot of questions. He wanted people to search out the truth for themselves. Get into the habit of asking lots of questions in your devotional time. Get your children thinking. Once you develop the habit, you'll find it becomes very easy to think of thought-provoking questions, even while you're reading a story.

Van Dyke once said, 'Opportunities swarm around us, thicker than gnats at sundown. Every day we walk through a swarm of them.' Creative ideas are like that. Once you train your eyes to see them, they come thick and fast. But you must be looking for them. And if you feel you haven't got a creative bone in your body – don't worry! Creative ideas are given by God to be shared. Borrow the ideas of others and make them your own. There are plenty enough ideas to go around! [12]

As I re-read that passage I'm struck again by the principle of sharing that's woven throughout this chapter. Sharing our own stories. Sharing our thoughts. Sharing companionable meals. Sharing a great book. A gezellige home is a place of warm connection. It's where we share laughter, adventures, challenges and faith.

Marriages, friendship, faith and family all hold the potential to discover the great joy of sharing our lives with someone else. And that, mamas, is the very essence of gezellig.

CHAPTER FOUR

Starting Out on the Homeschooling Journey

The mother's heart is the child's schoolroom.

—Henry Ward Beecher[13]

When I first started homeschooling, I would ask any homeschooling mother I met what their day looked like. My aim wasn't to copy them; rather, to glean any ideas that might help me structure my morning. At last I settled into what seemed to work for our family. I'm going to share a simple outline of what we did, hoping it might be of some help to those of you who are yet to settle into a routine. But let me add here, it's important we each find our own rhythm and pattern, because our families are all so different. You may have a child with special needs, or a husband who does shift work. So, please don't think I'm offering this to you as a template that you should follow. Not at all! But I know how helpful it was for me at the start to borrow a friend's ideas and then tweak them to fit our family as the months and years went by.

We're probably all familiar with the object lesson illustrating the importance of putting the biggest stones into the jar first and only then filling it with the smaller stones. If you put the small stones in first, the big stones won't fit in the jar. This principle proved important for our homeschooling day.

Our mornings began with chores, and then by about 9 am, we'd gather in the lounge for family devotions. This part of our day became the very heartbeat of our homeschooling and created a foundation on which the children would build their lives and characters. I'm not going to go into any depth about this here as I've written about it in *The Gift of Values* series. If you need help establishing a family devotional time, I encourage you to read them or any of the many books available.

After devotions, I would read to the children. Oh, the books we've read! For me, reading aloud is one of the big rocks that needs to go in first. And it's been one of the greatest joys of our homeschooling. Mamas, never underestimate the learning and character growth that flows from this. There is a closeness that develops as we read together and yet I hear of so many mothers who stop reading aloud to their children as soon as they're able to read books themselves. I encourage you – don't cheat yourself of this blessing! I was still reading aloud to Jacob when he was seventeen. We'd sit facing each other at opposite ends of the sofa, our legs stretched out side by side on the cushions, and the cat and dog snuggled in there as well.

This read-aloud time was one of the best parts of our day. It was hard to curtail with the children all begging for 'just one more chapter!' When I had finally closed the book amid groans and complaints, I would then read from some other textbook. It might be *The Story of the World or The History of Medicine* or a geography book. They all listened to this. A lot of it went over the younger children's heads, but it didn't seem to matter. They just enjoyed being together with the rest of us, and despite them sometimes hassling their siblings and generally causing a ruckus, we enjoyed having them there.

Following that, the older children would head off to the kitchen table to write in their journals while I helped the younger children with their reading. This sometimes involved the use of word games, memory cards and fun activities.

After a while, we would join the older children at the table, where the little ones would do their journal stories. At this point, I would oversee the younger ones' work and help the older ones with their maths.

When the older children had finished their maths, they'd go on to their other work – English, science, etc – while I helped the young ones with their maths. Art and project work usually followed this if there was time before lunch.

We loved the afternoons! Soccer, Lego, music practice, computer time, baking, reading, on the farm with Daddy, fun with friends, making tree huts and forts...

This simple routine provided an easy structure to follow. And with creativity and flexibility thrown into the mix, we had a template that worked for us.

I'd been homeschooling for six years before I finally made the call to extend the older children's book work past lunchtime. I had resisted this move for some time, not liking the thought of relinquishing my free afternoons, but it wasn't as hard as I'd thought it would be. We soon settled into our new timetable. The older children continued working after lunch with independent schoolwork while I managed to do some much-needed housework and other projects. As the structure of our homeschooling days changed and developed, we all changed with it, growing and learning together, students and teacher alike.

Mamas, as you navigate these different stages in your homeschooling, I encourage you to accept help when it's offered. You may have a willing grandparent keen to be involved. Grab them! Our own children loved it when Nana Boom came once a week and taught the girls sewing and knitting while Grandpa challenged Josiah to games of chess. When we moved from Hamilton to Whangarei, my elderly parents asked if they could homeschool the children one morning a week. What a huge blessing!

They loved spending quality time with their grandchildren, and my children relished their Wednesday mornings doing art with Grandma while listening to audiobooks. Grandpa did Bible memorisation with them and helped them with their maths. I remember driving the children up to G and G's one morning, and Milly piping up: 'I reckon G and G must be the oldest teachers in the world!' Perhaps she was right. At 90 years old, it could well be a record.

You may be reading this and thinking, 'I'd give anything to be offered that sort of help!' Well, don't wait to be offered. Ask! Invite family members to get involved. There may be an uncle or grandfather who would love to teach carpentry once a month. Or a keen quilter who would love to share her passion for quilting. Ask around and see what skills some of your friends may be willing to share.

I remember how daunted I felt as I began preparing the application for my very first homeschooling exemption. I know it can easily loom large in the minds of those just starting out. But mamas, there's no need to be anxious about it! Other homeschooling mums will be more than happy to share their experience, and there's also professional help to guide you through the process – experienced homeschooling mums who have set up businesses to help you with this potentially daunting task. The internet is your friend here – just google something like 'help with homeschooling exemptions' and you'll discover all levels of support.

One last word of advice, mamas, as you begin your journey. Don't travel alone. Find some fellow pilgrims who will cheer you on when the going gets tough, and who will encourage you with their own enthusiasm and wisdom. Join a local homeschool group and become committed. Don't just attend when select activities interest you. For you and your children to really benefit from the group, there needs to be more than just attending the occasional activity. The real joy and support will come as both you and your children build friendships and relationships through consistent attendance.

We were blessed to have a homeschooling family living just up the road from us for several years. We decided to work together on a project about Amy Carmichael, which culminated in a wonderful Indian feast with everyone dressed up in saris or turbans. One term, I taught the boys from both families one morning a week while my friend Leatitia taught the girls. It made for different interaction and the children all enjoyed the change of teachers.

Several years ago, Chris and I had the joy of travelling through England and Europe. However, I remember realising at one stage that I'd become so focused on where we were planning to go next that I was missing out on where we were at that present moment. Parenting and the homeschooling journey can be just like international travel. Mamas, don't squander the precious blessings of today by wishing you were on a different stage of your journey. If you have little ones, don't look ahead with longing to the time when they can read by themselves or make their own bed. Don't wish you were at the stage of no more nappies. Enjoy your babies and toddlers! Don't hanker for the day when your teenage son won't need you alongside him as he grapples with fractions or long division. Don't become so focused on getting your children through to graduation that you miss the blessings of the stage you're currently in. Homeschooling is a journey, not a destination. Each one of these stages is precious, and so fleeting. Carpe diem. Seize the day. Seize today.

I love the story I heard of a tired mother who was washing the dishes at the end of a long, busy day when she heard her young son's urgent voice: 'Mummy! Come here! Quick! I want to show you something.' She called back to him, 'Not now, darling. Mummy's busy.'

He called for her again and she was about to give him the same answer when she realised that she'd been saying that to him throughout the day: 'Not now, darling. Mummy's busy.' Too busy to read a book. Too busy to play outside. Too busy to help with the jigsaw.

She dried her hands and went to find her son. He grabbed her hand, led her onto the back porch, and said, 'Look!'

For the next twenty seconds mother and son sat on the back doorstep and watched the final fling of the sun as it set in pinks and golds and crimson. And I'm sure you can guess what that mother was thinking. *I could have missed this.*

Mamas, enjoy the journey! Don't miss discovering the wonders of Italy because you're dreaming of exploring Greece.

CHAPTER FIVE

Till the Stars Come Out at Night

*There was never a child so lovely, but his
mother was glad to get him to sleep.*

—Ralph Waldo Emerson[14]

In 2004, to celebrate its 70th anniversary, the British Council compiled a list of the seventy most beautiful words of the English language from a survey of over 42,000 people. 'Mother' topped the list.

I remember the night my twin sister Penny and I sang at a women's conference. Earlier in the day we had met a wonderful woman and her middle-aged daughter. The daughter had special needs and the intellectual age of a five-year-old. When Penny and I began playing our guitars and singing, she jumped up from her seat and joined us at the front, clapping her hands and singing loudly. We were delighted. But then I noticed her mother slip out of her seat and make her way to the back of the audience. I felt disappointed, sure she was going to stand at the back and beckon her daughter to sit down. How wrong I was! Moments later she came dancing down the aisle, twirling long red ribbons. Dancing past us, she joined her daughter at the front. The audience erupted with clapping and cheering, but not before I'd heard the happy, proud whisper of the daughter: 'Mummy!'

Hearing that word of love, I experienced a rush of joy. Mummy. Mother. Mama. It doesn't get better than that. And I certainly don't take it for granted.

In 1986, I was working as a missionary in Kuching, on the island of Borneo. In June, I needed to fly to West Malaysia for a few days to renew my visa. I arrived in Kuala Lumpur on my thirtieth birthday. I remember feeling so alone that day. Thirty years old and still single. My twin sister had been married for eleven years and had four children. Her life and heart and arms were full. Mine seemed so empty. I remember how bleak I felt that day. I cried in my hotel room, thinking that perhaps I would never marry; that I might never know the joy of being a mother. I often think how amazing it would have been if God had shown me a photo that day of me with Chris and our six children. How thrilling that would have been! How reassuring. But he didn't. Instead, he asked me to entrust my future into his hands.

The next six months held many joys and challenges for me. Then came the day a Malaysian Muslim government official called me in to their office and told me that it had come to their notice that I was involved in missionary work. They informed me that I had just three days to leave the country. This sudden unexpected turn of events stirred a tumult of emotions. Leave? I had expected to stay on the mission field for years. What was happening? I didn't know what to do, where to go. I had no idea what the next step in my life would involve. But I took comfort from the writings of Hudson Taylor: 'Life turns at times on a small pivot. God's hand was on the helm. The closed door is as much God's providence as the open door, and equally for the good of his servant, and the accomplishment of his own great ends.'[15]

Three days later, I said a heart-breaking goodbye to my friends and the small village church where I worked. As I boarded the plane, I felt sad and confused. I had no inkling of all the good things God had in store for me.

I had no idea that this painful time in my life would prove to be that small pivot that Hudson Taylor wrote about – the 'turning' of my life's course that would lead me to the next great adventure and my greatest dream – marriage and motherhood. On my return to New Zealand, Chris and I renewed our friendship, and it wasn't long before friendship blossomed into love. We were engaged six months later. God has blessed us with three sons and three daughters. Six precious children, three of them born when I was in my forties. God is good. It still thrills me every time I write 'mother' when filling out my occupation on a form.

When my darling mother was in her 91st year, she needed hospital-level care. We found her a private room in a wonderful aged-care facility not far from where we lived. I loved visiting her, and over the months, grew to know and love many other residents. Ninety-year-old Annie always cuddled a teddy bear or a doll. Whenever she became upset, she would call out in a trembling voice, 'I want my mum!' Her cry never failed to move me.

I always love the part in the movie *Hook* where Wendy looks with pity at the despicable Captain Hook and tells him, 'You need a mummy.' It makes me think of the passionate words of Catherine Booth, co-founder of the Salvation Army, on her deathbed: 'Try to raise up mothers. Mothers are the want of the world.'[16]

So, dear mamas, ours is a blessed calling. And a demanding, challenging one. Recently, while reading the Bible, one phrase captured my imagination: 'From the first light of dawn till the stars came out at night.' How beautiful. If I close my eyes, I can picture both the sunrise and the heavens ablaze with stars. These poetic words come from the book of Nehemiah, which recounts the rebuilding of the walls of Jerusalem.

Therefore, I stationed some of the people behind the lowest points of the wall at the exposed places, posting them by families, with their swords, spears and bows. After I looked things over, I stood up and said to the nobles, the officials and the rest of the people, 'Don't be afraid of them. Remember the Lord, who is great and awesome, and fight for your families, your sons and your daughters, your wives and your homes.' When our enemies heard that we were aware of their plot and that God had frustrated it, we all returned to the wall, each to our own work.

From that day on, half of my men did the work, while the other half were equipped with spears, shields, bows, and armour. The officers posted themselves behind all the people of Judah who were building the wall. Those who carried materials did their work with one hand and held a weapon in the other, and each of the builders wore his sword at his side as he worked. But the man who sounded the trumpet stayed with me.

Then I said to the nobles, the officials and the rest of the people, 'The work is extensive and spread out, and we are widely separated from each other along the wall. Wherever you hear the sound of the trumpet, join us there. Our God will fight for us!'

So we continued the work with half the men holding spears, from the first light of dawn till the stars came out (Nehemiah 4:13–21).

This great work that Nehemiah and all the people committed to reminds me of another monumental building project – motherhood! The descriptions of Nehemiah's building project fit hand in glove with motherhood.

It's a huge work

Nehemiah and the people continued at their work from the 'first light of sunrise until the stars came out at night'. What a great analogy of our parenting commitment. It will demand our time, energy, emotional strength – everything! It reminds me of a song in the movie *The Sound of Music*. Mother Abbess sings her challenge to Maria as she prepares to return to the von Trapp family. She tells her that the dream of becoming mother to the seven von Trapp children will require all the love she can give, day after day, for as long as she lives.

Raising our sons and daughters is going to take every bit of the strength, courage, inspiration and commitment we can give. And endless hours. We mothers are familiar with the star-lit hours.

It's a vital work

Just as the walls of Jerusalem were vital for its safety and protection, so too our parenting is vital for the wellbeing and development of our children. We need to catch the vision for our mothering and be intentional in all we do. We need to teach our children how to make their beds, how to persevere with a tough math problem, how to handle relationship challenges, how to practise good hygiene… The possibilities are endless and diverse. Most importantly, as believers, we need to be discipling our children in the Christian faith; teaching them how to fear the Lord and love him with all their hearts. We mustn't leave this to their Sunday School teachers. More of this in a later chapter.

Hearting

I love the stone walls that beautify the surrounding countryside where we live. Chris and I built a dry-stone wall at our home and found it extremely challenging! It seemed like every stone I put in place, Chris took out, saying it wasn't quite the right fit. It was both frustrating and discouraging. But we eventually finished the wall, and with the left-over rocks, I decided to build my own stone wall without any meddling from Chris. I managed to build one around a crab apple tree that my sons had given me one Christmas. Chris restrained himself from advising, and both of us are amazed that it is still standing (of sorts).

But before our first foray into dry-stone walling, I spent hours researching about it on the internet, watching how-to videos and reading articles. And I stumbled across a beautiful truth, which resonated deeply with me. An important part of building a dry-stone wall is the process of *hearting*. This involves filling the wall centre with small stones as you build. These small stones give the wall strength by filling any gaps and reducing movement; they help to transfer the wall's weight to the ground. What a beautiful analogy! Mamas, we must never underestimate the power and influence of the little everyday things we do. Each day, we face countless small jobs, little interactions, endless acts of service. But each time that we offer our children a small word of encouragement or love, we are *hearting*. Every time we 'die to self' and go that extra mile, we are hearting. The small things we do every day are vitally important. Tucking our little ones into bed, the goodnight cuddle and kiss, the lullaby, the story that you feel you just haven't got time for, the evening meal – *hearting*.

It's a challenging work

I read a cartoon strip on a plane one day that made me laugh out loud. Homer Simpson says to a friend, 'I won't lie to you – fatherhood isn't easy like motherhood.'[17]

In 1900, London newspapers allegedly published the following advertisement:

> MEN WANTED FOR HAZARDOUS JOURNEY.
>
> *Small wages, bitter cold, long months of complete darkness, constant danger, safe return doubtful.*
> *Honour and recognition in case of success.*
>
> Ernest Shackleton[18]

Shackleton later said, 'It seemed as though all the men in Great Britain were determined to accompany me. The response was so overwhelming.'

So, mamas, what about this challenge?

> WOMEN WANTED FOR DEMANDING JOURNEY
>
> *Small wages, little recognition. Total commitment and self-denial required.*
> *Long hours guaranteed. Endurance stretched to the limit.*
> *Patience essential. Commitment vital.*
> *Rewards immeasurable and eternal.*
>
> Father God

There will be times when you feel exhausted (from the first light of dawn till the stars come out at night!), wrung out, terrified, hurt, confused... there will be times you feel like a failure.

I love the Calvin and Hobbes comic strip by Bill Watterson where Calvin waves to his mother with a cheery smile and says, 'Hi! It's me! Your big accomplishment in life!' The next frame shows his mother sprawled on the sofa, telling her husband, 'I'm depressed!'[19]

Are you feeling like Calvin's mum? I'm pretty sure we've all been there at some point on our mothering journey. When my twin and I were born, Mum had her hands full, with a toddler and an older son as well. Penny and I were not naughty children – just lively, active and noisy. When Mum took our dachshund Hamish to the vet because he wasn't eating or sleeping, the vet asked her if there were young children in the house. He then diagnosed poor Hamish with a nervous breakdown and prescribed time away from the twins to recover. Mum survived those busy years without a similar breakdown because of Dad. As soon as he got home from work on Friday night, he took over our care so Mum could go out for the evening with her friends. This regular break kept her going through each demanding week. Thanks to Dad's ongoing support and love, she never had to join Hamish at the sanatorium!

When Nehemiah felt discouraged, he asked God to strengthen his hands. Mamas, let's ask God to strengthen our hands and our heart.

There are enemies

Just like in Nehemiah's situation, we will encounter persistent, aggressive enemies. We live in a culture that is opposed to godly parenting. Our adversary, the devil, has launched an attack at the very heart of Christians, churches and families. In Nehemiah's time, his enemy, Sanballat, constantly tried to demoralise the builders. It was not a one-off attack. He was relentless. When he failed with one tactic, he employed another. We need to do just what Nehemiah did – set a watch, a guard. Be vigilant in prayer. Pray and ask God to strengthen our hands for the work.

We need not be afraid.

Nehemiah encouraged the people to not be afraid, but to 'remember the Lord, who is great and awesome and fight for your brothers, your sons and your daughters, your wives and your homes' (Nehemiah 4:14). I love this! We need not be afraid. Rather, let's remember how great and awesome our God is, and fight for our families.

Fatigue, discouragement and opposition are all par for the course in this huge and challenging role that stretches from the first light of dawn till the stars come out at night. But mamas, let's celebrate our wonderful calling! Don't let anyone tell you that being a mother is not as important as having a much-respected career. Let's thank God for each of our children and ask him to help us be the best mother we can possibly be. And if any of you are torturing yourself with all the 'if only I'd...' Stop! Let go of your failures. Start again today. Today is a new day, fresh with possibilities and promise. And best of all, 'The Lord's unfailing love and mercy still continue, fresh as the morning, as sure as the sunrise' (Lamentations 3:22, 23 GNT).

CHAPTER SIX

Creating a Family Mission Statement

*Live in the moment and make it so beautiful
that it will be worth remembering.*

—Ida Scott Taylor [20]

Several years ago, I read an inspiring chapter in Stephen Covey's book *The 7 Habits of Highly Effective Families* about the effectiveness of creating a family mission statement. I remember trying to explain to Chris with great enthusiasm what a family mission statement was, and his somewhat less-than-overwhelming response. But I persisted and made him listen as I re-read the chapter out loud. Despite the somewhat clunky and formal wording of 'mission statement', I recognised that what was glimmering and catching my eye was a pearl of great price. So, let me try to explain what captured my heart.

Covey wrote that a family mission statement is a combined, unified expression from all the family members of what your family is about and the principles you choose to govern your family life. Putting it more simply, it's deciding what kind of family you want to be and then identifying the principles that will get you there. Just as we must intentionally build our marriages, so too we need to intentionally build our families.

We decide together what we want our family to look like, and that becomes our goal, our destination. It will act like a huge, powerful magnet that draws us towards it and helps us stay on track. It gives us a compass. When we clearly define who our family is and what our important beliefs are, it will give our children a feeling of stability. They will know that we are totally committed to them; that we have been from the very moment of their birth or adoption. Even if our teenagers don't take much notice of the words, they will sense a togetherness and a commitment.

Once you've defined your shared values and vision, and each family member has committed to it, then you can be demanding when it comes to standards.

When Chris and I decided to build our own house, he spent many hours designing, planning, drawing and researching. He even created a small model of the house. Those plans became the blueprint for the years that followed as we moved from the foundation to the block laying to the timber work. The plans became tattered and dirty from our constant use of them, but they served their purpose. They kept us on track. Without them, it would have been an unmitigated disaster.

The same principle applies to baking or cooking. Someone has created a recipe which, if followed carefully, will result in a delicious cake or meal.

So, too, with building a family. We decide what sort of family we want ours to be and then we draw up plans of how we will build it. That's what a family mission statement is.

Stephen Covey said it was the best thing they ever did. The process took them eight months. In the end, they had ten things that they decided they wanted to write into their mission statement: *The ability to work, to learn, to communicate; to solve problems; to repent; to forgive; to serve; to worship; to survive in the wilderness; to play and have fun.*

I think it was the surviving in the wilderness bit that caught Chris's attention. So, we decided to have a go at creating our own.

What did we want the Boom family to look like? Using Covey's book as a guideline, we began. Let me highlight the process.

Begin

We followed Covey's first suggestion to the letter. *You need pen, paper and popcorn! Make it fun.* Fun? I can do fun. I pinned up a large sheet of brown paper to our kitchen Welsh dresser and then brought out the popcorn. If this process is going to take a while, you want your children to look forward to the planning sessions, not dread them. Chocolate, popcorn, potato chips – whatever works for your family!

The first thing you need to do is to introduce the concept and get them on board with you. All of them. Your teenagers and your young children. You must help them understand what it is you're trying to build and how you need a plan. Now, I know some teenagers may not be excited about this and may groan and complain, but you can bet that, deep down, there will be at least a tiny spark of gratitude that their parents are trying to build a joyful, committed family.

At the time of crafting our family mission statement, we were living in our hundred-year-old barn while building our new home. That provided us with the perfect analogy to help explain to our children what we were trying to do.

Choose the family scribe

Give a different person this honour each time you work on it. Their job is to record all the suggestions and comments – a very important job!

Gather ideas

Start by asking for one word from each person that they think highlights something important in the family. I remember some of ours were fun, kindness, adventures, music, celebration. Write each one on your paper or blackboard. Then start asking the big questions. This is where Mum and Dad may have to bite their tongue and not react. There'll be time later to discuss and resolve things. Now is the time to just listen and write up the answers.

- What do you like about our family?
- What embarrasses you about our family?
- What makes you feel comfortable here?
- What is the purpose of our family?
- What do you think we do well together?
- What makes you want to come home?
- What makes you want to bring your friends home?
- What makes you not want to bring your friends home?
- What makes you feel sad? Angry?
- What makes you feel loved?
- What kind of relationships do you want to have with each other?
- How do you want to be treated by each other and spoken to?
- What are the unique gifts of each family member?
- What is our marriage about? (The marriage vows are our first mission statement!)

These are just some ideas. I'm sure lots of your own will surface as you start. Remember, everyone's ideas are important. Make sure that when someone speaks, the whole family listens.

You might need to stop one child from dominating the conversation, and make time to intentionally draw out your quieter child. Start with questions that you know they'll find easy to answer. Don't set them up for failure. For example, you could ask your little one, 'Do you like it when we do something fun together as a family?' If they nod, write the word FUN up on the board. After a while, they'll become more confident about participating and offer their own suggestions. I remember everyone chuckling when six-year-old Jacob said, 'More pocket money.' We wrote it on the paper. It won't take long before you've covered the paper with ideas and words, and you'll be wishing you'd chosen a bigger piece.

It's important at this stage that you don't become defensive and react to some things that come up. If one of your children says, 'I wish we didn't argue as much,' don't jump in with a feisty, 'We do *not* argue!' The important thing is that everyone understands that this is the beginning stage of deciding what we want our family to be like. Then we must aim to work out what changes need to be made. The important thing to remind the family is that everyone will benefit.

Write a rough draft.

You may change this many times. We spent months with our mission statement in draft form. We looked at it, talked about it, and tweaked it again and again. It's important you don't rush into finalising it until every member feels happy with it and you can all say, 'This is our mission statement. We're ready to commit to it. This is what we want our family to look like.'

Write your final draft.

This is the fun part! Make it personal to your family. You might decide to set it down in a song, cross-stitch it onto a wall hanging, carve it into a piece of wood, craft it into a poem, write it into an acrostic using the first letters of your surname – anything! I didn't want ours to be too wordy. I felt it needed to be succinct and easy to remember. And I wanted it to be something very visual. While this part of the process is exciting, it can also be somewhat intimidating. You may find you dither, like we did for some time. Our rough draft sat for months in our barn, and I didn't know quite where to go with it. Then one day, I had an epiphany! At that moment I knew what we should do with our mission statement. I had recently bought a wooden tree from Spotlight, thinking I might use it for our family tree. But then my brainwave hit. Because our surname Boom means 'tree' in Dutch, my recent purchase was the perfect place to write our mission statement. The word 'gezellig' had been written up on our brainstorming piece of paper (by me) and it seemed to encapsulate so many of the values we'd decided were important to us. So, I wrote 'A Gezellige Home that Honours Jesus' on the trunk of the tree. And then we wrote all the other words on the branches and leaves: warm hospitality, fun, encouragement, cosiness, creativity, music, faith…

It worked! Our mission tree now sits on the windowsill by our dinner table as a constant reminder of what we want the Boom family to be. Our destination. Our flight plan. Our compass.

To finish this chapter off, let me share with you Covey's three big no-nos about creating your family mission statement.

Firstly, don't 'announce' it. It may be tempting for you and your husband to just work it out together and then announce it to the children, but don't do it! Each family member needs to feel a sense of ownership.

Secondly, don't rush it. The process is as important as the end product. It will take time. If you have young children, you'll need to hold a series of short times together. More popcorn. More chocolate. Be patient and take as long as you need.

And lastly, once it's completed, don't ignore it. The actual writing of the statement is just the beginning. You must then translate it into the very fabric of your being, into the everyday moments of your everyday family life. If your mission statement involves being a family of fun, make sure you plan for a fun evening of board games or a game of soccer on the front lawn. If it's being a family that reaches out to others, work out how you're going to achieve that. The important thing is to write it on your hearts. Talk about it often, learn it, memorise it, review it, measure yourself against it regularly.

I love the story Covey shares in his book *The 7 Habits of Highly Effective Families* of one family who created a tee shirt as part of their mission statement. They were all wearing them on a family outing when they stopped for gas. The garage attendant said, 'Hey, you guys look like a team!' Exactly! Covey tells the story that three months later, the three-year-old in the family got cancer and had a long challenge with chemotherapy and isolation. Every time he had to go to hospital for treatment, he asked to wear his special t-shirt. It soon became stained with vomit, blood and tears. But when he pulled through, the whole family wore their shirts in his honour.

That's what I'm talking about!

CHAPTER SEVEN

A Student of Love – Marriage

God, the best maker of all marriages, combine your hearts in one.

—William Shakespeare [21]

In 2013, my parents celebrated their 70th wedding anniversary. Seventy years together! It's hard to imagine. At the time, Dad was caring tenderly for Mum, who had suffered a stroke, joyfully fulfilling the vows he had made to her 70 years earlier.

When we marry, we make a promise to love, cherish and obey till death do us part. But how do we live out that vow? What do we need to do to ensure our marriages stay healthy and our love keeps growing and deepening? How do we survive the dark times together?

In 1987, I promised to love, cherish, honour and obey Chris, in sickness and in health, for better, for worse, for richer, for poorer.

Worse. Poorer. Sickness. These words represent times that will not be easy. But how wonderful to know that 'love endures all things' (1 Corinthians 13:7). On Mum and Dad's 70th wedding anniversary, the local paper asked them to share their key to a successful marriage. I love what Dad told them: 'Great marriages don't just happen. They are built.'

I wanted to include a chapter on marriage in this book about homeschooling because I know the impact our relationships have on our homeschooling endeavours. If our marriage is thriving, it's more likely our homeschooling days will be productive and satisfying. However, if we are struggling in our marriage, this stress cannot help but overflow into our teaching days.

I know some of you reading this book are in difficult marriages. You're disillusioned and broken. Some of you are single parents. Some of you may feel trapped in dull, unsatisfying marriages. Others are blessed with a wonderfully happy marriage. No matter which applies to you, please don't skip this chapter. Many of the principles I'm about to share can be applied to other relationships as well. My prayer is that each one of you will be inspired to look again at your relationship and find new enthusiasm to work at improving it. Even the tiniest changes we make have the potential to bring about changes far more wonderful than we've ever dreamed. And when positive change happens in our marriage, the benefits will overflow into our homeschooling.

The Scottish minister Samuel Rutherford gave this profound advice: 'In fair weather mend your sails.' We need to invest in our relationships in the peaceful times, when things are sweet between us and uncomplicated. Here are just a few simple ways to make huge deposits into your marriage:

Go on regular dates

I know this isn't easy when you have little ones, but commit to setting aside some special time together, even if you can't leave the home. Later, when the children are older, you'll be able to go out more. You're going to have to fight for these dates and lock them into your calendar, because any number of things arise that could potentially bump that scheduled date off the calendar.

Find things you enjoy doing together

When our children were little, Chris and I made furniture together. Many nights would find us out in the garage building a Welsh dresser or a rimu table. When we bought our own property, we revelled in being able to work alongside each other – laying brick paths by moonlight once the children were asleep, landscaping and planting trees, building chicken sheds and tree houses. Keep in mind that we can all learn to enjoy new things. There are probably some of you who have learnt to enjoy watching a rugby game on TV just so you could share that time with your husband. Well done! And husbands who have agreed to do some dancing classes, just because his wife is keen to learn how to waltz. (Chris suffered his way through one term, and I loved him for it.)

Talk together

Learning to communicate is like learning a new language. We need to study and practise, practise, practise. Share your thoughts and the daily happenings in each of your lives; talk about the book you're reading, etc. One couple I know decided early in their marriage to set aside one hour every Monday night to talk together. In that regular time, they discussed anything and everything – their finances, their children, their sex life, the challenges they were facing, etc. One hour. It doesn't sound like much. But it was regular and locked in place. And 43 years on, the couple credit that one regular hour of conversation as having helped them build a strong, loving, enduring marriage.

Read books aloud together

I remember the joy of Chris reading *The Hiding Place* with me in front of the fire one winter. This year, we've been reading *All Creatures Great and Small* by James Herriot. There are so many wonderful marriage books to discover, as well as fantastic classics, so have a go at this, mamas. Turn off the television and read together.

Keep your love for Christ alive

Our marriages and relationships all reflect the condition of our faith walk. Do you want to be faithful to your husband? Faithfulness is a fruit of the Spirit. It is something that grows. If we continue to grow in our faith and walk in the Spirit, this area of our lives will also flourish. I remember years ago hearing a pastor tell the congregation, 'All our lives, we need to be both a student and a teacher.' Always learning. Always sharing what we've learnt. As homeschooling mothers, I'm sure we all share the same desire for our students. We want them to learn. Whether it's mathematics, reading or science, we want our children to discover the love of learning. But here is an all-important lesson to be learnt, for both student and teacher alike. *Love* must be learnt. Katherine Ann Porter wrote, 'Love must be learned, and learned and learned again. There is no end of it. Hate needs no instruction but waits only to be provoked.'[22]

Mamas, let's become students of love. Let's learn how to love our husband and our children. How do we learn to do anything? We study and we practise! Let me list several areas where we need to enrol as a student of love.

Learn to control our tongue

Proverbs 18:21 tells us that death and life are in the power of the tongue. It also says that we eat the fruit of our own lips. If only we heeded this! What we say, how we speak to our husband or children, can bring life. Or it can bring death. And we ourselves will reap the fruit of it in our own lives.

King David speaks of his own radical intention: 'I will watch my ways and keep my tongue from sin; I will put a muzzle on my mouth while in the presence of the wicked' (Psalm 39:1).

Sometimes, mamas, we need to put a muzzle on. I think we could all benefit from developing the habit of counting to twenty before we say anything inflammatory. This pause may help us calm down just long enough to think better of it. Rash words have the power to wreak havoc in our family. Proverbs 12:18 says, 'There is one that speaks rashly like the thrusts of a sword, but the tongue of the wise brings healing.' The poet Henry Longfellow wrote: 'Silence is a great peacemaker.'[23]

We must learn to stop throwing verbal bombs. Our words determine the general atmosphere of our home more than anything else. Positive, encouraging, loving words will create a home where people, big and little, can thrive. A gezellige home. So, let's learn to speak words of love. Practise saying something positive and loving every hour.

Think about this great quote by Herder: 'Do not discharge in haste the arrow which can never return. It is easy to destroy happiness, most difficult to restore it.'[24]

I remember the time I flicked through a *House and Garden* magazine and saw a photo of a beautiful country kitchen. Above the bench hung a carved wooden sign that read *Love is Spoken Here*. I showed the photo to each of the children and asked them to pick out one thing that they liked about the kitchen.

Despite there being countless interesting objects in the kitchen, all the children chose the sign. It was a great talking point that morning. After school was over for the day, Samuel carved me a similar sign which now hangs above our kitchen sink. Love is Spoken Here. We often look at it and refer to it. What a great reminder of an important truth.

It would be helpful if we ask ourselves, 'What have my words been like this past week?' And, mamas, we need to be honest with the answer. In Job 31:6, Job prays, 'Weigh me in honest scales.' Absolutely!

Learn to encourage

This follows on from the first point. In Proverbs 31, we read that when the wife of a noble character speaks, her words are wise, and 'the teaching of kindness is on her tongue' (Proverbs 31:26 NASB).

I love that! The teaching of kindness. Kind words. In marriage, kind words work miracles. We all need to learn to speak them. At certain times, one or other of you will need to be reassured of the other's commitment. Remember and repeat your vows. There is great power in them. Say them again to each other. There is power in the spoken word. Find something about your husband that you appreciate, and then thank him for it. Compliment him whenever you can. Mark Twain quipped he could live for two months on a good compliment. Truth is, we all thrive on positive feedback. It motivates us. Approval and encouragement in one area will often motivate a person to change in other areas. Powerful stuff!

Learn to turn away anger

Did you know we can learn how to prevent anger from decimating our relationships? Proverbs 15:1 says, 'A gentle answer turns away wrath, but a harsh word stirs up anger.'

Are your words harsh? If they are, cry out to God to help you change them to words of kindness. Your husband and children will eat the fruit of it. And so will you. Ask God to teach you how to give a gentle answer.

Learn to abandon a quarrel

Proverbs offers important advice about quarrels: 'The beginning of strife is like letting out water, so abandon the quarrel before it breaks out' (Proverbs 17:14 NIV).

Abandon the quarrel. Hmm. Do you find it difficult to drop an argument? I remember the time Angel, our Jack Russell terrier, jumped into the river to grab hold of a possum that Chris had just shot. It was bigger than her and she struggled to drag it up the steep riverbank. After several futile attempts, she gave up and started swimming in circles, holding onto her prize and slowly sinking. We were all shouting at her, 'Let it go!' But she wouldn't. In the end, my son had to climb out on a tree branch, reach down and pull both her and the possum out. It was a moment of great clarity to me. Sometimes I hold on to things which are, in fact, drowning me. It might be anger, unforgiveness, bitterness, hurt...

I have a great quote by Douglas Jerrold written on my bathroom notice board: 'The "last word" is the most dangerous of infernal machines, and the husband and wife should no more fight to get it than they would struggle for possession of a lighted bombshell.'[25]

Proverbs 20:3 (NASB) says, 'Keeping away from strife is an honour for a man, but any fool will quarrel.'

Watch out that you don't develop a contentious spirit. Quarrelling can easily become a habit. A dangerous, destructive habit. As the adage says, you can win the battle but lose the war.

Learn to yield

Ecclesiastes 10:4 (NKJ) tells us that 'yielding allays great offences.' The willingness to yield is listed as one of the fruits of wisdom (James 3:17). If a moving person or a vehicle yields, it means they slow down or stop in order to allow other people or vehicles to pass in front of them. Road rage is often the result of someone refusing to yield. In the same way, fights and quarrels and 'great offences' will blight our relationships when we refuse to yield. Rather, we should learn to give way. Surrender. Relinquish control. Hand over. Be reasonable. Each one of these meanings of the word reflects a valuable application to marriage.

Learn to give a blessing

Oh, the power of speaking a blessing! 1 Peter 3:8 says, 'Let all be harmonious, brotherly, kindhearted and humble in spirit, not repaying evil for evil, or insult for insult, but giving a blessing instead.' Mamas, let's speak a blessing over our children and our husband every day.

Learn to forgive

Hurts come. Your husband will hurt you. Your children will hurt you. And you will hurt them as well. That is why we must learn to weave forgiveness through all our relationships. Listen to what Proverbs says: 'He that covers a transgression, seeks love' (Proverbs 17:9 NKJV). Forgiveness births love. In the love chapter of 1 Corinthians 13, we are told that love keeps no record of wrongs. Yet how many of us have compiled a list of all the things our husband has done to hurt us? All his wrong-doings. Mamas, we need to delete this list.

There is timeless advice in Ephesians 4:6: 'Do not let the sun go down on your wrath.' If there is something brewing between you and your husband, take the time to sort it out before you go to sleep. I realise that sometimes this may seem impossible given the magnitude of some issues, but at least there could be a mutual recognition of the problem and a spoken commitment to work on it on the morrow. William Arthur Ward wrote that 'forgiveness warms the heart and cools the sting.'[26] Such a beautiful paradox.

Let's make use of the three powerful resources we always have available to us: 'love, prayer and forgiveness.'[27]

Learn to change

We all need the revelation that we can't change another person's heart or behaviour – only God can. Once we understand this, our focus will shift from trying to change our spouse to working on changing ourselves. Trying to control another person's behaviour is an exercise in futility. It makes us susceptible to chronic stress – the stress that wears us out, makes us sick and irritable and causes us to see everything from a negative state of mind. The only person we can control in this world is ourselves.

If you're in a difficult marriage, you may be grappling with challenging, painful realities. Perhaps your husband is addicted to alcohol, drugs, or gambling. He may often explode in anger, break promises or run up debt. As you contend with your own disappointment and hurt, your challenge will be to find that place of rest, where you come to know and understand that only God can change the heart. Once you find that place and work on changing your own response, other changes will happen within the relationship.

When we're dealing with a relationship problem, a great place to start is by acknowledging our own part in the problem, and then asking God to renew our heart and set a right spirit within us.

This prayer will help create in us a willingness to change our own attitude and response.

One of the first things we may need to change is our dialogue. We need to steer clear of all blaming. If we fling accusatory 'you' statements at our husband, the conversation will deteriorate rapidly. If, however, we learn to use 'I' statements that focus on how we think or feel about the situation, our words will promote healing and change. Mamas, we can learn to do this. We can change the way we communicate with those we love.

One other area we often need to change is in our habits. Habits can be lethal… the way we talk to and treat others is often the result of an entrenched habit.

Many years ago, when I was on an elephant safari in Nepal, the guide took us out one evening to see the elephants at rest. He asked us to guess what creature these massive animals are most afraid of. Several people suggested a mouse. He shook his head. 'They fear the tiny ant. If an ant crawls up an elephant's trunk and enters the brain, it can make the elephant go mad.' He then told us that an elephant will sleep with its trunk in its mouth to avoid this happening. I hurried back to my small hut, found my diary and wrote it down so I'd never forget it. What a great lesson! Small things matter. Small persistent habits can destroy our marriage. Criticism; harsh, angry words; sneering; belittling comments – these can become habits. And all of them have the potential to be lethal. Like the elephant, we need to avert the danger. How appropriate that the elephant's strategy was to put its trunk in its mouth – yet another reminder of how important our words are. So, mamas, let's be ruthless as we analyse our habits and then let's make the necessary changes.

Learn to resolve conflict

Conflict is to be expected in any relationship. And, in fact, it is often the instigator of positive change. But if it's not handled properly, it can destroy what we've spent years building. Sometimes, for varying reasons, we just want a fight! But that sort of conflict is always destructive. It's like smashing down parts of our own wall. Instead, we need to decide whether we've actually got a problem, or perhaps just a difference. You may be an extrovert and love parties, while your husband's personality makes him crave quiet nights at home. Perhaps you're great at starting projects, while he's adamant about sticking with the old project until every last boring detail is finished. Or maybe one of you is a morning person, the other a night owl. In these cases, the solution is learning to accept your differences rather than trying to fight it out and make your partner change. The experts encourage couples to try to recognise the ways that their differences are marriage-strengthening assets. Learning the art of accepting and valuing your husband for who he is – instead of complaining about shortcomings – may help the two of you find better solutions to problems.

So, how do we resolve the inevitable conflict in marriage? I think one of the biggest keys is picking the right time to deal with it. Problem-solving is least likely to work when you're tired, hungry, overloaded, stressed or trying to do something else at the same time, such as making dinner or catching up on work from the office. If your husband has just sat down to relax in front of the TV after a big day, chances are he won't appreciate you trying to initiate a deep and meaningful conversation. Save the big talks for a better time. You may need to plan a time away to discuss the really big issues. Whatever you do, don't start a heavy talk late at night. Fatigue inflames many fights.

When you manage to find some time to talk about the conflict, resist the temptation to use confrontation. Keep your voice soft. Instead of slamming into the talk with an aggressive attitude and loaded words of blame or criticism, start by talking about how you feel and then asking for your husband's input. Ask for God's help with this. Wisdom is gentle and reasonable. Rather than using inflammatory statements such as 'You always' or 'You never', learn to tackle the issue with gentleness. Even though it's hard to remember when emotions are running high, we need to remind ourselves that our spouse is not the enemy. We have an enemy of our souls, the devil, and he is the one who seeks to drive us apart.

If things get too heated during your discussion, take time out. You should do this early and often. As soon as either of you feels too upset or negative to follow healthy problem-solving steps, it's time to take a break. You can agree to this response ahead of time. This tactic will prevent you from saying things you may regret later. Stop the discussion right away, go to separate rooms or outdoors, and calm down. Take a walk, read a book, cook a meal. Try not to spend your time chewing over the conversation. When both of you have calmed down, revisit the issue, asking God to give you the gentleness of wisdom. And here's an important point, mamas. Make sure each of you has equal opportunity to share. If you tend to dominate the conversation, you'll have to learn to listen more. Or perhaps you may need to learn to open up and share what you're feeling. Either way, these are things we can all learn.

If your marriage is fraught with conflict, I encourage you to do a course on conflict resolution or read a book about it together. Learn, learn, learn.

No one enjoys conflict. But we need to remind ourselves that problems offer us the opportunity to build our marriages and show each other how much we care as we search for solutions together.

Learn to pray together

For those of you who are married to a Christian, this is one area that holds great potential for both growth and blessing. Our prayer journey is something that is constantly developing and growing as we walk with the Lord. And when we marry, a whole new possibility opens up – that of praying with our husband. However, over the years, many women have confided in me that they rarely pray with their husband, and when they try to, it's awkward and difficult. Some husbands are reluctant; others flatly refuse to do so. But I'm convinced this is something we can learn to do, and I know that it holds great blessing.

So, how do you learn to pray together? I encourage you to start small. It may be just a simple prayer together at night, thanking God for the day, and praying for each of your children. Or perhaps holding hands in the morning and praying for a blessing on each other's day. From these small beginnings, you'll become more comfortable to pray together about every aspect of your family life.

It was one of the things I loved about my parents. They prayed together about everything. But I know that it didn't just happen. They worked at it for over seventy years of marriage. They *learnt* how to do it.

Bless you, dear mamas, as you finish reading this chapter. I know that for some of you it may have been a difficult read. Some of you may have lost your husband; some of you perhaps have never been married. Some may be facing the devastation of a marriage breakup. Each one of you will face different challenges. But I hope all of you can take some of these principles and apply them to any of your relationships. Because I know that great relationships don't just happen. They are built.

Heart to Heart with Rosie Boom

CHAPTER EIGHT

Joy on Our Homeschooling Journey

*Enjoy the little things, for one day you may look
back and realise they were the big things.*

—Robert Brault[28]

Cold rain drizzled from grey winter skies as Eliza and I began the long journey home from a concert in a distant town. The trip included a 50 km stretch of isolated country road. We were singing together to pass the time when the car coughed and spluttered. I pulled over and listened in alarm as the engine died completely. After several unsuccessful attempts to start the car, a sneaky suspicion began to gnaw at my mind. Turning on the key, I watched as the petrol indicator refused to move from the empty sign. With a groan, I looked across at my young daughter. How could I have done it again? Only the day before, I'd run out of diesel in our family van. And now here we were, stuck in the back of beyond with no cell phone coverage, and not a car in sight.

It was a long forty minutes before a car finally appeared. I turned on my hazard lights to show we needed help, but the car raced past us, splashing us with mud. Another twenty minutes passed before a second car roared up the road with loud music thumping.

I suddenly felt isolated and vulnerable. Jumping back into the car, I put on my indicator and made as if we were about to pull out onto the road. An hour later, a passing farmer came to our rescue. Thankful and relieved, I chattered to him as he poured in some petrol. Without thinking, I said, 'Can you believe it? This is the second time this weekend that I've run out of fuel.' I regretted it straight away. He looked up at me and said, 'And what colour is *your* hair?'

I blushed and muttered an embarrassed reply, but once we were on the road again, Eliza and I had a good laugh about my faux pas. It wasn't until she dropped off to sleep that I had the luxury of uninterrupted thought. I began thinking about the homeschooling journey, and how easy it is to 'run out of petrol' on that journey as well. I thought of some women I've met at conferences who have expressed feelings of isolation and the inability to go any further. They'd run out of fuel. I've felt like that myself more than once. And, sometimes, it seems like there's no one around to help. Or worse, someone goes racing past in their fancy sports car without even slowing down, spraying us with mud. I determined then that I would always try to watch out for those who have run out of fuel on their homeschooling journey, stranded on a lonely road, needing help.

The whole embarrassing incident became a wonderful lesson for me as God applied it to my homeschooling. It began with a simple question. Why had I run out of fuel? The answer was obvious. I'd stopped looking at the gauge. I'd become distracted.

Mamas, we need to keep our eye on the gauge. We need to watch ourselves and read the signs. Are we snapping at the children or at our husband? Are we impatient or severe with the children? If that's the case, maybe all we need to do is 'fill up' with a few litres of sleep. Get a few early nights. Yes, I know. Easier said than done. I know only too well the temptation to burn the midnight oil. I get carried away doing some of my own projects, revelling in the quiet without the constant interruption of little ones.

But I have also paid the price the next morning, attempting to teach with my head thumping and my nerves frayed.

We also need to beware of over-commitment. If we always feel tired, it's time to examine our life and identify the things that absorb precious hours, leaving us ragged. In order to homeschool successfully, there are certain things we need to put aside for a while. We can't do everything. There will be changes and sacrifices we must make if we're to enjoy the journey.

I remember years ago running out of petrol in my beat-up orange Arabella Borgward car simply because I didn't have the money with me to buy some. I had tried to make it home on an empty tank, but alas! Here lies another important truth. Filling a vehicle up with fuel costs us. So does homeschooling. And I don't just mean the literal financial cost of only having one income because the mother has chosen to stay home from work to teach the children. There are other costs as well. It will mean you are no longer as free as you used to be to go out to coffee with your friends or play tennis. The answer to this is to count the cost and then pay it joyfully.

Another common reason for running out of petrol (I speak from experience) is trying to eke more miles out of one tank of gas than is feasible. Again, this can serve as a fitting illustration to those of us on our homeschooling journey. We need to ensure we're setting realistic goals for our homeschooling. We mustn't try to achieve the impossible. Unrealistic goals set us up for failure and lead to despair. I remember reading a book once that discussed the importance of regularly examining our expectations. The author explained that if there is a wide gap between our expectations and the actual reality of our experience and life, it has the potential to become a gaping hole through which we lose our 'joie de vivre' – the joy of life.

Mamas, are you expecting too much of your five-year-old? Do you hold an unrealistic expectation of how tidy your home should be?

Perhaps you have set unrealistic goals for your child with learning difficulties. This will set both you and your child up for failure. Instead, learn to set realistic goals and narrow the gap between your expectations and your reality.

When my children were quite young, I talked to them about this very thing. We discussed what realistic and unrealistic goals were, and then I asked each child to think of an example. Katie was nine at the time and had just started taking piano lessons. When I asked her for an example of an unrealistic goal, she said, 'I'm going to become a concert pianist in three months.'

I clapped my hands. 'Perfect! Now think of a realistic goal.'

She thought for a moment, and then replied, 'I'm going to study hard and sit Grade 8 by the time I'm 16.'

I applauded her again. That was indeed a realistic goal. It would take hard work, and plenty of practice, but she could do it. And she did.

This would be a good place to talk about the importance of setting realistic educational goals for individual children. For those of you with large families, it's important to remember that not all your children will be ready to learn to read at age five.

By the time Samuel was five and Jacob was four, I had taught four other children to read without too many dramas. I decided that since the youngest two were so close in age, I would teach them to read together and thus kill two birds with one stone. (I shudder to think how appropriate that saying might have been. Yikes.) It wasn't long before I realised that my youngest son was finding reading a lot easier than his older brother. I persevered for a while until my father, a retired teacher, gently suggested to me I needed to use a different approach for each boy. I heeded his advice and let Jacob advance at his own speed while spending more time with Samuel on the basics. How glad I am that I did that! I was to discover a few years later that Samuel had challenges with dyslexia.

If I had pushed him to achieve my unrealistic expectations, I would have crushed him in the process and set him up for failure.

As homeschooling mothers, we can also fall into the trap of setting unrealistic goals for ourselves. Perhaps it's that we endeavour to teach our children, keep the house spotless and cook gourmet meals every night. Don't fall into that trap, mamas. I know so many women who shy away from hospitality because they feel the need to serve up meals akin to a five-star restaurant. What a shame. Proverbs 17:1 (NASB) says, 'Better a dinner of herbs where love is, than a fattened ox and hatred with it.' A hearty soup and fresh buns (that don't have to be home-made!) served with pleasant conversation and merry laughter will make for a memorable meal.

The encouragement you receive from others will also fill your petrol tank. This is especially important for those of you who are homeschooling on your own without the support of a partner. Find someone who can speak encouragement into your life. Someone who will warn you if you're setting unrealistic goals. Someone who will cheer you on across the miles. The word 'encourage' means to stimulate someone with approval and hope; to inspire with courage and hope. 'Inspire' means to 'breathe life into'. How we all need inspiration and hope! In a later chapter, I'll talk about the absolute importance of letting God's word speak encouragement into your life. It's amazing how one word from God can transform your perception of your homeschooling.

Mamas, you are on a long homeschooling journey. You are going to need to keep your tanks full – emotionally, spiritually and physically.

Isaiah 40:31 (NKJV) says, 'But those who wait on the Lord will renew their strength. They will mount up with wings like eagles, they shall run and not be weary, they shall walk and not faint.' Whenever we spend time with the Lord, petrol is being poured into our tank. Nothing can take the place of that. And yet, too often we cheat ourselves of this infilling. We are too busy. Too tired.

Too distracted. I love the challenge William Booth left his family and friends on his deathbed: 'Tend to the fire, brethren, tend to the fire. For it is the nature of a fire to go out.'[29] A fire will not burn forever on one load of wood. We can start our homeschooling journey with full tanks, but we must refuel.

CHAPTER NINE

Don't Wreck Your Engine

There is nothing in the world of art like the songs Mother used to sing.

—Billy Sunday[30]

Even my clear-headed, sensible husband Chris has put petrol in our diesel van on two occasions. I must confess to feeling rather gratified when it happened. And relief that it wasn't my mistake – again. I still chuckle when I remember the look of astonishment on Chris's face as he realised his mistake.

Mamas, it's every bit as easy to use the wrong fuel on our homeschooling journey. When Chris filled the van with petrol instead of diesel, the mistake wasn't obvious as we drove out of the service station. But just a short distance up the road, the engine spluttered and died. In the same way, the wrong fuel seems to provide impetus on our homeschooling journey, but before too long, the engine chokes up and dies.

Let me list just a few of the wrong fuels I've discovered over the years.

Trying to please man rather than God

Perhaps you're trying to prove to your sceptical relatives how well your children are doing out of the school system, or how well Johnny is reading. Without realising it, you become stressed and tense and lose the joy of teaching. Wrong fuel!

Guilt

This is an emotion we've probably all wrestled with. We torment ourselves with questions: Am I doing enough? Am I preventing my child from experiencing the positive aspects of school? Will my child hate me for making him different?

When we feel sick in pregnancy and are struggling to put together a lesson, we feel guilty. This guilt pushes us to try harder and harder until we burn out. Wrong fuel.

Worry

Again, we're tortured by a raft of negative thoughts: perhaps my child will resent me in later years for homeschooling him. How will I ever stay ahead of my smart teenager? Perhaps I'm missing an important subject that my teenager will need in order to pursue his dream job.

Worry can generate a response and a lot of exhausting action, and it may seem that it's motivating us in the right direction. But all too soon the worry leads to a meltdown or maybe to us giving up on our homeschooling altogether. The future can be a heavy weight. One day is enough for us to bear. Worry is a wrong fuel.

Let me share one of my all-time favourite Pooh quotes:

The wind was against them now, and Piglet's ears streamed behind him like banners as he fought his way along, and it seemed hours before he got them into the shelter of the Hundred Acre Wood and they stood up straight again, to listen, a little nervously, to the roaring of the gale among the treetops.

'Supposing a tree fell down, Pooh, when we were underneath it?'

'Supposing it didn't,' said Pooh after careful thought.[31]

Comparison

Oh, this is a killer! And we've all fallen prey to it, I'm sure. Theodore Roosevelt is reported to have said that comparison is the thief of joy. How many times have we been robbed of joy by comparing our life, our children, our situation, our skills, our available resources, our schoolroom (or lack of it) with someone else? What a trap! Next time you're tempted to draw a comparison, say to yourself, 'I will not be robbed! Begone, thief!'

Mamas, enjoy the freedom to be yourself. Homeschooling in the Boom household will look different to how it looks in other homes. And that's good. Instead of giving the thief access, give thanks daily for what you have. Be grateful.

Comparison will also rob your children. Many a parent has fallen into the trap of trying to motivate a child by comparing him/her to a sibling who is doing better in a particular subject. 'Come on, darling! Look at Johnny! He's done all his work already and his printing is so neat.' You get the idea. But this comparison is anything but motivating. It may produce a grudging response for a time, but it can cause deep insecurity or resentment that really compromises the inner workings of the engine.

Opportunities to indulge in the dangerous habit of comparing our life with others present themselves again and again. You may look with longing at other women who spend a whole day in town, having coffee, browsing the shops. Or perhaps you dwell on the fact that so-and-so can afford to have someone clean her house once a week or hire a tutor to help with science. You may be tempted to draw comparisons between a family's bona fide, tidy, well-organised 'schoolroom' and your own messy kitchen table, strewn with books and paper and pens. Don't go there! Don't entertain thoughts that will steal your joy: if I had only one child instead of six to teach… if my children were as bright as her children… if I could afford all those wonderful books, that amazing curriculum…

If you indulge in those thoughts, they will rob you of motivation and joy. Wrong fuel.

Pride

You may think that it's good to allow a sense of pride to be a driving force in your homeschooling. Perhaps it appears to generate a striving for excellence. 'My children are intelligent. We'll show the nay-sayers of homeschooling how successful it can be.' However, God is very clear about the pitfalls of pride, and the Bible contains many warnings for us. 'Pride goes before destruction, and a haughty spirit before a fall' (Proverbs 16:18 NKJV).

Rather, let's teach our children with humility, asking God for his help. Pride is the wrong fuel.

Wrong values

If we hold mere academia as our goal and ambition, ignoring the weightier things such as godly instruction and character building, we will soon run out of impetus.

It may not be until the teenage years, when we suddenly realise our son knows algebraic expressions but doesn't know how to make his own bed. Wrong fuel.

None of the above are suitable fuels for the homeschooling journey. In the end, they just wreck the engine. God never intended these to be the motivating force, the fuel, for our homeschooling. So, what *are* the right fuels?

Doing it as unto the Lord.

In Colossians 3:23, Paul encourages us to put our whole heart into whatever we do, as if we were doing it for the Lord and not for men. When we remember it is God who called us to teach our children, and that he is the one whose approval we need, the engine runs sweetly.

We need to remind ourselves constantly that what we are doing is one of the most important things we could ever give ourselves to. A high calling. One that will demand whole-hearted commitment and whole-hearted dedication. Jim Elliot, missionary to the Aucas of Ecuador, once said, 'Wherever you are, be all there!'[32] What fantastic advice. Whole-hearted parenting and whole-hearted homeschooling will prove less stressful and exhausting than trying to do it with a divided heart.

I recently read a small passage in a book that shared the testimony of a humble mother who lived on a New Hampshire farm:

> 'I walked down the furrow of a field with the Governor of New Hampshire in my arms, and the Governor of Massachusetts clinging to my skirts.' She said that afterwards, long afterwards, in her old age. For she knew not then, and no one knew, that her two baby boys would be governors of two New England states.[33]

That begs the question: Who is clinging to your skirt? Who do you hold in your arms? Only God knows! And he is asking you to do your very best to teach these small children to love and fear him. When you truly catch this vision, it will be excellent fuel in your tank.

Treating each child as an individual

This may seem obvious, but we need to be constantly reminded of it. We need to see the individual strengths of each child and celebrate them. As I mentioned earlier, Samuel struggled with dyslexia, but he was such an earnest child and a deep thinker. He always listened carefully when I was trying to explain something to him. The way I taught him differed from how I taught Jacob or Milly. And there was great joy in that! As homeschoolers, we need to remind ourselves often that we don't just have one 'class' to teach. We have individual students who have differing learning styles and different giftings and interests. Ask God to help you understand the needs of each child and seek his wisdom.

Hearing God's word of promise for each child

Over the years, I've encouraged many of you to seek God and ask him for a specific word for each of your children. I can't stress the importance of this enough. One word, one promise from God about your child will provide fuel enough for many, many miles. I'll share my personal testimony about this in a later chapter.

Godly encouragement from other mums

This is a wonderful source of fuel for your journey! Don't isolate yourself.

I've met many women who have become so focused on the work they want their children to achieve in a term that they won't spare the time to meet with other homeschoolers.But for me, it's somewhat like tithing. We may feel we can't afford to tithe, but when we do, the Lord blesses us and we find we can, in fact, make ends meet.

For those of you live in isolated places, try to have regular phone or email contact with someone who can speak encouragement and wisdom into your life

Thankfulness

What a wonderful fuel this is! I believe that gratitude is one of the most powerful forces for good in our lives. Make a habit of counting your blessings. The fact that we're permitted to homeschool our children is a huge blessing. Thank God for it every day. Thank him for your children. Yes, I know they are noisy and messy and demanding, but what a privilege it is to be a mother! I still remember the longing I had in my heart to be a mother when I was single at thirty. As mentioned earlier, I'd wondered then whether I would ever find love and have children. In later years, when I battled through a difficult or tiring day, I'd remind myself of that and give thanks to the Lord for allowing me to have six beautiful children. Hallelujah!

On this note, let me also encourage you to take every opportunity to celebrate. You can do this in a myriad of different ways, but the result will be an outpouring of gratitude to God for something – an achievement, a milestone reached, a blessing, a challenge overcome. The Bible is replete with examples of God's people celebrating.

Prayer

Ask for God's help. You'd think this would be obvious, but it's amazing how often we forget to do it.

Try to make a habit of daily inviting the Holy Spirit, the teacher, into your classroom. And let your children hear you doing this. Every prayer results in more fuel in your tank.

Remembrance

Now this is an excellent fuel! In C.S. Lewis's book, *The Silver Chair*, Aslan gives Jill Pole important instructions that she must not forget: 'Remember! Remember! Remember the signs!'[34] The Bible is full of exhortations for God's people to remember and not forget. Do you remember what God first said to you about homeschooling? Do you remember the lessons and truths you've learnt along the way? We all need to keep re-reading the map. I encourage you to read the Word every day. Read good books that will inspire you on the journey.

In his book *The 7 Habits of Highly Effective Families,* Steven Covey explains that during any flight, a plane can be off course up to 90% of the time. This can be because of winds, air traffic, weather conditions, etc. But the pilot gets the plane back on course because before take-off, he locked the destination into the flight plan. As homeschooling parents, we need to have a flight plan. We need to lock in our destination. And then we need to reassess our flight plan regularly. A good habit to develop is to ask yourself often, why am I doing this? Call back to mind your goals and the real reason why you homeschool. Remember!

My goals were to teach my children to love the Lord with all their hearts and minds and souls; develop their characters and help them grow into kind, godly adults; equip them with everything they need to fulfil the plans God had for their lives; and enjoy my children. Remembrance stirs up the heart and fans the flickering embers into flame. It gets us back on course. It's a great fuel.

Patience

I've laughed many times at being told, 'Oh, I could never homeschool! I'm not patient enough.' I'm always tempted to reply, 'Oh? And you think I am?' I doubt if any of us were 'patient enough' when we started. But the good news is that patience is a fruit of the Spirit, and it grows. We can learn to be patient.

I love the verse in Hebrews that says, 'We do not want you to become lazy, but to imitate those who through faith and patience inherit what has been promised' (Hebrews 6:12 NIV). Faith and patience. I like to think of them as two shoes that we wear on our journey. One step with faith. One step with patience. Again and again.

When an interviewer asked heavyweight champion Jim Corbett what it took to be a champion, he said, 'Just fight one more round.'[35]

Paul writes in Corinthians, 'We get knocked down, but we get up again and keep going' (2 Corinthians 4:9 TLB).

Mamas, be patient with your child. Be patient with yourself. Keep the long view in mind and persevere. When a farmer or gardener sows seeds, they must then be patient. In fact, all of nature is a lesson in patience. Ralph Waldo Emerson wrote, 'Adopt the pace of nature: her secret is patience.'[36] The plant will not appear overnight. Some seeds need long, dark weeks beneath the ground before they put forth their tender shoots. So too with us. Every morning as we teach our children, we are planting seeds in their hearts. Here's a great promise for us in Isaiah: 'He will give you rain for your seed which you will sow in the ground' (Isaiah 30:23 NASB).

An ancient Egyptian proverb asks the question, 'What two things can scale the mighty pyramids?' I love the answer. 'The eagle and the snail.' What a wonderful illustration this can be of homeschooling. Sometimes our days go brilliantly, and it feels like we're soaring through the heights like an eagle, catching the wind currents and celebrating the uplifting power of the Lord.

Other days, we feel like we're crawling our way up the steep slopes with progress slow and painful, leaving a trail of slime behind us. But on both days, we are scaling the mighty pyramid.

A sense of humour

This is wonderful fuel for the journey! Mamas, never lose the ability to laugh at yourself or with your children. We need to lighten up, mamas. Relax our shoulders, take a few deep breaths and let ourselves laugh.

I talked recently with a lady who told me she had always found it difficult to laugh. She was desperate to change the feel in her home, and she knew laughter was a key. I told her she could learn how to laugh. I suggested that if she was reading aloud to the children and came across a funny incident, instead of just smiling, she should practise giving a chuckle. Or better still, a hearty laugh. It may seem forced at first, but soon enough, laughter will become an easy response.

We need to be intentional about introducing laughter and humour into our homes. We can do this by choosing funny books to read together. I still remember the joy of watching Jacob's little legs swinging with excitement as he laughed uncontrollably at Eeyore's ridiculous house dramas. Choose a funny movie to watch together on family night. Old family videos are great for this.

Joy

The holidays were over, and the new school year loomed ahead. Part of me was dreading it. I felt tired and uninspired – not a good way to start the year. But then I read about the oil of joy: 'Giving them a garland instead of ashes, the oil of joy, instead of mourning, the mantle of praise instead of the spirit of fainting, so they will be called oaks of righteousness, the planting of the Lord, that He might be glorified' (Isaiah 61:3).

The night before the new term was to start, I asked Chris to anoint me with olive oil and pray that I would have great joy in my teaching. The next morning at devotions, I shared with the children about the wonderful strength joy brings to our lives and then I anointed each of them with the oil of joy. It was a wonderful time. My tiredness dissipated, and, in its place, came fresh joy and creativity. And the children responded with excitement and enthusiasm. We were going to have a good term.

Many of us are familiar with the verse, 'The joy of the Lord is your strength' (Nehemiah 8:10 NKJV). Joy is the ultimate fuel. Nothing gives us more energy and strength than this. Again, like patience, this is one of the fruits of the Holy Spirit, and it will grow and increase in our lives as we walk in the Spirit. But we can also discover joy by looking for it. There are so many joys in homeschooling that we can sometimes overlook in our busyness. When you see your older children caring for the little ones, when you hear them pray true heart prayers, and when you see character development in their lives, give thanks and take joy!

Let me close this chapter with a wonderful quote from Fra Giovanni in the 15th century:

> I salute you. I am your friend and my love for you goes deep. There is nothing I can give you which you have not got. But there is much, very much, that while I cannot give it, you can take. No heaven can come to us unless our hearts find rest in today. Take heaven! No peace lies in the future, which is not hidden in this present little instance. Take peace! The gloom of the world is but a shadow. Behind it, yet within our reach, is joy. Take joy! And so I greet you, with profound esteem and with the prayer that for you, now and forever, the day breaks and the shadows flee away.[37]

Mamas, God wants to give you joy in your homeschooling. May your tanks be full as you continue your homeschooling journey. Take joy!

CHAPTER TEN

Hand in Glove – Structure and Creativity

Think left and think right and think low and think high.
Oh, the thinks you can think up if only you try!

—Dr Seuss[38]

Creativity and structure. They may seem diametrically opposed, but, in fact, they fit together like hand and glove. Both will enrich our homeschooling. As I write this, I'm thinking of the beautiful relationship my parents had. They were married for seventy years, and over that time they learnt to recognise their differences as a strength. Dad's sensible, down-to-earth pragmatism beautifully balanced Mum's creativity. Two different strengths, but they made for a wonderful marriage. In the same way, structure and creativity can live together with great harmony and blessing.

It seems that every homeschooler I've met has a leaning towards either one or the other of these two important elements. That's certainly true in my own life. But I'm convinced that great blessing lies in store for those who learn how to cultivate both. The days when I fail to get something out of the freezer in the morning for the evening meal take their toll. The thought, 'What am I going to make for dinner?' hangs over me like an annoying cloud all day.

In contrast, when I'm organised and get the meat out, then I can happily forget about it until it's time to prepare the meal. This holds true for my homeschooling. Having a plan to follow brings structure and peace into my day. It takes time and effort to work out a plan, but in the long run, it really pays off for me. Being a creative type, I'm naturally more inclined to just go with the flow and follow my creative inspirations. But I've learnt to undergird my creativity with a foundation of structure.

I think it's important for us to ensure our children have some structure in their schooling. As they grow older, they need to know how to work within a time frame and the importance of meeting deadlines. They also need to know that, as adults, they'll be required to do things they won't particularly enjoy. Any career choice, no matter how thrilling, will entail boring moments, tough days and unlikeable aspects. Deadlines. Exams. Long hours. They're all part of an adult's world, and having a measure of discipline and structure throughout your schooling will help prepare your children for that.

Right. That said, now I can share the fun part! Creativity. The very word excites me. It beckons you from the timetable with the promise of learning something exciting and refreshing. I remember the joy of bundling up in jackets and gumboots and taking a walk on a winter's morning after devotions. The books could wait. Spontaneity is important. Surprise your children with an outing, a visit, an adventure of some sort. My children still remember the days I watched them head off to begin their schoolwork, only to call them back and tell them, 'Actually, today we're not going to do any book work. I'm going to read to you all day, for as long as my voice holds out.' How I loved the look on their faces! Spontaneity makes for memorable days.

I don't think anyone would argue the fact that some people are naturally more creative than others. But that doesn't mean those who are less creative need to be compromised. Creative ideas are made to be shared, borrowed and copied.

No one will begrudge you borrowing their ideas. This might be a good place to mention the wonderful input other people can offer your family. If an auntie offers to teach the children art, grab the opportunity! You'll be amazed by the creative help you might receive if you mention to your extended family that you'd welcome their involvement. I've mentioned earlier the joyful afternoons of sewing with Nana, chess competitions with Grandpa, and art with G and G.

All of us need to make a point of asking God to help us develop creativity. Every day, ask the Lord for ideas and then watch out for them. Train yourself to be alert. Remember Van Dyke's cloud of opportunities swarming around us, thicker than gnats at sundown? Seize the opportunities to be creative. Ludwig van Beethoven said, 'You ask me where I get my ideas. That I cannot tell you with certainty. They come unsummoned, directly, indirectly. I could seize them with my hands – out in the open air, in the woods, while walking, in the silence of the nights, at dawn, excited by moods which are translated by the poet into words, by me into tones that sound and roar and storm about me till I have set them down in notes.'[39] I love it!

One of the best things we can do to inject creativity into our days is to capitalise on our children's current interests and passions... spiders, explorers, whales, stars. Mamas, let's use our freedom as homeschoolers to explore their different interests. It's all too easy to revert to what's comfortable or planned and miss these wonderful teaching moments. They might present themselves when you're reading aloud and one child asks a question. If you're watching and alert for creative ideas, you won't see this as an annoying interruption but rather the chance to discover some treasure. For example, if you're reading a book about Florence Nightingale and one of the children asks you about their great-grandmother called Florence, take the time to talk about your own family history. Study the family tree. Share with them whatever stories you know of Great-Grandma Florrie.

If you don't know any, ring up the grandparents and ask them about their memories of her. It's amazing what significant moments occur when you take the time to follow these leads.

Look for creative ways that you can share about your own reading material with your children. This can be a huge blessing. I mentioned before the need for us to be both teachers and students all our lives. What is God saying to you? What truth are you discovering? What book are you enjoying? You just need creativity to help make it age-appropriate for your family. Hence the need for us to be a student for life ourselves! (And what better way to make sure you keep learning than by homeschooling?)

Creativity comes into its own in times of chaos. We've probably all experienced times when some life challenge or drama upends our homeschooling. In the previous chapter, I shared Stephen Covey's analogy of a plane flight and how a plane can be off course up to 90% of the time. This is where creativity shines. Mamas, don't stress if your planned schedule is disrupted for a while. The arrival of a precious new baby can throw our schooling routine into chaos. No matter! Use this as an opportunity to teach your children important life skills as they help Mummy cope with the housework, etc. Sickness can cast a dense fog over our path for a while. Accidents can burst into our lives and shatter all our well-laid plans. It's alright. Ask God to help you find creative ways of dealing with what life has thrown at you. In time, your plane will come back on course.

The wonderful thing about homeschooling is that we can be flexible and change our programme. I encourage you to not do the same thing every morning for an entire term. Go for a walk on a crisp winter morning and make white clouds with your breath. Look at the spider web necklaces strung along the fence lines. Designate a reading day with no lessons. Make hot chocolates with marshmallows before you start devotions. Let the children make something while you read.

It helps to make the experience rich and is a wonderful way to end up with meaningful mementos. My boys often designed wonderful Lego creations while the girls knitted or cross-stitched. Go on a surprise field trip or have an art day. Have a cheese making morning. Stay in your PJs all day. Make a puppet show or put together a play. We often did spontaneous unrehearsed plays, which usually ended in great hilarity. They made for memorable days and helped the children remember the verse or story they were acting out. Make beds in the lounge and let the children stay up late to watch the Olympics. Enjoy a sleep-in the next morning! Have your own Olympics day on the back lawn. We put foam mattresses on the lawn and designed different classes for the children to compete in. Watch a special movie together. When our family suffered a bout of whooping cough, we stayed in our pyjamas all day and watched *Anne of Green Gables*. That week shines in our memory as a precious family experience. Have a chess or Chinese checkers tournament. Do the world map puzzle together. Play some of the educational games you've bought at homeschooling conferences and never used! Play Scrabble. Stay up late and look at the stars. Teach your children how to find south from the Southern Cross. Invite another family over and get all the children to help you to prepare a special meal. Do some baking for a sick friend. Work on making a quilt. Let the children raid your rag bag and be willing to teach some cavemen (that story is told in *The Barn Chronicles*). The list is endless! But I hope you get the idea. Let's celebrate the freedom we have to be creative in our homeschooling. Let's determine that we won't become trapped in dry, mundane book learning. And let's always keep in mind that one of the most important things we'll ever teach our children is life skills. Mamas, let's bring learning alive.

God, the Creator, is more than willing to share his creativity with us. Let's ask him every day for ideas and then make sure we're listening.

I've found that often the ideas come as a small prompting that I could easily ignore if I'm not watching and listening for it. In *The Gift of Values – Volume One*, I write about the creative idea that God gave me when I cried out to him in frustration one morning. 'A Pocket of Beans' tells the story of how one small creative idea that dropped into my mind transformed a wretched, trying morning into a profound learning moment. The key is to be listening. Time pressure, haste and hurry all crush creativity.

An important question we mamas need to ask is, 'How can I encourage creativity in my child?' Part of the answer lies in giving our children space and time to develop their own creativity. If we are constantly hurrying them up, their creativity will never flourish. Harvard Business Review journalist Dana Rousmaniere writes, 'Creativity takes time, requiring people to struggle down several blind alleys before finding the right solution. That's why a lot of creative activity may look suspiciously like loafing around until a breakthrough happens.'[40] And I know only too well how we homeschoolers hate the idea of our children 'loafing around'!

Journalist Clare Thorpe described boredom as one of the most important factors in creativity – 'a silent muse that has inspired countless great songs, novels and paintings.'[41]

Much of the world has enjoyed the detective stories of Agatha Christie. She claims that 'there's nothing like boredom to make you write.'[42] So true!

I love the fact that science has linked daydreaming with creativity. It would be interesting to compare the amount of daydreaming that takes place among children today with that of children who lived before the internet age. I would guess the results would show a huge decrease. Herein lies a real challenge for parents in this technological age. The internet. We need to teach our children how to handle this powerful, yet potentially destructive tool. And mamas, we need to teach by example. Are we bored?

Too often, our default is to scroll through countless feeds on our smart phone. Do your children see you turning to the screen for entertainment while you wait at the doctors? Or do they hear you engaging in conversation with the lady sitting nearby? If we model the former behaviour and allow our children to revert to screen time whenever they're bored, we are short-cutting the magic that can come as a result of boredom. Limit your child's screen time. Limit your own. Offer them alternatives. You can suggest they go outside and build a tree hut or play a game. But don't feel that you're obliged to come up with an option they approve of. Mamas, let's bring back boredom. Let's re-instate daydreaming. And let's watch our children become creative again.

CHAPTER ELEVEN

Susanna Wesley's Apron

Mother – that was the bank where we deposited all our hurts and worries.

—T. DeWitt Talmage[43]

When my mother died in 2014, I felt like I'd lost my main cheerleader. The one who prayed for me the most. All my life, I was aware of her prayers for me. Whatever I was going through, I knew Mum was lifting me up to the Lord with love and compassion. She carried me in her heart.

I can still picture her in the kitchen, wearing one of the many beautiful aprons she'd made, cooking Anzac biscuits or bumblebees. Her calico apron with appliqued flowers and leaves and butterflies is one of my precious possessions. I love to put it on in the evening as I cook dinner and remember her.

My mother told us that when she was pregnant with her first child at the start of World War Two, she would go outside and wave her apron at Dad as he flew overhead in his plane, letting him know she hadn't gone into labour.

I recently read a story that someone posted on the internet about Grandma's apron. I loved it. It resonated with me on so many fronts.

Grandma used her apron to protect her dress because often she only had a few dresses. It was also because it was easier to wash aprons than dresses and aprons used less material. Her apron served as a potholder, drying children's tears, and on occasion it was even used for cleaning out dirty ears. When Grandma went to the chicken coop, her apron was used for carrying eggs, fussy chicks and sometimes half-hatched eggs to be finished in the warming oven.

When company came, her apron was an ideal hiding place for shy children. It was amazing how fast Grandma could dust when unexpected guests dropped in. When the weather was cold, Grandma would wrap it around her arms to keep the chill away. The aprons wiped away the perspiration created while bent over a hot wood stove.

Many of Grandma's aprons hauled in firewood, chips and kindling to keep her stove working. In the garden it transported many vegetables, pea pods when the peas were shelled. In the fall, her apron would bring in the apples to be canned and many of the windfall apples for juice.

When dinner was ready, Grandma would walk out onto the porch, wave her apron, and the menfolk knew it was time to come in from the fields for dinners. It will be a long time before someone invents something else that will replace the memories from Grandma's apron.[44]

Susanna Wesley gave birth to nineteen children, but only ten of these survived to adulthood. She homeschooled each of her children, including her daughters. Educating girls was not a common practice in the 1600s, but she wanted all of them to read, write, reason and love God. Because of this practice, some call her 'the Mother of Homeschooling'.

When she couldn't find good textbooks for her children to read, she wrote her own books on whatever subject she wanted them to study. Some books she wrote were on reasoning, the Apostles' Creed, the Lord's Prayer and the Ten Commandments.

Susanna's marriage to Samuel Wesley was not an easy one. They disagreed on many things, from money to politics. On a number of occasions, Samuel went away for long periods of time, leaving her to raise the children alone. Susanna's life held many hardships and challenges. Nine of her children died in infancy. One of her children was crippled. Another couldn't talk until he was six years old. Because of her husband's actions, debt plagued the family. At one time, they threw him into debtor's prison, leaving Susanna struggling to find money for food. On two separate occasions, fire destroyed the home they lived in and the Wesleys lost everything they owned. It was a challenging and busy life. Susanna worked the gardens, milked the cow, schooled the children and managed the entire house herself. She struggled to find a secret place to get away with God. Her longing for some quiet time alone with God forced her to come up with a creative solution. She established a habit which soon came to be respected by every person in the household, from the youngest toddler to the oldest domestic help. Sitting in her favourite chair with her Bible, she would throw her long apron up over her head, forming a sort of tent. Quite different to the tabernacle as in the days of Moses, but a 'tent of meeting' nonetheless. When Susanna was under her apron, everyone knew she was not to be disturbed, except in the case of the direst emergency. There, under the shelter and privacy of her apron, she prayed for her husband and children.[45]

What an inspiring example of a praying mother. In answer to her fervent prayers, it's estimated that her son John Wesley preached to nearly a million people in his lifetime. He held evangelistic services in the open air to accommodate audiences in the tens of thousands.

Travelling on horseback, he regularly preached three or more times a day, often beginning before daybreak. Even at seventy, he preached, without the help of modern amplification, to an estimated crowd of thirty-two thousand people. His brother, Charles Wesley, became a beloved hymn writer of over 6,500 hymns. He wrote some of my favourite hymns. 'Amazing love! How can it be that thou, my God, shouldst die for me?' Beautiful.

We can all learn from Susanna Wesley's apron of prayer. Let me share with you just a few thoughts about praying for our children.

The song 'Make my Life a Prayer to You', written by Keith Green, was one of my favourite songs in the 70s. Praying without ceasing. Continuous prayer. My whole life a prayer.

1 Thessalonians 5:16-18 says, 'Rejoice always; pray continually; give thanks in all circumstances, for this is God's will for you in Christ Jesus.'

Mamas, let's constantly turn our hearts and minds to God, asking for wisdom, for guidance, for strength, for help, giving thanks, praising. Prayer should be our first response in an emergency. As we run towards a screaming child, our hearts should fly to God in prayer.

In the Old Testament, we read about the Israelite priests who carried the names of the children of Israel on the ephod, close to the heart. In the same way, we can carry our children close to our heart, constantly lifting them up to God in prayer.

There are many forms of prayer. Possibly all of us who are married have at some point lain in bed next to our sleeping husband and prayed silently. As parents, we've sat or knelt beside a sleeping child and poured out our hearts to the Lord in silent prayer. It's a beautiful thing to commune with the Lord in our hearts.

Psalm 139:1–4 tells us that God knows our thoughts. 'You have searched me, Lord, and you know me. You know when I sit and when I rise; you perceive my thoughts from afar. You discern my going out and my lying down; you are familiar with all my ways.

Before a word is on my tongue, you, Lord, know it completely.' What a wonderful truth. We can pray silently, and God hears and understands perfectly.

When Chris and I were travelling through Europe, we went to a church service where, at one point, the song leader encouraged the congregation to shout and make a loud, joyful noise before the Lord. I love to rejoice and sing and shout, but it just wasn't how I felt that night. I didn't want to shout. I felt quiet. Contemplative. I remember asking God, 'Can you hear my whisper above all this noise?' Immediately, I felt a deep peace and an assurance that he had heard the silent cry of my heart. He hears our whispered prayers. He hears our wordless prayers. No matter what cacophony of noise surrounds us, our silent prayers are heard by God.

Many years ago, when I was working as a nurse on night shift, I cared for a two-year-old girl with a huge abdominal tumour. Her prognosis was not good. On one of my night rounds, I discovered her lying wide awake, her eyes large and frightened. I picked her up and carried her over to the window, where we looked outside at the stars and the twinkling streetlights. She lay still in my arms, and within a few minutes fell asleep as I sang to her in a soft voice. I remember gazing down at her blonde eyelashes resting gently on her cheeks and feeling overwhelmed with a sense of compassion. Tears rolled down my face as I felt God's love for this precious little girl. When I arrived on duty the next night, I discovered they had transferred her to Auckland Hospital for surgery.

Three years later, I was sitting in a doctors' waiting room and picked up a Women's Weekly magazine. A headline on the front cover caught my eye. 'Miracle Child'. I turned to the article and began to read. I remember how my arms went all goose bumpy when I discovered it was the same little girl – completely healed. The tumour had disappeared before the surgeons could operate. The doctor had written 'miracle' on her discharge form.

I'm sure many people had been praying for this little girl. But I believe that compassion also works miracles. Although I hadn't prayed for her healing when I'd held her that night, I had experienced an outpouring of compassion and love. And as Michael Fairless writes, 'To have love is to work miracles.'[46]

Our tears are also prayers. King David cries out, 'Lord, hear my prayer! Listen to the words I cry to you. Look at my tears' (Psalm 39:12 ERV).

God sees our tears. He *hears* our tears. When Hezekiah became ill, he wept bitterly and cried out to God. And God answered him: 'I have heard your prayer, I have seen your tears' (2 Kings 20:5 NKJV).

Mamas, when we toss on our bed, concerned about one of our children, crying and praying, we need to remember that God keeps count of our tears. He gathers them up and puts them in his bottle. They are recorded in his book (Psalm 56:8).

The American theologian Timothy Keller writes, 'All the laments in the Psalms suggest that there are three things we need to do with our tears: expect tears, invest the tears and pray the tears.

'Weeping allows us to enter into our loss in a profound way, and when given to God, weeping becomes deeply hallowed prayers.'[47]

Deeply hallowed prayers. I love that. To know that our tears don't go unnoticed by God. In Psalm 6:6–9, David writes, 'I am worn out from my groaning. All night long I flood my bed with weeping and drench my couch with tears. My eyes grow weak with sorrow; they fail because of all my foes. Away from me, all you who do evil, for the Lord has heard my weeping. The Lord has heard my cry for mercy; the Lord accepts my prayer.'

Hallelujah! Mamas, let's keep praying for our children in faith, and water those seeds with our tears. I'm pretty sure dear Susanna Wesley would have wept many times in her apron tent, and then used her apron to dry her tears.

Then there are desperate prayers. The prayer of pain and desperate need – unrehearsed, from the gut, short, compelling. 'God, help me!' 'Jesus, son of David, have mercy on me!'

I love how the prophet Daniel cries out to God: 'O Lord, listen! O Lord, forgive! O Lord, hear and act!' (Daniel 9:19 NKJV).

When Chris's dad was in hospital, he looked with distrust at the tiny pill the doctor had prescribed him. Then he complained to me, 'This pill is so small!'

I laughed at the time, but later, God spoke to me from that little incident. How easy it is for us to presume that long prayers are more effective than short heartfelt prayers. If all we can manage is a gut-wrenching 'O Lord, forgive!', that will more than suffice.

Writing this reminds me of a wonderful miracle that happened when I was a young nurse. The Emergency Department of our small hospital was quiet and empty that afternoon as I was about to sit my State Finals practical exam. Because we had no patients at the time, the examiner asked me to set up Room 2 for a mock head injuries admission. She watched as I prepared the room. She wouldn't have known I was praying the whole time. *Lord, help me remember everything. Help me glorify you in this exam and in my nursing.* I wheeled the emergency trolley in and took a last glance around the room. 'I've finished,' I said, hoping with all my heart that I was.

At that very moment, we heard a sound that sent cold shivers shooting up my spine and then back down to my toes. A car raced towards the hospital, blasting its horn constantly. As it turned into the Emergency entrance, my heart began to pound. I prayed as I ran out to the ambulance entrance. *Oh God, help whoever it is that needs our care.*

A tall man leapt out of the driver's seat, shouting that his young daughter had been run over by a car.

Within minutes, Room 2 became the scene of a life and death drama. Everything was all there, ready for her. *Thank You, God. Thank You. You knew she would need this. Save her life, Father.*

The prayers rose and fell in my heart as I cut away her sleeve.

Within half an hour, Nicky was rushed to theatre, where the surgeons performed an emergency operation to release the blood haemorrhaging into her brain.

The next morning, I arrived at work to find that I had been transferred from Accident and Emergency to Intensive Care. I had one patient to care for – a little girl with head injuries. Nicky. I walked in just in time to hear her mother cry out, 'Oh God, if you save Nicky's life, I'll serve you the rest of my life!'

Faith rose inside me. 'She'll be alright,' I told the grieving mother. 'You just wait and see.' And then I told her how the Lord had arranged for the room to be all set up, ready for her daughter.

I was there the day Nicky opened her eyes and said, 'Hello, Mummy.' I heard Karen's joyful prayer as she opened her heart to the love of Jesus. We became best friends and sang together in an outreach band for many years.

I'll never forget that night. It was the night I earned my stripes. But for me, it was the night of answered prayers.

Years ago, I copied a quote that my grandpa had written in the back of his Bible: 'There is no better use of the word of God than to turn it into prayers.'

Mamas, it is so powerful to pray Scripture! I love to turn the verses I'm reading into prayer. One of my favourites is from John 17:11, a prayer that Jesus himself prayed: 'Holy Father, protect them by the power of your name.' Our children need protection! Pray that they will find it in the shadow of his wings (Psalm 91). Pray that the fear of God will keep them from evil (Proverbs 16:6); that they will walk in the ways of good men and keep to the path of the righteous (Proverbs 2:20); that the fear of God will be with them to keep them from sinning (Exodus 20:20). You get the idea. If God highlights a special verse to you, write it down, memorise it. Use it!

In Hosea 11:10–11 it says, 'He will roar like a lion. When he roars, his children will come trembling from the west. They will come from Egypt, trembling like sparrows, from Assyria, fluttering like doves. I will settle them in their homes, declares the Lord.' I think we can pray with hope and confidence that Jesus Christ, the lion of Judah, will roar in our children's lives, and that they will return to him.

There's another type of prayer that I want to mention. Borrowed prayer. The disciples asked Jesus to teach them how to pray and he gave them the Lord's Prayer. Some believers may prefer the freedom of praying in the Spirit to the traditional prayers used in the liturgy of more orthodox churches. Yet so many written prayers are beautifully and powerfully crafted. I have a book beside my bed in which I've written a few prayers that I prayed many times during a period in my life when I found it hard to get to sleep.

> If I lie restless on my bed, your word of healing peace be said.
> If powerful dreams rise in the night, transform their darkness into light.[48]
> Dear Lord, watch with those who wake or watch or weep tonight, and give Your angels charge over those who sleep; tend Your sick ones, rest Your afflicted ones, shield Your joyous ones, and all for Your love's sake. God, we go into this night, confident that the dawn will break tomorrow. Grant that when we come to die, we may go gladly and in hope, confident in the resurrection. Amen.[49]

The Apostle Paul wrote that he hoped he would have sufficient courage for whatever lies ahead. I've borrowed his prayer many times.

> Yes, and I will continue to rejoice, for I know that through your prayers and God's provision of the Spirit of Jesus Christ what has happened to me will turn out for my deliverance.

> I eagerly expect and hope that I will in no way be ashamed, but will have sufficient courage so that now as always Christ will be exalted in my body, whether by life or by death. For to me, to live is Christ and to die is gain (Philippians 1:18–20).

I pray a shortened version of this prayer anytime I'm running towards a hurt, screaming child, not knowing what I'll find. 'Lord, give me sufficient courage!'

I know you can find many examples of great prayers to pray for your children on the internet. It may be helpful to print these out on a bookmark and keep it in your Bible for easy referral.

Let me share with you a portion of Psalm 143, which makes a beautiful daily prayer. It covers all the bases!

> Let the morning bring me word of your unfailing love, for I have put my trust in you *(an ever-growing awareness of God's great love)*. Show me the way I should go, for to you I lift up my soul *(much-needed guidance)*. Rescue me from my enemies, O Lord, for I hide myself in you *(protection and deliverance)*. Teach me to do your will, for you are my God *(personal direction)*. May your good Spirit lead me on level ground *(companionship and provision on our journey)*. For your name's sake, O Lord, preserve my life; in your righteousness, bring me out of trouble *(deliverance and divine intervention)*. In your unfailing love, silence my enemies, destroy all my foes, for I am your servant *(and a powerful declaration of faith and commitment)* (Psalm 143:8–12).

We could pray this prayer every day of our lives. I encourage you to memorise it and teach it to your children.

I love the quote that says, 'The prayer "Thy will be done" is the softest pillow on which we could ever lay our head' (Anon). 'Thy will be done!' This is not just a submissive relinquishing; it is also a decree. I used an exclamation mark in that prayer because it captures the authority and power of those words. Lord, let your will be done in my life. In the life of my child. Amen and amen!

In 2 Chronicles 20, we read the account of the combined attack of several armies on King Jehoshaphat and his people. Among the alarm, the trembling and the fasting, the King prays a wonderful prayer, which I have often used myself: 'For we have no power to face this vast army that is attacking us. We do not know what to do, but our eyes are on you.' Our eyes are on you. How beautiful. And the story records that the place of feared and imminent defeat instead became the Valley of Berakah – the place of blessing.

Let me finish this chapter by touching on one area that we homeschooling mothers all seem to wrestle with. Worry. We all experience worries. None of us are immune. Perhaps it's worries about what this new year will hold. Worries about health or finances. Worries about our children. Worries about our marriage. Worries about our homeschooling. Dutch author Corrie ten Boom wrote, 'Worry does not empty tomorrow of its troubles. Rather, it robs today of its strength.' How true!

The Message Bible gives us God's antidote to worry in Philippians 4: 'Don't fret or worry. Instead of worrying, pray. Let petitions and praises shape your worries into prayers, letting God know your concerns.'

Our Father knows what we need. We mustn't let the worries of daily life rob us of our strength. Instead, we must learn to cast all our cares upon him, knowing that he cares for us. We must learn how to shape our worries into prayers. When we're struggling to teach our dyslexic child how to read and begin worrying that she will never learn, we must shape those worries into prayers:

'Father, thank you for my precious child. You love her even more than I do. Help me have the faith and patience to keep teaching her without frustration or impatience. Give me creative ideas. Help me speak hope into her heart. And, Holy Spirit, I ask that you speak hope into my own heart also. Amen.'

Mamas, let's pull our aprons over our heads and pour out our hearts in prayer to the One who hears.

CHAPTER TWELVE

Help! I'm a Cracked Vessel

Behind every great child is a mother who's pretty sure she's screwing it all up.

—Anon

One of my favourite missionary stories is that of Evelyn 'Granny' Brand. She holds special significance to those of us who are homeschooling because she also taught her two children at home for a number of years. Her son, Dr Paul Brand, writes how he used to do his schoolwork up a tree in India. He went on to study medicine and became a pioneer in developing tendon transfer techniques for use in the hands of leprosy patients.

Evie Brand, nee Harris, was baptised as a young girl of 11, and from that time on her heart burned with a passion for missions. She devoured missionary stories. One pamphlet that deeply moved her was written by a young man named Jesse Brand, entitled *How the Gospel First Came to the Mountains of Death*.

Some years later, Jesse Brand came to her church and preached. As young Evie sat listening to him, it seemed as if his words were directed straight at her. 'Could you do this,' he seemed to ask, 'you, a pampered, clean, fashionably dressed city girl?

Could you stand bodily contact with filth, lice, open sores, clutching fingers, disease, poverty, starvation?'

'Yes!' she hurled back in silent defiance. 'With God's help, I can do these things.'

And when Jesse read from Isaiah, 'Whom shall I send and who will go for us?' Evie felt faint with excitement. 'Here I am!' she responded silently. 'Send me!'

In time, Evie did go to India, and there she soon met up again with Jesse Brand. They married in August 1913 and began a life of ministry among the outcast inhabitants of all five mountain ranges of South India. Jesse was a man of many talents. He worked among the outcasts as a doctor, dentist, preacher, agronomist, teacher, counsellor and builder. Jessie and Evie had two children, Paul and Connie. As the children grew, the Brand family trekked over the mountain ranges together and the children became a valued part of the team. Evie homeschooled them until Paul and Connie returned to England to pursue their education.

Jesse was rarely ill, but in July 1929, he came down with a severe bout of malaria that soon turned into black water fever – one of the most lethal complications of that disease. He died on 15 July, 1929. He was 44.

I remember crying as I read Evie's diary entry recorded in Dorothy Clarke Wilson's book *Granny Brand*: 'How can I bear it without Jesse? The world has lost all its colour. Oh Jesse, Jesse! You had so much to give and I so little. Why couldn't I have been the one to go? Why? Why?'[50]

As she walked through the valley of grief, Evie poured her tears and questions and brokenness into her diary, and it makes for painful reading. However, after some time, she came to a place where she wrote, 'I am a broken vessel, yes. But slowly time is piecing together the fragments. And even a battered, mended pitcher can be a conveyor of living water.'

I want to emphasise one word in her diary entry above. *'But* slowly…' But. A small word, but a powerful one. Note how many times the word 'but' appears in 2 Corinthians 4:7–9: 'But we have this treasure in jars of clay to show that this all-surpassing power is from God and not from us. We are hard pressed on every side, but not crushed; perplexed, but not in despair; persecuted, but not abandoned; struck down, but not destroyed.'

Hard pressed on every side, but not crushed. Perplexed, but not in despair. Persecuted, but not abandoned. Struck down, but not destroyed. Each of these refers to the deliverance that God can bring to any 'impossible' situation.

Have you ever felt perplexed on your homeschooling journey? Hard pressed? Knocked down? Persecuted? I know I have. But…! Mamas, we have this treasure in jars of clay. Why? So that the all-surpassing power is from God and not from us.

Jars of clay. This is such an encouraging thought. God doesn't just call trained teachers and those with a PhD to homeschool. No, he calls us. You and me. Ordinary mums, of average intelligence perhaps, but (there's that word again!) called. I remember the joy of meeting one mother who confided in me she'd struggled throughout school and dropped out at a young age, still unable to read fluently. Years later, when she felt God call her to begin homeschooling, she learnt how to read alongside her children. Her testimony is that God is with us in our weakness. Our brokenness.

Think for a moment on these wonderful verses: 'Brothers and sisters, think of what you were when you were called. Not many of you were wise by human standards; not many were influential; not many were of noble birth. But God chose the foolish things of the world to shame the wise; God chose the weak things of the world to shame the strong. He chose the lowly things of this world and the despised things – and the things that are not – to nullify the things that are, so that no one may boast before him' (1 Corinthians 1:26-29).

Mamas, you may not feel super intelligent, but God chose you! You may not feel qualified to teach your gifted 13-year-old son, but God chose you. Hallelujah! Not many of us are 'of noble birth', or 'wise' or 'influential', but God has chosen us. And then he equips us and helps us do what we could never do in our own strength or with our own abilities. That way, we can't boast about our achievements. I'm sure we've all felt tempted by the rather agreeable prospect of being able to boast about our children. Wouldn't it be nice to be able to tell the grandparents or Uncle Jack about how well the children are doing in their schoolwork? But God has other measuring standards.

We are not perfect. We are jars of clay. We make mistakes. All of us. Sometimes we may fall flat on our faces. Proverbs 24:16 (GW) has another wonderful 'but': 'A righteous man may fall seven times, but he gets up again.'

During our homeschooling year, we may be knocked down, but we can get up again and keep going. And we can encourage ourselves that even through our mistakes and shortcomings, God's glory and power will shine through.

I love the Indian fable of the water bearer's two pots:

> A water bearer had two large pots, one hung on each end of a pole, which he carried across his neck. One pot had a small crack in it, while the other pot was perfect and always delivered a full portion of water. At the end of the long walk from the stream to the master's house, the cracked pot always arrived only half full. For two years, this went on daily, with the bearer delivering only one and a half pots of water to his master's house. Of course, the perfect pot was proud of its accomplishments, and felt fulfilled in the design for which it was made. But the cracked pot was ashamed of its own imperfection, and miserable that it could not accomplish what it had been created to do.

After two years of enduring this bitter shame, one day the pot spoke to the water bearer by the stream. 'I am ashamed of myself, and I apologise to you.'

'Why?' asked the bearer. 'What are you ashamed of?'

'For these past two years I have only been able to deliver half my load because this crack in my side causes water to leak out all the way back from the stream to the master's house. Because of my flaws, you have to do all this work, and you don't get full value from your efforts.'

The water bearer felt sorry for the cracked pot, and in compassion said, 'As we return to the master's house, I want you to notice the beautiful flowers along the path.'

Indeed, as they went up the hill, the cracked pot took notice of the sun warming the beautiful wildflowers on the side of the path and was cheered somewhat. But at the end of the trail, it still felt the old shame because it had leaked out half its load, and so again the pot apologised to the bearer for its failure.

The bearer said to the pot, 'Did you not notice that there were flowers only on your side of the path, and not on the other pot's side? That's because I have always known about your flaw, and I took advantage of it. I planted flower seeds on your side of the path, and every day while we've walked back from the stream, you've watered them. For two years, I have been able to pick these beautiful flowers to decorate my master's table. Without you being just the way you are, he would not have this beauty to grace his house.'

This story emphasises an important truth. Each of us has flaws. We are all cracked pots. But the Lord can use our flaws to grace the Father's table. In God's great economy, nothing goes to waste.

Your school year may have started with grand plans and intentions and a perfectly planned curriculum, but now it's turned to custard. My guess is we've probably all experienced terms or even whole years like that. It doesn't take much to throw a perfectly planned term off-kilter. And then it's easy for us to succumb to feelings of guilt or inadequacy. But we mustn't be crippled by a sense of failure. We mustn't fear our shortcomings. Rather, we need to acknowledge them before God, and then watch him make something beautiful out of our life.

I love the quote by American poet Edwin Markham: 'Defeat may serve as well as victory to shake the soul and let the glory out.'[51]

Mistakes. Defeat. God can take these and turn them into wonderful successes. I remember reading about Spencer Silver, a 3M research laboratory worker who attempted to create a strong adhesive. However, his attempt ended in definitive failure. His glue stuck to objects, but they could be easily peeled off. He put the invention aside but didn't discard it. Four years later, another 3M scientist named Arthur Fry remembered the super weak adhesive Silver had created. He decided to try using some of it to glue markers in his church choir hymnal instead of using bookmarks that kept falling out. It worked perfectly. With the weak adhesive, the markers stayed in place, yet could be removed without damaging the pages. A decade after Silver developed the weak glue, 3M began distributing Post-it Notes nationwide. Today, they are one of the most popular office products available. The initial failure became a tremendous success. As Michel de Montaigne claimed, 'There are some defeats that are more triumphant than victories.' [52]

What crack has appeared in your pot? Maybe you're struggling to teach your child with learning difficulties how to read. Perhaps one of your children is constantly being naughty, prompting you to lose your temper. Perhaps you're suffering from terrible morning sickness. Maybe you have a sick child.

Any of these situations can appear as a crack in your vessel, and you feel you're leaking precious water. All your enthusiasm, hope, energy, optimism – you name it – is draining away. Or perhaps a school subject is leaking through your crack. You might be exhausted after sleepless nights with the new baby, and the thought of trying to explain long division is simply a bridge too far.

I'm reminded of the time when our family took in a newborn baby who was awaiting adoption. She was only going to be with us for ten days, but that stretched out to over a month. She fretted a lot and was hard to settle at night. At times I took her for long midnight walks along our country lane to make sure her crying didn't disturb the other children's sleep. I became exhausted and soon started fretting that I wasn't doing enough schoolwork with the older children. It wasn't until later that I realised how much my children learnt through this time. As they took turns bottle feeding the baby, we discussed teenage pregnancy and all the potential outcomes. They cuddled this precious wee girl and rejoiced that the young mother had chosen to adopt her to a loving family rather than abort her. But they also witnessed the great sadness of the maternal grandmother who was grieving the 'loss' of her first grandchild. They felt the pain of the young father who desperately wanted to keep his baby. No textbook could have prompted so much learning or the forming of lifelong beliefs and values in my young children. Light shone through my cracked vessel.

Of course, not all the cracks will have to do with your homeschooling. There may be cracks appearing in your marriage, your personal health, your extended family, your older children's lives. If this is happening, seek God and do all you can to mend the cracks. But also remember that God has chosen the weak and the foolish things, and he can shine through those cracks.

Here's the bottom line, mamas: we are not perfect, and neither are our children. They will make mistakes. Abraham, Isaac and Jacob were all cracked vessels, and yet they are all mentioned in Hebrews 11's hall of fame. King David. Peter. In Luke 22:31, we see yet another wonderful example of the significance of the word 'but': 'Simon, Simon. Behold, Satan has asked to sift you as wheat. But I have prayed for you, Simon, that your faith may not fail. And when you have turned back, strengthen your brothers.'

When our imperfect children fail and make mistakes, just as Peter did, there are several things we need to do as parents.

- We need to remember that God loves them even more than we do! He is still on their case. He has prayed for them.
- We must never give up hope. Rather, we need to be proactive and encourage our own hearts with Scripture. I encourage you to ask God for a word of promise for each child.
- We mustn't take the blame for their mistakes. Perhaps some of you are hurting from children who have made big mistakes and are choosing to live their lives in a way that appals you. Yes, you can in all honesty admit that you are not a perfect parent, and that you made mistakes in your parenting, but don't collapse under that in condemnation. Our children have free wills – a God-given gift. They must choose their own path.
- Instead, we must continue to pray for them to come to their senses as the prodigal son did. And mamas, remember, when your prodigal is gone from your sight, and you don't even know where he or she is, God knows. He sees what country they are in. He is still working in their lives.
- We mustn't try to walk their walk for them. That is a burden too heavy to carry. You cannot walk someone else's journey of faith. You can't make their decisions and choices for them.

All you can do is keep your own heart firm and steady in the love of God and keep praying that they will have a revelation of Christ for themselves.

- We've got to be willing to let them fail sometimes. Perhaps some of you are scrambling around trying to prevent your child from making a mistake; trying to do all the hard work for them so they won't fail an exam. Don't do it! None of us want to see our children fail, but we must resist the urge to rescue them all the time. This can be so difficult, but it's vital. And we must remember that many of the great lessons in life are learnt through failure.
- Here's the good news, mamas! We can bring our cracks, our failings, our imperfections to Jesus. He doesn't love us because we are a success. God wants our hearts and our love, not our success or achievements. His love is not based on our performance. We need to remind ourselves of this truth often. Our children need to hear it daily. Romans 5:8 says, 'God demonstrates his own love for us in this: while we were still sinners, Christ died for us.' While we were sinners, he loved us.

The Pharisees were concerned about their outward appearance, and Jesus likened them to whitewashed tombs. They looked good on the outside, but inside was a whole different story. Are you trying to hold it all together so that when people look at you they think you're a homeschooling marvel? Don't fall into that trap. Be honest before God and ask for help. Don't be afraid to admit there are problems. And remember Evie's words, 'even a broken pitcher can be the conveyor of living water.' [53]

Granny Brand gave her brokenness to God and continued to minister among the hill tribes for five decades until her death in 1974 at ninety-five.

Life-giving water poured through her cracks and helped transform the mountains of death. In the same way, mamas, God can use each one of us as we commit our shortcomings and failings to him. The water of life will pour through our cracks and transform our lives, our family and our homeschooling.

CHAPTER THIRTEEN

Selah Moments

Being a mom has made me so tired. And so happy.

—Tina Fey[54]

Psalm 46 introduces us to a small word that appears three times in the psalm. Selah. It was written as an instruction calling for a break in the singing of the psalm. 'Be still and know that I am God. Selah' (Psalm 46:10). The Amplified Bible adds 'pause and calmly think about that' to each verse where 'selah' appears.[55] When we see the word in a psalm, we should 'pause to weigh carefully the meaning of what we have just read or heard, lifting our hearts in praise to God for His great truths'.

As I considered this small but important word, it reminded me of two significant examples of the concept of selah.

With Katie and Eliza involved in classical music, I've been blessed with many opportunities to listen to the music of Mozart, Chopin, Schumann and other great composers. Music is the perfect example of the need in our lives for selah. Claude Debussy stated it plainly: 'Music is the space between the notes.'[56]

Music needs the rests. It needs the space between notes. Rest notes are a vital part of musical structure. They keep the other notes from stringing together in a breathless and chaotic noise.

The rest note creates a deliberate pause, a temporary break in the action.

This concept of the rest note – an interval of silence within a piece of music – is an essential part of the 'music' of our homeschooling. Now, I can just imagine some of you reading that with a grim smile. You might tell me that there's no such thing as 'music' in your homeschooling. More like a cacophony of strident, discordant noise. Yes, I've had days like that. But it doesn't have to continue like that. We can re-write the music. Mamas, we must write in some rests. They, and only they, will transform a ghastly muddle of discordant notes into a beautiful symphony.

Of course, our written language includes these rest notes as well. We place a full stop at the end of our sentences, and we use breaks between paragraphs that convey different ideas. Without the structure of punctuation, sentences run into a long, jumbled, confusing stream of mumbo jumbo. Without notes of rest in our homeschooling, we can feel like our days and weeks are blurring together.

My advice to those of you who are enthusiastic new mums starting out on the homeschooling journey is to make sure you learn to create selah moments, both for yourself and for your children. You must be intentional about this. They won't just happen of their own accord. We must write them in. And that will mean saying no to certain things and not over-committing ourselves.

When my twin sister and I were young, Mum survived the huge workload and gruelling schedule by a regular weekly night out. As soon as Dad came home from teaching at school on Friday, Mum would give him a quick rundown of what we would need before bolting out the door. She met up with friends and they went to a movie or the library or shopping. Knowing that she had that break to look forward to helped her navigate the maelstrom of twins. For you, it might be a soak in a hot bath with a candle going or a good book to read. Or a short walk outside to enjoy the beauty of nature (by yourself).

It's amazing how a short selah moment can restore our good spirits and our energy. It doesn't have to be a holiday in Rarotonga. (Okay, that would be nice, but…) In fact, the big getaways are not what's needed as much as regular small selah moments. Plan for them. Make them happen. Write the rest notes into your sheet of music.

Another wonderful example of the need for selah moments is our own heartbeat. When we're healthy, our amazing hearts keep up their steady rhythm throughout our entire life. Medical staff monitor our heart's health by taking our blood pressure. The reading consists of two numbers in a ratio, with the reading 120/80 being a good blood pressure. The top number is called the systolic pressure, the bottom number the diastolic pressure. These two readings represent the force your blood exerts against your arteries at different stages in the heartbeat. The systolic pressure is a measurement of the pressure of blood in the arteries when your heart muscle contracts. The diastolic pressure is a measurement of the pressure of blood in the arteries between heartbeats (when your heart is resting and refilling with blood). This is the heart's 'selah' moment. After the contraction, the heart chambers relax and dilate and refill with blood. If the diastolic reading is high, it shows that the resting tension of our blood vessels is high, and our heart is not getting the rest it needs.

'Diastole' comes from a Greek word meaning to expand, to bring together, to make ready. When the heart goes into its diastolic phase, the heart is expanding, refilling and preparing for the next contraction. I love this concept. In the same way as our physical heart is 'made ready' by diastole, our spiritual hearts are expanded and 'made ready' by selah moments. And boy, do we need this 'being made ready' in our homeschooling!

Mamas, this is the healthy heart rhythm we need to develop and maintain in our homeschooling. Contraction. Rest. Contraction. Rest. We can often feel the need and pressure to be doing, doing, doing. Momentum is great, but the pauses are vital.

As homeschooling mums, we are susceptible to the tyranny of the urgent. In fact, very often it seems that everything in our busy day is urgent. Jonny desperately needs to go to the bathroom while Jane is having a meltdown over what you've just asked her to do. And out of the corner of your eye you see your baby son crawling towards the fire. We must learn how to navigate these moments and do our own form of 'mama triage'. But this all too familiar scenario also highlights the desperate need for us to factor in some selah moments whenever we can.

One of my homeschooling friends took stock of her frantic days and realised she needed to do something, or else she'd burn out. So, she put in place a simple rest time in the middle of the afternoon for *all* the children. She had several young ones who were still having an afternoon sleep, but two of her children had outgrown that stage. She explained to the older ones that they were going to have 40 minutes on their beds with some special books (kept aside for this time) while she had a rest. She set the timer and told them they weren't to come into her own bedroom until the timer went off. It took a wee while before they got the gist of it, but they soon learnt to appreciate that quiet time and even looked forward to it. By making this simple change to their daily routine, it's possible my friend avoided suffering a major 'homeschooling heart attack'.

We all need selah moments. Susanna Wesley created hers by pulling her apron over her head. The children knew they were not to disturb her unless it was *very* important.

Selah moments restore our souls. Psalm 23 tells us that our Shepherd leads us beside quiet waters of rest. There, he restores our soul. Homeschooling is very much a heart exercise. It involves our souls. And oh, how we need this promised restoration!

Let Jesus lead you to quiet waters of rest. Follow his leading. Don't throw up thousands of excuses as to why you can't possibly spare the time. You *need* to spend time beside the quiet waters of rest. These moments of stillness help bring things into perspective. As Psalm 46 says, 'Be still and know that I am God.' Selah moments help us remember why we're homeschooling. It's so easy for us to lose our way sometimes. But so often, the path back to 'our way' leads beside those quiet waters. Time spent there restores our joy, which in turn renews our strength.

Selah moments also keep us sharp. Ecclesiastes 10:10 (NKJV) says, 'If the axe is dull and one does not sharpen the edge, then he must use more strength.' How often do we try to keep working with a blunt instrument? We make the mistake of thinking we haven't got time to stop and sharpen the axe. But rest time is *not* wasted time. Your selah moments will sharpen your axe. You will be more efficient. More effective. Imagine the marathon runner who realises he has a tiny pebble in his shoe. Will he begrudge the time it takes to stop running and remove the stone from his shoe? Possibly, but he also knows without a doubt that if he doesn't, he will not run a good race.

Are you needing inspiration for your homeschooling? Schedule some selah moments. They will fill your heart with much-needed inspiration and new energy. It works in exactly the same way as when our physical heart moves into diastole and our heart chambers fill with blood. New inspiration. New creativity. New passion. An infilling of creativity and inspiration. We are 'made ready' for tomorrow's workload. This is vital for healthy homeschooling. Without it, we become stressed, and symptoms of heart disease begin to appear.

So, mamas, be still. Listen. Pray Samuel's prayer: 'Speak, Lord, for your servant is listening' (1 Samuel 3:9). We will hear the voice of the Lord as we quieten our hearts and listen in the selah moments.

I watched a short TED Talk by Julian Treasure called *5 Ways to Listen Better,* in which he recommended having three minutes of silence a day. This requires a proactive, disciplined effort. A walk in nature is one of the most effective ways to relieve stress. But make sure you turn off any music or podcasts and listen instead to the silence. I wonder if Phillip would have heard the Spirit instruct him to join the chariot if he had been listening to an iPod. Hmm.

Psalm 19:1–2 (NASB 1995) teaches us that 'the heavens are telling of the glory of God; and their expanse is declaring the work of his hands. Day to day pours forth speech, and night to night reveals knowledge.' Nature has a message for us if we care to listen.

In Psalm 62:1 David prays, 'Truly my soul silently waits for God.' Does mine? Truly? Sadly, silence is almost a forgotten art. We fill our days with music and talking and podcasts – all valuable in themselves, but we should never let them dominate our time. We need to factor in times of silence. I have had some very special times when I've been travelling on my own (a fairly recent phenomenon). My initial default action has been to turn on some music, but then I've felt a small prompting to turn it off. Each time I've followed that prompting, I've had a precious time with the Lord; I've heard him speak to me and I've received some wonderfully creative ideas.

One of the most beneficial things you can do in your selah moments is to read the word of God. But remember to take time to ask God to speak to you before you read.

A word of caution here: selah moments can be stolen from you. Let's imagine you manage to escape your busy life for a few glorious minutes. You sit down in the shade of a large oak tree and close your eyes. And then you hear the ping of a Facebook notification or a text message or email. You tell yourself you'll just make sure it's nothing important… Before you know it, your time has gone and all you've done is scroll through endless posts. I know. It's happened to me.

So, leave your devices in another room. The Bible tells us that when Jesus went up to the mountain to pray, he was there alone (Matthew 14:23). Don't let the crowds find you during your selah moments. And that includes the internet crowds.

As homeschooling mothers, our lives move fast. Our days are full. Our homeschooling is all consuming. Mamas, is it time to insert a rest note? Have any of you had a selah moment this last week? If not, plan for one. Be still and know that he is God! And as you do this, I pray your hearts will be filled again with passion, strength and inspiration.

CHAPTER FOURTEEN

Starry, Starry Night

The hand that rocks the cradle is the hand that rules the world.

—W. R. Wallace[57]

When the children were little, Chris and I used to take them into town to visit Nana and Grandpa every Friday night. We'd enjoy a meal of fish and chips together, Nana would read to the children before bed, and then Chris and I would enjoy a special adult time with Mum and Dad. We all looked forward to Friday night. We locked it in every week without fail unless we were out of town.

One Friday night, after we'd carried six little sleeping children out of the car and inside to their own beds, Chris and I stood on the drive and marvelled at the beautiful starry night sky stretched above us. It took our breath away. We lived in the country, with no city lights to compete with the stars. As we stood there, hand in hand, we made a plan…

The next night after dinner, we told the children they didn't have to go to bed till later – that they were going to do something special with us. They jittered with excitement. When it got dark enough, I slipped outside. Climbing the fence, I laid a blanket on the ground and piled it with pillows and extra blankets. And then Chris began slinging the children one by one over his shoulder and carrying them outside.

I'll never forget the joy of lying in the paddock with my husband and children and looking up at the night sky. It was magical. We lay there for some time without speaking. After a while, Chris began pointing out the Southern Cross, the Pot and the satellite orbiting above us. And then I shared how I always think of Abraham when I look at the stars and remember how faithful God was to him. I told them how God took Abraham outside and told him to look up at the stars. We lay on our blankets gazing up into the same sky, and it was as if the centuries, the millennia, dissolved away. We were with Abraham, looking up, and hearing God speak the promises over his life.

'And he took him outside and said, "Now look toward the heavens, and count the stars, if you are able to count them." And he said to him, "So shall your descendants be." Then Abraham believed in the Lord and it was counted to him as righteousness' (Genesis 15:1–6 NASB).

Count the stars, Abraham! If you can! How amazing! God has a plan for our lives, and he wants to speak to us – each one of us. He cares for us. Loves us. Oh, how our children need to hear that. What better place to tell them than under a starry, starry sky?

'When I consider Your heavens, the work of Your fingers, the moon and the stars, which you have set in place; What is man that You think of him, and a son of man that You are concerned about him?' (Psalm 8:3–4 NASB).

It's an incredible and humbling thought to realise that of all God's creation – the starry heavens, the towering redwoods, the surging ocean, the leaping gazelles, the majestic mountains – we are his most perfect and treasured creation. When God created man, he smiled and said it was very good. I love the quote of St Augustine: 'People travel to wonder at the height of the mountains, at the huge waves of the sea, at the long course of the rivers, at the vast compass of the ocean, at the circular motion of the stars, and yet they pass by themselves without wondering.'

What powerful truths to think about while lying beneath the starry sky. Our God made the heavens and the earth by his outstretched hand and there is nothing, *nothing*, too difficult for him (Jeremiah 32:17).

It was an unforgettable evening. It didn't matter that only half the stars we'd seen the night before were visible because of some cloud. It was still breathtakingly beautiful.

I was unprepared for what would happen the following night. I went outside to collect an armful of firewood and stopped to look up at the night sky. The sight almost took my breath away. There wasn't a single star in the sky. Not one. It looked like someone had pulled the light switch and plunged the heavens into utter darkness. I stood staring up into the inky blackness, thinking over the three different skies I'd seen in as many evenings. The first had been ablaze with millions of stars. The second studded with pockets and sprinkles of stars, cloud hiding the rest. And now, this sky. Black as velvet. Empty. Nothing. I remember staring up in astonishment and then speaking aloud to myself: 'Life's like that.' A pause. Then, 'Homeschooling's like that!'

It was a revelation. A profound insight into life's mystery. Whether or not we see them, the stars are always there. But in the course of a lifetime, there will be times when we walk beneath each one of these skies. Some days are ablaze with promise and hope, and everything is right with our world. Each time Chris has handed me one of our precious newborn babies, all the stars are shining above us. My heart is full, bursting with gratitude and love. My life is alight with the promises of God. But I have also experienced days and nights of worry, doubt, heartbreak and fear. Clouds have rolled in and obscured all but a smattering of distant stars. Where has my confident assurance gone? Why am I feeling such confusion? Such indecision? Why is nothing as clear as it was a year ago? A month ago?

I remember the day I drove down our country road and Milly's little voice piped up from the back seat: 'Mummy, you can't even see our beautiful mountains!' Sure enough, a low mist had descended and hidden them from view. I stopped the car to look. And think. Clouds can roll into our lives, and we can lose that feeling of certainty and confidence. Homeschooling had seemed so right, so perfect for our family. But now we're wrestling with feelings of inadequacy and doubt. Should I be doing this? Is this the right path for my children? What if I'm ruining their futures? The sure promises and clear direction we knew at the start of our journey seem muted. Faded. Obscured.

And then there's the season when we must walk for a time beneath an empty sky. Not one star visible. For the longest night we lose all vision, all hope. It feels as if the promises of God have failed. Disappeared. Despair, discouragement and doubt flood into our hearts. Jesus himself hung on a cross beneath a darkened sky. Three hours of darkness, culminating in the painful cry, 'Eloi, Eloi, lama sabachthani?' (Mark 15:34).

'My God, my God, why have you forsaken me?'

I will never forget the day all the stars disappeared from my homeschooling sky. It coincided with the time I was caring for the wee baby awaiting adoption. I was sleep-deprived and exhausted. Vulnerable. Let me share with you the account that I wrote of it from my book *The Gift of Values – Volume One:*

> 'Well, I'll run away!'
>
> I couldn't help smiling at the feisty little thing that stood in front of me. With curly blonde hair and the bluest of eyes, Milly looks like a little angel. But I don't think angels could ever be as stroppy or strong-willed as my six-year-old daughter.

Starry, Starry Night

The drama was over schoolwork. I teach my six children at home, and the other five were all keen, teachable students. But not my Milly. For the past few months, she had become quite unteachable, complaining and groaning at everything I asked her to do. She was the only one that had ever threatened to run away from home!

'Oh no, you won't, Miss Milly,' I said with a smile. I bent down and kissed her freckled nose. 'You will do your work, and we'll have a good time at school today.'

How wrong I was. That day was to be the worst of my homeschooling and mothering career. Milly was determined to push me to the limits. She argued, dilly dallied, disobeyed and complained. I can't even remember what finally pushed me over the edge.

'That's it!' I shouted. 'That's it! I can't take it anymore. You're going to school!' I pushed away from the table and stormed into my room. Milly followed me, wailing.

I sat on my bed, trying to gain control of my frustration and the sense of failure that threatened to swallow me up.

Milly was crying now and pleading with me. 'No, Mummy! I'll be good. I promise.'

She looked so vulnerable, but something had happened inside my heart. I felt hard and brittle in my defeat.

'I used to love homeschooling,' I snapped. 'But you've ruined it for me!'

Did I say that? How could I have said something so cruel? Milly flinched, and her face crumpled. Immediately, I gathered her in my arms and kissed her.

'Oh Milly, I'm so sorry. Mummy's just tired, that's all.' I stroked her wet face.

We sat there holding each other until we had both stopped crying. But I couldn't escape the empty, despairing feeling inside.

Horrible, dark thoughts began tormenting me. She can't run away now – she's only six. But she might when she's sixteen. It was as if I were staring into a future of rebellion and pain. All the hope and optimism I'd ever had for my precious daughter's life seemed to shrivel up and die.

Eliza, my ten-year-old, came into the room and said in a sweet, caring voice, 'I've finished all my schoolwork now, Mummy. Shall I take over teaching Milly for the morning?'

That made me feel worse. I had never felt such a failure.

That night, after Chris and I had put them all to bed, I retreated to my room and fell to my knees. 'Dear God,' I prayed, 'You've got to help me. I'm scared. I've lost hope for my daughter. All I can see is rebellion and heartache ahead. Please, give me a word, a promise for her life. Something I can hold on to.'

I was almost too scared to face the next morning. I couldn't bear another day like the one I'd just had. After reading a couple of Psalms and trying to encourage my heart, I went into the office to check my email. There was just one. Four lines from a missionary friend in Asia. I'd written to her that week and told her Milly had fallen on a tree root and broken her collar bone.

'I was so sorry to hear about dear Milly's accident. But it will take more than a broken bone to slow her down! She's a champion!'

She's a champion! The words leapt off the screen and straight into my wounded heart. It was as if God had spoken from heaven. I began weeping with joy. Hope filled my heart again. God had spoken to me. He saw my Milly as a champion! I laughed and cried as I spoke the truth out loud again and again. 'She's a champion! Milly's a champion!'

And so, with just three words, the Lord turned despair into hope, my sense of failure into a sense of purpose. I'm training a champion – a little blonde, blue-eyed girl with that extra grit, determination and strength that a champion needs.

My Milly's a champion![58]

What sky are you walking under, mama? Can you see the stars? Let me encourage you: whether or not you see them, they are still there. What we all need to do is equip ourselves to walk beneath an empty sky.

Peter tells us, 'We have the prophetic word made more sure, to which you do well to pay attention as to a lamp shining in a dark place, until the day dawns and the morning star arises in your hearts' (2 Peter 1:19 NASB).

The prophetic word. I know about the power of that. 'She's a champion' rose like the morning star in my despairing heart.

I remember the amazing word God gave me on the afternoon I discovered I was pregnant with Jacob. It was so clear; so wonderful. Over the coming weeks, I treasured the promise in my heart, like Mary. And then came the day I went to the bathroom and discovered I had started spotting. Fear washed over me like a tidal wave. The only other time I'd bled in my pregnancy, I had lost the baby. But in less than a heartbeat, the morning star rose in my heart. I remembered the word God had given me eight weeks earlier. All fear vanished in an instant. I knew with absolute certainty that I would carry my baby to full term and deliver a healthy son. Hallelujah! What incredible power a word from God has! I encourage you, mamas, ask him for a word of promise for each of your children. And on the nights when there are no other stars in the sky, that morning star can burn on your horizon.

When Jacob was four, he came into my office and pointed across me to something on my desk. 'Mummy, pass me my photos, please.'

I looked at the things scattered on my desk but couldn't see any photos.

'My photos, Mummy! There!'

I looked again to where his little finger pointed and saw some plastic binoculars lying on a plate. I picked them up. 'These?'

He beamed at me. 'Yes!'

Taking the binoculars, he went to the window, pulled back the velvet curtain, and held the binoculars to his eyes. When I asked him what he was doing, he replied, 'I'm looking at the stars!'

How can I ever forget the understanding that flooded my heart at that moment? It was as if I heard a voice from heaven saying, 'Pick up the word of God. You will see the promises of God shining like the morning star.'

I had just been teaching the children about Galileo the day before. We had read the remarkable account of the first time he had put his eye to the telescope and how the stars 'leapt towards him'. He fell backwards and then dropped to his knees and worshipped God, overawed by the beauty he had just seen.

Each one of us can feel the same wonder that Galileo experienced if we use the telescope of God's word. Stars of promise will leap towards us.

Do you need a star to rise in your heaven tonight? Do you need to find new strength and encouragement for your homeschooling journey? New hope for your child? Go to the Word. No matter how we feel, God remains. His promises are true, whether the skies are clear above us or not. He can give you a fresh word of promise to hold on to.

My mother often used to quote, 'Two men looked out through prison bars; one saw mud, the other stars.' I always loved that.

Let me close this chapter with a wonderful extract from Tolkien's *The Return of the King*. Sam Gamgee is sitting desolately in the tower of Cirith Ungol, at journey's end.

> At last, weary and feeling finally defeated, he sat on a step below the level of the passage floor and bowed his head into his hands. It was quiet, horribly quiet. The torch, which was already burning low when he arrived, sputtered and went out; and he felt the darkness cover him like a tide.

And then softly, to his own surprise, there at the vain end of his long journey and grief, moved by what thought in his heart he could not tell, Sam began to sing. His voice sounded cold and thin and quavering in the cold dark tower; the voice of a forlorn and weary hobbit that no listening orc could possibly mistake for the clear song of an elven lord. He murmured old childish tunes out of the shire, and snatches of Mr Bilbo's rhymes that came into his mind like fleeting glimpses of the country of his home. And then suddenly new strength rose in him, and his voice rang out, while words of his own came unbidden to fit the simple tune.

> *Though here at journey's end I lie*
> *In darkness buried deep*
> *Beyond all towers strong and high*
> *Beyond all mountains deep*
> *Above all shadows rides the sun*
> *And stars forever dwell*
> *I will not say the day is done*
> *Or bid the stars farewell.*[59]

What a perfect encouragement for those of you who feel you're at journey's end. Do not bid the stars farewell. No matter how dark the heavens are above you, 'above all shadows rides the sun and stars forever dwell.' The clouds will pass. Stars remain.

CHAPTER FIFTEEN

The God of Hope

There is no way to be a perfect mother, and a million ways to be a good one.

—Jill Churchill[60]

Our homeschooling group planned a trip to the Waitomo Caves – a labyrinth of caves, sinkholes and underground rivers. When we reached a huge underground cavern, our guide informed us of its amazing acoustics and asked for a volunteer to sing a song. The entire group turned to look at me. What song do you think I sang?

John Newton's mother was a devout Christian who taught him the Bible from an early age. She died of tuberculosis before he turned seven, and his ensuing life story is one of increasing rebellion and godlessness. Press-ganged aboard HMS *Harwich* in 1744, he began a life at sea, one that would involve him both being a slave and the captain of several slave ships. He described his life as one of 'moral abandon'. But there came a time when he recognised his need for forgiveness and cried out to God for mercy.

When I read his story, I marvel at the goodness of God and the power of his 'full redemption' (Psalm 130:7). How far can a man drift from God and yet be brought back? Oh, the wonders of God's love! The song I sang beneath the glow worms was, of course, John Newton's 'Amazing Grace'.

His song is arguably the most famous of all hymns, loved and sung by millions around the world.

I wonder what Newton's mother would have thought if she could hear her son's song of redemption ringing in the underground cave. How she would rejoice that her son had found salvation – the boy she had sung to, prayed for, loved and read the Bible to! Her early death spared her those years of heartbreak as Newton rebelled and lived his life of brokenness and sin.

Newton was an ardent admirer of John Bunyan's work *The Pilgrim's Progress* and was invited to write the preface to the 1776 edition. I have no doubt he would have loved this quote of John Bunyan's: 'No child of God sins to that degree as to make himself incapable of forgiveness.'[61]

Mama, your child is not beyond the reach of God's love and forgiveness. Never lose hope for your child. Never stop praying or believing. 'Put your hope in the Lord, for with the Lord is unfailing love and with him is full redemption' (Psalm 130:7).

As much as we don't want to hear it, homeschooling is not the all-encompassing assurance against rebellion, wrong choices and mistakes. It does not destine us to have perfect little graduates pop out the other end of the homeschooling manufacturing chute. Listen to God's anguished cry: 'Hear me, you heavens! Listen, earth! For the Lord has spoken: "I reared children and brought them up, but they have rebelled against me"' (Isaiah 1:2).

Some of you know the pain and heartbreak of watching a child turn from all you've taught them, choosing instead to walk in ways that appal you. The book of Hosea reveals God as a spurned lover and a hurting parent. He knows the pain we feel when our children fail, when they hurt us by their choices. But take heart from Psalm 130's message of hope! He can turn their hearts and lives around and show them his full redemption, just as he did for John Newton.

We can have so many fears regarding our children – sickness, rebellion, hurt backsliding... Linda Dillow writes: 'I worry that they might take drugs; that my daughter might get pregnant, that my husband might be unfaithful, that I might get breast cancer, that we might be unable to face the bills next month...' [62] But we must learn not to forecast grief. God doesn't want us to live a life of countless fearful imaginings. French philosopher Michel de Montaigne said, 'My life has been full of terrible misfortunes, most of which never happened.'[63] The Bible gives us a different scenario than that. 'How blessed is the man who fears the Lord, who greatly delights in His commandments... he will not fear evil tidings; his heart is steadfast, trusting in the Lord' (Psalm 112:1, 7 NASB 1995).

Listen to the word of hope in Jeremiah 31:16–17: 'This is what the Lord says: "Restrain your voice from weeping and your eyes from tears, for your work will be rewarded," declares the Lord. "They will return from the land of the enemy. So there is hope for your descendants," declares the Lord. "Your children will return to their own land."'

Hallelujah! There is hope for our children. And herein lies a significant challenge to us as parents: we need to give our children hope. So, how do we do that?

In John Bunyan's classic allegory *The Pilgrim's Progress*, Christian and his friend Hopeful wander from the true path and are captured by Giant Despair. He imprisons them and daily goads them to take their own lives: 'Your only way out of this place is by death. So why are you waiting? Make an end of yourselves! Why should you choose life, seeing it is attended by so much bitterness?' And he provides them with a noose, a knife and a bottle of poison to facilitate their act of despair. I love the way Bunyan describes the friends' conversation as Christian and Hopeful discuss their dilemma and what they should do:

Perhaps the giant is right,' said Christian. 'Perhaps death would be better than the miserable life we lead.'

'Not everything is in the hand of Giant Despair,' said Hopeful. 'Who knows but he may have one of his fits and forget to lock us in? Let us not be our own murderers.'

In this way, Hopeful moderated the mind of his brother.'[64]

Later, Christian remembers he has a key in his pocket – an old key called Promise that might just fit the lock. 'Try it,' said Hopeful hopefully.

Ah! Don't you just love Hopeful? He speaks hope into his friend's heart when he is at his most vulnerable. He encourages him to try the key forgotten in the depths of his pocket. Most of us, at some stage in our lives, will languish for a time in Giant Despair's dungeon. Some of you may be incarcerated there right now and can't see a way out. I think back to a time in my life when I was in Giant Despair's dungeon, and a friend spoke five powerful words that released me from the giant's grip: 'The story's not over yet!'

Hopeful's words are so powerful: *'not everything is in the hands of Giant Despair.'* He listens to Christian's fears and despair and then speaks hope into the heart of his friend. Oh mamas! We need to do this for our children. We need to remind them that God holds their lives in his hand; that he will bring them out of the giant's dungeon of despair. We need to speak hope. Let's listen to our children's fears and anxieties and then balance them with a word of wisdom.

Bunyan's allegory perfectly illustrates the truth that death and life are in the power of the tongue. Let's use that God-given, life-giving power to speak life into despairing hearts. Tell your children that God has a good plan for their lives: a plan that they can spend the rest of their lives discovering. Teach them God's word – the source of hope. Talk to them about the times we all face when the enemy of our souls attempts to convince us that there's no hope for our situation.

We as parents can be to our children what Hopeful was to his friend Christian – a voice of moderation. As we remind them of God's promises and his faithfulness, we can moderate the gloomy, depressing thoughts in our children's minds and hearts. So many children look at the current state of the world and despair. It's as if the beautiful dreams they might have had of finding true love and having children have been robbed from them. Everywhere they look, they see heartbreak, marriage breakups and dysfunctional families. They can feel overwhelmed with all the talk of global warming and the dire state of the world. Speak hope, mamas. Tell your children that they *can* find a job, that marriage *can* be wonderful and last a lifetime, that there is healing for hurt and freedom from addictions. There is hope for their future. Jeremiah 29:11 (TLB) shares a powerful message of hope: '"For I know the plans I have for you," says the Lord. "They are plans for good and not for evil, to give you a future and a hope."'

God wants to give us a purpose in this life and a hope for the next month, the next year, all our life – something we can give our lives to.

Our teenagers and young adults need to find out what God's plan is for their life. The apostle Paul writes to the Christians at Philippi, 'I press on to take hold of that for which Christ Jesus took hold of me. Brothers and sisters, I do not consider myself yet to have taken hold of it. But one thing I do: forgetting what is behind and straining toward what is ahead, I press on toward the goal to win the prize for which God has called me heavenward in Christ Jesus' (Philippians 3:12-14).

Encourage your children to cry out to God for his leading, to ask him every day to reveal his will to them. Remind them to include God in their plans. He is the one who knows best what they should do with this year, and the next... urge them to seek him earnestly about the future and discover what he wants them to do.

Some years ago, our pastor interviewed a group of young children during the church service, asking each one what they wanted to be when they grew up. It was delightful listening to their answers.

I remember hearing my Samuel say in a loud voice, 'A builder.' That small group of children also held aspiring astronauts, firemen, circus acrobats, doctors, mothers and ballerinas.

I'd hazard a guess that none of them will make it to NASA, but does that matter? I'm sure we've all cherished dreams that never eventuated. But that doesn't lessen the positive impact of having a dream. Dreams can provide powerful motivation. I think back with a smile to some of my childhood dreams and feel glad that I had them. I explored and entertained several exciting possibilities. And although I never became an archaeologist or competed in the show jumping at the Olympics, they were wonderful dreams! Encourage your child to talk about any dreams they have and don't crush them. That doesn't mean you tell them they can be anything they want to be. Rather, you can just explore the options with them and ask questions such as 'What do you think he needed to do to become an astronaut?' Don't feel compelled to inform them that less than 700 people have trained as astronauts.

It's important that we speak specific words of hope into each of our children's hearts. I've encouraged you already to ask God for a word for each of your children – something that you can hold on to. When you receive a promise or an encouraging word, share that life-giving word with your child. Speak a blessing over their lives.

As I think about the importance of hope, I'm reminded of an important aspect of life that is all too often overlooked – the positive impact and blessing of good old-fashioned hard work. It's more valuable than we'll ever know! It's a known fact that idleness breeds despair. Going back 150 years, young people worked hard on the family farm or in the family business and were expected to contribute to the general running of the home. The family needed their help. I've met many mothers who feel bad about asking their children to do any work around the house. Don't fall into that trap, mamas! You're not doing them any favours by allowing them to opt out.

I encourage you to make sure that all your children have chores to do, and I don't mean just the paltry contribution of making their own bed. Parental expectations have diminished over the years to a meagre level of responsibility. It might be a good idea to re-examine your own attitude to asking your children to work around the home, and then reassess the allocation of family chores. It's important that your children know that their contribution around the home is needed.

Let me finish this chapter by encouraging you to take hold of the hope that the Bible offers. Hebrews 6:18–19 tells us that this hope will be 'an anchor for the soul, firm and secure.'

If you're struggling with feelings of despair over a certain situation, a child you're homeschooling – whatever – my prayer is that 'the God of hope will fill you with all joy and peace as you trust in him, so that you may overflow with hope by the power of the Holy Spirit' (Romans 15:13).

CHAPTER SIXTEEN

Homeschooling up a Tree

Be thankful they can run wild, like the young animals they are.
Better a broken bone than a pair of cowards or weaklings.
Childhood should be a time of freedom and adventure.

—Jesse Brand[65]

Okay, so you have chosen to homeschool your children, but let me ask you a very important question. Are you enjoying the freedom and creativity it allows? Are you making the most of this incredible opportunity?

Jesse Brand, missionary to India, put few limits on his children's freedom. As his son Paul grew taller, he climbed higher and higher in the spreading jackfruit trees. The trees had a sticky sap that played havoc with his skin. But Jesse pooh-poohed his wife Evie's fears and reminded her that childhood should be a time of freedom and adventure.

Evie was almost as ingenious a teacher as Jesse, although reading, writing and arithmetic were less intriguing to the children than monkeys, ants and spiders, especially to Paul. Whenever there was a composition to write or sums to add, he would sit and stare out the window.

'Come, Paul,' Evie said one day, 'I know where you'd like to be.'

From that day on, Paul Brand did his sums high in a tree near their house. When he'd finished, he would drop them down to Evie, who sat below. If they were wrong, he had to climb down and get them, re-ascend his tree, and start again. For years, this was his schoolroom.

When I told my children about Paul Brand, my Milly took it a step further. Here's a brief excerpt from my book *Where Arrows Fly*:

> Despite the usual reluctance to start the new year of study after the lazy summer holidays, Milly quickly settled into the more structured routine of school days. And true to her word, on the hottest days, Mum read to them down by the river in the cool shade of the trees on the riverbank. As they lay on their backs and looked up into the hairy branches and leaves of Old Man Willow, she told them of Paul Brand, who used to do his schoolwork up in a tree in India.
>
> 'But he must have worked hard,' she cautioned them when she saw the glazed, lazy look that had come into their eyes at the sound of doing school up in a tree, 'because he became one of the foremost surgeons involved in reconstructive surgery for lepers.'
>
> 'Really?' said Jacob. 'That's pretty cool.'
>
> Milly laughed and gave him a poke in the side. 'So, you could still become a singing doctor even if you did your schoolwork up a tree, Jacob. What a relief.'
>
> He made a face at her. 'I never said I was going to be a singing doctor.'
>
> 'Yes, you did.'
>
> 'No, I didn't.'
>
> 'Yes, you did. We all…'
>
> 'That'll do, kids,' said Mum as she put her book down. 'Jacob won't be a doctor of any sort unless we get some decent work done. Off you go. Get started on your lessons.'

But the idea of Paul Brand doing his schoolwork up in a tree held a certain appeal to Milly. That afternoon she sneaked away from the others out to Dad's workshop, found a few macrocarpa off-cuts and nailed them together to make a small box. Then she drilled some holes in six pieces of flat timber and threaded rope through them to make a ladder. A few more holes in both sides of her box and some more rope, and she was ready.

She climbed up a large totara tree beside her hen house and tied her ladder to a sturdy branch. She practised pulling it up and down a few times. It worked perfectly. She had to be able to pull it up after she was in the tree. She didn't want any of the others to climb up there and join her. Then she tied the box's two ropes around the branch and slowly lowered it to the ground. It was a bit wobbly, but it should work.

She climbed down the ladder and ran in to the barn to get a few books. It took a while to get them balanced well enough, so they didn't fall out, but on the third attempt, she successfully pulled up her schoolwork. She smiled to herself. She couldn't wait for the morning. [66]

Years on, Milly's ladder is still hanging from the tree, calling us, beckoning us. I always smile to myself as I drive past it on my ride-on lawnmower, remembering the wonderful freedom it held for Milly. I'm convinced that nature is more important in our lives than any of us realise. We homeschooling mamas can miss out on so much it can offer if we become obsessed with 'traditional' learning models.

Richard Louv coined a provocative phrase in his 2005 book *Last Child in the Woods* – 'nature deficit disorder'. Arguing that modern-day children were being cheated of the benefits of nature by the urbanisation of human society, he claimed digging in the soil and wandering in the woods was essential for any child's development.

Louv presents evidence that spending time outdoors helps relieve the symptoms of ADHD. He claims there is irrefutable evidence that time spent outdoors produces significant student gains in social studies, science, language arts and mathematics.[67] I believe him.

Of course, there are legitimate reasons why we've moved away from encouraging our children to get involved in adventure activities like rock-climbing and horse-riding and canoeing. There are risks. Our generation has become obsessed with safety. Few children walk to school anymore because of stranger danger. The powers that be frown upon climbing trees, and beautiful oak trees have been felled in school playgrounds and replaced by 'safe' artificial climbing gyms. Aaargh! Even parks and nature walks have signs everywhere warning people not to 'walk off the trail'. I love Jesse Brand's attitude. Let them climb. Let them explore. Better a broken arm than a cosseted coward or weakling.

I'm so thankful my parents shared his belief. My three years of childhood spent in the jungles of New Guinea were the best gift any parent could offer their child. My sister, brother and I ran wild and free in the jungle, exploring, building, adventuring. I'm sure our mother felt nervous about us running barefoot through the jungle, but she didn't stop us. Thank you, Mum and Dad!

While risks go hand in hand with adventure, Louv argues that there are risks attached to not offering children the opportunity for adventure. 'If you lose these activities, some children will not bother – they will grow obese and vegetate and play computer games. Others, of course, will make their own activities, and some of these will be dangerous and some will be deeply anti-social.' [68]

Mamas, we are so blessed to be able to homeschool our children! We can make sure our children know what it's like to run through the woods, explore the creek, climb trees and build huts. They do not need to suffer from 'nature deficit disorder'. Let's take a long, hard look at our homeschooling day and factor in some nature time.

Plenty of it! For those of you who live on a farm or lifestyle block, it will be easy to get them out into nature. But for those of you who live in the city, you're going to have to be more creative and intentional. Don't sit at night with your husband and bemoan the fact that your son spends hours and hours on his device. Don't complain that your daughter is obsessed with Facebook. Yes, the computer age is guilty of tempting our children to stay indoors. But mamas, you can't just confiscate their devices. Give them an alternative. Replace them. Buy your child a pet. (Yes, I mean it!) Enrol them in archery, orienteering or sailing classes. Introduce your older son to the local search and rescue club. There are endless options.

Three years ago, Chris and I visited the Lakes District in England. Top on my list was to visit Beatrix Potter's home at Hill Top Farm. I also wanted to see the lakes and imagine the Swallows and Amazons racing each other to the island. I loved every minute of my day. That evening we bought fish and chips and found a spot in the local cemetery of Ambleside to sit and enjoy dinner. Imagine my surprise when I paused in my eating and read the gravestone that we sat beside. It was the grave of Charlotte Mason, who pioneered the use of living books – books written by passionate authors in a narrative style. Some of you may use her method. She encouraged families to head outside at least once a week, each member armed with their own personal nature notebook. Children are encouraged to make entries that include pencil drawings, sketches, descriptions and lists of birds and animals they see. These activities cultivate within them a love and a joy of nature. Charlotte Mason knew how important nature is.

Mamas, we live in a beautiful world. Use the freedom of your homeschooling to explore it with your children. Go on walks. Do scavenger hunts. Collect flowers and press them. Plant a garden. Buy your child a bug-watching kit. Do a tramping trip. Scour the beaches for beautiful shells. Search the internet or your public library for ideas. They are endless!

And Nature will generously supply you with countless teachable moments, wonderful adventures and great joy.

Let me finish this chapter with a beautiful quote from Martin Luther: 'Our Lord has written the promise of the Resurrection, not in books alone, but in every leaf in springtime.' [69]

CHAPTER SEVENTEEN

The Gift of Music

Without music, life is a journey through a desert.

—Pat Conroy[70]

So many of my earliest memories involve music: watching Mum and Dad waltzing to 'Sail Along Silvery Moon'; hearing Mum play 'Remembrance' on the piano; Grandma and Grandpa taking Penny and me as four-year-olds to sing at an old folks' home (I remember we sang 'Side by Side' and 'Twinkle Twinkle Little Star'); listening to Mum singing 'After the Ball' and 'Sentimental Rendezvous' in her clear, soprano voice; big brother John teaching Penny and I how to play 'Sloop John B' on our three-quarter size guitars; standing between Mum and Dad at the Anglican church and listening to their voices as we sang a Fanny Crosby hymn... I could go on and on.

And as I grew, music continued to influence and enrich my life. When Chris and I married, we began singing together and writing songs. Over the next ten years, we had six children, and they all performed with us at our family concerts. What a blessing that was! Music was woven into the very fabric of our lives.

Berthold Auerbach said that music washes away from the soul the dust of everyday life. I remember my favourite line from Tennyson's writing: 'Music that gentlier on the spirit lies than tired eyelids upon tired eyes.' [71]

Such music will enrich our lives.

As parents, we can give this gift to our children – all of them. It's not just for the child prodigy, the budding Mozart. Every child should have the opportunity to discover the joy of music. Perhaps your own childhood was devoid of music. If so, I encourage you to make sure your own experience doesn't limit your child's. You may have had no positive experience at all with music, but that doesn't mean you can't successfully introduce your child to a passionate love of music, and in the process, find great joy yourself.

So, *how* do we introduce our children to the love of music? First and foremost, start young! I hope that many of you have already developed the habit of singing to your unborn child. From the safety of your womb, they will learn to recognise and love your voice. As soon as your child is born, sing to her, rock him to the music, dance with them held close to you.

Rhythm marked our first experiences in the womb (mama's heartbeat), including sound (mama's voice, and the *shhh* of the amniotic fluids – a universal calming sound), and movement (the rocking of mama walking). Little wonder that when we calm our babies, we instinctively rock, pat rhythmically and *shhh* or hum to them. I love that! The wonderful power of music.

There are so many physical benefits from singing. Did you know that singing releases dopamine (a feel-good endorphin) in your brain, and can make you feel calmer and happier? Even humming has a similar effect.

Recent studies have also shown that singing together increases empathy towards others – even strangers who sing together. Faith communities and traditional societies all over the world use music regularly for this purpose. Mamas, we want to foster empathy in our families, don't we? So, let's sing with our children at bedtime! And let's sing as we work together in the garden or travel in the car.

A wee word of caution here. Young children will take to heart what people say about their voices. Many of Katie's adult students have shared with her that one negative comment from a parent/teacher/friend when they were as young as seven meant they never sang in front of others again. Let's encourage our children! And mamas, whatever you do, don't be embarrassed to sing yourself – your voice is the most beautiful voice in the world to them! In fact, why not tell them you feel the same way about their voice – that when you hear them singing, it fills your heart with love?

I will never forget the thrill I had one evening of hearing three-year-old Josiah singing to himself in bed. I stood transfixed out of sight in the hallway, my heart overflowing with love as he sang the song that I'd just taught him that day. His high (very high!) little voice wavered and trembled, but it sounded to me like an angel singing.

> *Count your blessings name them one by one*
> *Count your blessings see what God has done*
> *Count your blessings, name them one by one*
> *And it will surprise you what the Lord has done*

It won't be long before your little crawler discovers the pot cupboard and bangs on an upturned pot with a spoon. Noisy, yes, but great fun. My two-year-old grandson, Obi, loves it when Daddy holds him high and lets him 'play' the row of pots hanging above my Homewood stove. All the distinct tones and pitches delight him. Daddy's arms grow tired long before Obi's had enough of the game.

I included a lot of music in my homeschooling, but still wish I'd done more. As homeschooling mothers, we have wonderful opportunities every day to fill our homes with music. My daughter Katie is a music therapist and has shared some great ideas for you to try:

- A fun thing to do with your young children is to play games with songs – is the music loud or soft? Fast or slow? Have them try to copy a short musical phrase you sing. Encourage them to clap with the music.
- Have some fun with drumming. Bring out the pots and the bongos and the xylophone. A set of bongos offers a lot of enjoyment. (Our set looks decidedly shabby, and sports two beautiful felt pen horses drawn by Emily on the skins when she was five.)
- Body percussion is a fun way of learning how to drum and keep a beat. Use combinations of stomps, knee or chest slaps, clapping and finger clicks to make simple repeating beats. Ask your children to copy what you do and vary the beat and rhythm from simple to complex, fast to slow. This will encourage gross motor development and stimulate the same part of the brain that controls the walking gait.
- In the same way, have some fun using music to play freeze games (great for developing impulse control). Dance while the music plays and freeze when it stops. Small sounds can be shown by small movements. The children will make some fun connections and respond with lots of laughter. You could take turns mirroring each other: go round the circle and follow each other's movements, no matter how silly or simple.
- Listen to all kinds of different music together. Remember that four children will probably have four different tastes in music. One activity that children enjoy is the listening game. Get them to close their eyes and then play a piece of music for them to listen to. Then ask them to write on a piece of paper (or discuss) anything they can about the music. Was it loud? Fast? Gentle? Did they like it? How did it make them feel? Did they picture anything as they listened? Did it make them think of something?

Were they able to recognise any instruments? When they've finished, tell them what the piece of music was called and who wrote it. Then listen to it again together. Some ideas for you to try would be 'The Swan' by Saint-Saëns, or Gershwin's 'Summertime'. The list is endless. Of course, it doesn't need to be classical music – try all sorts. Children love doing this, and it soon raises their awareness and appreciation of many types of music while training them in the art of listening.

- Learn to improvise. This can be an incredibly rich experience to share with your child – even a little one who is banging on the piano. Respond to the way they play and do the same thing with them: single fingers, black notes only. (The black notes on the piano form what's called a pentatonic scale, which means there are no clashes to be found! That makes it possible for the least musical among us to create a beautiful harmonious sound.)
- Now, this suggestion might be difficult, but I think it holds merit. Be interested in your teen's music preferences as it can be a window into their lives and a point of connection with them. Recognise that what sounds pleasant to each person is what they're familiar with. The more you listen, the more your ears and brain will understand and appreciate different styles of music.

One thing I would encourage you to do is to read books about different musicians and composers. This can be a tremendous source of inspiration! Itzhak Perlman overcame the disabilities of polio to become one of the world's greatest violinists. Share with your children the incredible story of Beethoven's struggle with progressive deafness and how he composed the *Ninth Symphony* when completely deaf.

We did a project about Fanny Crosby, who became blind during the first year of her life. She developed a strong Christian faith and wrote over 8,000 hymns. The great composer Haydn was once asked why his church music was always full of gladness. He replied: 'I cannot make it otherwise. I write according to the thoughts I feel. When I think upon my God, my heart is so full of joy that the notes dance and leap from my pen.'[72] As you read about the lives of such people and listen to their music, your children will also learn real life values.

Whenever you have the opportunity, expose your children to different types of music. Take them to concerts and let them see young musicians and singers perform. Nothing can quite compare to a live performance.

I will never forget the evening I took two of my daughters on a special date. Katie was nine and Eliza six. I didn't tell them where we were going, just that they needed to get dressed up. The very fact that they could stay up late caused much excitement and anticipation. But when we arrived at the theatre and they saw the members of the Symphony Orchestra tuning their instruments and heard the excited buzz of the audience, they both edged forward in their seats, their eyes large with anticipation. What an evening! We sat enthralled the whole time, and I had as much joy watching my girls' reaction as I did in listening to the beautiful music. I might have guessed then that music would play a big part in both of their lives.

Two years later, I read in the local paper that a young classical singer was going to perform in the Hamilton English Garden as part of the city's annual music festival. Music by Candlelight. It sounded wonderful! I decided to take my daughters to hear her sing. Again, their excitement was palpable as we sat in the beautiful garden under clear skies, with candles twinkling in the dark. The singer was just nineteen and my girls loved seeing her all dressed up in her evening gown. At half-time, I leaned over to them and whispered, 'Who knows? Maybe one day you'll sing at something like this?'

But despite that comment, I would never have guessed that my little girls would both end up having careers in music.

It would be just eight years later that I had the joy of hearing Eliza perform *Si, mi chiamano Mimi* in the same gardens at Dame Malvina Major's Music Under the Stars concert. She has since completed her master's in classical singing and is currently employed by the Bavarian State Opera House in Munich.

Katie also did a music degree. After the three years, she moved to Cambodia, where she developed a music curriculum for the Cambodian prisons. On returning to New Zealand, she set up a music teaching studio. As well as teaching private students, she began teaching at schools and community groups. She then went on to complete a Master of Music Therapy at Victoria University. Now a registered music therapist, Katie has established a music therapy centre in Northland, supporting children and adults with disabilities, mental health needs and trauma.

The time may come when your child is keen to learn an instrument. Wonderful! (But expensive.) However, if you can afford it, it will be money well spent. For some, a good option may be the afterschool or Saturday morning classes held at schools, where you pay a small fee per term. This way, your child can decide which instrument they really want to learn at minimum expense. They can go on to join the local youth orchestra and discover the joy of playing with others. Sistema New Zealand offers free, intensive, ensemble-based music lessons to inspire children through orchestral music-making.

The ukulele is an easy instrument for children to learn, with strings spaced closer together than a classical guitar. This means little hands can learn to play a lot earlier than if they started with even a half-sized guitar. Learning three basic chords will mean your child can play hundreds of songs! Keep a folder somewhere easily accessible with some simple songs that have the chords written above the words.

Here's an important tip from Katie: instruments are much more likely to be played when they are within sight and easy reach. You may find that a guitar in a case (although well protected) is seldom played. Instead, make or buy simple guitar or ukulele hooks for your lounge or bedroom wall. In the same way, a piano that is left with its lid open is more likely to entice someone walking by to sit down and play – of course it will gather more dust, but better a used dusty piano than a silent clean one.

Right from the start of their music tuition, encourage your children to perform whenever possible. Grandparents are great for this! Remember, music was made to be performed and shared with others. Offer the gift of music to residents at rest homes by going with your family or homeschool group to sing and play for them. Before you go, learn a couple of older songs together. 'Lili Marlene', 'Side by Side', 'You are My Sunshine', 'Danny Boy', 'Amazing Grace' and 'One Day at a Time' are all favourites with the older generation.

One of my favourite memories of singing to the old folk at a hospital care facility was when one outspoken woman demanded at the end of our concert, 'Sing "Jesus Loves Me" again!' At that, a 100-year-old lady told her in no uncertain terms, 'Alright. They can sing it once more, but after that we need to get lunch ready because our men will come in from the fields soon.'

Offering impromptu or planned performances is a wonderful and rewarding activity. Trombonist James Kraft said that practising is like putting money into the bank. And performing is like taking money out of your bank account. Obviously, you can only withdraw as much as you have put in. (I could add that spending money is a lot more fun than saving it!)

While we're talking about practising... the reality is, this can often be painful! Many of you will groan at the thought of trying to fit piano or violin practice into an already full schedule. Add to that the noisy and persistent complaints of a reluctant child who hates practising.

No matter how excited your child is at the beginning when they get their first guitar or penny whistle or violin, they are going to reach a point where they don't feel like practising. Countless articles are available online with ideas of how you can motivate your child to continue and not give up. I encourage you to read them. When you take a genuine interest in your child's musical journey (which includes the passage through dreary valleys), you'll discover ways to help them navigate those difficult times and come out the other side.

If your child is struggling, it's important that you listen to their complaints. Be willing to consider the possibility that they might be learning the wrong instrument or have the wrong teacher. If your child isn't connecting with their teacher, chances are they'll be feeling negative about the whole experience. Keep looking until you find a teacher who can share concepts in a way that interests your child, and who understands your child's learning style. If your child likes their teacher, they'll be more willing to learn and eager to practise. Another thing to consider is finding a teacher who can support your child to not only learn to read music but also to play by ear. This way, they will develop the skills to play a much wider range of music and will usually be far more motivated to practise when they can play a piece from a recent Disney movie or a worship song from church. A simple app or website for finding chords to popular or traditional songs and worship songs is Ultimate Guitar. You can use the 'transpose' function to change the key to one that your child knows how to play in. Print out the songs and keep a folder on your piano. As your child becomes familiar with playing the worship songs you sing at church, the possibility of them joining the youth band will become more and more attainable. And what a joy it is to see them playing an instrument at church!

If your child has chosen to learn a classical instrument, don't presume that they should sit the classical instrument exams.

For some, this will be motivating, but it may mean that children end up practising the same three pieces for the better part of the year. It's an all-too-easy jump to boredom from there.

Now, mamas, here's a thought to challenge you: what about *you* learning an instrument? Never too old, they say! There is something so very special about a family playing and enjoying music together. I recently listened to Sheku Kanneh-Mason, the young cellist who performed at the Royal wedding of the Duke and Duchess of Sussex. Remarkable! I cried as I listened to one of his performances. But each of Sheku's six siblings shares exceptional musical talents. Have a listen to them playing together and be inspired. Never mind that few of us could ever hope to achieve that level of expertise. What matters is that playing music together can be a profoundly rewarding and enjoyable experience which binds a family together.

Mamas, the discovery of music will be a wonderful, ongoing journey in your child's life; something that will enrich the rest of their lives. Enjoy the journey with them!

CHAPTER EIGHTEEN

Terrific Teens

Teenagers who are never required to vacuum are living in one.

—Fred G. Gosman[73]

Mark Twain once advised parents that when their children turned 13, they should put them in a barrel, close the lid and feed them through a hole in the side. When they turn 16, Twain suggested parents close the hole.

All joking aside, this chapter deals with one of the most common questions I get asked by homeschooling mothers. It triggers a raft of emotions when discussed in a group setting – fear, doubt, anxiety, guilt…

'How do I navigate the teenage years?'

The years when our children change from boy to man, girl to woman, are both exciting and challenging times. As parents, it can be the time when we begin to wring our hands and wonder if we're doing enough to prepare them for adulthood. The list of things we know we should be doing seems to stretch before us like the never-ending median strip on the highway: teach them life skills, navigate relationship turmoils, ensure they succeed with their studies, help them find the right career, teach them to make their bed…

It's a time of great change for our teenager, not only physically, but emotionally, mentally, spiritually and socially. It's a time when they begin asking questions like 'Who am I?' 'What do I believe?' 'How do I fit into this world?' It's the time when they're searching for their identity as individuals.

The teenage years also seem to turn up the heat on our own inadequacies as mothers, and we often berate ourselves about all the things we've failed at or neglected to do. As our children enter the teenage years, we suddenly realise we can count on one hand the number of years we have left to teach them everything they still haven't learnt – all the things they still don't know! Life and homeschooling become a pressure-cooker course. That can lead to frustration, impatience and despair – on both sides! But despite all this, the teenage years can be incredibly exciting and rewarding.

The most important thing to remember during these years is that our teenagers need us! I remember laughing out loud the first time I saw the TV advertisement in which a jubilant father ejects himself from his teenager's car after his son finally gets his restricted driver's licence. But the advertisement carried an important message. Drivers on a restricted licence are seven times more likely than other drivers to be involved in a fatal or serious injury crash. Data also shows that young, restricted drivers are more at risk of having a serious crash in the first 6 to 12 months of driving solo on their restricted licence than at any other time. Think about that! Your teenager needs you. Amelia M. Arria, PhD, director of the University of Maryland's Center on Young Adult Health and Development wrote, 'The years when kids are between 13 and 18 years old are an essential time for parents to stay involved.'[74]

So, mamas, whatever you do, don't press the eject button!

I realise I will be merely touching on a subject here that is the sole theme of countless books. I encourage you to read those books and learn, learn, learn.

But let me share with you a simple acrostic of the word 'teenager', which may help you remember a few important truths as you navigate these years.

T – Time

Be there! Be present in your teen's life. Don't abdicate when things get tough. Dedicate the time you need to stay connected. This may take the form of late-night discussions on your teen's bed, endless hours watching soccer games or listening as your teen pours out his angst or disillusionment with the world. The bottom line is that teens need to be connected to their family. Research shows that teens engage in fewer high-risk behaviours such as smoking, drinking, abusing drugs or becoming sexually active when they are connected to their family. We need to be there for them. And here's an encouraging fact – a survey report revealed that most teens want to spend more time with their parents.

When Chris and I were raising our children, Dr James Dobson was a huge inspiration. We would listen to his radio show as we did woodwork in the garage, and treasured his sensible, wise advice for parents. I pored over his books. He was our parenting guru. Recently, I read this extract that he wrote about his teenage years:

> When I was sixteen years old, I began to play some games that my mother viewed with alarm. I had not yet crossed the line into all-out rebellion, but I was definitely leaning in that direction. My father was a minister who travelled constantly during that time, and Mom was in charge. One night, we had an argument over a dance I wanted to go to, and she objected. I openly defied her that night. I said, in effect, that I was going and if she didn't like it, that was just too bad. Mom became very quiet, and I turned in a huff to go into my bedroom.

I paused in the hall when I heard her pick up the phone and call my dad, who was out of town. She simply said, 'I need you.'

What happened in the next few days shocked me down to my toes. My dad cancelled his four-year speaking schedule and put our house up for sale. Then he accepted a pastoral assignment seven hundred miles south. The next thing I knew, I was on a train heading for Texas and a new home in the Rio Grande Valley. That permitted my dad to be at home with me for my last two years of high school. During these years, we hunted and fished together and bonded for a lifetime. There, in a fresh environment, I made new friends and worked my way through the conflict that was brewing with my mom. I didn't fully understand until later the price my parents paid to do what was best for me. It was a very costly move for them, personally and professionally, but they loved me enough to sacrifice at a critically important time. In essence, they saved me. I was moving in the wrong direction, and they pulled me back from the cliff. I will always appreciate these good people for what they did. [75]

Reading that shocked me. I read it several times. Dr James Dobson? The loved and respected founder of Focus on the Family? A rebellious teenager? I kept going back to the part where his mother simply told her husband, 'I need you.' And he responded. He dropped everything and saved his son. They moved house and father and son began hunting and fishing together. Where before he'd been absent, now he was present. And millions of parents, myself included, are so very thankful he did.

Let's search for ways we can stay involved in our teen's life. Invite their friends over for meals. Be interested in their sporting endeavours. Get involved if you can. Chris has had the joy of playing both soccer and hockey with his three sons. I can watch from the side-line and shout encouragement – 'Go, darling!' – and one of them is sure to have the ball. What a joy.

And mamas, I mentioned in an earlier chapter the importance of the family meal table. Here is a regular opportunity to spend quality time with your teen. Make the most of it!

E – Encourage

Our teenagers need our encouragement. The teen years can be a time of uncertainty, a time of harsh self-examination. We mustn't add to their stress by focusing on their failings and shortcomings. You may disapprove of their clothes, the length of their hair, their music, the state of their room… there will probably be any number of things that you could pick on. But whatever you do, don't get into the habit of only criticising. Anger never motivates teenagers. Remember the illustration of the caricature? I used it in reference to marriage, but it is equally as relevant to our teenagers. Look for the good things in your teen. Mention them as often as you can. Thank your teenager for any thoughtful action they do, be it however small. Tell your daughter she looks beautiful when she's heading out the door. Encourage them in their studies. I remember my mother offering suggestions for an English essay. I may not have taken them, but it was comforting to know she was interested, and that she was there for me if I needed help.

E – Enjoy

These years can be wonderful! This is the age when your teen can give you a decent game of table tennis and beat you at chess. You can enjoy some great adventures together. So, plan them! We must be proactive about this sort of thing or otherwise the months and years slip past and before we know it, our son or daughter is leaving for a new city to go to university.

Our family has enjoyed some wonderful adventures together. We've kayaked and tramped the Abel Tasman. One year we did the Tongariro Crossing and canoed the Whanganui River. And we are still planning family adventures with our adult children. Finances needn't be a prohibiting factor. New Zealand has so many places to explore, mountains to climb, rivers to kayak. You don't have to be restricted to the famous ones with entry fees.

It's probably wise to ask your teen what they'd love to do (and be open to their suggestions!) rather than just put forward your own ideas. It might push you out of your comfort zone, but that could be a good thing. You may need to get fit. Or you may have to learn to enjoy a sport you never really had time for before. Do it for your teen, mamas!

N – Nurture

I love this word. To nurture means to care for, to tenderly look after. To protect. Our teens need tenderness. We must keep reaching out to them with tenderness, even when they are touchy and prickly. Now, this can be a real challenge. It's not easy to keep reaching out to someone when they respond with an off-hand or even hostile demeanour or action, but we must. Your big, tall son needs your hugs. He may spend hours working out in the gym and be developing broad shoulders and large biceps, but he still needs your physical touch. If he'll let you tuck under his arm and hug him around his waist, great! But if not, squeeze his shoulder when you walk behind him. Give him a neck massage. Any small touch is significant.

A – Ask questions

Now, mamas, we have something on our side here! Teens tend to be egocentric and think about themselves constantly.

So, a great way to communicate with them is to ask them questions about themselves. Not interrogation, mind you, but genuine interest. You may share a few titbits about your own day and then ask about theirs. How was the concert? Did you have a good game? How was the date? What do you think about this event, or that person? How are you finding your different school subjects?

Find out what movies they've been watching. Ask who they like to be with and why. Be genuinely interested in their friends and invite them over for meals. If you persistently, gently and sincerely ask questions, your child will soon realise that you want to be a part of their life. That you care about how they're feeling. Of course, there's no guarantee they'll open up to you, but they very well might. Even when you ask to be let into a painful experience or emotion, they may surprise you and offer a response freely, but you may also be fobbed off. That's okay. At least they know you care; that you're interested. If they shut you out, you can always tell them, 'It's okay. I realise you may not feel like talking about it right now. I know what that's like. But if you want to talk about it later, come to me and I'll listen.'

Experts encourage parents to sit down when they're attempting to communicate with their teen. Sitting while you talk communicates to your child that what he or she is saying is important to you; that you really want to hear it. You are not about to turn and disappear out the door, called away by some trivial thing. So, when the two of you begin a conversation, pull up a chair. If you're standing in the kitchen, sit up on the counter. If your teen is sitting on the floor, don't be shy about joining him there. Or best of all, flop on their bed!

A word here about your mobile phone. When you begin a conversation with your child (or anyone!), put it well away from you or turn it off. That will send out a very clear and essential message – 'I'm listening.'

Many of you may have had your small child take hold of your face and turn it towards them, wanting your full attention. That's what human beings crave – loving, undivided attention. Eye contact. Physical contact. Focus. Let's make sure we give all of these to our teenager.

G – Grapple

This is a real action verb. It conjures up images of a fisherman wrestling to land a huge marlin. Or two powerful men wrestling with each other while the onlookers cheer. It shows a struggle. A fight.

Some of you may have read the book *Don't Sweat the Small Stuff* by Richard Carlson. He encourages his readers to stop getting stressed and upset by minor issues.[76] Great advice! His book makes for great reading for parents of teenagers in many respects.

But, and it's a big but, we mustn't ignore the big stuff. If you have an inkling that there's something big going on in your teen's life, don't ignore it or hide from it. No one wants to face big issues if it means confrontation and disappointment and potential hurt. But grappling with big issues is one requisite of being a mother. We can't ignore them or wish them away. Painful as it is, we must face them with our child. One antonym for grapple is 'dodge'. How often have we as parents defaulted and dodged the hard stuff? Too many times. Rather, we must grapple with the big stuff.

Mamas, there is help available for you if you are grappling with serious issues. Ask for help. Get professional help if you need to. And may God give you courage and strength as you work through these issues with your teen. Remember, he needs you. She needs you.

E – Educate

Those of you who are just starting out on the homeschooling journey will probably look ahead (like we all did!) and think the stage of graduation and adulthood will never come; or at least, it's so far in the future that it doesn't warrant thinking about. Not so! It will surprise you how swiftly things change. I remember starting out teaching just two children. But very quickly, one, two, three, four more were added to the Boom classroom. I couldn't even imagine the time when it would get smaller. But my 23 years of homeschooling raced by. One by one, the children graduated, and my schoolroom began shrinking every year. So, mamas, enjoy every minute. Remind yourself what a gift these years of education are and give yourself wholeheartedly to it.

Of course, when we discuss education, I'm not just talking about maths and English. Our teen's education involves a lot more than just academia. At the end of the day, how much Latin do I remember after my high school years? Amo, amas, amat… That's about it. My goal has always been that each of my children will finish their homeschooling with four things:

❖ Faith

I've listed this first because for me, this is the number one. My prayer has always been that my children will each develop a robust, firm faith in the Lord Jesus, and a close relationship with him. This is the most important part of my schooling – teaching my children in the ways of God. Teaching them what it is to fear him, to trust him and to serve him. This will be the best gift we can give our teenagers. I'm convinced that Sally Clarkson is right when she says, 'In the absence of biblical conviction, children will go the way of culture.'[77]

We need to remind them they cannot live in the shadow of their parent's faith, but their faith must become their own. To do this, we need to help them discover how and where they can find answers to spiritual questions. We need to teach them how to study the Bible for themselves. Mamas, we can do this! We have the time in our homeschooling days to dedicate to this. But please, if you're feeling overwhelmed by this responsibility, don't be! There are countless resources that can help you. Over the years, I've bought dozens of books to inspire and help me with this important task. I encourage you to make use of such books. Learn and then teach, learn and teach... all our lives, a student and a teacher.

I'll offer some of my own suggestions in a later chapter, but for a more in-depth coverage of this topic, you could read *The Gift of Values* series. I wrote those books as a practical guide to inspire and help parents teach their children about the Christian faith.

As your children read the Word, they will discover in its pages how to get through the hard times they will inevitably face, courtesy of belonging to the human race. And as we devote time to helping them deepen their faith, they will come to realise that they, and they alone, are accountable to God for how they live.

❖ Character

This is potentially the most important area of your child's education – the development of a godly, noble character. A character that has been shaped and formed by the Holy Spirit. Men and women of integrity. Men and women who will be a blessing in society. Men and women who will make wonderful husbands and wives, fathers and mothers.

When a 100-year storm hit our place, we were astonished to see how many massive trees had been uprooted by the wind. But there was a common denominator – they all had shallow root systems.

So much of the real 'work' of parenting involves the hidden places of the heart. We can't see the roots that are growing deep and strong in our children's lives. We catch glimpses of progress and growth, and we rejoice. But, unfortunately, it is all too easy for us to become focused on the outward appearances – the trunk, the branches, the leaves. The storm forcefully reminded me that a tree is only as strong as its roots. It's not what's visible on the top that counts. It's the strength and depth of what lies below.

This is something we need to be constantly assessing. Is my child learning to be kind? Is she learning to think before she speaks? Is he learning that strength must be tempered with gentleness? Do they know how to be a good listener? Do they know how to forgive? Do they know how important honesty is?

Time given to teaching these values is not wasted time. Mamas, remind yourself of this when you're feeling stressed about your teenager's algebra! I once heard an employer say he didn't give a toss for university degrees and such like. All he wanted was to find a young man who would turn up to work on time each morning. Someone who was teachable and reliable. They would learn the rest on the job.

❖ Qualifications

When your child begins their high school years, you need to help them walk a path that will get them to where they want to go. This is exciting! Enjoy the process of discussing all sorts of career options. Introduce them to as many varied occupations as you can. Let them catch a vision for the future and an understanding that what they sow now in their last few years of school, they will reap the benefits of for years to come.

I remember taking 16-year-old Jacob with me to one of my X-ray appointments and suggesting he could be a radiographer.

'No? What about physiotherapy? Now, there's a great career!' Jacob didn't end up doing either of those, but he gave me full marks for trying. In the end, he settled on civil engineering. That meant my job as his homeschooling mama involved helping him get whatever qualifications he needed. We spent hours together researching his options. Should he do Cambridge exams or sit NCEA Level 3 with Te Kura Correspondence school? Was ACE (Accelerated Christian Education) a good option for him? If so, how would he cover calculus? Could he do that as a single subject with Te Kura? It was an exciting time.

Each of your children will be different. Each of them will walk a different path and end up in quite different careers. But for each of them, you need to begin their high school years with the end in mind. Don't dread these years, mamas! It's a thrilling time; one bursting with potential. Let them catch your enthusiasm, your hope for their future.

❖ Life skills

One of the most important qualifications our children are going to need is life skills. Don't neglect this! We need to equip our children with the wherewithal to thrive in everyday life and relationships. Teaching our children life skills is way more important than maths and geography. Do you believe that? You'll probably say yes. But does your school day reflect that? Count how many hours of science you're likely to do this year. Now compare it with how many hours you've allocated to teaching life skills. Aha. It may be time to take a good long look at your timetable.

When I fell off a log and broke my leg in 2008, I suddenly needed to rely on my husband and children to do everything. That's when the hard work paid off. Teaching life skills takes a lot of time and effort – every bit as much as science. Don't ever resent the time needed to teach your children to cook or light the fire or do the washing. More on this in the next chapter!

R – Release

Oh boy! This is hard. I was dreading the time when Eliza would leave our home to go to university. I'd already said goodbye to Josiah and then a year later to Katie. There were lots of tears. But looking ahead, I knew I had a couple of years before Ellie left, and I was content with four of my children still tucked in the nest. But time marched on relentlessly and there was no stopping it. The day I helped Ellie pack is etched in my memory. I wrote a song, trying to capture my conflicting emotions.

Fly, My Darling, Fly

I sit on your bed and watch you pack
Take down your paintings from the walls
You empty your desk and chest of drawers
Excited, you chatter through it all
And I sit and listen with an empty heart
Try to silence my dread
This time's been coming since the day you were born
But still catches me unprepared
You're eighteen and dreaming of the future
You're ready to take wings and fly
You fold your clothes and spread your wings
And gently tell me not to cry
Mama, there's no need to cry

Why is it when I sit and watch you now
I just can't see you're eighteen at all
You're my little girl in a calico hat
Dancing with her daddy at a ball
You're surely not old enough to drive a car

Or cross the busy street on your own
How can I let such a young thing go
And venture so very far from home?
When did I glance away long enough
To somehow miss you growing so tall?
If I blink a few times, perhaps
I'll see you're eighteen after all.

Oh Ellie, I'm going to miss you
Your laughter, your sweetness and love
What will fill the empty space
When you've flown from your family like a dove?
I will carry you in my heart
Whisper your name in my prayers
Rejoice in all the joys you're finding
And treasure each visit you make here
I will cherish each and every memory
And smile with confidence at future's face
I will pray for your constant protection
Entrust you to his grace
God's amazing grace
God's unchanging grace
Fly, my darling, fly
Spread your wings and soar
Fly, my darling, fly

Parenting in a nutshell. The joy and the pain. But what a wonderful, thrilling thing to watch your young fledgling try her wings and fly – soar – as you release her to God's plans and purposes.

Mamas, the teenage years will hold both challenges and rewards – at times fraught with concern and stress, but also bursting with possibilities and joys. May God strengthen your hearts as you navigate these years, and equip you to love and guide your teenager into adulthood with wisdom, patience and optimism.

CHAPTER NINETEEN

Life Skills

Nothing is lost until your mother can't find it.

—Anon

Very early in my homeschooling, a friend lent me a book called *What Every Child Should Know Along the Way: Teaching Practical Life Skills in Every Stage of Life* by Gail Martin. The children and I so enjoyed this book! It covered a huge range of topics – etiquette, survival skills, common courtesy, household chores, etc. And best of all, the author had compiled lists of age-appropriate chores. We had so much fun going through the list that corresponded to each of my children's ages. With great excitement, they ticked off all the things they already knew how to do. There was a lot of laughter as they joshed each other and pointed out tasks that as yet they were unable (or reluctant) to do. Emptying a mouse trap stood out as an unwelcome skill. Seven-year-old Samuel was chuffed to be able to tick so many of his boxes. Make my bed. Tick. Chop kindling. Tick. Light and tend a fire. Tick.

The lists astounded me. Each age category listed things that hadn't even crossed my mind. How to change a fuse wire. To be honest, I hadn't the foggiest. Chris was called in for that one. (Did the book have a mummy list? I can't remember...) How to change a light bulb.

Milk a cow. Make a simple dinner. Bake a cake. Fix a bike puncture.

I printed out each of my children's age-appropriate list and we began...

It became a fun part of our homeschooling – one that I made an intentional effort to keep up with. To this day, I'm glad my sons know that, in our family at least, taking a dead rabbit or rat out of the house and burying it is definitely a boy's job.

In this chapter, I'll list some areas that I've put together over the years to give you an idea of what you can cover in your life skills course. I won't separate mine into ages, however. I'll leave you to do that. Of course, the internet is a mine of information if you search for 'age-appropriate chores'. It might surprise you how the standards or expectations have slipped, however!

Financial skills

If there's one thing your children need to learn, it's how to handle money. It reminds me of Mr Micawber's advice in David Copperfield: 'Annual income 20 pounds, annual expenditure 19 pounds 19 shillings and sixpence, result happiness. Annual income 20 pounds, annual expenditure 20 pounds ought and six, result misery.' [78]

Chris and I gave our children a clothing allowance when they reached a certain age. It was amusing to see how they spent that first allowance. Several of them didn't spend a cent. One blew it all the next day on a pair of label shoes. They all learnt over time that they only got to spend the allotted money once. And a month can be a long time to wait before the next allowance comes due!

- How to handle pocket money. Spending, saving, giving
- How to stay out of debt; only buying what you can pay for
- Learning to live within your means
- Learning how to wait for something you desperately want

- Understanding the dangers of hire purchase and credit
- Learning the principles of giving
- How to work out a budget, including a savings plan
- Opening a bank account and learning how to use it
- How to use an EFTPOS card wisely
- How to set up internet banking
- Making online purchases

These are just a few ideas to get you thinking. Again, there are some excellent resources available to help parents teach their children about money. I encourage you to invest in them.

Physical health

As parents, we spend a lot of time and energy teaching our young ones about basic physical hygiene. We teach them how to clean their teeth, get dressed, brush their hair. But all too often, we abdicate from our role in helping the older children navigate the adolescent years, scared away by their prickly manner or terse response. I'm sure we've all met young people whose appearance shows they haven't got a clue about the importance of general hygiene. Their breath may smell, there's a telltale sweat patch under their armpit, crumpled and dirty clothes... not a good look. But even more important than that is their physical health and wellbeing. Does our child understand how important a good night's sleep is? Is he able to monitor his screen time and limit it to an acceptable amount? (Probably not! He'll need help with this, I'm sure.) Does our teenager realise how harmful junk food can be? Or the devastating impact of alcohol and drugs? There are so many things you can cover in this area, and it will differ between age groups. But it's something we all need to be reminded about, irrespective of our age.

- Establishing and maintaining a personal hygiene routine. Regular brushing and flossing of teeth, daily shower, use of deodorant
- Learning to shave
- Developing a healthy diet
- Understanding the perils of addictions
- Exercise
- Maintaining a reasonable bedtime
- Moderation in screen/media time
- Dressing modestly

General life skills

One of my dear friends had the delightful habit of always putting on the kettle as soon as you arrived at his place. He did it before asking if you had time for a cuppa, and it always made me feel so welcome. Entertaining guests is a skill. We can teach our children how to welcome a visitor. This (and so many other skills) is something that you can role-play with your children. It can be a lot of fun. Have one of them knock at the door and then take turns being the one to make the visitor welcome. Eye contact. A warm smile. A firm handshake. (Okay, here is the perfect opportunity to have fun trying all sorts of handshakes – not to be used in real life!) Greeting people is an important skill. You can have fun illustrating the appropriate ways of greeting people in different scenarios. You'll greet a family member or close friend differently than you will an unfamiliar adult – peers, seniors, people of the same gender as you, younger, older. Introducing yourself is a skill that needs to be taught and learnt. It will stand your young adult in good stead when he has his first interview.

Life Skills

I'll list below some ideas you can have fun with; some serious, some good fun. The important thing is that you take the time to show them exactly what you want. The first time one of my daughters hung out the washing by herself, she draped everything in half over the line. I realised my mistake and took a few minutes to show her how to hang the clothes so they dried in the shortest amount of time. Once you've demonstrated a new skill, you then need to watch them for the first few times they do it on their own. Follow up with regular checks over the next wee while. It might seem like a bit of a hoo-ha to do these steps, but it's worth it!

- Plan a menu and prepare simple meals
- Sew on a button
- Do the grocery shop, looking for the best bargains
- Let your older children watch you fill out your tax forms and GST
- Fill the car with petrol (stories of the father filling up with the wrong fuel might be appreciated here)
- Write a resume and prepare a CV
- For country folk: how to milk a cow and make butter
- Light and maintain a good fire
- Chop kindling
- Make the bed properly (young ones can learn this early on, even mitre corners!)
- Change the bed sheets
- Clean the toilet
- Time management
- Vacuum
- Dust
- Load the dishwasher
- Garden work – mowing, gardening, weeding, raking, trimming bushes and trees

- Hang out the washing
- Problem-solving
- Ironing
- Sweeping and washing the floor
- Routine maintenance of a vehicle such as checking fluids and changing oil
- Change a car tyre
- Empty a mouse trap (woohoo!)
- Change a light bulb/fuse
- How to answer the phone (boy, do some people need to learn this!)
- Make coffee/tea

You get the idea! Of course, in many of these skills, there's a safety aspect that needs to be taught. Boots on to chop the kindling!

Relationships

Our lives are made up of relationships – family, friends, employers, neighbours and loves. It stands to reason then that the more we can teach our children about how to make the most of these relationships, the happier their life will be. Again, this is something that can be taught and learnt. People who knew Dr John Watson said he had a 'genius for friendship'. But he didn't just inherit it somehow; he *studied* how to be a good friend. And then he practised what he learnt.

I'm sure we all share the same dream for our children: that they grow up to be blessed with enduring, happy marriages; that they will have good friends; that they will enjoy a satisfying relationship with their siblings; that they will be reliable, valuable employees; that they will be fantastic employers; that they will be compassionate, caring people. But it won't just happen. They need to develop the skills needed for maintaining these relationships.

- How to apologise
- How to resolve arguments
- Making friends
- Nurturing friendships
- Learning to listen
- Sportsmanship
- Empathy
- Respecting the opinions of others
- Accepting praise from others
- Learning how to say no
- Saying please and thank you
- Dealing with anger and frustration
- Asking questions appropriately
- Accepting responsibility for one's own behaviour
- Dealing with insults in an appropriate manner
- Initiating a conversation with others
- Accepting 'No' for an answer
- Complimenting others
- Receiving compliments
- Compromising on issues
- Cooperating with peers
- Coping with taunts and verbal/physical threats/aggression
- Seeking attention in an appropriate manner
- Waiting one's turn
- Asking permission
- Interrupting others appropriately

The list could go on and on! I suppose that's why we need to enrol in this class as lifetime students. Let's keep learning, mamas! And let's joyfully devote some time in our busy homeschooling days to teach these all-important skills to our precious children. And while you're doing it – have some fun with it!

CHAPTER TWENTY

I Can

Whether you think you can or think you can't, you're right.

—Henry Ford [79]

An adult son asked his father one day, 'Dad, will you take part in a marathon with me?' Despite being middle-aged and having a heart condition, the father agreed. They successfully completed the race together and then ran other marathons, the father always agreeing to his son's request that they do the race together. Then one day, the son said, 'Dad, let's do the Ironman race together.' After a moment's thought, the father agreed.

Ironman is the toughest triathlon ever. The race encompasses three endurance events – a 3.9 kilometre swim, a 180.2 kilometre bike ride, and then a gruelling 42.2 kilometre run.

I will never forget the emotion I felt as I watched Dick and Rick Hoyt (Team Hoyt) compete in their first Ironman event. Rick Hoyt has cerebral palsy and is confined to a wheelchair. For the 3.9 kilometre swim, Rick lay in an inflatable boat, which his father pulled as he swam. Watching the father towing his son just about undid me. I recalled the wobbly legs and burning lungs I'd experienced when I did my one and only women's triathlon.

I cried as I watched the father carry his son up the beach and place him in a special seat in the front of his bicycle. Together they set off on the cycling leg of the race, with Rick's face beaming. 180 gruelling kilometres. Then they ran the marathon, with Dick pushing his son's wheelchair ahead of him. I couldn't stop the tears. What incredible love! After the race, Rick said to his father, 'When I'm running, it feels like I'm not handicapped.'

The video finished with a scene in which Rick was sitting at a special computer that helps him communicate. He typed the words I CAN. And then the rest of the verse appeared: '… do all things through Christ who strengthens me' (Philippians 4:13).

Father and son competed in over a thousand races, including 32 Boston Marathons. They captured the hearts of millions of people worldwide, and in 2013, they were honoured with a bronze statue erected near the starting line of the Boston Marathon. Beside it is plaque with the words: 'Yes, You Can!'

Rick said, "When my dad and I are out there on a run, a special bond forms between us, and it feels like there is nothing Dad and I cannot do." [80] What an amazing example Dick Hoyt is of the power of a father's love. His commitment. Dedication. Perseverance. As I watched the video for a third time, I thought about my homeschooling journey; the race I was running. And it highlighted to me my own weakness and the need I have for my heavenly Father to help me run my race.

If someone were to write the job description of a homeschooling mother, we'd probably all read it and freak out. It would seem impossible. Our first reaction would be to cry, 'There's no way I can ever do all this! How can I teach algebra? How am I supposed to help my child write an essay when I haven't got the foggiest idea myself? How can I teach my child to be kind and honest and diligent? How am I supposed to teach my older children, look after the little ones, feed the baby and still have dinner on the table by 6pm?'

The list could go on and on. But the wonderful thing is, we can! Through Christ. We *can* be the mother we long to be for our children. We *can* create a home filled with peace and joy. We *can* teach our children to love God (and do their maths). We *can* homeschool our children with learning difficulties. How can we achieve all these things? We *can* do all things through Christ who strengthens us.

Consider for a moment these phrases: 'I can jump', 'I can dance', 'I can hope', 'I can swim' and 'I can teach'. They all contain verbs. Action words. But verbs also include state-of-being words. God can also help you *be*: 'I can be loving', 'I can be joyful', 'I can be peaceful', 'I can be kind', 'I can be good', 'I can be faithful', 'I can be gentle' and 'I can be self-controlled'. I can learn to be patient if I abide in him.

Paul writes, 'My grace is sufficient for you, for my power is made perfect in weakness' (2 Corinthians 12:9). This verse is such a comfort to us when we feel keenly aware of our weakness and overwhelmed by the enormous task ahead of us.

Jesus tells his disciples, 'Remain in me, and I will remain in you. No branch can bear fruit by itself; it must remain in the vine. Neither can you bear fruit unless you remain in me. I am the vine; you are the branches. If a man remains in me and I in him, he will bear much fruit; apart from me you can do nothing' (John 15:4–5).

I can't read this passage without pausing on that last phrase: apart from me you can do nothing. This destroys the concept of a homeschooling superwoman! But with him, in him, we can bear much fruit.

So, dear mamas, no excuses! We can meet everything that homeschooling demands, through Christ's help.

A student once asked his professor, W. Page Pitt, which he thought was worse – blindness, deafness or having no arms or legs. Pitt himself was sightless in one eye after the age of five, with only 3% vision in the other eye.

However, he refused to go to a school for the blind, choosing rather to attend a public school. He completed college and became a professor of journalism, with a reputation for demanding excellence. [81]

In answer to the student's question, Pitt replied, 'None of these. Lethargy, irresponsibility, lack of ambition or desire, they're the real handicaps.'

He often told his students, 'You are not here to learn mediocrity, you're here to learn to excel. If I send you on a story and you don't get it because you've got a broken leg, call me from the ambulance. And I'll forgive you. But don't give me excuses! They wound me, and your explanations pour salt in the wound.'

Wow. What a challenging statement. 'Don't give me excuses.' Can I expect (demand) that same excellence from my children? From myself? I know only too well how easy it is to raise all manner of excuses as to why I can't possibly do something. My children are no different. I'm convinced that one important thing we need to be teaching our children is that they can do all things through Christ, who gives them strength. Their biggest enemy is not the challenges they face. It's complacency, negativity, self-imposed limitations and laziness. Rick Hoyt faced huge limitations, but he claimed Philippians 4:13 as his own.

We consistently need to remind ourselves and our children that with God's help we can rise above circumstances that ordinarily spell failure. Mamas, our children need us to help them rise above their 'I can'ts'. They need to know that they can draw on Christ's strength in every challenge and every situation.

How many of you have ever won a three-legged race? If so, what was the key to your victory? There is only one way you can ever win a three-legged race, and that's by getting into the swing of togetherness – keeping in step with each other. Co-operation.

Paul mentions this very key.

'So, I say, live by the Spirit, and you will not gratify the desires of the flesh. For the flesh desires what is contrary to the Spirit, and the Spirit what is contrary to the flesh. They are in conflict with each other, so that you are not to do whatever you want. But if you are led by the Spirit, you are not under law. The acts of the flesh are obvious: sexual immorality, impurity and debauchery; idolatry and witchcraft; hatred, discord, jealousy, fits of rage, selfish ambition, dissensions, factions and envy; drunkenness, orgies and the like. I warn you, as I did before, that those who live like this will not inherit the kingdom of God. But the fruit of the Spirit is love, joy, peace, forbearance, kindness, goodness, faithfulness, gentleness and self-control. Against such things there is no law. Those who belong to Christ Jesus have crucified the flesh with its passions and desires. Since we live by the Spirit, let us keep in step with the Spirit' (Galatians 5:16–25).

Keeping in step with the Holy Spirit. In all our homeschooling, let's not forget this important truth. Let's teach our children what it means to keep in step with God. The wonderful thing about the analogy of the three-legged race is that it illustrates what we need to do if we ever fall. When we get out of step, or fall, the challenge is to get back in step. In a three-legged race, this involves both people. One cannot do it on their own. To apply this analogy to our Christian walk, it involves repentance on our side and forgiveness on God's.

I encourage you to take your children outside and let them enjoy a three-legged race. Then use it to explain the importance of keeping in step with the Holy Spirit, and of how to get back in the race.

Homeschooling is also very much like a three-legged race. As parents, we need to keep in step with our children. When they have a bad day and stumble and fall, we must help them get up. Often a soft answer will work wonders with a strong-willed child, whereas a harsh, grumpy word would alienate them completely.

So, how do we stay in step with the Spirit? Let me share four simple steps that apply to both us as the mother and to our children.

1. Ask God every day to fill you with the Holy Spirit

Our relationship with God is not a static one. We need to be constantly growing and deepening our love for him. Isaiah 55 offers the invitation to come and drink. Our lives should overflow with living water. But for this to be so, we need to keep on drinking and keep on being filled. The Greek translation for Ephesians 5:18 is '...be being filled with the Spirit.' Keep on being filled constantly and continually.

I should take this opportunity to quote the whole verse, because in this day and age of alarming rates of alcohol consumption, this is a vital truth. 'Do not be drunk with wine, which leads to debauchery. Instead, be filled with the Spirit...' We all want our children to live free from the curse of alcoholism. This is one key. Instead of drunkenness, be filled with the Spirit.

Mamas, I encourage you to invite the Holy Spirit into your home and classroom every day. He is the Teacher. Ask for his help. Ask him to fill your life with the wisdom and strength that he alone can bring. And encourage your children to do the same.

2. Listen to his voice

I've already written about the need for selah moments, and how important it is to hear God's word. One word from God can make all the difference. The daily input of the Holy Spirit in your life will transform your schoolroom. If you are in step with the Holy Spirit, he will help you live a life of purity and power, overflowing with joy and peace.

My son Josiah is a keen guitarist and songwriter.

He once told me he's always listening and watching for an idea for a song. I'm the same. A little snippet of conversation, one line in a book, one small quote – they've all inspired me to write songs.

Charles Haddon Spurgeon, known as the 'Prince of all Preachers', encouraged all his students to carry a small notebook with them wherever they went and to write things down as soon as they observed or heard them. He taught them how to train their eyes to see and their ears to listen. He reminded them often that illustrations for their sermons filled their days if they just learnt how to recognise them.[82]

This holds true for us, homeschooling mamas. Creative ideas, teachable moments, illustrations and inspirational ideas fill our days as well. We just need to train ourselves to listen and see. I remember the day I was struggling to help Samuel spell the word 'people'. We'd tried writing it out every day for two weeks, but he still couldn't get it right in a test. And then I listened to the gentle prompting of the Spirit. I made some play dough and helped Samuel to build the word. It worked like magic!

3. Be careful not to grieve him

'And do not grieve the Holy Spirit with whom you were sealed for the day of redemption' (Ephesians 4:30 NKJV).

How do we grieve the Holy Spirit? What hurts him? Offends him? Saddens him? These are all questions you can ask your children. Get them searching for the answers in the Bible. Once they understand that God has given the Holy Spirit to be their companion, their counsellor, their helper and their best friend, they will value his friendship. Tell them he will always be with them. His gentle voice will speak to their hearts and consciences. And their lives will be blessed beyond imagining if they learn to listen to him.

4. When we sin, we must get back into step with the Holy Spirit

Our repentance and God's forgiveness! I mentioned this earlier. God has promised to forgive our sins when we come to him in repentance. The truth of forgiveness and repentance is one of the fundamental truths of the Christian faith. But are we teaching it to our children? Try to develop the habit of looking for little ways you can illustrate this to your younger children. Talk about deeper aspects of it with your older children. The concept of repentance and forgiveness is not something you teach once a month. It needs to be a constant revelation.

Let's say you have an awful morning and snap at the children, complain at your husband and kick the cat. Right. Stop what you're doing and think for a moment. Am I in step with the Holy Spirit? No? Then what do you need to do to get back in step? You choose your response.

First of all, ask God to forgive you. When you've apologised to your children and your husband, give the cat a loving stroke. Once you're back in step, you can explain to your children what just happened. Here's a fun quote from Dr Seuss to share with your children: 'You have brains in your head. You have feet in your shoes. You can steer yourself in any direction you choose.' [83]

Every now and then, Chris and I get out of step. Most of the time it's over some silly little thing. I hate it. It's not long before I'm desperate to get back in step. I long to walk in unity and harmony and love. You will know how easy it is to get out of step with your children as well. Learn to value unity. Work hard for it. That means taking time to resolve conflicts and talking through hurts. It means listening to each other. Forgiving each other.

So, mamas, we need to stay close to Jesus. We need him in our daily lives as mothers. We need him in our schoolroom. Let's remind ourselves every day that we can fulfil this wonderful calling of being a homeschooling mama. How? By abiding in him. We need to recognise that without him, we can do nothing. But we can take encouragement in the fact that if we abide in him and stay in step with the Holy Spirit, we will bear fruit that will remain.

CHAPTER TWENTY-ONE

Family Traditions

*As a mother, my job is to take care of the possible
and trust God with the impossible.*

—Ruth Bell Graham [84]

Last year on our wedding anniversary, Chris and I stayed in a beautiful old lodge, run by an elderly Dutch widower. Over the next few days, I watched him carry out some beautiful personal traditions. Every evening, he donned his woollen cap and took a stroll around the small town (so very Dutch!), he lit a candle at every meal (not just dinner), set his plate and silver cutlery on a white linen tablecloth on a small corner of the cluttered table and ate his meal while listening to classical music. I loved it. When I asked him about his ritual, he told me he'd been doing the same thing for decades.

Most families I know have their own traditions. I love hearing about unique family traditions and have adopted some myself because I've loved them so much (why *not* light a candle at breakfast?).

So, what is a tradition? How does it differ from a routine or a habit? According to Brett and Kate McKay, traditions, whether big or small, differ from routines and habits in that they are done with a specific purpose in mind and require thought and intentionality.

They are behaviours and actions that you engage in again and again – regular rituals that you perform at the same time and/or in the same way.[85]   And, mamas, do you know what the best thing is about traditions? They strengthen the family bond. Researchers have found that families that engage in frequent traditions report stronger connection and unity than families that haven't established traditions together.

Traditions create a deep bond that comes from knowing you're a part of something that's special and unique to your family. They offer comfort and security; a sense of knowing that 'this is what we do; this is who we are'. For a child to know that Mama will tuck her into bed each night with a prayer and a lullaby is incredibly reassuring. A comforting constant. Something they can depend on.

Traditions also help tell a story about our family. They provide an important source of identity. When I was living in Borneo, my friend, who was Chinese, gave birth to her firstborn son. She then followed the traditional Chinese postpartum care – a tradition called 'Sitting the month'. This was so different from anything I'd experienced during my nursing. Different cultures have passed down many such traditions through multiple generations. Continuing to observe them in your own family is a wonderful way of teaching your children about your family's cultural and religious history. The important thing is to decide which traditions are compatible with your family's belief system and values and leave the ones that conflict with your faith.

One of the main purposes of traditions, whether religious or secular, is to impart and reinforce values. Through daily family prayer, we re-enforce the importance of faith; regular family dinners or activities highlight the value and importance of family.

Traditions come into their own during times of change and grief. Maybe you've moved to a new city, and everything is different and strange for your children.

But if you've established a tradition of having pizza every Saturday night, continuing to do that will give them a certain feeling of stability amongst all the change.

I treasure a letter I received from a young reader shortly after the 2010 Christchurch earthquake. She told me that in all the fear and chaos, the time she felt safest was cuddling in bed with the whole family, listening to Daddy read aloud from my book *Where Lions Roar at Night*. The wonderful power of traditions!

In her book *Ask the Children*, Ellen Galinsky, co-founder of the Families and Work Institute, describes a survey in which she asked children what they remembered most about their childhood. Most of them responded by describing simple, everyday traditions like family dinners, holiday get-togethers and bedtime stories.[86]

So, how do we create family traditions? In her book *The Book of New Family Traditions* Meg Cox suggests that in order to start a new family tradition, we must first find a purpose and then make it personal. The two P's. Purpose and personal. When considering a new tradition, first ask, 'What's the purpose of it? What do I hope my children and family get out of it? Am I wanting to instil a certain family value with the tradition?'[87] The answers to these questions will help ensure we develop *meaningful* family traditions.

Once we know our purpose, our next task is to make the tradition personal. I have a dear friend who has established a wonderful family tradition. Every year, they celebrate the purchase of their farm with a Thanksgiving dinner. Friends and family share a lamb on the spit. It's full of purpose and it's very personal.

Before we go any further, let me add a thought here. As you know, families have seasons. Traditions that worked well when your children were toddlers might not have much relevance when they're teenagers (although I've still sung the lullaby to my 21-year-old son).

There have been some traditions I've heard of that I've wanted to start straight away, but deep down I realised it'd be better to wait until the children were just a tad older. We have the liberty to create and eliminate traditions when needed.

And a caution before we proceed! Mamas, please don't go overboard (as I have done at times). I hesitate as I offer suggestions for establishing traditions because I know that some of you may read them and beat yourself up for what you perceive as your own lack. We are all different! Our families are unique. Some of you will love this idea of family traditions; others won't be interested at all. And that is absolutely fine. I also know it takes two to establish many of these traditions. Some of you may have a husband who can't see the point in any of this and baulks at the idea of every single suggestion (except perhaps praying for the evening meal). Decide what's really important and just go for that! You don't have to name it as a tradition. Just do it. It's the doing of it, not the naming of it that's important. Here are some ideas for you to think about.

Daily connection traditions

These are the small things you do every day to re-enforce your family values and identity. One of the greatest blessings in our family was the daily time we shared in the morning, reading the Bible together and praying.

A lot of daily traditions will spring spontaneously from everyday life. Mealtimes provide an abundance of options. Remembering the idea of the two Ps, the purpose of mealtime traditions might be to promote connection and conversation. You could have everyone share something that they're grateful for that day, or a family news time when everyone takes their turn sharing something positive and negative that has happened to them during the day.

'Got any stories? Learnt something?' (Doesn't that sound like the sort of question we homeschoolers would love to ask?) This is a fun one: each person shares something interesting that they've read or heard during the day. This helps open a door into each other's lives and minds. (Oh, the random facts we've learnt at the dinner table! Did you know a ladybug can eat up to 500 aphids a day? You're welcome in my garden anytime, Mrs Ladybug.)

Connection traditions like these will foster family togetherness while helping protect your mealtime from degenerating into a rushed meal, with everyone looking at their cell phones.

Evening walks can be a lovely tradition. They're a great time to get some fresh air and digest the day's events along with your dinner. And research has shown that not only does walking help solve problems, it can also strengthen families.

Many of our favourite traditions centre around bedtime. Reading a story to the children in front of the fire after bath time. Daddy's crazy rides to bed. A Bible story. A prayer. Singing a lullaby. There are so many beautiful ones out there. I used to sing 'La La Lu' (from the movie *Lady and the Tramp*) to our children, except I would change a few of the words. Instead of 'Oh, my little star sweeper,' I would sing their own name: 'Oh, my darling Katie.' They loved it. (And there's an example of the other P principle – make it personal.)

I also wrote a lullaby of my own, and from then on, the children could choose which one they wanted me to sing. Mine was short and simple.

Tonight, as you sleep, God will watch over you
Tonight, as you cuddle your teddy and you
(Here they would grab a teddy if they didn't already have one)
Close your eyes tight and drift away
(So cute watching them squeeze their eyes tight)
He'll be watching you; He'll be loving you
Tonight

I really hope each one of you will choose a lullaby and sing it to your children every night. A lot of mothers have told me they're embarrassed to sing one because they don't think their voice is good enough. Don't you believe it! It doesn't matter what sort of voice you have. Your child grew in the womb listening to your voice and loving it. To them, your voice is the most beautiful voice in the world. Sing, mamas! Sing.

Weekly connection traditions

I've mentioned earlier our own tradition of joining Mum and Dad Boom for dinner every Friday night. We did this for twenty years. The impact that this tradition had on our family is immeasurable.

Many families enjoy a family game night each week. This is a cheap way to bond and have fun together as a family. You might need to remind some of the family not to get too competitive, though! Make sure everyone is enjoying it.

Movie night is another loved tradition. Enjoy watching a great family movie and eating popcorn together. But don't forget to bring out some of the old family videos – great for a laugh and family bonding.

For many families, Saturday morning breakfast means a big cook-up with eggs, hash browns and bacon. And Saturday night might mean pizzas. You can design the perfect fit for your family. It means a lot to a child when she can say to a friend, 'Wanna come over to my place for dinner tonight? We're having pizzas. We always have pizzas on Saturday night.' Right there, whether she realise it or not, your daughter is cashing in on the fact that she belongs to a family who does things together regularly.

One weekly occurrence shared by the vast majority of New Zealanders is Saturday morning sports. This is a marvellous opportunity for creating some family traditions.

Sports is such a huge thing in many children's lives and if possible, you, as the mother, should try to be a part of it. Be their greatest cheerleader! Get to as many games as you can. The tradition might be as simple as getting a McDonald's ice-cream after the game. Perhaps you head home for a special lunch and then a spa. Whatever it is, the purpose is to be a part of your child's life and stay connected.

For Christian families, one of the most regular weekly traditions is attending church together. This has been, and continues to be, such a blessing in our family. We hear the same message and can talk about it together later. We sing together (beneficial for our health) and connect with friends and people of all ages. We have time to still our hearts from our busyness and draw near to God.

I used to love hearing the tenor voice of my father as he stood beside me to sing the hymn. And then to hear my mother's beautiful high voice, loud and clear above the others. As a young teenager, I could feel the solid ground of their faith beneath my feet.

Monthly connection traditions

Okay, here's one I read about that I thought was great. Full moon walks. How romantic. A full moon occurs roughly every 29 days. Every month, year after year. While you may have got used to seeing it, don't forget that a full moon rising is a magical sight – especially for kids who haven't lost their sense of wonder. Take a walk outside at night to watch. Such a simple but beautiful tradition. Maybe I'll suggest this one to Chris.

Another one that someone shared with me is the monthly 'Box of Goals'. At the start of the month, each family member writes down one goal they want to accomplish in that month and places the piece of paper in a beautiful wooden box that the family had made.

At the end of the month, they empty the box and review their goals to see how everyone did. Then they write a new goal for the new month. I love it!

I talked about Daddy or Mummy dates in an earlier chapter. But I must mention it again in this family tradition chapter. Special one-on-one dates with Mummy or Daddy have to be one of the best traditions ever! I first heard of this idea from a friend when my children were small, but I tucked it away as a keeper. These one-on-one dates don't necessarily require money and don't have to be elaborate or hugely exciting. The important thing is that it's regular quality time with your child.

Life changes and milestone traditions

Milestone traditions celebrate events that may occur only a few times, or even just once, for your immediate family. But they become traditions as one generation passes them on to the next.

This could include graduation and 21st birthday traditions, and new home traditions. In the classic movie *It's a Wonderful Life*, George Bailey and his wife, Mary, give a lovely housewarming gift and blessing to a family that's just moved into a new house. Mary offers the couple a loaf of bread with the blessing, 'May this house never know hunger.' She gives them a box of salt, 'that life will always have flavour.' Then George Bailey hands the couple a bottle of wine, with the wish that 'joy and prosperity may reign forever'.

Birthday traditions

There are so many possibilities here. The birthday child gets to choose what's for dinner, the birthday child's height is measured and recorded in a special book, you create a time capsule on a child's eighth birthday with a note (written by himself) listing some things he likes and a personal note to himself. Then it's put away and opened a decade later when he's eighteen. Fun!

You might decide on a certain handmade gift that each child will receive on their 21st birthday. I know that for many mothers, recording some of the funny things that their child has said or done in a special book and then reading from it at each birthday celebration is a wonderful tradition.

Chris and I decided that when each child turned 18, we would give them the 'Boom necklace' – a silver tree of life (Boom means tree in Dutch). My brother Peter had made the original for me on my 50th birthday. Our family verse also talks about a tree, so that makes the tradition personal and significant: 'Blessed is the man who trusts in the Lord, and whose hope is the Lord. For he shall be like a tree planted by the waters, which spreads out its roots by the river, and will not fear when heat comes; but its leaf will be green. And it will not be anxious in a year of drought, nor will cease from yielding fruit' (Jeremiah 17:7–8).

Years ago, at H.E.A.R.T., someone told me about their family tradition of taking each child away for a special trip when they turned 12. Mother and daughter; father and son. I remember loving the idea but feeling like we'd missed the boat with my oldest son, who had already turned 13. But I quickly realised I could make it whatever age I wanted! Fourteen it was. We decided that on each trip we'd make sure the children were involved in some form of mission – one of the best things we've ever done! The children looked forward to that for years as they grew up, and used to spend ages guessing where they would go. Milly was determined that she would go to Steve Irwin's Zoo and have snakes draped around her neck. She cried the day he died, realising she would never meet him. But she ended up joining me on a mission trip to Fiji instead.

What a joy it was to sing with my beautiful 13-year-old at churches, with fragrant frangipani leis (not snakes!) draped around our necks.

Yearly traditions

These can range from things as simple as garlic planting on the shortest day of the year to special harvest celebrations or Thanksgiving dinners. One of our loved yearly traditions is our annual camping trip to the Kai Iwi Lakes. We have built so many special memories there. For several years, we ran our very own Kai Iwi Triathlon. We had different age brackets – some children did their 'swim' on a flutter board. I remember my elation at winning the over 50s race (Okay, so I was the only one in it. No matter – I completed it with a personal best). We inevitably had at least one rainy day during our camping, and one year we decided to set aside that day to each write a story. Budding writers squirrelled away in a tent or on the beach, hard at work, glancing about them every now and then to make sure no one was sneaking up behind them, trying to see what they were writing. Oh, the secrecy! The stories ranged from adventure to science fiction to romance, and we had so much fun reading them out loud that night after dinner amid much applause.

You may decide that every year your family will attend the Anzac Day dawn parade, followed by a special breakfast. Or perhaps choose one exciting family adventure to go on every year. The important thing is that it is something your children can plan on and look forward to because they know it's a tradition.

Special day traditions

These will vary from culture to culture. Chris and I had the joy of travelling to India with our daughter Katie and celebrating her engagement to Aakarsh with his family, sharing in some of their beautiful family traditions.

New Year's Eve

Many cultures have their own New Year's Eve traditions. I remember the year I was in Singapore for Chinese New Year. The noise was deafening! For the Boom family, New Year has always meant making oliebollen – a Dutch doughnut. Chris and I have a tradition of hosting a New Year's Eve party with lots of young people, culminating in a noisy celebratory jump into the swimming pool on the stroke of midnight. We also set aside half an hour during the party to read aloud from *The Book of Years*. This is the special book where I write in bullet point format all the significant happenings in the Boom family for that year (it's amazing what you forget if you don't write things down). This is always a time of gratitude and thanksgiving.

I read of one family who has a New Year tradition called 'Putting Regrets to the Fire'. Each family member writes one of their regrets from the past year on a piece of paper. Then they throw the regrets onto a bonfire or into the fireplace to symbolise a fresh start.

Traditions abound at Easter and Christmas! Try to find something that will be special to your family. When the children were little, I made a patchwork advent quilt with twenty-five pockets. Each pocket held chocolate and a card with a portion of the Christmas story written on it. We would take turns reading the verses and eating the special chocolate hidden in that square. *The Christmas Miracle of Jonathan Toomey* became a yearly read, but for the children, the tradition they still love best is setting up our homemade pottery nativity set. Guffaws of laughter fill the room when someone unwraps Jacob's special wise man and camel. They are always given pride of place by the stable. Memories of making the nativity characters together during an electrical storm years ago come flooding back, and we are a young family again, full of love and joy.

Putting on a Christmas play or puppet show is another wonderful tradition, as is sneaking up to the neighbours' or grandparents' house on Christmas Eve and surprising them with a rendition of 'Silent Night'.

Oh, I love traditions! Just writing about them makes me feel warm inside. They create such a deep bond and sense of belonging. Have some fun with this, mamas! Think of a purpose and then make it personal with your very own tradition. Your children will thank you for it.

I read a story from *The Book of New Family Traditions* by Meg Cox about a family who developed their own secret message. They would squeeze each other's hand three times to signal the words 'I love you'. So simple. On her wedding day, the father squeezed his daughter's hand three times as he walked her down the aisle. No one else saw it or felt it. It was a tiny, intimate moment tucked away amid a very public event; a tradition shared between father and daughter. Yet the daughter said years later that it was one of the most moving moments of her life.[88]

CHAPTER TWENTY-TWO

Peace in Our Homeschooling

My people will live in peaceful dwelling places, in secure homes, in undisturbed places of rest.

—Isaiah 32:18

Children learn best when they're surrounded by an atmosphere of peace. I'm guessing that we all want our children to love their experience of homeschooling so much that they will choose to homeschool their own children as well. But for this to happen, they must know peace and joy in their own experience. And we, the mothers, have the prime task of creating a peaceful home. The good news is that a peaceful home is not out of reach. Even two strong-willed people can learn to live in peace together. (So can eight strong-willed people!)

I remember reading a story about a wealthy man who commissioned an artist to paint something that would depict peace. After a great deal of thought, the artist painted a beautiful country scene. Cows chewed their cud in green fields, birds flew in the blue sky and a lovely little village lay nestled in a distant valley. When the artist gave the picture to the man, he noticed a look of disappointment cross his face. The man said to him, 'I'm sorry. This isn't a picture of true peace. It isn't right. Please go back and try again.'

The artist returned to his studio, thought for several hours about peace, then went to his canvas and painted. A beautiful picture took shape of a loving mother smiling down at the baby asleep in her arms. Convinced that this portrayed true peace, he hurried to present the picture to the wealthy man. But again, the man refused the painting and asked the painter to try again.

Discouraged and tired, the artist returned to his studio. Disappointment and irritation welled inside him as he felt the sting of the man's rejection. Bowing his head, he prayed for inspiration, and moments later he had an idea. He rushed to the canvas and began to paint. When he'd finished, he took it back to the man. The artist held his breath as he studied the painting in silence for several minutes.

At last, the man turned to him with a smile. 'Thank you. This is a picture of true peace.'

And what was this picture of true peace? The painting showed a stormy sea pounding against a cliff. The artist had captured the fury of the wind as it whipped black rain clouds laced with streaks of lightning. The sea roared in turmoil, waves churned and lashed the rocks, and a tree bent beneath the force of the furious thunderstorm. But in the middle of the picture, on a small ledge in the cliff, the artist had painted a small bird, safe and dry in her nest; at peace amidst the storm that raged about her.

Mamas, peace does not mean a family free of struggles, disagreements or troubles. Every home will experience those. Peace means a nurtured togetherness that affords a place of rest in the wildest of storms. It is walking in step and in harmony with one another, even when you don't see eye to eye. It is learning to forgive and to seek the good of the other.

There are many storms in life – financial worries, family breakdown, illness, depression… but in the midst of these storms, the Lord is stretching his hand out to you with a most precious gift.

Peace. Don't forfeit that for anything. 'Peace I leave with you; my peace I give you. I do not give to you as the world gives. Do not let your hearts be troubled and do not be afraid' (John 14:27).

The thesaurus offers an extended list of antonyms for peace: disagreement, discord, agitation, disharmony, distress, fighting, frustration, upset, conflict, war and worry.

You might read those and think, 'Those words perfectly describe my home. My family.' Maybe they do. But you can change that. Let's look at a few of those antonyms.

Discord

Every mother has experienced the stress of having one child stirring up all the rest. It's like hearing the jarring tone of an instrument that is out of tune. Not pleasant. But as mothers, we are called upon daily to be a peacemaker. I suggest illustrating this to your children by playing a sweet chord on the piano and then following it up with a jarring one. Then talk to them about discord. Discuss what it means. Explain that when we choose to be considerate, kind and caring, we will live in harmony with each other. And everyone will benefit.

Frustration

It's easy for us to become frustrated with a child when we're trying to teach them a new concept (or an old one) and they're struggling to grasp it. Any goal-setting you do needs to be achievable. We need to remember that when a child is feeling inadequate or embarrassed, the only clue we might get of how they're feeling is their naughty and uncooperative behaviour. Our frustration may also come from holding unrealistic expectations for that child. If something isn't working, drop it and move on to a different subject.

Tomorrow's attempt may be a completely different experience, with your child willing and receptive to learn.

Agitation

Recognise that this may indicate a deep fear or concern in your child. Gently try to discover what is causing it.

Fighting between siblings

Oh, mamas, we all know about this. It wears us down and makes us frazzled and grumpy. This is where we need to set definite boundaries and be consistent in enforcing them. My parents always used to tell any fighting grandchildren, 'No fighting in here. This is a house of peace.' How many times did I hear those words? But our children learnt to respect them.

Consistency in parenting is one of the hardest things to maintain. When we allow certain behaviour, or let it slip past our notice or do nothing about it, we sacrifice peace in the process. Tiredness is often the culprit here. The thought of having to get up and intervene is just too much. I remember seeing a cartoon depicting a father slumped on the sofa, watching his daughter storm out of the room. He offers a half-hearted response: 'Somebody stop her!'

All too often I've felt like that. Too exhausted to do what I need to do. Maintaining peace can be hard work. Maintaining consistency is definitely hard work. But in the long run, your consistent reaction will pay huge dividends.

Conflict with a child

No matter how much calming music you play, conflict will happen within the family. You may go through a period when one child seems determined to disrupt and annoy you. Don't despair! Recognise that you will have some good days and bad days. Keep working towards peace. Work on developing your relationship with that child. Go on dates together. Factor in plenty of one-on-one time. And always remember that sometimes the best thing to do is call a break from schooling and get outside for a few minutes. It works wonders.

Worry

The classic homeschooling worry – 'Am I doing enough?' I remember the time when this question tortured me. All the children were sick with whooping cough, and I had been dragging myself around for days, also feeling ghastly. Every morning, I tried to deal with the worrying question by insisting we did at least a wee bit of school. But the worry of my lack tormented me. On a second visit to the doctor with the children, he looked at me and asked me how I was. I told him it was an effort to get out of bed in the morning – that I'd love nothing more than to stay tucked up in bed all day. With a smile, he suggested that perhaps my body was trying to tell me something. Maybe I should listen to it? I gave him a wan smile and reminded him I was a homeschooling mother. But he insisted on listening to my chest, and then informed me I had pneumonia. I stared at him in shock and with a growing sense of relief. 'I have? I *have*?' I felt overjoyed. The doctor told me to ring Chris and ask him to come home. I was to go to bed. Doctor's orders. I had permission to be sick. My worries about not doing enough gave way to a wonderful sense of peace.

I would take time to recover and then I would start again. Oh, the power of a doctor's certificate! I think perhaps many of us need a doctor's certificate for time out. We need to be realistic about what we can or can't achieve and let the peace of God rule our hearts. In Philippians 4:6–7, Paul encourages us to refuse to be anxious about anything. Rather, we are to present our requests to God in prayer. If we do that, the peace of God, which transcends all understanding, will guard our hearts and our minds in Christ Jesus.

Over the years, I discovered that one simple way of promoting peace in my home was by ensuring that my homeschooling mornings were set apart. I learnt not to try and do other things at the same time. I discovered by trial and error that trying to squeeze a small painting job or a photo book creation in while supervising bookwork often resulted in a tetchy mother. Interruptions are painful things. I realise that some can't be avoided, but I know from experience that a lot can be.

Minimise the potential for interruptions by letting family and friends know your mornings are busy. Organise phone calls and visits for after lunch. If someone rings you while you're doing schoolwork, explain to them you're busy teaching and ask them to ring you back in the afternoon. It doesn't take long for friends and family to understand that your mornings are sacrosanct.

Minor irritations and annoyances often fill our homeschooling days. These can rankle and irk us, and nettle and rile our children. They may be small, but they seriously compromise our peaceful atmosphere.

I had a bout of hiccups the other day. They were so annoying! As I drank water backwards from a cup and then tried holding my breath, I thought of how hiccups are a great illustration of the small irritations that can frequent our homeschooling days. A hiccup is an involuntary contraction or jerk of the diaphragm that may repeat several times per minute.

Once triggered, the reflex causes a strong contraction of the diaphragm followed by the closure of the vocal cords, resulting in the classic *hic* sound. At the same time, the normal peristalsis of the oesophagus is suppressed. (On that note, it's interesting how easy it is for all normal schoolwork to grind to a halt as we deal with a bout of 'hiccups'.)

What are some hiccups that we can encounter? The baby wakes up just as we sit down to tackle maths with Johnny, the cat brings in a live bird, constant struggles with spelling (in fact, even the spelling differences of hiccoughs or hiccups highlights one of my own challenges in homeschooling – teaching spelling to my dyslexic son), big brother teases his sister and causes a flood of tears, the phone rings, the dog vomits on the floor… The list of hiccup bouts is endless.

What should we do? First, we need to realise that hiccups are a commonplace thing, which will usually resolve spontaneously. Don't get worked up about the little irritations. In his book *Don't Sweat the Small Stuff*, Richard Carlson shares simple ways to keep the little things from taking over our life.[89] Whenever you can, use the interruptions and irritations to teach something important. Rescue the bird from the cat's jaws and teach your children the joy of kindness. Play with the baby and revel in the joy of family. Hiccups are a fact of life, and a fact of homeschooling.

A word here about haste. One cause of hiccups is eating too fast. I know for myself that little issues often arise if I'm trying to do things too fast or teach things in a hurry. Mamas, relax. Don't rush through everything. Slow down. I have had my worst homeschooling days when I've been in a hurry. A.A. Milne wrote in *House at Pooh Corner* that 'the little stream didn't run and jump and sparkle along as it used to do when it was younger, but moved more slowly. For it knew now where it was going, and it said to itself, "There is no hurry. We shall get there someday." [90]

I recently enjoyed reading John Mark Comer's book *The Ruthless Elimination of Hurry*. The subtitle is *How to Stay Emotionally Healthy and Spiritually Alive in the Chaos of the Modern World*.[91] What a wake-up call to those of us whose lives are dominated by a sense of hurry! He speaks about the importance of silence and solitude, sabbath, simplicity and slowing down. If your homeschooling seems to be fraught with hurry, I recommend you read this book.

Just a word here about our homeschooling schedule. When we set too strict an agenda, and strive to keep it, come what may, peace often disappears out the window. There should always be time in our homeschooling day to follow unexpected and exciting diversions. Flexibility and peace often go hand in hand.

Billy Graham said, 'Peace-making is a noble vocation. But you can no more make peace in your own strength than a mason can build a wall without a trowel, a carpenter build a house without a hammer, or an artist paint a picture without a brush. You must have the proper instrument; you must know the peace-giver. To make peace on earth, you must know the peace of heaven. You must know Him who "is our peace." [92]

We need him. He is our peace. The Prince of Peace. And his promise is to keep our minds in perfect peace if our minds are steadfast, trusting in him.

'You will keep in perfect peace those whose minds are steadfast, because they trust in you. Trust in the Lord forever, for the Lord, the Lord himself, is the Rock eternal' (Isaiah 26:3–4).

Mamas, let's fix our hearts and minds on him and ask him every day to make us his instrument of peace within our family.

Lord, make me an instrument of your peace
Where there is hatred, let me sow love
Where there is injury, pardon
Where there is doubt, faith

Where there is despair, hope
Where there is darkness, light
And where there is sadness, joy.
O Divine Master, grant that I may
Not so much seek to be consoled as to console
To be understood as to understand
To be loved as to love
For it is in giving that we receive
It is in pardoning that we are pardoned
And it's in dying that we are born to eternal life
Amen.

—St Francis of Assisi

What better way to close this chapter than to proclaim the Aaronic blessing over our families and homes?

'The Lord bless you and keep you; the Lord make his face shine on you and be gracious to you; the Lord turn his face toward you and give you peace' (Numbers 6:22–26).

CHAPTER TWENTY-THREE

The Strong-willed Child

*Play helps build a warm relationship between family members
and create a bank of positive feelings and experiences
that can be drawn upon in times of conflict.*

—Carolyn Webster-Stratton[93]

This is an exciting chapter to write. I once asked a group of mothers to raise their hand if they had a strong-willed child. Two-thirds of the audience raised their hands. I then told the mothers who hadn't raised their hands that I really hoped they would also get a strong-willed child someday. Everyone laughed. But I meant it differently than they thought I did. I assured them I meant it as a positive thing: that strong-willed children are an absolute blessing – a gift from God! Every mother should have at least one!

Self-motivated and passionate, our strong-willed children often develop into outstanding leaders. I remember Chris and I climbing a mountain with our family and watching our little three-year-old daughter leading the way. She kept this up for a good hour, but I could see from the set of her shoulders that she was finding it harder and harder. When Daddy offered to carry her for a while, she looked at him with stricken eyes and wailed, 'But then I wouldn't be the leader anymore!'

As teenagers, strong-willed children can often resist peer pressure and hold fast to their convictions with an integrity that compliant children don't always have. Instead of defining them as stubborn or difficult, we need to see their God-given potential and rejoice in their ability to hold the course and not be swayed by other people's opinions.

When my blessing arrived, it seemed like she exploded into the family with a burst of brilliant colours. Our lives became that much more exciting and colourful. She made things happen. She created so much fun. Yes, there were outbursts and tears. She goaded and argued. Everyone knew when she was sad or upset. We all felt the impact of her emotions. But that wasn't just in the negative sense. I remember how I had to brace myself at the door of the playcentre when it was time to pick her up. When she saw me, her little face would light up with such joy and love. She'd drop whatever she was doing and run to me, leaping up into my arms and wrapping my neck in a fierce hug. I felt so incredibly loved. It's important we remember that God himself created our son or daughter with a strong will. I believe our champion children have a God-planned destiny that will need every scrap of pluck and determination God has given them.

So, mamas, how do we parent our little champions? What can we do to guide our child through the stormy patches and the overwhelming emotions that so often swamp them? How do we survive the constant challenges and exhausting confrontations? Let me offer you some tips that I've learnt along the way.

Reaffirm your love for your strong-willed champion every day

Do it often throughout the day. You'll need to train yourself to look for ways to affirm them and find the good in them.

If they're in an obnoxious mood and are saying things that have perhaps wounded you, ask God to help you look past it and into their own turmoil. Speak peace and love. Hug them often. Physical touch is so very important. If they resist your attempt to hug them, give their shoulder a loving squeeze instead. Tempt them to cuddle up beside you on the sofa by reading another chapter of their favourite book.

Go on dates together

This works wonders. It didn't matter how moody or challenging my little champion had been during the week, she would become soft and gentle whenever we spent quality time together on a date. I treasured those times! If you've been in a heated conflict with your little person and it seems like there's no hope of it ending, change tack. Surprise your child with an unexpected trip to the library or lunch at a café. Spend one-on-one time together as often as possible. Share as many experiences as you can; choose their company, invite them into your life. And always remember to laugh together. Humour is an undervalued parenting tool. But it lowers defences and is brilliant at reconnecting hearts.

Beware the habit of always saying no

I used to enjoy the old McDonald's advertisement on TV which featured a child bouncing around the room, full of energy, firing questions at his father:

'Can I parachute out my bedroom window?'
'No.'
'Can I grow a moustache?'
'No.'
'Can we go shark fishing?'
'No.'

'Dad, can I have a pet monkey?'
'No.'
'Bee keeping?'
'No!'
'Can we go to McDonald's?'
'N... Yes! Yes, we can!'

How easy it is to get into the habit of telling our little champion, 'No'. When you can say yes, say it! It is all too easy to end up constantly fighting our child, obstructing them, resisting them. Confrontations will come, but try to make them as few as possible. I remember one *Focus on the Family* radio broadcast where Dr James Dobson talked with a woman who was having regular arguments with her fourteen-year-old daughter. When he asked her the cause of their arguments, she explained that her daughter wanted to shave her legs – something which she had forbidden. Dr Dobson listened carefully and then told the mother the answer to the problem was quite simple. He said, 'Ma'am, I strongly encourage you to take your daughter shopping this afternoon and buy her a razor.'

What great advice! We need to be constantly asking ourselves, 'Is this really important? Is it worth fighting over?'

That leads me to the next point.

You don't have to engage in every battle to which you're invited

It takes two to have a power struggle. You can sidestep a lot of power struggles with a bit of wisdom. Avoid pushing your strong-willed children into a corner. If you do, they will bristle and fight back. It is all too easy to push them into full-on defiance. Instead, look for win/win situations. Our little champions need to learn the art of negotiation and compromise (they're going to need that skill in their adult lives also).

And we need to listen to them. Imagine your daughter is doing a puzzle by the fire, and you're desperate to get her to bed so you can finally relax after an exhausting day. Instead of telling her in a curt voice, 'Right! Bed, now!' you'd be better to say, 'Okay, darling, in five minutes you need to start getting ready for bed.' She might look at you with pleading eyes and say, 'But, Mama! I can't finish this puzzle in five minutes!' This is the perfect opportunity to let her know you've heard her and that you understand where she's coming from. A harsh response will precipitate a meltdown. But a gentle response offering a term of negotiation will make for a happier evening. 'Oh, so you've nearly finished it. Well done! Would ten minutes give you enough time to complete it? Or can I help you finish the last bit?'

This isn't permissive parenting. It's listening to your child and negotiating, so you both win. You still set the limits. But you've taken the time to listen to their perspective. And at the end of the day (excuse the pun!), five or ten minutes won't make much difference.

Let's say you're experiencing daily battles with your three-year-old son as you try to dress him in the morning. He does *not* want to wear that clean shirt you've got ready for him. He wants to wear his beloved Zorro outfit that he's been wearing all week and that's splattered with mud. This is a perfect opportunity to teach him about negotiation. You can ask him why he especially wants to wear his Zorro outfit today. He may tell you it's because he loves it. You can then ask him if he knows why you want him to wear the clean shirt. When he shrugs and pulls a face, you can tell him it's because later you're going into town, and you want him to wear something that doesn't reek of mud and tomato sauce. Then you can negotiate.

'Right. You can wear your Zorro outfit until we need to leave for town. Then we'll swap it for this clean shirt. I'll pop your Zorro clothes in the wash while we're away and it'll be all clean for you to wear tomorrow. Deal?'

I hope you hear what I'm trying to say. I am not advocating giving in to all the demands and challenges of your stroppy young child. Not at all. But I am saying that we should be constantly looking for opportunities to teach them how to negotiate an impasse. Laying down the law doesn't achieve that. Learning to navigate challenging situations will be something your strong-willed child will have to become proficient in. He will soon discover that, throughout all areas of his life, he will face situations where he can't demand or expect his own way. He needs to be au fait with the tools of diplomacy – communication, co-operation, compromise.

Offer your strong-willed child choices

These choices need to be ones you can live with. When we simply order them to do something, they will often bristle and argue, especially if they feel they're being made to go against their own conviction. But when we offer choices, they feel more in control of their life. And that is so important to them. Children who feel more independent and in charge of themselves will have less reason to oppose you.

You may also find that a daily conflict over some small matter dissipates if you offer a choice. An apple or a pear. Now or in ten minutes.

Avoid the phrase 'Because I said so'

It doesn't work well with strong-willed children. But let me ask a question: does it work well for any children? Or adults? Who likes to be told in a harsh voice what to do, and then given no explanation as to why they should do it? It feels dismissive and uncaring. As Dr Laura Markham writes, 'No one likes being told what to do, but strong-willed kids find it unbearable.' [94]

'No' is not a complete thought. It is an imperative, a command. It doesn't teach. It tells. If you want your child to learn to think like an adult, take the time to explain your adult thinking.

When God promises to give Abram and Sarah a son, Abram asks God to let Ishmael, son of Hagar, be the promised one. And the Lord replies, 'No.' But he doesn't leave it there. He goes on to explain to Abram the plan he has for his descendants: 'No, but Sarah your wife shall bear you a son, and you shall call his name Isaac' (Genesis 17:19 ESV).

Mamas, there is a better way of coping with the situations that sometimes lead to us giving that ultimatum. Instead of firing out the 'Because I said so!' line, try this: 'My answer is no. Here's why…'

And if they come back to you in five or ten minutes with the same request, tell them, 'My answer is still no. The reason is still…'

If they persist in whining, it's time to use what Lyn Lott describes in her book *Positive Discipline* as the 'Asked and Answered' tool.[95] It's a simple concept. Let's say your child is whining about your decision not to allow them to kick their soccer ball in the living room and keeps nagging you about it. Lott suggests we respond with, 'Have you heard of "asked and answered?"'

Then briefly review the question and answer: 'Did you ask me if you could kick the ball in the living room?'

'Yes.'

'And what was the answer?'

Your child will mutter, 'No.'

Next, ask, 'Do I seem like the kind of parent who would change her mind when you ask me the same thing over and over?'

At this point, your child will probably protest, roll her eyes, walk away, or a combination of these. Ignore it. From now on, anytime your child repeats the question you've already answered, simply say, 'Asked and answered.' He'll quickly get the point and stop whining so much.

Of course, the big problem we are concerned about as their mother is the lack of obedience. We all want to raise a child who is responsible and does the right thing, even when it's hard. But we don't want blind, reluctant obedience. We need to keep in mind the truth of what H. L. Mencken writes: 'Morality is doing what's right, no matter what you're told. Obedience is doing what you're told, no matter what's right.' [96]

We don't want our child to obey simply because someone bigger than them tells them to do something. That could be dangerous if they encounter an adult who tells them to do something wrong. We need to be teaching our children about right and wrong, and equipping them to make wise decisions. We should teach them that if they feel uneasy about something that someone has told them to do, they should check it with an adult who they love and trust.

Limit the number of rules

Set your child up for success by keeping your rules few and clear. Nothing vague. Deciding on your family rules may take a lot of brainstorming. Write everything down that you feel is important, and then try to combine like with like. Simplify, simplify, simplify. One child told her parents, 'We've got so many family rules! God only gave ten.'

This process will take time and perseverance. But it's worth it. It's like a writer trying to edit a wordy 5,000-word chapter down to 2,500. Difficult but essential. If we can make our family rules succinct and well-defined, it becomes a lot easier to enforce them. And then, of course, each rule needs to be explained to the children in age-appropriate terms.

Be consistent

Set the boundaries and hold to them. Don't allow a behaviour one day and then jump on it the next. Your child needs to know that you'll follow through on the consequences of naughty behaviour each and every time.

Invite co-operation

We all dream of cheerful co-operation from our children. But, remember, if we want to invite co-operation, we must first issue the invitation to co-operate! Barking out commands and orders isn't an invitation. A strong-willed child is very much their own person with their own agenda. It will help if we focus on inviting co-operation instead of demanding obedience.

One way we can promote co-operation is by designing daily routines together. Routines are wonderful things. They help diffuse many explosive situations, especially when your child has helped choose the routine. When we talked as a family about setting down rules and limits, it surprised me that my strong-willed children were the ones who diligently followed them and often had to remind me of them. I discovered that they often loved to co-operate.

At some point, mamas, you'll realise that your child has her own inner world of thoughts, plans, worries, hopes and dreams. Her own agenda. And that these inner thoughts are all-important to them. Getting a glimpse into her inner world will help you understand her so much more. My moment of revelation came one day when we were about to go on a picnic. Three-year-old Milly's voice piped up from the back seat: 'Mama! You got sunscreen? Towel? Water?' I listened in amazement as she listed all sorts of things she deemed necessary for our trip to the river. I hadn't even realised she *knew* some of the words.

And then I understood the reason behind some of her previous meltdowns as a two-year-old when we set off on a trip. She had her own agenda, and sometimes Mama wasn't getting things right! I was forgetting important things. Her new ability to communicate opened a door for her (and me!) and helped us navigate those potentially stressful times. From then on, I asked Milly to help me plan and prepare for our expeditions, and she rose to the challenge beautifully.

Choose your words carefully

This is so important. We must learn not to use inflammatory words. Listen to this dictionary definition of inflammatory: 'If you accuse someone of saying or doing inflammatory things, you mean that what they say or do is likely to make people react very angrily.'[97] Hmm. I've had children 'react very angrily'. When we resort to using inflammatory language, our little firecrackers will explode. Instead, we need to ask God to help us use kind, gentle words that turn away wrath' (Proverbs 15:1).

Don't over-react

Strong-willed children are passionate and often say things they don't really mean in the heat of the moment. They wear their emotions on their sleeve and blurt out things they may be feeling at the time, but don't really mean. Let those unkind words go. Don't hold on to them. Don't react out of your own hurt or hold onto it.

Ask for forgiveness whenever needed

Unfortunately, when locked in battle with our strong-willed child, we may say or do things that we bitterly regret. This is where we need to be ready to apologise and ask for their forgiveness.

It never fails to move me how quickly children respond to a genuine apology. How many times have little arms been flung around my neck in a passionate, forgiving hug? We need to do this for our own sake, but also to model forgiveness for our child. Nothing is more essential to the maintaining and nurturing of relationships than forgiveness.

Pray that God will get a hold of their lives

This may seem obvious, but it is so very, very important. When my nine-year-old champion came home from a church camp and told me about the experience she'd had with God where she cried for two hours in his presence, my heart rejoiced! It was a turning point in her life. She wanted to please him and do what was right. Never stop praying for this life-changing experience for your child.

When they disappoint you, keep on loving them

Remember, many a successful, God-fearing adult has come through difficult, rebellious younger years. It's our God-given task to guide our children, teach them and encourage them. And above all, love them.

So, mamas, rejoice in your strong-willed son or daughter! Thank God for the gift they are to your family and the world. Thank him for the colour they bring to your home and family. Ask for his help as you train your champion, and remind yourself often of all their wonderful qualities: they're self-motivated, impervious to peer pressure, they have oodles of leadership qualities, they're energetic, fun, passionate...

And pray, pray, pray that they will passionately love God with all their hearts, and passionately serve him – again, with all their heart. And a whole-hearted response is something our strong-willed children know all about! They do it so very well.

CHAPTER TWENTY-FOUR

Hiding in the Shadows

A mother understands what a child does not say.

—Jewish proverb

Does one of your children often feel left out? Overlooked? Shy? One of our challenges as homeschooling mothers is to make sure that in our busy, demanding days, no child is overlooked or neglected. Easier said than done!

When my brother Peter was just two years old, his world imploded with the arrival of two squalling, demanding twin sisters. Our oldest brother John took it in his stride, but Peter, now the middle child, struggled with his new position in the family. One day, Dad took Peter to the zoo. That afternoon, as Mum sat on the sofa feeding the twins, Peter stood silently beside her for a while. And then, without warning, he spat at her face. Shocked, Mum wiped her cheek and then looked at her son. She saw straight into his heart. Reaching for his hand, she asked him in a gentle voice, 'Why did you do that, darling?'

Returning her gaze, he said, 'Cos me's an angry camel.'

Later, Dad explained to Mum that he'd told Peter on their visit to the zoo that camels spat when they felt angry.

Dear brother Peter faced a difficult road ahead. Mum tried her best to make sure visitors interacted with him as well as fussing over the twins, but it wasn't easy for him. Our children may not face the challenge of being in the shadow of cute twin sisters, but there are countless other scenarios that might produce the same result. Let me list a few.

- A strong-willed child overpowering a gentle child
- Different personality types. A lion versus a beaver
- A louder child speaking over the top of a quieter child
- An articulate child who dominates family conversation
- A demanding child sucking all our attention
- Focusing on our high achiever and all their demands
- Focusing on our slow learner and neglecting our independent child
- A 'good' child neglected because of the 'naughty' child
- A new baby
- One child being more talented than another at sport or music
- Demanding toddlers
- Ongoing dramas and problems with teenagers

So, mamas, how can we stop this happening? How do we ensure each of our children feels heard and noticed and loved? I think being aware of the potential problem is the first important step. Train yourself to listen. Observe. Watch sibling interactions. Ask questions. If we do these things, we'll soon realise if one of our children is in the shadows. We'll become aware of the potential issues. But to do this, we need to be intentional and schedule special time with each child.

Susanna Wesley's household organisational skills are the stuff of legend. She knew from personal experience that quality one-on-one time with a parent is scarce in a family with lots of children, yet so very important. So, she set a rotating schedule which ensured she spent an hour alone with each of her children before bedtime on a designated night each week. She wrote a letter to her absent husband about the responsibility she felt of watching over her children's souls: 'I observe the following method: I take such a proportion of time as I can spare every night to discourse with each child apart. On Monday I talk with Molly, on Tuesday with Hetty, Wednesday with Nancy, Thursday with Jacky, Friday with Patty, Saturday with Charles.' [98]

You might be thinking 'Impossible!' But is it? You could make it twenty minutes instead of an hour and fit it in at other times of the day. The important thing is keeping your finger on your child's pulse.

As we homeschool our children, we need to be factoring in the differences in their learning styles, their personalities and their capabilities. Despite it often being the easy option, we mustn't lump all the children together in our teaching sessions. It works for some subjects but not for others. We all have our strong and weak subjects. And that's OK. Our children need to know that. You may need to create special time and space for someone who's struggling with a particular subject.

I mentioned earlier about my decision to teach both Samuel and Jacob to read at the same time, and how that could have been a disaster if it weren't for some wise advice from my father. Sam, Jacob and I would sit together on the sofa and read a chapter of their Early Reader's Bible, with them taking turns to read a page each. After reading his page out loud, Jacob would fidget beside his older brother as he struggled with his page. I remember the day he burst out, *'The'*, Sam! It says *'the'*. You've already read it twice on this page.'

He wasn't being mean. Not at all. He just couldn't understand why Samuel was struggling with such an easy word. But it wasn't easy for Sam. 'The' was frustratingly difficult.

From that day on, I taught them to read one-on-one, and let them progress at their own speed. (Oh, the blessings of homeschooling!) Yes, it required more time from me, but it was well worth it.

A common place where we can encounter problems is at the dinner table. Some children can tend to dominate the conversation. We mustn't let that happen. We need to make sure the noisy children don't interrupt the quieter ones and that everyone gets their say. That will mean teaching your other children to wait patiently while your reticent child searches for the right words to express what he wants to say. Don't let an eager, articulate sibling butt in and blurt out his news for him.

Do you have a compliant child? One who always does their chores without being asked, and always listens when you speak? One who never makes a fuss at bedtime and always eats their dinner? One who always wants to do the right thing? Mamas, we can often overlook these children. Perhaps a toddler is throwing a tantrum and demanding our attention. Or little Johnny is defying our instruction and is making a beeline for the electric fence. We need to act fast and deal with these things as they happen. But in the meantime, our compliant child has done exactly what we asked without a fuss. The important thing is to ensure that this child gets special one-on-one time with us later. She needs to know how much we appreciate what she does without being told and with no fuss. We need to reward her good behaviour even though it's not out of the ordinary. Too often we reward our naughty child for 'first time obedience' and yet forget to reward the child that always obeys us as soon as we ask them to do something. We also need to think about what reward our compliant child might appreciate. Rather than some sort of prize, she may revel in the special opportunity to show her work to Daddy or Grandma and Grandpa.

What about our introverts? Susan Cain sparked a worldwide conversation when she published *Quiet: The Power of Introverts in a World That Can't Stop Talking*. Her book has helped many people change the way they see introverts and the way introverts see themselves.

She describes the problem of the 'extrovert ideal' and points out that the extrovert, with their confident, loud, out-going, gregarious, alpha traits, is no more important or valuable than the introvert with their quiet fortitude. Our world needs thinkers. We need gentle, sensitive, serious people with a preference for reflection. If you're lucky enough to have one of these children, don't try and make them into an extrovert. Celebrate their personality. Cain writes, 'At school you might have been prodded to "come out of your shell" – that noxious expression which fails to appreciate that some animals naturally carry shelter everywhere they go, and that some humans are just the same.'[99]

Psychologists agree that extroverts and introverts differ in the level of outside stimulation they need to function well. Mamas, perhaps our introvert child is more than happy to rest for a while in the quiet shadows – something we should also think about. If you read Susan Cain's book, it will prompt you to take a good long look at each of your children, your husband and yourself! And I'm sure it will cause you to love them even more and appreciate the fact God has made us all different.

For those of you who are struggling with big issues involving one of your children, the challenge will be making sure the others don't get lost in all the emotional turmoil. Whether it's caring for an ill child, discovering your teenager is on drugs, or helping your young adult cope with a broken relationship, many scenarios can arise that demand your attention and exhaust your emotions. You will need to be super intentional to make sure the other members of the family don't get swept aside in the tsunami of your grief or anguish.

There will be times when you have to fight to maintain the family connection and closeness.

Anxious children often retreat into the shadows to cope with their fears. Perhaps they dread meeting a new person or attending a group session. In many cases, we can help them prepare for these challenging events and the unknown by rehearsing some scenarios. Familiarity with an experience will help reduce the anxiety it may otherwise generate.

I love the concept of 'social stories'. According to Carol Gray, the creator of the aid Social Stories, the goal of a social story is 'to share accurate social information in a patient and reassuring manner that is easily understood by its audience.' [100]

As homeschooling mamas, we have the time and the flexibility to use this technique to help an anxious child deal with a challenging situation, such as going to the doctor or dentist. We can create 'social stories' that will help our child know what to expect, and give him tools he can use to navigate stressful situations. By carefully explaining and rehearsing an activity as many times as needed, our child will become less anxious about the challenging experience. If we take the time to prepare them patiently for new situations and new people in advance, we can gently coax our frightened child out of the shadows where they're hiding.

In any family, no matter how close, there's the potential for a child to begin to feel unnoticed, unheard, unloved. Mamas, let's be aware of this and make sure we correct their wrong perceptions. And let's try to make the necessary changes to ensure it doesn't happen. May our homes be a place where our children with differing personalities and giftings thrive in a warm, caring, supportive environment. *Gezellig*!

CHAPTER TWENTY-FIVE

Love is Spoken Here

One of the best parts of being a family is that you can encourage one another. You can put courage into one another. You can believe in one another. You can affirm one another.

—Stephen R. Covey[101]

Some years ago, I met an engaged couple at an event in Auckland and asked them when they were getting married. The girl's eyes flicked to her fiancé sitting near her and then she told me in a low voice their wedding wasn't for another five years. That surprised me, but then her fiancé shocked me by saying in a cutting tone, 'Yeah, it's a long time, isn't it? But I'm not too worried. If it doesn't work out, there are plenty of other fish in the sea. Or should I say, whales in the ocean.'

I was appalled. His cruel words felt like a punch in my own gut. I could only imagine what his fiancée must have felt like. But at the same time, I knew instinctively that she was probably used to him speaking about her in such a brutal way. Unless they made some radical changes in the way they spoke to each other, their relationship was doomed to failure.

Many children have grown up hearing the saying 'Sticks and stones may break my bones, but words will never hurt me.' Yet nothing could be further from the truth.

Proverbs 18:21 contradicts the sticks and stones saying with the weighty words, 'The tongue has the power of life and death.'

Mamas, this verse prompts an important question – one we should ask ourselves often: are my words bringing life or death to my marriage, to my family?

Mark Twain once quipped, 'I can live for two months on a good compliment.' [102] In reality, if we only give or receive such a meagre token once every two months, our relationships will soon starve.

I mentioned in an earlier chapter about the sign Sam carved for me which is hanging in our kitchen. *Love is Spoken Here.* I look at it every day and pray that love will be the language of our home.

Ephesians 4:29 is such a beautiful verse. 'Do not let any unwholesome talk come out of your mouths, but only what is helpful for building others up according to their needs, that it may benefit those who listen.'

I remember the day we read this verse together and talked about words of affirmation and encouragement. Then I told the children, 'Today we are only going to speak affirming words.' Quick as a flash, Josiah said, 'I'm staying in my room!' We all laughed, but his quip illustrated the difficulty we all have of only speaking the language of love.

When I first read Stephen Covey's book *The 7 Habits of Highly Effective Families,* I shared with the children his chapter about creating a beautiful family culture.[103] Milly was just four at the time, but she really grabbed hold of the concept. From that time on, if any of her siblings (or parents) did something naughty or said something a bit mean, she would tell them in no uncertain terms, 'That's not a bufiful family culture!' She kept us in line, and we all loved it. It was such a cute reminder from a tow-headed little person. Learning to speak the language of love is essential if we want to create and maintain a beautiful family culture. A *gezellige* home.

Mamas, take time to make the little comments that speak approval and love to your child. Sadly, it is often not so much that a child isn't loved by her parents, it's more that she doesn't feel loved. We need to communicate love to our child in a language they understand. Gary Chapman writes about this in his book *The Five Love Languages*, encouraging his readers to ensure they're speaking the language their spouse or child understands.[104] These can be physical touch, words of affirmation, quality time, gifts or acts of service. They are all vitally important. But each of your children will especially respond to one or two of them.

It's important for us to remember that it's not just the 'dictionary' meaning of words that heal or destroy. The *perceived* meaning of words can also wreak havoc in a person's soul. Body language, past experiences and the current moods of both the speaker and the listener all contribute to the atmosphere that the words are spoken in. And it's the atmosphere that determines what the listener actually hears.

Impulsive, hasty words are destructive. Sarcasm, nagging, belittling, ridicule and criticism – all destructive! These words can never be recalled. Herder writes, 'Do not discharge in haste the arrow which can never return. It is easy to destroy happiness, most difficult to restore it.' [105]

Criticism is a destructive habit that can often sneak into our families. If you realise that you've begun to always answer with a harsh or critical word, stop! Criticism is way more destructive than any of us realise. Although it may seem to prompt some necessary action by our partner or child, its impact is always negative.

Jean-Paul Sartre wrote, 'Criticism often takes from the tree caterpillars and blossoms together.' [106] Picture your child as a beautiful tree laden with blossoms – blossoms that will go on to produce fruit. Determine that your harsh words will not strip the blossoms from the tree. Mamas, if this has become a habit, you need to work hard at breaking it and then form a new habit.

Ask God for help as you learn a new way of speaking. The psalmist prayed, 'Set a guard over my mouth, Lord; keep watch over the door of my lips' (Psalm 141:3). Our lips are a door that we can either open or shut. Measure your words.

James 1:9 encourages us to be quick to hear and slow to speak. Too often we have it the other way round. Quick to speak and slow to hear. Research indicates that the average person listens for a mere 17 seconds before interrupting and interjecting their own ideas or thoughts. The goal of listening is to discover the other person's thoughts and feelings. To understand. Our motivation must not be to 'set the record straight'. Mamas, if we learn to wait before we speak, we will protect the relationships and people we love. And if/when we make a mistake and say something that tears down instead of builds, let's be quick to ask for forgiveness.

I've always loved the story of the young lad who begged his dad to come outside and play darts with him. He told his father, 'I'll throw, and you say, "Wonderful!"'

My own children have often said a similar thing. To be honest, I've said it. It's not just children that need encouragement. We all need affirmation and approval. We all need someone who will stand beside us and tell us that we're doing OK. Someone who believes in us. Someone who will encourage us. There are few things more uplifting and inspiring than having someone who loves you cheering you on, applauding your attempts and encouraging you to try again. Conversely, it is hard to thrive when you feel that no matter what you do, it's never quite good enough. Criticism is so very destructive. If all a child hears is, 'What a lousy throw!' he will soon stop picking up the dart at all. As parents, we have dozens of opportunities each day to say 'Wonderful!' to our children. We need to be lavish with our encouragement. We should look for any opportunity to say 'Well done!' If your five-year-old has done his best to tidy his room, make sure he knows you're proud of him.

If there are still a few toys and dirty socks scattered on the floor, never mind. Encourage him with what he has done and help him finish the job. He'll try even harder to please you next time.

Recently, I had the privilege of being the marriage celebrant at my brother's wedding. Before they shared their vows, I spoke to them of the importance of the words they were about to say to each other. Words of love. Words of promise. Words of commitment. I told them that these words would be some of the most beautiful, the most powerful words they would ever utter. In the beginning, God said, '"Let there be light," and there was light' (Genesis 1:3). In the same way, the words of their vows held the power of creation. And the words that I was to speak as the marriage celebrant would have the power to call into being and pronounce a new creation – their marriage. Husband and wife. It didn't take them long to speak their vows, but they will spend the rest of their lives putting them into practice, honouring them, living them out.

Words are incredibly powerful. Ask any writer or songwriter about the power of words. Or any child. Or wife, or husband. They can bring joy to someone who's sad, they can make a person feel loved and valued, they can give hope to someone in despair, and they can strengthen and gladden the heart. Words can build our marriage and make it strong and beautiful. James 3 says the tongue is like a rudder of a huge ship. Words will direct the very course of our life.

But in the same way, words also have the power to tear down, destroy and wound...

Harsh angry words, thoughtless words and unkind words – they all hold the power of death. Of course, we all make mistakes and say things we wish later we'd never said. When that happens, we need to speak new words that will bring healing. 'I'm sorry. Will you forgive me?' We can't build beautiful, enduring relationships without these words.

But it's not just angry, harsh words that hold the power of death. Too often, we speak other things over our own lives. The Lord said to Jeremiah, 'Do not say, "I am too young." You must go to everyone I send you to and say whatever I command you. Do not be afraid of them, for I am with you and will rescue you," declares the Lord' (Jeremiah 1:7–8).

We all have excuses that we throw up when the Lord asks us to do something. We might be too young, too old, not talented enough, not intelligent enough, not bold enough, no good at public speaking – the list could go on and on.

You might have had similar excuses when you first felt the call to homeschool. 'Oh, I couldn't possibly do that!' But his word to us is, 'Do not say…'

We need to remind ourselves that if he has called us to this huge task, he will be with us and will equip us with everything we need to do his will. So, what do *you* need to stop saying?

Mamas, let's use this incredible power that God has given us. Let's speak life every day into our marriages, our relationships, our children and our homeschooling. Let's speak life to our hurting world.

Learning to speak the language of love is just like learning any foreign language – German, French, Mandarin, Spanish… You need to study the language. Learn it. Practise it. In the same way, we must practise speaking the language of love (and teach it to our children just as if we were teaching them French).

Now, you may be wondering what this language of love sounds like. Let's think about it as we read 1 Corinthians 13:

Love is patient

The language of love might sound like this: 'It's alright, darling. I can wait while you sharpen your pencil.' Such a small thing, and yet how easily our day disintegrates when we're impatient and snappy with the children.

Love is kind

'What's the matter, sweetheart? Are you feeling sad? Come here and let Mummy give you a cuddle.' Proverbs 31 says of the wise woman, 'The teaching of kindness is on her tongue.' Therese of Lisieux said, 'One word or a pleasing smile is often enough to raise up a saddened and wounded soul.' [107] Mamas, we can raise up our sad or wounded children by the words of our mouth, by a kind, gentle smile. 'The tongue of the wise brings healing' (Proverbs 12:18).

Our children need our kindness. Our husband needs our kindness. I think simple kindness is one of the most important things in a marriage. I love the part in the movie Captain Corelli's Mandolin when the Greek doctor is walking with one of the villagers on an evening and asks him, 'Do you love your wife? If you love your wife, my advice is, be nice to her. Bring in the wood before she asks for it. If she's cold, put a shawl around her shoulders. And bring her a flower every time you come in from the field.'

The whole world is in desperate need of kindness. And much of the time, all that's needed is the smallest word or touch. But we mustn't just think kind things, we need to say them. We need to do them.

Love always protects

The language of love will say to a frightened child, 'It's alright, darling. I'm here with you. Don't be afraid.'

I hope you get the idea. I think it would be good for all of us to memorise 1 Corinthians 13; etch it in our hearts and minds, so we think about it, pray it, speak it and live it every day.

Love speaks a blessing. This is something we can do every day – speak a blessing over the people in our life. Take every opportunity to encourage each other. To thank each other. For those of us who are married, let's reaffirm our vows.

(I often speak out our wedding ring promise as I put my rings on in the morning: Chris, I give you this ring in token and pledge of my constant faith and abiding love).

As homeschooling mamas, let's speak a blessing over our children every day. When you go into your sleeping child's room to pull up the covers and tuck him in, speak a blessing over him. When you comfort a frightened or anxious child, speak a blessing. When your child is grappling with rebellious attitudes, speak a blessing. Proclaim God's word over their life and speak of the promises and blessings he has for those who will follow him. The blessing can turn a life around.

Just this week, I had the thrill of being present at the birth of my daughter Katie's son. As I held Moshe in my arms for the first time, I sang *The Blessing* over him. Such a precious moment. Such a privilege. But as his grandma, I want to continue to speak a blessing over his life – whenever I pray with him, sing him to sleep or play alongside him. I will tell him how much I love him, how precious he is to his family and to God, and how we will always pray for him and be there for him. I want him to grow up in the sunshine of our love and our blessing.

Mamas, may love be spoken in your gezellige homes.

CHAPTER TWENTY-SIX

The Fear of God – A Treasure Key

He will be the sure foundation for your times, a rich store of salvation and wisdom and knowledge; the fear of the Lord is the key to this treasure.

—Isaiah 33:6.

I love the verse in Psalm 34: 'Come, my children, listen to me; I will teach you the fear of the Lord' (Psalm 34:11). What a beautiful way to call our children each morning to begin school.

As a Christian parent, one of my greatest desires was that each of my children would develop their own faith and relationship with Jesus, and that they would hold to the paths of the righteous. I longed for them to choose to live godly lives, following the commandments and seeking to please the Lord in all they did. I knew that while they lived in our home and under our guidance, we could help them make wise choices and protect them from many of the evil influences that saturate our society. But I knew it needed to be more than our supervision and controlling of their environment. It needed to be their own heart choice.

Perhaps you have a sixteen-year-old son who loves to spend time on the computer. As his parent, you have a window of opportunity to teach him moderation, to make sure he goes to bed at a reasonable hour, to get daily exercise and fresh air, to help him learn how to live and work in this modern digital age while avoiding the pitfalls of the internet. It's a big ask for any parent. Many families wrestle with this challenge and often face painful confrontations with their teenagers. But the scary thought for many is 'what about when he leaves home and goes to university? Who will tell him then that he's spending too much time online? Who will make sure he gets enough sleep? Who will remind him he needs to be oh so careful with what he looks at online?'

It can be a frightening thought to realise that while he has you now as a very present 'shepherd of his soul', at some point he is going to leave the fold and be on his own, far from your daily involvement and godly input. He must walk his own walk. Make his own choices.

But let me encourage you! Your child has a helper, a friend who is with them always, everywhere they go. God has promised never to leave or forsake us. He has given us the Holy Spirit as our helper, our companion, our teacher, our friend.

Our job as parents is to help our little ones learn how to listen to the voice of the Lord. We need to teach them to be sensitive to the gentle voice of the Holy Spirit and to listen to the voice of their conscience.

Moses told the people of Israel, 'Do not be afraid. God has come to test you, so that the fear of God will be with you to keep you from sinning' (Exodus 20:20).

The fear of God. It holds more blessings for us than we could ever realise! The prophet Isaiah speaks of the fear of the Lord as a key to great treasure (Isaiah 33:6).

Do you want your children to avoid evil? Teach them the fear of God. 'Through love and faithfulness sin is atoned for, through the fear of the Lord evil is avoided' (Proverbs 16:6).

Do you want them to walk in good and righteous paths? Teach them to fear God. 'Thus you will walk in the ways of the good and keep to the paths of the righteous' (Proverbs 2:20). I love that verse! I've often prayed that each of my children will keep to the paths of the righteous.

Do you want your children to have the protection of God over their lives? Teach them how to fear the Lord. 'The angel of the Lord encamps around those who fear him, and he delivers him' (Psalm 34:7).

Do you want them to enjoy a long life? The fear of the Lord is the key to this treasure. 'The fear of the Lord adds length to life' (Proverbs 10:27). 'The reward of humility and the fear of the Lord are riches, honour, and life' (Proverbs 22:4 NASB).

Do you pray every day that your children will escape the snares of the enemy? (I hope so.) Again, the fear of God will protect them. 'The fear of the Lord is a fountain of life, turning a person from the snares of death' (Proverbs 14:27).

Moses encouraged the people of Israel to love the Lord with all their heart and soul and strength. He then told them they were to teach God's commandments to their children, talking about them throughout the day as they sit at home or walk along the road. He promised that those commandments would bring a blessing, not just to their own lives, but to the lives of their children and their grandchildren. Hallelujah!

Listen to his heart cry:

> 'These are the commands, decrees and laws the Lord your God directed me to teach you to observe in the land that you are crossing the Jordan to possess, so that you, your children and their children after them may fear the Lord your God as long as you live by keeping all his decrees and commands that I give you, and so that you may enjoy long life. Hear, Israel, and be careful to obey so that it may go well with you and that you may increase greatly in a land flowing with milk and honey, just as the Lord, the God of your ancestors, promised you' (Deuteronomy 6:1–4).

In April 2020, I had the wonderful joy of becoming a grandmother. Josiah, my oldest son, and his wife Sarah had their first child, Obadiah John, while we were in lockdown with COVID-19. What a blessing this little boy is to our family! I've looked forward to becoming a grandma for years and was overjoyed to welcome my first grandbaby into my heart. But with this joy comes a new sense of responsibility. I have the mandate to teach God's commands not just to my children, but also to my grandchildren:

'Only be careful and watch yourselves closely so that you do not forget the things your eyes have seen or let them fade from your heart as long as you live. Teach them to your children and to their children after them. Remember the day you stood before the Lord your God at Horeb, when he said to me, "Assemble the people before me to hear my words so that they may learn to revere me as long as they live in the land and may teach them to their children"' (Deuteronomy 4:9–10).

So, I will do my very best to help Josiah and Sarah teach little Obadiah to love and fear God. I must mention here that King Ahab's palace administrator was a man named Obadiah. He was a devout believer in the Lord. While the wicked Jezebel was killing off the Lord's prophets, Obadiah hid a hundred prophets in two caves, fifty in each, and supplied them with food and water (1 Kings 18:3–4). What great courage that must have taken! But he feared God more than he feared his evil sovereign. I look forward to sharing that inspirational story with Obi.

Some of you may feel a bit confused reading this chapter, unsure what the fear of God actually is. Many people confuse the fear of God with being afraid of God. Believers have no reason to be scared of him. We have his promise that nothing can separate us from his love (Romans 8:38–39). He has promised that he will never leave us or forsake us (Hebrews 13:5).

However, a biblical fear of God includes understanding how much God hates sin. Some years ago, I asked my young children what they thought it meant to fear God. One of them quoted a verse we had memorised together:

'And he passed in front of Moses, proclaiming, "The Lord, the Lord, the compassionate and gracious God, slow to anger, abounding in love and faithfulness, maintaining love to thousands, and forgiving wickedness, rebellion and sin. Yet he does not leave the guilty unpunished"' (Exodus 34:6–7).

Compassionate. Gracious. Abounding in love and faithfulness. A God who is slow to anger. Forgiving. What a beautiful description of our God! But he is also a God who cannot leave sin unpunished. A righteous judge. One who is to be feared.

One author wrote that the fear of God means respecting him. While the concept of fearing God includes respect, I think there's much more to it than that. Fearing God means having a reverence for him that impacts the way we live our lives. Every small detail of it. It makes us want to do what pleases him with all our hearts. We know that he delights in those who fear him and who trust in his love (Psalm 147:11). We hate the idea of disappointing him. We want to obey him and keep his commandments. We know that all of us, young and old alike, will stand before the judgement seat of God. We hate evil. Proverbs 8:13 says that 'to fear the Lord is to hate evil; I hate pride, arrogance, evil behaviour and perverse speech.'

King Solomon sums up the whole duty of man in a succinct six-word sentence: fear God and keep his commandments. 'Now all has been heard; here is the conclusion of the matter; fear God and keep his commandments, for this is the whole duty of man. For God will bring every deed into judgement, including every hidden thing, whether it is good or evil' (Ecclesiastes 12:13–14).

The whole duty of man. Wow. Teaching our children the fear of God is no small thing. The fear of God is lifesaving. Life-giving.

The source of huge blessing. The key to great treasure.

Now, dear homeschooling mamas, let me share a wonderful truth. Deuteronomy shows us that the fear of the Lord can be both *taught* and *learnt*. It is something we can teach our children, and yes, they can learn it, just like they learn to read or write.

Listen to the instruction Moses gave to the priests when he handed them the written law:

> You shall read this law before them in their hearing. Assemble the people – men, women and children, and the foreigners residing in your towns – so they can listen and learn to fear the Lord your God and follow carefully all the words of this law. Their children, who do not know this law, must hear it and learn to fear the Lord your God as long as you live in the land you are crossing the Jordan to possess (Deuteronomy 31:11–13).

There it is, mamas. It's as simple as that. Read God's word to your children so they can listen and learn to fear God. Assemble and read.

I remember half a century ago when we used to gather for morning assembly at school. We would sing hymns and a teacher would pray for God's blessing on the day ahead. I still remember singing *To Be a Pilgrim.* Somehow the words of that song captured my heart with an understanding of the Christian life and pilgrimage. But this didn't happen at a Christian school. No, this was a secular girl's high school. How times have changed! I'm not even sure if modern schools still have assembly. I guess they probably do, but I'm certain that assembly time now won't involve singing hymns or prayer unless it's at a Christian school.

But mamas! We can call an assembly just like Moses did. We can gather our little ones together every morning and read to them from the word of God. We can let them hear stories about the great power of God and the miracles of Jesus.

We can share with them the beauty of the Psalms and the Beatitudes. We can read to them of the exploits and adventures of David and Abraham and Esther.

We can teach them the Ten Commandments. Let me encourage you to take your time doing this. Make sure they understand what each one means. And then show them in Scripture how Jesus explained that love – loving God and loving your neighbour – was the fulfilment of *all* the law.

Mamas, one of the greatest gifts homeschooling has given us is the gift of time. So, when you read to your children, take the time to talk about what you're reading. Ask them questions and let them ask their own. Teach them how to turn the word of God into prayer. Set aside time to memorise passages of Scripture together. A beautiful prayer to memorise is from Psalm 86:11(NKJV): 'Teach me Your way, O Lord; I will walk in Your truth; Unite my heart to fear Your name.'

As you read God's word to your children, they will encounter stories of sin and moral failure, of anger and murder. Balance these with Scriptures of a holy God who will judge sin, but who made a way for the sinner to be forgiven and cleansed. It's important they understand about the wages of sin and both God's grace and judgement. I heard someone speak about this, saying that before anyone can truly understand the good news, first they need to understand the bad news. Without an understanding of the wages of sin, Christ's death on the cross will mean nothing to your child.

During King Josiah's reign, Hilkiah the high priest finds the lost Book of the Law. When Shaphan the secretary reads it aloud, there is a great outpouring of repentance. The knowledge of sin came from the reading of God's commandments. As American evangelist Dwight. L. Moody said, 'The best way to show that a stick is crooked is not to argue about it or to spend time denouncing it, but to lay a straight stick alongside it.' [108] God's word is that straight stick.

When your child becomes aware of the 'crookedness within', he will be ready to understand the glorious gospel. The good news. Read to them about how Jesus died Once your child experiences the love and forgiveness of God, they can then learn how to live a life that pleases him. They can discover what it means to walk carefully before God, listening to the gentle voice of the Spirit.

What a wonderful gift the conscience is! It is our ever-present teacher, and as Vincent van Gogh called it, our compass. If we can teach our children to listen to the quiet voice of their consciences, we will be giving them a lifelong gift. Once our children realise that their conscience is on their side, trying to help them, it will have a tremendous positive impact in their lives.

Ask them if they can think of any time when they were about to do something wrong, and a little voice inside said, 'Don't do that.' They will all have stories to tell! Just discussing these times together will help them identify and recognise the voice of their conscience. Ask them to think of any time when they've done something wrong, and have heard a clear voice inside say, 'You shouldn't have done that.' Explain to them that the conscience is like a referee's whistle that blows whenever there's a foul.

And, mamas, make sure you use this opportunity to share with your children about times in your own life when you've heard your conscience speak to you. Tell them of the times when you listened to your conscience, but also the times when you chose to ignore it. Then discuss the consequences of both the different choices. This can be a wonderful learning moment, all built upon the understanding of God's word.

I remember an evening when I heard the unmistakable sound of one of my daughters crying in her bed just after I'd tucked her in. I went back to her room and asked her what the matter was. She threw her arms around my neck and sobbed. She told me she'd been keeping a bad secret.

She confessed that she and her sister had stolen a small stuffed toy from a shop a few days earlier and had enjoyed playing with it in secret. She told me they were planning to return it the next time we went to that shop.

'But I don't understand,' I said. 'Why have you chosen to tell me about it now?'

'Because of the movie, Mum! I want to be able to enjoy the movie!'

Ah. Suddenly I understood. She had been so excited about going to see a movie with her friend the next day. But as she lay in bed, she knew her conscience wasn't clean. She wanted to put things right so there'd be no reason for her not to enjoy her special day.

We prayed together and then talked about what she would have to do to put things right. That night, she went to sleep with a smile on her face and a clean conscience. Never mind that she had to go with her sister and apologise to the shop keeper. Never mind that she had to help pay for the toy. Tomorrow would be a good day! As a French proverb says, 'There is no pillow so soft as a clear conscience.'

Let me finish this chapter with some beautiful verses from Deuteronomy:

> And now, Israel, what does the Lord your God ask of you but to fear the Lord your God, to walk in obedience to him, to love him, to serve the Lord your God with all your heart and with all your soul, and to observe the Lord's commands and decrees that I am giving you today for your own good?... Fear the Lord your God and serve him. Hold fast to him and take your oaths in his name. He is the one you praise; he is your God, who performed for you those great and awesome wonders you saw with your own eyes (Deuteronomy 10:12–13, 20–21).

The prophet Samuel tells the people, 'As for me, far be it from me that I should sin against the Lord by failing to pray for you.

And I will teach you the way that is good and right. But be sure to fear the Lord and serve him faithfully with all your heart; consider what great things he has done for you' (1 Samuel 12:23).

Samuel felt his responsibility to pray for the people. But he also understood the need for him to teach them the good and right way.

Let's do the same, mamas! Let's pray for our children every day that they will hold fast to God, that they will love him with all their hearts and with all their soul, and that they will fear him and serve him. And let's continue to teach them the way that is good and right. Every day, layer upon layer. Let them hear your joyful voice beckon them every morning, 'Come, my children, listen to me, and I will teach you the fear of the Lord' (Psalm 34:11).

CHAPTER TWENTY-SEVEN

The Way of Wisdom

He who knows all the answers has not yet been asked all the questions.

—Confucius[109]

Hands up all those who have made a mistake in their life. If I were to seek that response from a group of a thousand people, I'm sure there wouldn't be one person who could, in all honesty, keep their hand down. We are all in great need of wisdom – God's wisdom – no matter our age. Day by day, we need wisdom to protect us from making big mistakes that we will bitterly regret later.

What greater blessing could we give our children than the gift of wisdom – or at least, the teaching of wisdom? (Wisdom must be the choice of the individual, but we can teach our children the importance of choosing to hear Wisdom's voice). Godly wisdom will enrich their lives and spare them much trouble and heartache.

One of the daily responsibilities we carry as a parent is to teach our children about consequences. They need to understand that every choice they make, big or small, has consequences. We need to teach them how to make good decisions – in practical matters, matters of conscience and morality, in their choice of career, and their choice of friends and lifetime partners.

In the first nine chapters of Proverbs, there are thought-provoking subtitles about wisdom: Exhortations to Embrace Wisdom, Warning Against Rejecting Wisdom, Moral Benefits of Wisdom, Further Benefits of Wisdom, Wisdom is Supreme, and Wisdom's Call. The final one of these headings is 'Invitations of Wisdom and Folly'.

These headings beckon me to read the book of Proverbs with my children. The last one details two different voices that seek to shape our lives: the voice of wisdom and the voice of folly. Proverbs personifies them as Wisdom and Folly. Both cry out, calling to those who pass by: one luring the foolish into dark paths, the other appealing to all who pass by to turn and listen and gain wisdom.

We were watching a Charles Dickens movie one evening, and without any prompting, we all began calling out to the character who was about to be led astray by an evil man, 'Don't listen to him!' In the same way, Wisdom cries out to us.

Listen to her cry:

> My son, do not forget my teaching, but keep my commands in your heart, for they will prolong your life many years and bring you peace and prosperity. Let love and faithfulness never leave you; bind them around your neck, write them on the tablet of your heart. Then you will win favour and a good name in the sight of God and man. Trust in the Lord with all your heart and lean not on your own understanding; in all your ways submit to him, and he will make your paths straight. Do not be wise in your own eyes; fear the Lord and shun evil (Proverbs 3:1–7).
>
> Listen, my sons, to a father's instruction; pay attention and gain understanding. I give you sound learning, so do not forsake my teaching. For I too was a son to my father, still tender, and cherished by my mother.

Then he taught me, and he said to me, 'Take hold of my words with all your heart; keep my commands, and you will live. Get wisdom, get understanding; do not forget my words or turn away from them. Do not forsake wisdom, and she will protect you; love her, and she will watch over you.

The beginning of wisdom is this: Get wisdom. Though it cost all you have, get understanding. Cherish her, and she will exalt you; embrace her, and she will honour you.

She will give you a garland to grace your head and present you with a glorious crown. Listen, my son, accept what I say, and the years of your life will be many.

I instruct you in the way of wisdom and lead you along straight paths. When you walk, your steps will not be hampered; when you run, you will not stumble. Hold on to instruction, do not let it go; guard it well, for it is your life.

Do not set foot on the path of the wicked or walk in the way of evildoers. Avoid it, do not travel on it; turn from it and go on your way. For they cannot rest until they do evil; they are robbed of sleep till they make someone stumble. They eat the bread of wickedness and drink the wine of violence. The path of the righteous is like the morning sun, shining ever brighter till the full light of day. But the way of the wicked is like deep darkness; they do not know what makes them stumble. My son, pay attention to what I say; turn your ear to my words. Do not let them out of your sight, keep them within your heart; for they are life to those who find them and health to one's whole body. Above all else, guard your heart, for everything you do flows from it. Keep your mouth free of perversity; keep corrupt talk far from your lips. Let your eyes look straight ahead; fix your gaze directly before you. Give careful thought to the paths for your feet and be steadfast in all your ways. Do not turn to the right or the left; keep your foot from evil' (Proverbs 4:1-27).

Can you hear the cry of wisdom in those passages? Every morning at school, I want the wisdom cry to be heard.

God has given each one of us free will, the freedom to choose. We need to be preparing our children to handle that gift wisely. We need to teach them to cry out for wisdom. Teach them how to make excellent decisions. And we need to be doing this day after day, term after term, year after year. It's not a school subject that we touch on once or twice over the years.

In Proverbs 8, we read that wisdom takes her stand where the paths meet. The place of decision, of choice.

> Does not wisdom call out? Does not understanding raise her voice? At the highest point along the way, where the paths meet, she takes her stand; beside the gate leading into the city, at the entrance, she cries aloud: 'To you, O people, I call out; I raise my voice to all mankind. You who are simple, gain prudence; you who are foolish, gain understanding. Listen, for I have worthy things to say; I open my lips to speak what is right. My mouth speaks what is true' (Proverbs 8:1–6).

Where the paths meet. This highlights how important it is to listen to wisdom whenever we face the choice of which path to take.

Folly 'sits at the door of her house, on a seat at the highest point of the city, calling out to those who pass by, who go straight on their way, "Let all who are simple come to my house!" To those who have no sense she says, "Stolen water is sweet; food eaten in secret is delicious!" But little do they know that the dead are there, that her guests are deep in the realm of the dead' (Proverbs 9:14–18).

Who will our children choose to listen to? The brazen woman Folly or Wisdom?

Both Wisdom and Folly direct their cry to the 'simple'. The Hebrew word translated to 'simple' denotes someone without moral direction with an inclination to evil. So, here's another important question. Do you need some moral direction? Does your child?

If your child is lacking moral direction, this is God's heart cry: 'You who are simple, gain prudence; you who are foolish, gain understanding' (Proverbs 8:5). Or, as another translation puts it: 'Are you foolish? Learn to have sense' (GNT).

In the previous chapter, I shared the wonderful truth that the fear of God can be both learnt and taught. The same thing is true of wisdom. We are not born with it, but we can acquire it. We can 'get wisdom'.

So, how do we help our children 'get' wisdom (Proverbs 4:5)? Let me offer you a few simple ideas.

Share words of wisdom daily

Throughout Israel's history, the people learnt to fear God by hearing the priests read aloud the word of the Lord to them. In the same way, wisdom distils like dew whenever we read the Bible to our children. Make it a daily habit, mamas. 'Blessed are those who listen to me, watching daily at my doors, waiting at my doorway' (Proverbs 8:34).

It's fitting that Proverbs has thirty-one chapters – a chapter for each day of the month. Within those chapters is godly advice on relationships, work ethics, financial matters, treatment of animals, friendship, marriage, health and family. Read Proverbs aloud to your children. But don't neglect the rest of the Bible. Everything written in it is for our admonition.

Also, read the life stories of people who have chosen the way of wisdom. Glean from their lives. My own life has been greatly impacted by reading about the lives of people like Amy Carmichael, Isobel Kuhn and Corrie ten Boom, to name just a few.

Turn our ears and listen

Over and over in Proverbs, we read the exhortation to listen carefully. 'My son, pay attention to what I say; listen closely to my words' (Proverbs 4:20 ERV). Pay attention. Turn your ear. Listen closely.

Some years ago, Chris and I took the children to see the kauri forest. As we walked through the bush, marvelling at the giant kauri towering above us, the children laughed and chattered and made their normal racket. After a while, I said, 'Let's stop for a moment and listen carefully. What can you hear?'

We stopped walking, stopped talking, and closed our eyes. It was as if we were transported to another world. I would have liked to stay listening like that for a long time, but the little ones soon became restless, and before too long giggles and untoward noises punctuated the beautiful quiet. But in that short time, we had heard the heavy flight of the kererū, the song of a tūī, the wind in the trees.

There's no doubt about it: listening is a learnt behaviour, one that we need to cultivate. Let's teach our children that hearing differs from listening. They may hear a dog barking or a rooster crowing, but to listen for the call of the shining cuckoo or the musical sound of wind in a grove of rustling poplar trees is on a different level. It requires intentional action. We can teach our children to do this. I encourage you to make it a regular habit. Turn off any device that is making noise, close your eyes and listen. It needn't be for long. Just a minute will awaken the soul.

The psalmist writes about God's creation and tells us that every day it pours forth speech. Every night displays knowledge (Psalm 19:2). How much of that outpouring do we hear? It depends upon how well we listen.

Apply our hearts

There's a wonderful passage of Scripture that paints a very visual scene. I told my children to close their eyes as I read it to them, and to picture in their minds what it was describing. Could they see the overgrown, neglected vineyard? Could they picture the thorns and brambles? What about the tumbled-down stone wall?

> I went past the field of a sluggard, past the vineyard of someone who has no sense; thorns had come up everywhere, the ground was covered with weeds, and the stone wall was in ruins. I applied my heart to what I observed and learned a lesson from what I saw… (Proverbs 24:30–32).

Verse 32 of this passage holds a vital key to gaining wisdom. Yes, you can picture the scene. Yes, you've seen the ramshackle wall and the choking weeds. But just seeing them is not enough. The next step is applying your heart to what you've seen and learning a lesson. This is being proactive. Taking the time to ponder, to learn. If you fail to do this, you will merely walk on past with a tut-tut and gain no wisdom at all.

Respond to wisdom

'Therefore everyone who hears these words of mine and puts them into practice is like a wise man who built his house on the rock' (Matthew 7:24).

The teaching of wisdom always requires a response, an action. We mustn't be like the man who looks at himself in the mirror and then turns away and immediately forgets what he looks like (James 1:23). Rather, we must learn to listen to the Word and then do what it says.

Proverbs tell us that 'wisdom is found in those who take advice' (Proverbs 13:10). Not just hearing advice. Taking advice. What a great verse to discuss with your children.

Whenever we're reading the Bible to our children, we need to make sure that we highlight the need for a response. For example, if we've just read that true religion in the sight of God is to care for orphans and widows in their distress (James 1:27), we should follow it up with some questions: who knows what a widow is? Are there any widows in our church? In our community? How can we help them? What about helping orphans? Should we give some money to Tear Fund or World Vision?

Mamas, let's always encourage a response when we teach our children from the Word. I promise you that doing so will lead you on some exciting adventures!

Ask for wisdom

This is such a simple truth, but one that many people neglect. We need to ask. God loves to give generously! Teach your children (by example) to ask for God's help when they need to make an important decision. Let them hear you asking him for guidance. 'If any of you lacks wisdom, you should ask God, who gives generously to all without finding fault, and it will be given to you' (James 1:5).

The story is told of a young cleric who was in a public debate with an intelligent and formidable opponent. The older man spoke first, with great authority and compelling sharpness of thought and word. The spectators noticed the younger man scribbling on a piece of paper, again and again. It intrigued the audience. Was he writing down ideas, perhaps? Clever arguments? Things to remember?

When the older man finished presenting his argument, the audience was convinced that nothing the young cleric said could refute it.

But to their astonishment, the cleric rose and addressed every argument with a simple clarity of thought and persuasive truth. Later, someone found the scrap piece of paper and read what the young cleric had scribbled over and over: More light, Lord! More light! More light, Father! More light!

'You do not have because you do not ask God' (James 4:2). Throughout Proverbs, we are encouraged – implored – to call out for insight, to cry aloud for understanding. We are to hunger for wisdom and search for her as if for treasure.

Search for wisdom as if for hidden treasure

As mothers, we'll all be familiar with the scenario of a child losing something and then telling us in great despair that they can't find it – that they've looked for it everywhere. I've often asked a child, 'If I told you there was $50 hidden inside your lost book, would you look for it more carefully?' That often sends them scurrying off for another quick search. A common result of the whole scenario is that I end up taking the child with me as I conduct a thorough 'mummy look'.

This can be a good time to talk with your child about treasure. If you're going to be motivated enough to do a thorough search for something, you first must understand and appreciate the true value of what you're looking for. So, it's very important for us to teach our children about the blessings of the Christian life and the joys of walking in God's way.

Walk with the wise

'He who walks with wise men will himself be wise, but the companion of fools suffers harm' (Proverbs 13:20 NASB 1995).

This verse illustrates the importance of choosing good friends. How many times has our family talked about this truth over the last 24 years of homeschooling? Too many to count! This is not something we can teach our children once and then tick off our to-do list. Important truths like this need to be taught and discussed, again and again.

You may like to look up some great quotes on the subject. Here's one I love: 'If you lie down with dogs, you'll get up with fleas.' [110]

Reading great literature aloud together will offer many opportunities to discuss all manner of situations and moral issues (think of the dissolute James Steerforth in *David Copperfield* with his drinking and lack of moral compass). So too, will any stories from your own life. Share with your children age-appropriate accounts of any 'fools' that may have tried to tempt you to walk with them. And then talk about the friends in your life who have inspired you to follow God with all your heart.

Whether your older children are choosing to follow Christ or not, you can talk with them about the importance of choosing their friends carefully. You can share practical wisdom with them in a way that even your most rebellious teenager will listen to. Sharing real life stories of young people who have made both good and bad decisions provide great talking points. My children heard about drunk drivers I came across in my nursing who were discharged from hospital straight into prison, the young girl who eloped with a man her parents begged her not to date, the young man who played chicken on the road and ended up killing someone and spending four years in prison...

I love the scene in Bunyan's *The Pilgrim's Progress*, where Pilgrim reaches the house of the Interpreter. During his stay, the Interpreter takes him into a large room where a raging fire is burning hot against a wall. Beside the fire stands the devil. He holds a large jug, from which he pours water on the flames. Pilgrim stares in amazement.

'This is a strange thing!' he exclaims to the Interpreter. 'Why does the fire not go out?'

'Come with me,' replies the Interpreter. He leads Pilgrim through a door and to the back of the fireplace. There stands Christ himself. And in his hands is a vessel from which he is pouring the oil of grace upon the flames.[111]

This is a fantastic, visual allegory that can help to illustrate to your children several important truths. They will learn that, yes, we have an enemy of our souls, but we also have a champion and an advocate. One who is greater than the enemy. (Just a note: make sure they understand what an advocate is. It's easy for us to use words that go over their heads, and they won't always ask us what the word means.)

If you are blessed to have teenagers who are wanting to follow Christ, remind them regularly that he has wonderful plans for their life, and that the blessings of the walk of faith will amaze them. Use Bunyan's allegory to talk with them about the work of the enemy, and how he is always trying to douse the fire of our love and commitment to the Lord. Discuss with them the powerful influence that friends have in our lives. It would be good if we all examined each friendship in the light of the revelation Pilgrim received in the Interpreter's house. Does our friend throw water or fuel on our heart's fire of devotion to Christ? Paul says, 'Do not be misled: Bad company corrupts good character' (1 Corinthians 15:33).

Over the years, I've watched many Christian young people lose their passion as they chose to spend most of their free time with questionable friends. Some of these friends called themselves Christians, but their lives were full of compromise. I realise, of course, that an earnest young person may be helping to stoke their friend's smouldering fire. But they need to be careful. They should constantly assess the effect their friend is having on their faith, and if they realise it is predominantly negative, they should step away from that friendship.

Mamas, pray, pray, pray for your teenagers. Ask God to send them a friend who will inspire them and encourage them to follow Jesus. A wise friend. If your son or daughter has a personal faith, encourage them to ask God for godly friends.

Our older children will need so much wisdom as they approach the dating and marriage stage of their lives, so try and make these topics something you talk about regularly and often. Get them thinking by discussing important questions they'll need to ask: Does this person share the same values as me? Are we getting married for the right reasons? Do we have the skills and knowledge we need to make this relationship work? Can we pray together? Do they have a vision for serving God? Do we share the same expectations about marriage and children?

Many of these questions will be covered by a good pre-marriage course. When our adult child begins a serious relationship and is considering marriage, we should encourage the couple to enrol in one. The earlier the better! This is something my father was passionate about. He often spoke to my older children about the importance of doing a pre-marriage course and was always researching different ones that were available both locally and online.

Christian theologian and clinical psychologist Neil Clark Warren has written a book that I highly recommend. *Finding the Love of Your Life* offers ten principles for choosing the right marriage partner, drawn from the author's counselling sessions with thousands of engaged couples. The book is full of real life stories that illustrate the importance of each of these principles. Mamas, buy your teenager a copy! I personally know a number of young people whose lives and futures were turned around by Warren's common sense and godly wisdom.

Another important area to discuss with our children is the potential pitfalls of peer pressure. Wisdom knows that the advice of peers may often prove to be bad advice. The story of King Rehoboam illustrates this.

Rehoboam had two sets of counsellors – the elders who had served his father, Solomon, and the young men who had grown up with him – his peers.

The elders gave him wise counsel: 'If you will be a servant to this people today, will serve them and grant their petition and speak good words to them, then they will be your servants forever' (1 Kings 12:7 NASB 1995).

But his peers told him to say, 'Whereas my father loaded you with a heavy yoke, I will add to your yoke. My father disciplined you with whips, but I will discipline you with scorpions' (1 Kings 12:11 NASB 1995).

Unfortunately, Rehoboam listened to the advice of his peers and ignored the wise advice of the elders. And that led to big trouble.

Just like Rehoboam, our children will be offered differing advice. But we can teach them to ask good questions: what is this person's motivation for advising me to do something? Is it to appease their own conscience? To make them feel better? Do they have a vested interest?

Let me finish this chapter with just a brief outline of how to make a wise decision. My children are all adults now, but we still often sit in the spa and discuss any up-coming decisions they need to make. Here are a few pointers from our spa time:

Avoid pressured decisions

Take the time to pray and consider your options. We seldom make wise decisions in haste or impulsively. 'It is a snare for a man to say rashly, "It is holy", then after the vows to make enquiry' (Proverbs 20:25).

When the children were little, we held a Midsummer's Evening Strauss Ball at our place. We made young Samuel and Jacob top hats out of black cardboard and the girls curled their hair and got dressed in beautiful ballgowns.

The front lawn was ablaze with flares and candles and the strains of a Strauss waltz filled the night air. I was greeting visitors at the front gate when I noticed that six-year-old Milly looked different somehow. A closer look revealed that lots of Milly's ringlets had disappeared. It turns out she had impulsively cut them off 'cos they weren't curly anymore and got in the way'. Sigh. I found the ringlets under her dressing table months later.

Beware impulsive decisions! Take whatever time you need to look things over carefully and consider all your options.

Examine the voice that is speaking to you

Line it up with the word of God. Clamouring voices are not from God. He will never tell you to do something that contradicts the Word.

It's good to role-play this practice of examining voices with your children. Develop and act out different scenarios and ask them for ideas of how they would assess each one. What Bible verses do they know that might offer a clear course of action?

Ask for godly counsel

Invite people you trust to offer their suggestions on the best course of action. Don't attempt to work everything out by yourself. Years of experience can give a person a huge amount of wisdom. Give older people whom you respect the opportunity to share some of their hard-earned wisdom with you.

'Where there is no guidance the people fall, but in abundance of counsellors there is victory' (Proverbs 11:14 NASB 1995).

Be careful who you ask for advice. A friend may tell you there's nothing wrong with sleeping with your boyfriend. Yet the way of wisdom is clearly defined in the Word: 'It is God's will that you should be sanctified: that you should avoid sexual immorality' (1 Thessalonians 4:3).

You will always be able to find someone who will tell you what you want to hear. But what will it cost you? What are the consequences?

Consider your priorities

When it's time for you to make a decision, line it up with your priorities. What are your priorities in life? Family? Faith? Physical fitness? If you are offered a higher-paying job that disrupts your family life, wisdom would turn it down. If a certain course of action will sabotage your faith, wisdom will direct you away from it.

Be careful of making big decisions while discouraged

My mother often quoted a popular saying: 'Things always look better in the morning.' And do you know what? Most of the time, it's true! If you're feeling depressed, discouraged or confused, defer any big decisions until later. Experts recommend that, if possible, a person should delay making any major and permanent financial decisions for at least six months after the death of a spouse or close family member.

Eli Joseph Cossman, American entrepreneur and author, said, 'The best bridge between despair and hope is a good night's sleep.' [112]

Reverse a poor decision

Mamas, we need to make sure our children know that if they've made a bad decision, they can change it. German theologian Dietrich Bonhoeffer once said, 'If you board the wrong train, it's no good running back along inside it; you've got to get off the train.' [113]

Let's teach our children about how and when to get off a train. Let's show them how they can get their life back on course. None of our children are perfect. They're all going to make mistakes.

We need to equip them with the know-how they'll need to find their way back after a wrong decision.

I remember sitting on the beach at the Kai Iwi Lakes, having a game of chess with my son. Ten-year-old Katie came up beside me and then whispered in my ear, 'That was a silly move, Mummy.' She was right. Josiah put me in checkmate moments later. How many of us have suddenly realised that we've made a silly move in our life? The devil will try to convince us that there's nothing we can do. That it's all over. But that's not true. With God, there is always hope. Yes, there may be consequences we have to live with, but God is the God of 'full redemption' (Psalm 130).

Mamas, we have 12 years of schooling for each child, with approximately 180 days of schooling in each year. That's 2160 days. Listen to the prayer of Moses: 'So teach us to number our days that we may gain a heart of wisdom' (Psalm 90:12).

Oh, that we would number our homeschooling days and do our very best to teach our children the way of wisdom!

CHAPTER TWENTY-EIGHT

Homeschooling with Patience

If you think my hands are full, you should see my heart.

—Anon

My 21-year-old son Samuel tore the anterior cruciate ligament in his knee a year ago and has had to deal with countless frustrations and disappointments. No soccer. No volleyball. No sport at all for a full year. He had surgery to repair the ligament and then began a daily regime of exercises to strengthen his muscles. His surgeon and physiotherapist gave him clear instructions about what he could and couldn't do, and a strict timeline for his recovery. And dear Samuel stuck to it all religiously. I'm sure he was tempted at times to have just a little kick of the ball (in fact, I might have been guilty of trying to tempt him onto the volleyball court for just a wee game), but he refused to. He bore his restrictions with a patience that amazed me. Of course, he'd set his eyes on a goal: full recovery. He didn't want a premature return to sports, only to have the ligament rupture again. And recently, he was rewarded with the all-clear from his surgeon.

The word 'patience' originates from the Latin word *pati*, which means to endure, bear or suffer.

The Oxford Learners' Dictionary defines 'patience' as 'the ability to stay calm and accept a delay or something annoying without complaint.' [114] Samuel demonstrated that to me perfectly.

Yesterday, Chris repaired a favourite pair of boots that I had bought in a leather market in Rome. As I watched him glue the loose sole, I thought of a quote from the book of Hebrews: 'We want each of you to show this same diligence to the very end, so that what you hope for may be fully realised. We do not want you to become lazy, but to imitate those who through faith and patience inherit what has been promised' (Hebrews 6:11–12).

Some years ago, that verse formed a picture in my mind of a pair of shoes – one shoe named Faith, the other Patience. I pictured myself running my life's race, wearing those shoes. Faith and patience. Two attributes we need every step along the way.

Mamas, if you've embraced the calling to homeschool your children, you are going to need patience – big time! Patience as you teach reluctant or slow learners; patience as you grapple with difficult concepts and bad attitudes. Patience as you struggle to work with uncooperative children and a raft of untoward circumstances. And of course, you must not only learn to be patient with your children, but with yourself as well. Feelings of inadequacy may cause you to become frustrated and irritable. You may become impatient with yourself at how impatient you are with the children. What a steep learning curve this is for all of us! We know how important it is to create an environment where children thrive and learning blossoms. We know that an atmosphere of impatience does nothing to build that beautiful gezellige environment we long for. But it's so hard to be patient sometimes! It requires relinquishing our own agendas, our own timetables. And that's never easy.

Yes, patience is a virtue, but it's one that doesn't come naturally to most of us. Patience is something we must consciously choose and practise every day.

Our relationship with our children, as well as the ability to teach them, depends on it. But thankfully, patience is a fruit of the Spirit, which will grow in our lives as we walk with the Lord.

Growing anything takes time. It's unrealistic to expect something to grow overnight. And this is never truer than with our children. Conception to adulthood is a long time. There's a lot of growing that needs to take place, a lot of learning and a lot of teaching on our part. It will require patient shepherding, mentoring and wisdom.

If your school days are fraught with tension and emotional distress, and you spend your time fidgeting beside your child as she struggles with a maths problem, it's time to take a good look at yourself. Impatience surfaces when we realise that a goal that we have is going to cost us more or take longer to reach than we originally thought.

Perhaps your goal is to teach Johnny to read by the end of the term. But after a promising start, he becomes confused with unfamiliar words and begins to lose confidence. His reading becomes halting and painfully slow. And it dawns on you that teaching your son to read won't be as easy or as quick as you thought. Worrying questions crowd into your mind – am I a terrible teacher? Is he just being naughty? Does he need glasses? Does Johnny have dyslexia? What if I can't teach him to read? Your goal of achieving this important milestone in his life seems to be slipping through your fingers. When you sit beside him on the sofa, listening as he stumbles over words, you find yourself jiggling your leg or glancing at your watch. He becomes distracted and disinterested. When you talk to him, your words are clipped and there's a different tone in your voice. And Johnny hears it and feels it.

Anyone recognise this scenario? If you do, please don't beat yourself up about it. Most of us have been there. The important thing is that we learn how to handle our impatience. When we begin to feel churned up inside, we need to stop what we're doing and take time to recalibrate. Impatience does more harm than we imagine.

Instead of letting the tension grow, shut the book, and say in your kindest voice, 'You know what, Johnny? I think we both need a break. Why don't you go outside and have a bounce on the trampoline while I have a walk and get some fresh air?'

When he bounds off, relieved to have escaped, take a few deep breaths, and then get a glass of water. Yes, the experts recommend this if you're feeling impatient. (But let me clarify – by expert, I'm *not* meaning Chris, who thinks a glass of water is the cure for everything). Then head outside if you can and let the soothing power of nature calm your spirit.

Ask God to help you grow the beautiful fruit of the Spirit that you so desperately need – patience. Once you've settled the churning inside, ask yourself some hard questions. What triggers my feelings of impatience? Why do I feel in such a hurry? What goal do I have that is being delayed? How can I encourage myself and Johnny to persevere? When you examine your heart, you may discover that the cause of your impatience has more to do with a messy house and visitors arriving soon than it does with Johnny's hesitant reading. Or perhaps you're eager to get school finished so you can get outside and finish the window painting you started earlier in the week.

For myself, I've found that recommitting my goal to the Lord in prayer and asking for his help enables me to see the big picture rather than the current frustration. So often through my years of homeschooling I've told myself again and again, 'I have time. There's no hurry. I have tomorrow. And the next day. And the next.' This was especially helpful when I grappled with the challenge of teaching my son with dyslexia to read. I relinquished all deadlines. I refused to let myself get agitated. I reminded myself each day that some things can't be rushed.

Visit your vegetable garden if you have one and apply your heart to the lesson it teaches! Every seed is an example of patience. All of nature is a lesson in patience.

As philosopher Ralph Waldo Emerson wrote: 'Adopt the pace of nature: her secret is patience.' [115]

If you can, develop a regular habit of taking a break in your busy day to do absolutely nothing for a few minutes. Just sit in quietness and think. Don't watch television; don't even read. Do nothing. I've done this a lot lately, mostly when I'm driving in the car by myself. I've often got into the car and turned on some music without even thinking. But then I've turned it off, deliberately choosing quiet. Those times have been incredibly blessed. Time to think. Time to pray. Time to dream.

It may be hard at first, and you may even feel impatient after a minute or two, but by taking some time out, you can slow your world down. This is a practice that will be beneficial to your child as well. Some quiet thinking time without gadgets and devices. They may choose some quiet time by themselves to play with their Lego. If they have lots of noisy siblings, it's important for them to have regular times of solitude.

We've discussed in an earlier chapter some goals that we homeschooling mamas all share. It's important to remember that every one of these objectives is going to require a lot of patience on our behalf. They are not quick, 'easy-to-reach' goals. There will be setbacks and challenges along the way, both for us and for our children. Your child may become discouraged with his own progress. He needs to develop patience with himself. As St Francis de Sales said: 'Have patience with all things, but first of all with yourself.' [116]

I remember the time when my young children were creating a home movie called The Rescue. They all raided the dress-up wardrobe in the barn and began filming. I heard the director telling the actors that the emperor's guards had to search the castle (aka the barn). She'd instructed Samuel to pound on the door and shout, 'Open up in the name of the emperor!' But dear Sam got the words all muddled up, time and time again.

I listened from inside the barn and smiled as I heard some of his funny mistakes. But my mother's heart was hoping and praying that he wouldn't give up, and that the other children wouldn't become impatient and give the part to someone else. I felt like clapping when I heard Katie and Ellie tell him, 'Never mind, Samuel! Try again.' And we all cheered when he got his lines right.

It was an important lesson for Samuel and the other children. Everyone, adults and children alike, needs to be treated with patience. This is something we can model to our children. Next time you're sitting in a traffic jam, don't drum your fingers on the steering wheel and mutter vague complaints and threats to the other drivers. How you respond to delays, slower-moving older folk, interruptions with the internet, fellow motorists and your own family will demonstrate to your children the importance of patience.

An important habit for homeschooling mamas to develop is that of expecting the unexpected. Yes, we have plans, but things don't always (usually!) work out as planned. We must learn to accept the twist and turns in life gracefully. We must keep our expectations realistic. This applies not only to circumstances but also to the behaviour of those around you. Reasonable expectations foster patience. Unrealistic ones stir up impatience. When you expect things to happen NOW, it is likely you will get angry and demanding when things take time. In the same way, if we focus only on our child's shortcomings or failings, we set ourselves up for bouts of frustration and impatience. Remember, 'If you are patient in one moment of anger, you will escape a hundred days of sorrow.' [117]

I love how Paul describes the Lord's dealings with him: 'But for that very reason I was shown mercy so that in me, the worst of sinners, Christ Jesus might display his immense patience as an example for those who would believe in him and receive eternal life' (1 Timothy 1:16).

Immense patience. Mercy. How beautiful! That is how God deals with us. And he can help us develop that same immense patience with our loved ones.

What kind of patience is required for dealing with our younger children? Patience for constant noise and commotion (translation: whining, crying, and fighting), messes and accidents, interrupted sleep and the never-ending presence of a little person.

But teenagers are a whole different kettle of fish. It might involve moody and/or stubborn attitudes accompanied by rolling eyes and that annoying response 'whatever'. We may encounter neglected responsibilities in favour of something more fun, staying up too late, a messy room, a bad attitude towards study… each of these will test our patience.

When our children reach the teenage years, we suddenly realise we only have a few years left to teach them everything they still haven't learnt – all the things they still don't know! Our homeschooling morphs into a pressure-cooker course. And that can lead to frustration, impatience and despair, for both mama and child.

We may also develop an impatience to finish homeschooling with our teenager. Sadly, too many parents abdicate during the older teenager years. Remember the father who pressed the eject button as soon as his son passed his restricted driving test? Mamas, our teenagers need us. Don't abdicate or disappear. Don't become impatient with the process.

Those of you just starting off on the homeschooling journey will probably look ahead (like we all did!) and think that graduation and adulthood will never come, or at least, it's so far in the future that it doesn't warrant thinking about. Not so! It comes around so fast. My 23 years of homeschooling seem to have raced by. I remember the noise and mess and activity around the cluttered kitchen table. And yet, those six little people have grown up and have all graduated…

Patience, mamas! Put on your running shoes – faith and patience – and run the course set before you. And as you encounter the inevitable trials and challenges along the way, remind yourself of Helen Keller's wise words: 'We could never learn to be brave and patient if there were only joy in the world.' [118]

As you choose daily to be patient, your children will blossom and thrive, your schoolroom will become a place of peace, and your own heart will know contentment and joy as you continue to teach your children 'with great patience and careful instruction' (2 Timothy 4:2).

CHAPTER TWENTY-NINE

Dealing with Squabbles

*The heart of a mother is a deep abyss at the bottom
of which you will always find forgiveness.*

—Honoré De Balzac[119]

Squabbling. Scrapping. Bickering. Tattling. Sigh. There's nothing like it to wear you thin (writing that makes me think of Bilbo telling Gandalf, 'I feel thin, sort of stretched, like butter scraped over too much bread.' [120] Exactly! Our homeschooling days are often loaded with this sort of soul-wearying sibling interaction. Big brother teasing little sister. One child goading the other. A mischievous child stirring up trouble between the siblings. Tempers frayed and accusations flying. We all know how exhausting it is to be a referee in countless petty squabbles. Child psychologist Clara Linnros writes that siblings of preschool age squabble on average six to eight times an hour.[121] That can make for a long day, especially when you're trying to teach the older siblings long division and grammar.

Of course, we don't need to get involved in every squabble. It's good to let children learn how to sort things out themselves, but there comes a time when you need to intervene. The relentless regularity of these quarrels can make for a stressful and challenging day/week/year.

But keep in mind that while sibling conflict is unavoidable, it also provides our children with the opportunity to develop essential life skills. Anger management. Forgiveness. Conflict resolution. The family home is their practice ground. Their social training.

When conflict surfaces, often the first reaction in the heat of the moment is for one person to blame the other. This blaming tendency goes way back to the Garden of Eden, where Adam tells God that the woman made him eat the forbidden fruit. It's all too easy to jump to conclusions and blame the wrong person. Mamas, we need to be aware of this when we're trying to sort out some silly squabble. If we're tired and frustrated, we can easily make a snap judgement and mete out consequences for the wrong child.

Some years ago, I went outside to hang the washing on the line and discovered our young puppy, Lucy, standing beside a hen lying on the grass, sniffing it. At that moment, I realised all my worst fears. Lucy's sire had killed several hens and maimed others.

Lucy wagged her tail when she saw me, her whole body wriggling with excitement. I stared at her, horrified, furious! I knew I had to teach her a lesson before she became a confirmed chicken-killer like her father, so I gave her a real telling-off.

Then came the hard part. I went inside to tell my daughter, Milly, that one of her beloved chickens was dead. She looked at me aghast, then ran outside and knelt beside her hen. Lucy came creeping around the corner. Milly yelled at her, 'You bad, bad girl!'

At that precise moment, the hen opened her eyes. I stared in amazement as she flapped her wings. Slowly, the truth sank in. The hen was alive. In fact, she wasn't hurt at all. Seconds later, Cackleberry got up from her sunbathing and waddled off towards the hen house.

I glanced at Lucy, who still cowered beside us. I felt terrible. Poor Lucy had probably just seen Cackleberry sunning herself on the lawn and gone over to sniff her.

I picked Lucy up and rubbed her ears. As she licked my hand, I was determined to learn a lesson from this. How many times have I jumped to conclusions, and in my frustration, dealt out unjust punishment to one of my children? Too many. I am slowly learning not to make hasty judgements; slowly learning to wait until I've heard both sides of the story. It takes patience. I still make mistakes.

That night at dinner, the family had a good laugh at my mistake as the children told Dad all about it. But it hit home again the next day, with the case of the missing pencil.

'Who's taken my pencil?' demanded Milly.

Several of the children glanced up from their schoolwork and shook their heads.

'Jacob!' growled Milly. 'Where is it? You took my pencil!'

'No, I didn't,' said six-year-old Jacob.

'Yes, you did!' snapped Milly. 'That's mine! Give it to me.'

'But, Mum, I didn't!' squeaked Jacob as Milly reached over and tried to grab his pencil.

Time to intervene. 'Hang on a minute, Milly. Are you sure you haven't lost yours?'

'Yes! This is mine! I *know* he took it!'

Jacob clutched his pencil tightly.

I stood between them. 'Milly! Remember Cackleberry! You have a good look under your books before you accuse your brother of something he says he didn't do.'

Milly shot a grumpy look at Jacob and lifted her books. Lo-and-behold, there lay her pencil in full view. She had the good grace to look embarrassed. 'Sorry, Jacob,' she mumbled.

If your family is anything like mine, this sort of drama can happen almost daily. But instead of thinking of squabbles as just a frustrating, annoying part of homeschooling, start thinking of them as the perfect opportunity for teaching some important life skills.

It doesn't matter that the science lesson has to be paused for a while. There are more important things at stake!

Teachable moments often show up at the most inopportune times. But if we learn to recognise them and seize the opportunity, wonderful things can happen. When Johnny wrongly accuses his sister of scribbling on his page, you might decide to call it time for morning tea and then share with your children about times in your own life when you've been quick to blame someone for something, only to find out later that you were wrong. My children always loved it when I said, 'Do you know, I remember a time when I...' (especially if it was some dumb, silly thing I'd done).

In the aftermath of the 'hen that was dead but came alive again' incident, I seized the opportunity to do some fun learning with my family. Let me share some ideas I had after Cackleberry's mistaken demise.

- Ask the children what it means to be a good detective. Answers might include checking the facts and then checking them again (it's very easy to miss something at first glance), not accusing the first person who comes on the crime scene, carefully listening to what the other person is saying or hearing both sides of the story. The Bible warns us about this: 'The first to plead his case seems right, until another comes and examines him' (Proverbs 18:17 NASB). You might like to watch the movie *Basil the Mouse Detective* with your younger children and get them to watch out for some of these things.
- Ask the children how they would feel if their best toy disappeared or turned up broken? Or the chocolate bar they hid in the fridge 'for later' disappeared? Or the wonderful Lego creation they spent hours making lay broken on the floor? (These things happen, you know!)

Explain to them that when things like this upset us, we want to blame someone because we're feeling angry or hurt.
- Ask them to think of some good things to do when they're feeling like that. Tell them how effective a few deep breaths and counting to some number greater than ten can be! Discuss what often happens when we jump to conclusions. (Others get hurt.)
- Ask them to think about what they should do if they've falsely accused someone. This involves learning how to apologise. It needs to be more than a mumbled 'sorry!' In fact, I remember one hilarious morning when we acted out all manner of apologies. I told the children they each had to demonstrate different apologies, good and bad. I couldn't believe how creative they were! Some 'sorrys' were snarled, others were mumbled while the apologiser's evasive eyes looked at the ground or the ceiling. Others were spat out and then followed immediately by 'but you shouldn't have…' It was an entertaining and instructive exercise.
- And what needs to happen when you find the culprit who broke your Lego creation? What then? This is when we all need to learn to forgive. And it's also good to remember that we've all done things 'on accident!'
- What about making a family code to remind each other not to jump to conclusions? A gentle clucking of a hen may work wonders.

Mamas, if you (like me) have jumped the gun and reacted before finding out what really happened, admit your mistake and ask your child to forgive you. It will be a wonderful example of forgiveness that he can learn by.

In her book *Easing the Pain of Parenthood*, Mary Rae Deatrick says, 'If you have previously blown it with your child by speaking heart-damaging words, express your grief to him or her and ask his forgiveness. Turn the tables on failure by walking in words of forgiveness and love. There are hundreds of words to choose from. Take your pick. For myself, I am particularly fond of "forgive" and "love" and "care" and "appreciate" and "respect" and "need". They team especially well with "I" and "you".' [122]

Whereas you can ignore some conflict and leave it to the children to sort out, certain sibling conflict needs to be handled swiftly and consistently. A swift consequence will carry more weight than a dozen long-winded lectures. And if our response is consistent, the children will learn. For example, if two of your children are always fighting over their toys, Mum can walk in and remove the toy, calmly but firmly. 'If you fight over a toy, you lose the toy.' No arguments. Smile and walk away. After a while, they'll figure out that they're better off playing together or taking turns.

If your children are often coming to fisticuffs, you need to make sure that the consequence for their fighting is always more unpleasant than any pleasure they may have derived from the fight. It might mean an earlier bedtime, or the confiscation of some special toy, or the withholding of some enjoyable activity, or some time on their own to think about what has just happened. The important thing is to be consistent. With any consequence, you need to make sure it's one that you will have the energy and determination to enforce (not so jolly easy sometimes!).

Mamas, this awful pattern of squabbles and intense sibling conflict can be broken by our commitment to change the atmosphere of our home. Read the chapter about creating a gezellige home again. Determine you'll create your own family mission statement and get everyone's agreement on the acceptable and desired family culture – Milly's 'bufiful family culture'.

Perhaps you've let certain behaviours take root in your home simply because you're just too exhausted to deal with them. Don't beat yourself up about it; just ask God to give you the energy to set things right. Make small changes. Remember the story of the *Titanic*? Just a few slight adjustments of our course can make all the difference. Your children may be scratchy and grumpy because they're tired. An earlier dinner and bedtime might make all the difference. The problem of sibling jealousy may fade if you set in place one-on-one dates with each child. Some regular 'toddler-free' space for an older child might help them cope with the demanding, constant presence of a young sibling who adores his older brother and wants to follow him everywhere.

Ideally, we want to reach the place where we're doing more positive things to change the family dynamics rather than constantly dealing with negative behaviour. Anything that fosters togetherness will reap huge rewards. Family fun nights, playing board games together, reading great books together, going on family adventures…

Despite all this, I know there will be times when we feel stretched to the limit, like 'butter scraped on too much bread'. But take heart, mamas! Every time you deal with a squabble or intervene in a sibling fracas, you are teaching your children skills that will stay with them throughout their whole life, enriching their friendships, marriages and careers.

They will be learning life-long lessons at home amid the fray.

CHAPTER THIRTY

The Burdened Donkey

*My mother was the making of me. She was so true and so sure of me
I felt I had something to live for – someone I must not disappoint.
The memory of my mother will always be a blessing to me.*

—Thomas A. Edison[123]

Someone once said to Mother Teresa, 'I wouldn't do what you're doing for all the money in the world.' She replied with a smile, 'Neither would I!'

I shared in an earlier chapter about the time I cared for a newborn baby prior to her adoption. She was unsettled and cried a lot at night, and I became desperate for sleep. At the same time, my strong-willed child demanded my attention and fussed when I couldn't give it to her. Everything seemed to pile in on top of me. I felt tired and overwhelmed. After one ghastly night, I checked my emails before calling the children to devotions. Chris had sent me an email with a question written in the subject line: Do you ever feel like this? And he'd attached this photo.

Overloaded donkey[124]

I laughed till I cried. I was that donkey! Burdened down, helpless, unable to do anything or go anywhere. That morning, I printed off six copies of the photo and gave one to each of the children. We all laughed as we studied the pitiful donkey. And then I asked if the picture made them think of any verse in the Bible. Straightaway, Katie said it reminded her of Jesus telling those who were weary and heavy laden to come to him. Yes! Just the answer I wanted.

> Come to me, all you who are weary and burdened, and I will give you rest. Take my yoke upon you and learn from me, for I am gentle and humble in heart, and you will find rest for your souls. For my yoke is easy and my burden is light (Matthew 11:28).

What a beautiful verse! Are you weary? Come to him. Burdened? He will give you rest. How I needed to hear those words. We had a wonderful time that morning as we talked about the photo. I told them that the Bible teaches that we have an enemy of our souls who wants to burden us down so we can't move or go anywhere.

'Be alert and of sober mind. Your enemy the devil prowls around like a roaring lion looking for someone to devour. Resist him, standing firm in the faith, because you know that the family of believers throughout the world is undergoing the same kind of sufferings.

And the God of all grace, who called you to his eternal glory in Christ, after you have suffered a little while, will himself restore you and make you strong, firm and steadfast. To him be the power for ever and ever. Amen' (1 Peter 5:8–11).

But we also have an advocate! (There's that word again.) Someone committed to helping and supporting us. 'And if anyone sins, we have an Advocate with the Father, Jesus Christ the righteous' (1 John 2:1–2 NASB). We can cast all our cares and anxieties upon him because he cares for us (1 Peter 5:7).

I love what the Scottish evangelist Henry Drummond wrote about yokes. He said that a yoke is never intended as a burden. Rather, it is designed to make an animal's burden lighter and easier to carry.

> Attached to the oxen in any other way than by a yoke, the plough would be intolerable. Worked by means of a yoke, it is light. A yoke is not an instrument of torture: it is an instrument of mercy. It is not meant to give pain, but to save pain. And what is the burden? It is not some burden especially laid upon a Christian; it is what all men bear. It is simply life, the general burden of life which all must carry. Christ saw that some men took life painfully. To some it was a weariness, to others a failure, to many a tragedy and to all a struggle and a pain. And what he tells us is this: "Carry it as I do. Take life as I take it. Take my yoke and learn of me, and you will find it easy." [125]

After we'd read Christ's beautiful invitation, I asked the children to write something on each of the packages that were weighing the donkey down in the picture – things that they thought could make a person feel weary and heavy laden. We read them out when we'd all finished: worry, fear, sickness, failure, financial concerns (that was mine), guilt, responsibilities (another one of mine)... it made an impressive list.

As homeschooling mamas, we can fall into the trap of heaping burdens upon ourselves in our eagerness to do a sterling job. I've seen many fellow homeschooling mamas carrying the heavy burden of unrealistic expectations. If ever we need Christ's yoke to help us carry our burdens, it's in our homeschooling. We need to take his yoke upon us and learn from him, and then we'll find rest even in the midst of the challenge.

As we face the weeks and months and years of homeschooling, it's easy to feel daunted by all the challenges that we know it will hold for us. But here's an encouraging thought, mamas! All the great heroes of the faith, all the missionaries we read about, and the men and women whose biographies we devour shared a common factor: challenges. Every one of them responded to and engaged in a challenge.

God told Noah to build an ark. He did so amid the mocking and scorn of ungodly men. Abram faced a challenge: 'Leave your country, your people and your father's household and go to a land I will show you' (Genesis 12:1).

Joseph had God-given dreams, but the many years he had to wait until the fulfilment of those dreams can be summed up in the one word: challenges. Betrayal, slavery, temptation, abandonment, loss, years in prison…

What about Paul? He talks about sleepless nights, shipwrecks, floggings, bandits, and hunger.

God chose Joshua to succeed Moses and lead the people of Israel into the promised land. Joshua found the courage to fulfil this challenging role because of God's promise that he would be with him. 'As I was with Moses, so I will be with you; I will never leave you nor forsake you. Be strong and courageous, because you will lead these people to inherit the land I swore to their ancestors to give them. Be strong and very courageous' (Joshua 1:5–6).

Each of the disciples responded to a challenge, a call. They had to leave their nets, their business and their known way of life in order to follow Christ.

And then there's us, the homeschooling mamas! We have chosen to go against the popular education trend in our society and have embraced a calling that will test our strength, resolve, faith and commitment.

A mother of six children once told British evangelist Gipsy Smith that she wanted to be involved in evangelism and missions. He replied, 'Madam, the mission field does not need you. Your children need you first. They are your mission field.' [126]

How true. There is no greater task for us than to teach our children about the love of God and raise them to be people who will impact the world for righteousness. Such a big calling, one that could weigh us down like the burdened donkey. But let's come to Jesus with all our burdens, all our cares and all our worries and find his rest.

CHAPTER THIRTY-ONE

Refreshing at the Brook of Cherith

*There are only two lasting bequests we can hope to give our children.
One of these is roots; the other, wings.*

—Hodding Carter [127]

I had a dream some time ago of a woman kneeling on the ground. She wore a simple blue and white sari over the top of her everyday clothes, which reminded me of Mother Teresa. As I approached her, she looked up at me, and wailed, 'I'm so tired!' I woke from my dream with a 'knowing' that this woman was exhausted from all the work of the service she was doing in caring for others. A verse from Jeremiah also burned in my mind: 'I'll refresh tired bodies; I'll restore tired souls' (Jeremiah 31:25 MSG).

With the dream still vivid in my mind, I prayed for my fellow homeschooling mamas. We have all experienced times when we feel worn out, discouraged or exhausted. Our days are full and demanding.

In Jeremiah 31, we read an account of another dream. I encourage you to read it. It's a beautiful description of the restoration of God's people; of joy and gladness, of tears turned to laughter, of children returning from the land of the enemy, of hope for our children and of refreshing for tired bodies and restoration for tired souls.

Jeremiah finishes the account of his dream by saying, 'At this point I awoke, and looked around, and my sleep was sweet to me' (Jeremiah 31:26 NKJV).

How wonderful! I want a dream like that.

I remember a particular day some years ago when Chris and I were in the middle of building our house. I was feeling glum about something – the funny thing is, I can't even remember what it was now! But I recall slumping down on a pile of concrete blocks at the building site and Chris asking me what the matter was. 'Everything,' I told him.

My darling husband looked at me with a slight smile in his eyes, and replied, 'Oh. "Everything" is hard to fix!'

I chuckle to myself as I remember that conversation. How easy it is for me to become a bit of a drama queen. Perhaps we all need to watch out for exaggeration. If we're not careful, we can get into the habit of making mountains out of molehills and indulging in over-reactive responses to minor issues. I'm reminded of Amy Carmichael's encouragement in her book *Gold by Moonlight*. The book deals with physical pain, bereavement, suffering and trials – it's a beautiful, encouraging read.

Amy writes, 'Strewn among the big and really shattering things there are often tiresome trifles that can seem quite important and draw attention to themselves. And yet, "They are gone. Why write their epitaph?" As a way of dealing with the little ills of life it is excellent; a bad night, a bad day, a worry, a small pain, a petty annoyance. "It is gone. Why write its epitaph?" [128]

There you go, mamas. What a great way to keep a bad night or a bad day in perspective. 'Why write its epitaph?' has become a common phrase in our household.

I'm reminded of Elijah by the brook of Cherith. He had just triumphed over all the prophets of Baal and seen a huge demonstration of God's power.

But now he's hiding in fear from Jezebel, exhausted and discouraged to the point of wanting to die. He falls asleep, exhausted, beneath a bush. An angel of the Lord comes to him and wakes him up, offering him water to drink and bread to eat. After the meal, Elijah sleeps again and then is awakened a second time by the angel and encouraged to eat and drink some more. Strengthened by that food, Elijah travels forty days and nights to Horeb, the mountain of God. Once he reaches Horeb, God appears to Elijah and asks him a question. In answer, Elijah complains that the Israelites have rejected God's covenant, torn down the altars and killed the prophets. He then informs God that he is the only prophet left, and that he's a marked man. I love God's response. He informs Elijah that in fact there are 7,000 prophets still living who have not bowed the knee to Baal.

How easy it is to succumb to despair when we're exhausted; to exaggerate the situation and not assess it accurately. I have found that many of my lowest times have happened after some high point, some thrilling experience. Peter, James and John experienced this when they descended from the mount of transfiguration and then faced their inability to heal the young boy afflicted with seizures. On a smaller scale, it's like the blues children (and adults) often get when they come home to normal life after an exciting time away at camp.

I now know to prepare myself for the possibility of feeling blue or unmotivated following a high point in my life. When I feel a touch of melancholy, I tell myself that it will pass. Mamas, this can sometimes happen when we return to our homes and family after a wonderful weekend away at a homeschooling conference. We head home full of joy and hope and with the messages we've heard thrilling our hearts. We have such high expectations of sharing it all with our family. But then reality hits. We walk in the door and glimpse stacks of dirty dishes on the kitchen bench.

We've been hoping that hubby and the children would have cleaned the house and prepared a lovely meal to welcome us home. Instead, the house is a mess. No one has swept the floor the whole time we've been away, and there's no sign of any meal. At this point, it's easy to tumble headlong into a melancholic response.

God's promise is to refresh our tired souls. Like the woman in my dream, we reach a point where we collapse to our knees and wail to anyone who will listen, 'I'm so tired!' However, it sometimes takes us a good while to reach the point where we realise just how depleted we are. Mamas, let's learn to recognise the telltale signs earlier than that. Are you snapping at your children or your husband? Do little things send you into a flood of tears? Does the thought of having to tidy the lounge again make you feel exhausted? If so, it's time to take action.

After sharing my dream with the children, we had fun discussing what someone could do if they felt that tired. Let me share their entertaining but pertinent ideas and then add some of my own:

- Get good sleep. (OK, that's often easier said than done.)
- Drink plenty of water. (Someone has been listening to Daddy!)
- Eat properly. (This point gave me a great opportunity to talk about vegetables.)
- Have an energy drink. (Hmm… I wasn't so sure about that.)
- Don't stay up all night. (This I totally agree with! How many times have I set myself up for a meltdown by staying up late to do some writing? Or painting. Or to finish a project.)
- Prioritise. (Here, my children suggested that I didn't have to finish painting the windows if I was already feeling overloaded. From the mouths of babes… I agreed.

I often try to do too much; to squeeze too many things into my busy day. I acknowledged to them that I needed to pause and take a long, hard look at all the things that were crowding into my days. At that point a question began to niggle at the edges of my mind... is the woman in my dream me?)

- Train your children to help with the workload. Mamas, we need to do this! Don't rush around doing everything yourself. Delegate. Teach. Train. I know this takes time, and at the start, it would be way quicker to just do the job yourself, but oh! it's worth it in the long run.
- Accept the help of others. 'When Moses' hands grew tired, they took a stone and put it under him and he sat on it. Aaron and Hur held his hands up – one on one side, one on the other – so that his hands remained steady till sunset' (Exodus 17:12). We could all do with finding an Aaron and a Hur in our lives. Someone who will stand alongside us and encourage us in practical ways. Paul commends Onesiphorus, who searched throughout Rome until he found where Paul was imprisoned. He was not ashamed of Paul's chains and often refreshed his spirit (2 Timothy 1:16–18). How lovely to think of that young man visiting Paul in his dank prison cell and bringing such encouragement, simply by his company. Many times, Paul speaks of being encouraged and refreshed by the company of different believers – Stephanas, Fortunatus, Onesiphorus and Achaicus. And this illustrates a wonderful truth. 'Whoever refreshes others will be refreshed' (Proverbs 11:25).
- Pace yourself. Remember the tortoise and the hare.

- Don't try to do everything. Let some things go. I confess to not doing a lot of ironing. But I still felt somewhat chagrined when little Jacob ran past me one day as I was ironing a shirt for Chris. He screeched to a halt beside me and then asked in astonishment, 'Mummy, do you know how to iron?' Sigh.
- Factor in some rest time. We need to let the shepherd of our souls lead us beside quiet waters of rest. For it is there he restores our soul.
- But here's the biggie! In Psalm 73:26, 28, Asaph writes, 'My flesh and my heart may fail, but God is the strength of my heart and my portion forever... but as for me, it is good to be near God.' The New American Standard version puts the last portion of the verse as: 'the nearness of God is my good.' The nearness of God. This is where we find refreshment. We cannot hope to be strong in the Lord unless we know the nearness of God. Isaiah 40 reminds us that even young people get tired and grow weary. We can't do all that our homeschooling demands in our own strength. We need him! He will not grow tired or weary.

'Do you not know? Have you not heard? The Lord is the everlasting God, the Creator of the ends of the Earth. He will not grow tired or weary, and his understanding no one can fathom. He gives strength to the weary and increases the power of the weak. Even youths grow tired and weary, and young men stumble and fall; but those who hope in the Lord will renew their strength. They will soar on wings like eagles; they will run and not grow weary, they will walk and not be faint' (Isaiah 40:28–31).

In Acts 3:19, Peter encourages his listeners to repent and turn to God, telling them that times of refreshing come from the presence of the Lord. God gives us the wonderful promise that if we draw near to him, he will draw near to us (James 4:9). Times of refreshing. What a lovely thought. Once, when I was praying and lamenting that my spirit was so dry and tired, I heard the Lord gently chide me, reminding me I had been cheating my heart of the greatest source of refreshment – the word of God! The Apostle Paul writes that 'through the endurance taught in the Scriptures and the encouragement they provide we might have hope' (Romans 15:4).

Mamas, don't cheat yourself of the most vital and common way God strengthens us and renews and refreshes our spirits. Read the Bible. And as you read, ask and listen for a word from God. Isaiah 50:4 says, 'The Sovereign Lord has given me a well-instructed tongue, to know the word that sustains the weary.' Jot these words down in a notebook so you can look back at them. Write them in notes around your house.

I've greatly enjoyed reading a book by Linda Dillow called *Calm My Anxious Heart*. In it, she shares an old translation of Psalm 42:5. Let me share the more common translation and then the ancient one.

'Why are you in despair, O my soul? And why have you become disturbed within me? Hope in God, for I shall again praise him for the help of his presence' (Psalm 42:5). There it is again. His presence. Refreshing and help are found in his presence.

Now listen to this beautiful translation: 'Why droopest thou, O my soul, and frettest so upon me? Hope thou in God, for I shall yet praise Him for the help of His countenance.' [129]

I *love* that! Many times, my soul has drooped and fretted. I'm going to memorise that old translation so I can address my soul in the appropriate way next time it droops!

We all need to learn how to encourage our own souls in the Lord. King David did just that when he returned from a battle to find the enemy had destroyed the city and taken all the men's wives and children. The men wept until they had no more strength to weep. But then David 'strengthened himself in the Lord' (1 Samuel 30:6). No droopy soul for him. He put his hope in God, found strength, and then pursued the enemy and got everyone back, safe and sound.

No doubt about it, mamas – we have taken on a big job, a great calling, one that is going to demand our all. Unless we are being constantly refreshed, we will end up feeling depleted, exhausted and finished. We all reach a point in our 'marathon' when we feel like we just can't go any further. A new baby, sickness, menopause, financial stress, an ever-expanding classroom and any number of other demands might precipitate it.

When you think you've got no more to give, no more energy, no more joy, no more vision, God wants to refresh you. He wants to give you your second wind.

CHAPTER THIRTY-TWO

Finding Your Second Wind

If it was going to be easy to raise kids, it would never have started with something called labour.

—Barbara Johnson [130]

I had a good laugh one day while reading some definitions of the phenomenon of athletes finding their second wind. Listen to this one from Wikipedia: 'The phenomenon has come to be used as a metaphor for continuing on with renewed energy past the point thought to be one's prime, whether in other sports, careers, or life in general.' [131]

Past the point thought to be one's prime. That earned a genuine chuckle from me. I was well past my prime when I finished homeschooling Jacob! Reading that definition makes me think we all need to find our second wind so we can continue with renewed energy. I mentioned earlier that the homeschooling 'event' is most definitely not a sprint. It's a marathon. So, this analogy is a perfect fit. Documented experiences of the second wind go back at least 100 years, when athletes understood it to be a commonly held fact of exercise. Let me share some definitions I've read:

- The return of relative ease of breathing after the initial exhaustion that occurs during continued physical exertion.[132]
- Restored energy or strength.[133]
- Renewed ability to continue in an effort.[134]
- 'Finding your second wind is a phenomenon in distance running, such as marathons or road running (as well as other sports), whereby an athlete who is out of breath and too tired to continue suddenly finds the strength to press on at top performance with less exertion.' [135]

Out of breath. Too tired to continue. Exhaustion. Does that sound like you?

There is no doubt about it – we have taken on a big job, a great calling; one that is going to demand our all. We need the renewed ability to continue in an effort. We need to find our second wind.

Chattanooga Track Club president Bill Moran said that the sensation can be a godsend. 'To me, it just feels like you have something left in your tank. It's a confidence that, between your energy stores and your respiration, you feel like you can finish. Your body is telling your mind, "I can do this." [136]

Studies have found similar results when researchers have offered encouragement to subjects during exercise. It reminds me of the day nine-year-old Milly competed in her first Weetbix Tryathlon. The whole family went along to cheer for her. I felt nervous as I watched her dive into the pool with scores of other children. The pool became a mess of thrashing, surging arms and legs. I cried a few tears when I saw the first child emerge and realised it was my daughter. She did a quick changeover for the bike leg of the race and was off in a flash. When we saw her again at the end of that leg, I could tell she was exhausted.

'You can do it, Milly!' shouted Katie, as Milly pulled off her helmet and stacked her bike, ready to start the 1.5 km run. 'I'm so tired, Mummy!' wailed Milly as she ran past me.

'Just do your best, darling,' I yelled to her. I didn't know how she was going to finish it. The next minute, I saw my oldest son, Josiah, sprint after her. He ran beside her the whole way, encouraging her to keep going. We cheered and clapped as they crossed the finish line. Milly was all smiles when Hamish Carter, the Olympian triathlete, presented her with her medal.

So, how do we find our second wind? In Ezekiel 37, we read the thrilling account of the valley covered in dry bones.

> God asks Ezekiel a question: 'Son of man, can these bones live?' I said, 'Sovereign Lord, you alone know.'
> Then he said to me, 'Prophesy to these bones and say to them, "Dry bones, hear the word of the Lord! This is what the Sovereign Lord says to these bones: I will make breath enter you, and you will come to life. I will attach tendons to you and make flesh come upon you and cover you with skin; I will put breath in you, and you will come to life. Then you will know that I am the Lord."'
> So I prophesied as I was commanded. And as I was prophesying, there was a noise, a rattling sound, and the bones came together, bone to bone. I looked, and tendons and flesh appeared on them and skin covered them, but there was no breath in them.
> Then he said to me, 'Prophesy to the breath; prophesy, son of man, and say to it, "This is what the Sovereign Lord says: Come, breath, from the four winds and breathe into these slain, that they may live."' So I prophesied as he commanded me, and breath entered them; they came to life and stood up on their feet – a vast army.
> Then he said to me: 'Son of man, these bones are the people of Israel. They say, "Our bones are dried up and our hope is gone; we are cut off."

> Therefore prophesy and say to them: "This is what the Sovereign Lord says: My people, I am going to open your graves and bring you up from them; I will bring you back to the land of Israel. Then you, my people, will know that I am the Lord, when I open your graves and bring you up from them. I will put my Spirit in you and you will live, and I will settle you in your own land. Then you will know that I the Lord have spoken, and I have done it, declares the Lord'" (Ezekiel 37:3–14).

The breath of God. Our second wind. We may feel just like the people of Israel did – that our hope is gone and our bones are dried up. But a simple word from God will breathe new life, new energy and new hope into us. I've shared already about my own word from God that breathed new life into my own despairing heart in just three words – 'she's a champion!'

When I was in my early twenties and walking through a dark time in my life, it was the word of God that helped me through it. There's a verse in Psalm 119 that perfectly sums up my experience: 'If your law had not been my delight, I would have perished in my affliction. I will never forget your precepts for by them you have revived me' (Psalm 119:92 NASB 1995).

Mamas, let me encourage you again to read the Scriptures. No matter how busy and demanding your life is, try to make some time each day to read his Word. I know that for some of you, it will seem like I'm suggesting the impossible. But I also know how desperately important it is. This is the most common way God strengthens us and renews our spirits. Don't cheat yourself of it. When you open the Bible, take a moment and ask God to breathe into your spirit. And then speak it out: 'Dry bones, hear the word of the Lord!'

I love to read Ezekiel's account of the rattling and noise as those dry bones hear the word of the Lord and come to life. Hallelujah! God can open up our graves and bring us up from them (v13).

As he breathes into our spirit, we will find our second wind, and with it, the strength to continue with our homeschooling (even well past our prime).

An interesting phenomenon of the second wind is that an athlete never knows when it will kick in. So too with us. It may come when we least expect it, or in a way we least expect, but when it comes, we will find the strength and the energy to finish our course. I found my second wind unexpectedly one night when I tumbled exhausted into bed and turned out the light. Seconds later, a message began to glow on the ceiling above me. Dear Jacob had somehow stacked a pile of cushions and pillows on the bed and got high enough to write a message with his glow-in-the-dark stars on the ceiling. 'I love U'.

That simple message of love still delights me every night when we turn out our light. Back then, it was just what I needed to hear. It gave me the encouragement I needed to just keep persevering day by day.

I once read the story of a person who told his friend that the two great marvels of America were the Grand Canyon and Helen Keller. His friend replied with a wonderful rebuttal: 'I beg to disagree – the two great marvels are Helen Keller and Anne Sullivan.'

Theirs was a relationship that spanned 49 years. In the early years, Anne needed perseverance and patience to unlock the potential in her young pupil's mind and heart.

In 1916, Helen and Anne delivered a lecture in the small town of Menomonie, western Wisconsin. Let me finish this chapter with what the Dunn County News wrote about their talk:

> 'A message of optimism, of hope, of good cheer, and of loving service was brought to Menomonie Saturday – a message that will linger long with those fortunate enough to have received it. This message came with the visit of Helen Keller and her teacher, Mrs John Macy, and both had a hand in imparting it Saturday evening to a splendid audience that filled The Memorial.

> The wonderful girl who has so brilliantly triumphed over the triple afflictions of blindness, dumbness and deafness, gave a talk with her own lips on "Happiness", and it will be remembered always as a piece of inspired teaching by those who heard it.' [137]

I'm convinced that during her long involvement with Helen, Anne experienced the phenomenon of finding her second wind. Because she didn't give up despite huge challenges and setbacks. She found renewed strength and energy. She finished the course. And as a result, the world was enriched by the life of Helen Keller.

CHAPTER THIRTY-THREE

I Can Plod

I can plod. I can persevere in any definite pursuit. To this I owe everything.

—William Carey [138]

The title of this chapter comes from one of my all-time favourite quotes. William Carey is often called the father of modern missions. Born into a poor family, he left school at fourteen to become a cobbler. But he had both a passion and a remarkable ability for learning languages. He soon developed the habit of studying new languages as he mended shoes, balancing a book on his work bench. He came to faith in his teens and became deeply concerned with the Great Commission.

In 1793, Carey, along with his pregnant wife and young children, set sail on a gruelling five-month sea journey to India. Over the ensuing years, their life in India held countless trials and tests of faith. Carey suffered severe family losses, poor health, and at one point, lost ten years of translation work in a fire. But despite his trials, Carey's contribution to India is legendary.

Before his death, Carey was told that someone wanted to write about his life and achievements. His response was: 'If one should think it worth his while to write my life, I will give you a criterion by which you may judge of its correctness.

If he gives me credit for being a plodder, he will describe me justly. Anything beyond this will be too much. I can plod. I can persevere in any definite pursuit. To this I owe everything.' [139]

I can plod. I can persevere in any definite pursuit. To this I owe everything. Oh, I love those words! Carey knew the taste of failure and the sting of opposition. He knew what it was to be knocked down. But he also knew how to get up again. Proverbs 24:16 (GW) describes him perfectly: 'A righteous person may fall seven times but he gets up again.'

Carey also knew the power of simply plodding. So often, we feel that it's the fastest who wins the race. The brightest who wins the prize. The strongest who wins the fight. And yet, those who persevere often cross the finish line first. The plodders. Aesop immortalised this truth in his fable *The Tortoise and the Hare*.

Albert Einstein said, 'It's not that I'm so clever. It's just that I stay with problems longer.' [140] He knew how to plod. How to persevere. As did Thomas Edison! While inventing the lightbulb, he tried over 2,000 experiments before he succeeded. A reporter asked him what it felt like to have failed so often. I can just imagine the smile on Edison's face as he informed the young reporter that he hadn't failed once. He had invented the lightbulb. It just happened to be a 2,000-step process.

Oh, mamas, how we need to have that attitude! When we wrestle with the challenges of teaching a child long division, or we encounter serious issues with our teenager, let's remember that teaching and raising children is a 2,000-step process (at the very least!).

I love the scene in *Chariots of Fire* when a runner knocks Eric Liddell over in a race. I've seen it so many times and yet still my heart seems to stop as I join Liddell's trainer in watching Eric struggle to get up on his feet and re-join the race. 'Get up, lad. Get up.' [141] There always seems to be a bit of dust in my eye as he starts running again and overtakes all the other competitors to win the race.

I cheer along with the audience as he crosses the finish line. In a way, I feel like I'm joining the great cloud of witnesses Paul wrote about: 'Therefore, since we are surrounded by such a great cloud of witnesses, let us throw off everything that hinders and the sin that so easily entangles. And let us run with perseverance the race marked out for us, fixing our eyes on Jesus, the pioneer and perfecter of faith. For the joy set before him he endured the cross, scorning its shame, and sat down at the right hand of the throne of God. Consider him who endured such opposition from sinners, so that you will not grow weary and lose heart' (Hebrews 12:1–3).

There's no doubt about it. We will all experience times when someone or something knocks us off the racetrack. But great spiritual athletes of the past – those who have completed their events and finished their life race – fill the stands and are eager to encourage the new contestants. We can look to them and see inspiring examples of faith and endurance under every imaginable circumstance as they finish their race. Many of them knew the sting of personal failure, but found healing and redemption, and went on to finish their race. Cheering from the stands are:

- David, who committed adultery and murder
- John the Baptist, with his strange diet and bizarre wardrobe
- John Mark, who fled at Christ's arrest
- Mary, the prostitute
- William Carey, the plodder
- Simon Peter, who denied the Lord three times
- Job, who suffered the loss of children and property
- Stephen, who was hated and stoned
- Amy Carmichael who served God as a single woman in India
- Grandparents, uncles and aunts, friends... the list is endless.

Paul captures the essence of endurance in his letter to the Corinthians: 'We get knocked down, but we get up again and keep going' (2 Corinthians 4:9 TLB). The dictionary offers a few meanings of the word endurance, and each one is inspiring.

- 'The ability to endure an unpleasant or difficult process or situation without giving way.' [142] I smiled when I read the dictionary's example of how to use the word in a sentence: 'She was close to the limit of her endurance.' (Sound familiar, anyone?)
- 'The ability to continue or last, especially despite fatigue, stress or other adverse circumstances.' [143]
- 'The ability of an organism to exert itself and remain active for a long period of time, as well as its ability to resist, withstand, recover from, and have immunity to trauma, wounds, or fatigue.' [144]

Yes, mamas. There's no doubt about it. We need endurance on our homeschooling journey. We must remain active over for a long period of time. We are familiar with the heavy eyelids of fatigue (a rather disturbing image floats into my mind of yours truly being photographed by the children – fast asleep in the chair, the reading book fallen on my lap).

As we discuss the endurance needed for a long race, it's worth mentioning a simple truth. We need to lighten our load. It reminds me of a Russian proverb: 'Even a straw weighs on a journey of a thousand miles.'

We need to let some things go. Jettison whatever surplus weight we're carrying. It might be an excessive tidiness compulsion. Worry. Guilt. These will all weigh heavily on us.

But most importantly, we need to keep our eyes on Jesus. 'And let us run with perseverance the race marked out for us, fixing our eyes on Jesus, the pioneer and perfecter of faith' (Hebrews 12:1–2).

When a vast army comes to wage war against King Jehoshaphat, he determines to seek the Lord and proclaims a fast for all Judah. Both he and the people are alarmed and afraid. But Jehoshaphat stands before the people and prays: 'For we have no power to face this vast army that is attacking us. We do not know what to do, but our eyes are on you' (2 Chronicles 20:12). In answer to his prayer, Jahaziel prophesies that they are not to be discouraged or afraid because the battle is not theirs but God's.

It is so easy to lose heart. We can become alarmed, frightened. Vast armies may surround us, breathing threats. 'But our eyes are on you.' If we fix our eyes on Jesus, the author and perfecter of our faith, our courage will return, and with it, the strength and perseverance to continue.

We read in the faith chapter of Hebrews that Moses 'persevered because he saw him who is invisible' (Hebrews 11:27).

'Therefore, we do not lose heart. Though outwardly we are wasting away, yet inwardly we are being renewed day by day. For our light and momentary troubles are achieving for us an eternal glory that far outweighs them all. So, we fix our eyes not on what is seen, but on what is unseen, since what is seen is temporary, but what is unseen is eternal' (2 Corinthians 4:17,18).

We're all familiar with the story of Peter walking to Jesus on the water. The wind had buffeted the boat all night, and yet Peter had the courage to step out of the boat at Christ's beckoning. But when he takes his eyes off Jesus and looks instead at the wind, fear engulfs his heart, and he begins to sink (Matthew 14).

Mamas, let's fix our eyes on Jesus. Whether it's a storm or an army that surrounds us, let's turn our eyes to Jesus. Christ is the one who will enable us to run our race and finish our course. He is the one who gives strength to the weary. He keeps his promises. He is strong.

Are you feeling weary? Have you lost heart? Paul encourages us to 'consider him who endured such opposition from sinners, so that you will not grow weary and lose heart' (Hebrews 12:3). What does it mean to consider Christ? I think a good definition is 'to look attentively at; to think carefully about.' [145] As we read the Word, and fix the eyes of our heart on Jesus, we will find new strength. We will gather the endurance needed for the next step of our journey. There will be seasons in our homeschooling that are blessed with boundless energy, joy and great progress. Hallelujah! But there will also be seasons when we need to content ourselves with plodding. The Oxford Dictionary defines the word plod as to 'walk doggedly and slowly with heavy steps'. [146] Like William Carey, we will make slow but steady progress as we 'walk doggedly with heavy steps'. But mamas, let's raise a hallelujah here too. We can plod. We can persevere in any given pursuit. To this, we owe everything.

CHAPTER THIRTY-FOUR

Favourite Family Read-Aloud Books

You may have tangible wealth untold, caskets of jewels, and coffers of gold. Richer than I you can never be – I had a mother who read to me.

—Strickland Gillilan [147]

Author Emilie Buchwald said, 'Children are made readers on the laps of their parents.' [148] How true! When I was seven years old and living in Auckland, my parents took up teaching positions at the St Christopher's Anglican Mission school in Popondetta, Papua New Guinea. My siblings and I enjoyed three years of adventure in our new jungle home, where we become explorers in our own wild kingdom. We swam and fished in the rivers and made huts and gardens where we grew pineapples, peanuts and bananas. We chased huge emerald and blue butterflies. We ran barefoot and free, and imagined ourselves as Tarzan and Jane, swinging on vines through the jungle. Vivid, poignant memories. But one of the most enduring, significant memories I have of that time is of us all squashed in Mum and Dad's bed, listening to Dad read to us from *The Chronicles of Narnia* by Tilley light as the monsoon rains pounded the tin roof and geckos scuttled across the ceiling. Gezellig.

Many years later, when I became a mother, I had the joy of reading aloud to my six children every morning, and then listening to Chris read to them by the fire before bedtime. Over those twenty plus years, we devoured so many books – picture books, classics, mysteries, biographies, adventure stories… What a joy! When our last child left home, I grieved the fact that there would be no more reading aloud sessions. But then Chris and I realised that there was nothing stopping us from reading aloud to each other – just the two of us. Since then, we've enjoyed many of James Herriot's books together, among others, and have delighted in the closeness it brings. We are also looking forward to sharing many happy hours reading to our grandchildren in years to come.

Below is a list of some of our favourite books. Of course, I couldn't list them all, but there are enough books here to get you well and truly started.

The ages given are a guide only. The beautiful picture books can be enjoyed by children of all ages – including adults. Books in the 6+ category will be beyond their own reading age, but still can be enjoyed when read by a parent.

Enjoy, mamas! Reading aloud to your children not only brings great joy, but also helps impart spiritual truth, godly values and character growth. Read, read, read!

Picture books

- Beatrix Potter books
- Winnie the Pooh collection and poems by A. A. Milne
- *Wilfred Gordon McDonald Partridge* by Mem Fox
- *Fritz and the Beautiful Horses* by Jan Brett
- Paddington series by Michael Bond
- *The Four Seasons of Brambly Hedge* by Jill Barklem
- *Song and Dance Man* by Karen Ackerman

Favourite Family Read-Aloud Books

- *James Herriot's Treasury for Children* by James Herriot
- *The Christmas Miracle of Jonathan Toomey* by Susan Wojciechowski
- *Library Lion* by Michelle Knudsen
- *Mike Mulligan and His Steam Shovel* by Virginia Lee Burton
- *Curious George* by Hans A. Rey
- *When Jessie Came Across the Sea* by Amy Hest
- *The Gardener* by Sarah Stewart
- *Saint George and the Dragon* by Margaret Hodges
- *The Log Cabin Quilt* by Ellen Howard
- *Mr Brown Can Moo* by Dr Seuss
- Books by Shirley Hughes
- *Pancakes for Findus* by Sven Nordqvist
- *The Gift of the Magi* by O. Henry

6yrs+

- *In Grandma's Attic* by Arleta Richardson
- Little House on the Prairie series by Laura Ingalls Wilder
- *Pollyanna* by Eleanor H. Porter
- *The Matchlock Gun* by Walter D. Edmonds
- *The Adventures of Romy* by Penelope Foote
- *The Chronicles of Narnia* by C. S. Lewis
- *The Wind in the Willows* by Kenneth Grahame

8yrs +

- *The Drover's Road Collection* by Joyce West
- The Barn Chronicles series by Rosie Boom
- *All-of-a-Kind Family* by Sydney Taylor
- *The Great and Terrible Quest* by Margaret Lovett
- *Cheaper by the Dozen* by Frank B. Gilbreth

- *My Friend Flicka* by Mary O'Hara
- *Thunderhead* by Mary O'Hara
- *Freckles* by Gene Stratton-Porter
- *A Girl of the Limberlost* by Gene Stratton-Porter
- *Laddie* by Gene Stratton-Porter
- *Little Women* by Louisa May Alcott
- *Little Men* by Louisa May Alcott
- *Jo's Boys* by Louisa May Alcott
- *The Wheel on the School* by Meindert DeJong
- *The Basket of Flowers* by Christoph von Schmid
- *The Courage of Sarah Noble* by Alice Dalgliesh
- *The Perilous Road* by William O. Steele
- *Carry on, Mr Bowditch* by Jean Lee Latham
- *Charlotte's Web* by E. B. White
- *Miracles on Maple Hill* by Virginia Sorensen
- *The Great Turkey Walk* by Kathleen Karr
- *Mama's Bank Account* by Kathryn Forbes
- Little Britches series by Ralph Moody
- *Caddie Woodlawn* by Carol Ryrie Brink
- *The Railway Children* by Edith Nesbit
- *Otto of the Silver Hand* by Howard Pyle
- *Heidi* by Johanna Spyri
- Viking Quest series by Lois Walfrid Johnson
- *My Side of the Mountain* by Jean Craighead George
- *Duncan's War* by Douglas Bond
- *Jip* by Katherine Paterson
- *Becky Landers Frontier Warrior* by Constance Lindsay Skinner
- *Miracles on Maple Hill* by Virginia Sorensen
- *The Hiding Place* by Corrie ten Boom
- *The Trumpeter of Krakow* by Eric P. Kelly
- The Kingdom series by Chuck Black

Favourite Family Read-Aloud Books

- *The Silver Sword* by Ian Serraillier
- *Anne of Green Gables* by Lucy Maud Montgomery
- *I Am David* by Ann Holm
- *On to Oregon!* By Honoré Morrow
- *Where Lions Roar at Night* by Rosie Boom
- Trailblazer books by Dave & Neta Jackson
- *Hinds' Feet on High Places* by Hannah Hurnard
- *Seeking Allah, Finding Jesus* by Nabeel Qureshi
- *Death of a Guru* by Rabindranath R. Maharaj
- *The Secret Garden* by Frances Hodgson Burnett
- Ranger's Apprentice series by John Flanagan
- Brotherband Chronicles series by John Flanagan
- Redwall series by Brian Jacques
- The Green Ember series by S. D. Smith
- *What Katy Did* by Susan Coolidge
- *No One Went to Town* by Phyllis Johnston
- *Black Boots and Buttonhooks* by Phyllis Johnston
- *Runaway Settlers* by Elsie Locke
- *The Shakespeare Stealer* by Gary Blackwood
- *Adam of the Road* by Elizabeth Gray Vining
- *A Single Shard* by Linda Sue Park
- *Hittite Warrior* by Joanne Williamson
- *House of Sixty Fathers* by Meindert DeJong
- *The Golden Goblet* by Eloise Jarvis McGraw
- Books by Michael Morpurgo
- Books by Patricia St John
- *Children on the Oregon Trail* by Anna Rutgers van der Loeff
- Sadie Rose Adventure series by Hilda Stahl
- *Christy* by Catherine Marshall
- The Rocky Ridge Years series by Roger Lea MacBride
- *Goodnight Mister Tom* by Michelle Magorian

- *Pocahontas: True Princess* by Mari Hanes
- *Two Mighty Rivers: Son of Pocahontas* by Mari Hanes
- *The Great Trek* by Ion L. Idriess
- Biggles series by W. E. Johns
- Mandie Adventure series by Lois Gladys Leppard

These books represent just the tip of the iceberg. Have fun, mamas! And whatever you do, don't stop reading aloud just because your child has become an avid reader. If you have to, hide the read-aloud book! As I've stressed before, the joy of reading together and sharing the same emotions is invaluable. Gezellig, mamas. Gezellig.

CHAPTER THIRTY-FIVE

A Fence Around the Cuckoo

Try to raise up mothers. Mothers are the want of this world.

—Catherine Booth [149]

As Chris and I welcomed more and more children into our family, my classroom grew and grew. I became busier and busier. The washing pile seemed never-ending. I marked more and more papers and wrestled with algebra while trying to teach the youngest to read. But the time soon came when no new students enrolled in the Boom schoolroom, and the oldest pupils began sitting their final exams. I'll never forget the day when Josiah graduated, and my schoolroom shrunk just that little bit. I had the sudden awareness that things would change quickly over the next few years. I realised how important it was to enjoy every minute.

It was an exciting time as each of the children travelled somewhat different roads to their chosen careers. When Josiah and Katie turned 16, they began correspondence and sat NCEA Level 2 with Te Kura. Josiah then applied for a discretionary entrance to Massey University. Katie chose to have a gap year before starting a music degree at Vision College.

Chris and I will never forget the amazement and joy we felt when she told us that she wanted to stay at home and take over the homeschooling of her younger siblings for a year so that I could help Chris build our house. What a fantastic year that was!

Ellie sat NCEA Levels 2 and 3 with Te Kura, while Milly and Jacob earned their Year 13 certificates with ACE (Accelerated Christian Education). The biggest surprise came one morning in January when I received a phone call from a local builder offering Samuel an apprenticeship. Just like that, our plans changed. Instead of beginning Year 12 as expected, Samuel bought some tools and began the career he'd always dreamed of. It came as a real shock to his mama, though. I had presumed I'd have two more years teaching him, and I grieved that loss, but at the same time, I knew it was the right path for him.

So, for the last three years of my homeschooling journey, it was just Jacob and me – a very different but incredibly special time. How I treasure these years of homeschooling. What else allows you to spend beautiful, unrushed hours with your 17-year-old son, reading God's word and great books together and beginning each day praying together? I didn't want it to end. But of course, it had to.

Homeschooling my children has been my magnum opus, my life's greatest work. I spent twice as long teaching them as I did nursing. As the end of my homeschooling drew near, I experienced a vast range of emotions. I wondered what life would look like. Would I feel lost, and lacking in purpose and direction? Would I encounter melancholy, thinking about all the happy times we'd had? (Strange how easy it is for me now to let the struggles and difficulties take back seat!) Would I feel like there was a huge, gaping hole in my day? Each of these were potential realities. But I was determined to prepare for the transition. Someone said that life has a middle name – Change. While some people thrive on change, I've never been a fan.

I'm too content with what I have right now. So, when inevitable change approaches, I've learned that I must ready myself.

I began praying that God would show me my next big assignment; that I would catch a vision for the next season of my life. I realised that the busy, noisy bustle of a large family would give way to a quieter, slower way of life; that Chris and I would enjoy each other's company and do things together – just the two of us. As we both began to think about these changes, and experience evenings where there was just the two of us for a meal, we would look at each other and smile, and say, 'Back to where it all began. Just the two of us.'

I know that some of you reading this will think it sounds like a dream – that you can't wait for the solitude and quiet. The thought of enjoying a candlelit dinner for two sounds like heaven. And it is wonderful! But we all need to find the joy of whatever season we're in. Your time will come. In the meantime, try to enjoy the noise. Revel in the bustle and constant activity.

I can still picture my six young children around the table, laughing and ribbing each other as they did their schoolwork, and I marvel at what they've turned out to be. It was a mystery, of course, back then. When Josiah spent hours playing with Lego, I didn't know he'd become a property valuer. I might have guessed Katie would do something with music, but a master's degree in music therapy? I didn't even know such a thing existed. When three-year-old Ellie used to write *tip tip tip tip* over a page and then say, 'Uh oh!' while twinking the words out again and again, I never guessed she'd end up being an opera singer. I thought Milly might become a vet, but never guessed I'd have the thrill of seeing her choose nursing. Watching Samuel always creating things with his hands and being so keen to help Daddy with any building projects, I guessed he would become a carpenter. Now, I've had the joy of seeing my qualified builder build his own tiny home.

And little Jacob, so enthusiastic and excitable, creating great Lego structures and all kinds of drawings – a civil engineer? How marvellous!

I'm very aware that not everyone will resonate with the joyful feelings I experienced at the completion of my homeschooling journey. Perhaps when you think back over your experience, whether it was six months or ten years, all you can remember are the bitter struggles, the feeling of being overwhelmed and a ghastly sense of failure. You may reminisce with no warm nostalgia at all, just a huge relief that it's over. Perhaps you're beating yourself up that you didn't try hard enough; that you never did find the joy. Perhaps you chose to send the children back to school. But let me encourage you, dear mama. Never mind that it wasn't perfect; the very fact that you tried to do what you felt was best for your children deserves commendation. And you may never know the positive impact it had on your child's life.

Each one of us can finish phases in our lives with the feeling that we could have, and should have, done better. How vulnerable we are in that respect when it comes to parenting! But one thought never ceases to encourage me. God gave us these children, knowing that we wouldn't do a perfect job.

So, dear mamas, when the last assignment has been done and the last test sat, is this the end? In one way, yes. You can take a deep breath and give yourself a well-earned treat for having completed your homeschooling journey. But in another way, no. There is an ongoing need to show our children by our own example what it means to follow Jesus and walk in the fear of the Lord, to teach them wisdom, to offer them wise counsel and support. This will never end. We can still speak into our children's lives when they are twenty, thirty, fifty… They need a mother's input through the years of first jobs, first loves and first heartbreaks. We need to pray for them every day.

And we need to keep connected with them in whatever way we can. We must stay involved in their lives. We may not be folding their undies anymore, but they still need us to encourage and support them on their own journeys.

Last weekend, Jacob, our youngest, married Christina. Chris and I helped him carry out boxes of clothes and possessions to the car, and as we did, the season of raising a large family closed behind us. We became official empty nesters.

That night, I folded the last few socks and shirts he'd left behind and thought about the past three decades I've had of folding mountains of washing. From now on, I won't need to hold each pair of undies or socks up and ask, 'Whose are these?' Maybe that sounds wonderful to you busy mamas now, but I must confess, I had a wee cry that night. And when Pierre the cat prowled upstairs, meowing mournfully, looking for Jacob, I cried again. But only for a moment. There are two full hearts in this empty nest.

I poured out my thanks to God for the amazing journey I've had as a mother, and then turned my heart to the future, to new joys and to new adventures. Who knows? I may be needed to help teach my grandchildren in years to come. And I can always visit my grown children in their own homes and help fold their washing. But in the meantime, I have caught a vision for this next season of my life. I'm going to enjoy the companionship of my best friend and lover. Each day, I'm going to sit in my quiet office and write, write, write. I'm going to light a candle at each meal for two that Chris and I enjoy in front of our Homewood stove. I'm going to put on my overalls and help Chris build his implement shed and the pioneer cabin down by the river. I'm going to invite the children home for family dinners and revel again in their noisy laughter and banter.

Ruth Park grew up in New Zealand during the Depression and she wrote a wonderful memoir, which I've just finished reading.

It's charming, witty and poignant. The title refers to a quote on the front page of the book: 'The three wise men of Gotham loved the spring so dearly and could not bear to bid her farewell, so they built a fence around the cuckoo.' [150]

When I read that, I had a burst of self-realisation – I have loved my house being full of children and have loved homeschooling them. I've loved this season so dearly that I've been tempted to build a fence around it, so that it never ends. But I mustn't do that. The cuckoo must fly away at the end of spring. The children must fly from home. And I must be willing to let them go. But I can watch them fly away with my blessing and love. As someone said, we've been preparing them to walk away from us ever since we helped them take their first steps. Our challenge as empty nesters is to maintain a warm, loving gezellige home that they will still want to come home to. And bring their children to. Now that's a lovely thought.

Postscript

Thank you, dear readers for letting me share my heart with you. I've struggled with sending this book to the printer, knowing that I could have said so much more; that there are whole areas that I haven't even touched on. Important areas. But I realise that *Heart to Heart with Rosie Boom* was never destined to be an exhaustive resource, a complete encyclopedia of homeschooling wisdom. I'm content to know that as I've sat writing, I've 'seen' so many of your faces, thought of so many of your stories, and felt as though you've been sitting across the lunch table with me. I've tried to share my heart with you and encourage you.

Many of you have travelled the road with me over the years. Thank you for all your encouragement, wisdom and companionship! It's been a wonderful pilgrimage. But I also know that many of you will be new friends to me. I wish you all the best on your homeschooling journey! I hope and pray that something I've written may help you along the way and cheer and strengthen your heart. I hope we get to meet sometime. Till then, may the Lord pour out his richest blessings on your family. May he strengthen your hands when they hang down and fill your heart with resolve and joy. May your children thrive within the nurture of your love and may yours truly be a gezellige home.

With love,

Rosie

Acknowledgements

- Chris, my husband, best friend and companion for 35 years. You caught the vision with me to homeschool our children and have worked hard through the years to make it possible for me to stay at home to teach them. Thank you with all my heart. You've been with me every step of the way. And now, in our empty nest, you've supported me in writing this book, encouraging me whenever I became discouraged. You kept reminding me of how important it is for the next generation of homeschooling mamas to be cheered on by those who have gone before. I feel so incredibly blessed to have you as my companion for life. I love you.

- My precious children, Josiah, Katie, Eliza, Milly, Samuel and Jacob. I feel so incredibly blessed to have been your mama. Thank you for all the joy, the noise, the banter, the adventures, the cuddles and the love. My cup overflows. Thank you for letting me share some of your stories in this book. I so look forward to helping you in whatever way I can with your own parenting journeys.

- John, Peter and Penelope – my creative siblings. I can't even count how many wonderful sibling writing retreats we've been on together! Or how many times you've helped me get back on track and encouraged me to finish this book. What fun we've had together! Penny, our weekly writing days in our cabins have been invaluable. Thanks for believing in me.

- All the beautiful women who have shared the journey with me. Pilgrims together. Over the years, we've laughed, cried and prayed together. We've helped each other and shared much-needed counsel and comfort and encouragement. Thank you for your precious friendship.

- Chris Bovill, visionary and founder of H.E.A.R.T (Home Educator's Annual RetreaT). You received the idea of H.E.A.R.T, fresh from the heart of God, and you did it! And thousands of women have been blessed because of your obedience and hard work. Thank you, my friend, for inviting me to speak at the conferences, year after year after year. It has been my great joy.

- God, the Father of mercies and God of all comfort. My faithful friend and Saviour. You've led me and guided me my whole life long. You've given me blessing after blessing, and crowned the years with your goodness. Thank you with all my heart for my loving husband and six wonderful children. I feel so blessed to have been able to stay at home and teach my children these past 23 years. You are the one who has filled our home with joy. Your presence is gezellig to me.

About the Author

Rosie lives with her husband, Chris, on a small lifestyle block in Northland, New Zealand. They have six adult children, whom she homeschooled for 23 years. *Heart to Heart with Rosie Boom* is written from those years of experience.

Rosie spent three years as a young child in Papua New Guinea, where her parents were missionaries. After graduating from her nursing training, she spent a year in Borneo as a missionary, before marrying Chris in 1987.

Rosie has written eleven books and is the author of the multi-award-winning series *The Barn Chronicles*. She is a sought–after speaker at homeschooling conventions, women's conferences, schools and churches, where she loves to speak about faith and family.

For Speaking Engagements and Bookings

Contact Rosie at:

Boom Tree Publishing

Rosie Boom

Whangarei

New Zealand

Email: *rosie@rosieboom.com*

Rosie's Website and Blog: *www.rosieboom.com*

Scan the Q-Code below to access Rosie's website on your phone.

To order additional copies of this book:
Visit: *www.rosieboom.com*

Other books by Rosie Boom

The Gift of Values - Volume 1

Do you struggle with family devotions? Do you long to help your children develop values such as honesty and perseverance? Volume 1 covers the following values:

Honesty	Right Attitudes
Courage	Perseverance
Diligence	Obedience.

Written primarily for parents to use with their children this is a practical book, easy to use, with plenty of stories, inspirational quotes, creative ideas and personal sharing. Printed hardcover, brown leather look with gold foiling trim.

The Gift of Values - Volume 2

More creative ideas to teach your children the following values:

Self control	Compassion
Encouragement	Generosity
Patience	Forgiveness.

Printed hardcover, blue leather look with silver foil trim.

The Happy Prince

A re-telling of Oscar Wilde's story about a golden statue of a prince and the little swallow that alights at its feet one night on his way to Egypt. Includes a CD with the story told in a ten-minute song. Full page colour illustrations throughout.

Available from your local Christian bookstore or online at *www.rosieboom.com*

Other Books by Rosie Boom

The Barn Chronicles - Book 1

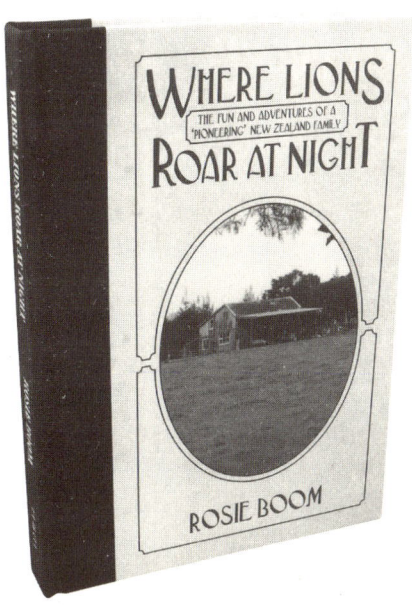

Where Lions Roar at Night - The fun and adventures of a 'pioneering' New Zealand family

Ten-year-old Milly had always dreamed of living in the country and owning all sorts of animals. So when her parents buy a piece of land and move their six children into a ninety-year-old barn, Milly can't believe her luck. But she never imagined that living the simple life would include mucking out a filthy water tank, gathering endless supplies of firewood, clearing the land, and rescuing animals in a 'hundred year' storm.

Nor did she expect to hear deep groanings in the night...

This book is the first in *The Barn Chronicles* series, and tells of the exciting, humourous adventures of the Boom family as they make their home in a 90-year-old barn. They are told in Rosie's unique style and are suitable for primary age readers, or to be read to children by parents.

Winner of the 2010 CALEB PRIZE for Best Children's Book

Available from your local Christian bookstore or online at *www.rosieboom.com*

The Barn Chronicles - Book 2

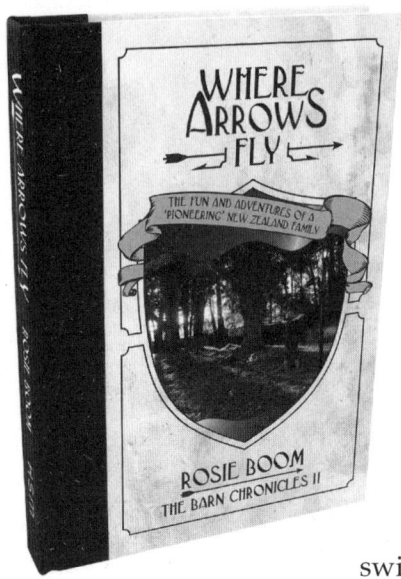

Where Arrows Fly - The fun and adventures of a 'pioneering' New Zealand family

As eleven-year-old Milly and her family begin their second year of living in the ninety-year-old barn, Milly has never been happier. While Dad and Mum are busy building the new family home, the children are messing about on the land. Their days are full of adventures - horse riding, camping in Lantern Waste, making huts, canoeing and swimming in the river, archery... and all the while, Milly's collection of animals continues to grow. But one thing is missing. Milly dreams of milking her very own cow. However when the time finally comes, Milly discovers that training a house cow is not as easy as she thought it would be...

Where Arrows Fly is the sequel to *Where Lions Roar at Night* and is the second book in *The Barn Chronicles* series by New Zealand author Rosie Boom. Read about the continuing adventures of the Boom family and the everyday joys and challenges of the 'simple life'.

Winner of the 2011 CALEB PRIZE for Best Children's Book

Available from your local Christian bookstore or online at *www.rosieboom.com*

The Barn Chronicles - Book 3

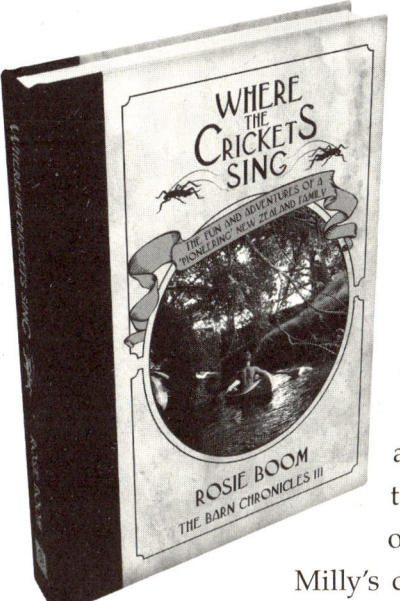

**Where the Crickets Sing -
The fun and adventures of a 'pioneering' New Zealand family**

Going on the pony trek to the beach is a dream come true for twelve-year-old Milly—trekking over high hills, swimming Peony in the sea, galloping along the beach. But when tragedy strikes, the excitement turns to tears.

Adventures, dramas, laughter and some tears are all part of the rich tapestry of the Boom family's third year of living in their ninety–year–old barn. Milly's days are full to the brim as she cares for her animals, milks her cow, enjoys adventures with her brothers and sisters, and helps Mum and Dad build the new family home. She is as happy as a cricket. But that doesn't stop her lying awake at night, dreaming of hitching Peony to a wagon, climbing into the high wagon seat and picking up the reins…

Where the Crickets Sing, the third book in *The Barn Chronicles* series, invites the reader to join the Boom family in another year of homesteading in rural New Zealand.

**Finalist in the 2012 CALEB PRIZE for Best Children's Book
Winner 2013 Christian Small Publishers International
Book of the Year Award Children's Category**

**Available from your local Christian bookstore
or online at *www.rosieboom.com***

The Barn Chronicles - Book 4

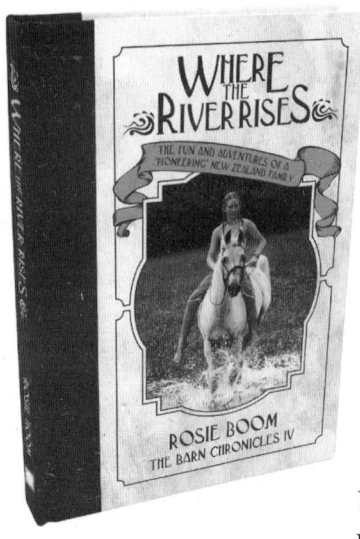

Where the River Rises - **The fun and adventures of a 'pioneering' New Zealand family**

As the Boom family begins a fourth year of living in their ninety-three-year-old barn, a terrible drought has Northland in its grip. The land turns brown, the Great River of Narnia falls, and the animals begin to suffer. As the relentless drought continues, thirteen-year-old Milly begins to think the rains will never come. But meanwhile there is a homestead to be finished and adventures to be had. There are calves to rear, gardens to plant and endless firewood to be collected.

By the time the drought finally breaks and the river rises again, The Ruins have been transformed into a home crafted with love, blood, sweat and tears. Milly can hardly wait to move in. The time has finally come to leave the barn and begin a whole new adventure...

"A modern–day *'Little House on the Prairie'*, and every bit as charming as that classic. My daughter sat spellbound as we read *The Barn Chronicles*. In an era where wholesome, entertaining children's novels are increasingly hard to come by, this series is a gem."

Lisa Taylor, mother, author of *Motive Games*

2013 CSP Book of the Year Award - Best Children's Book

Available from your local Christian bookstore or online at *www.rosieboom.com*

Other Books by Rosie Boom

The Barn Chronicles - Boxed Set

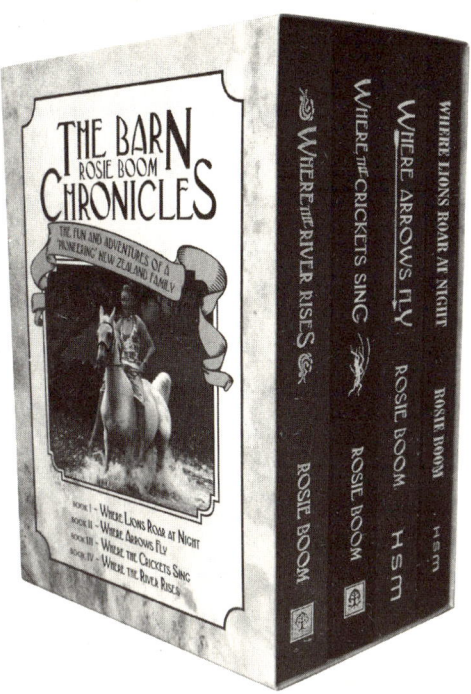

All four books of the award-winning series
The Barn Chronicles **now available in a boxed set.**

"*The Barn Chronicles* are amazing to read in the classroom. The children hang off every word, desperate to know what will happen next. Beautiful, real-life, wholesome read-aloud books. I am sure they will be favourites for many years to come."

Samantha Long, teacher

**Available from your local Christian bookstore
or online at *www.rosieboom.com***

Where the Jungle Calls

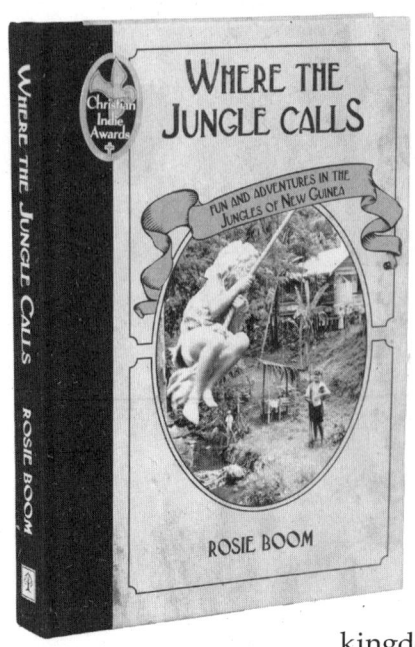

***Where the Jungle Calls -*
The fun adventures in the Jungles of New Guinea**

A long time before *The Barn Chronicles,* Rose lived in the big city. But one day her life changed forever …

Rose, Penny and Peter find themselves swept away into a great adventure, sailing the blue Pacific to a mission school deep in the jungles of Papua New Guinea. There they become adventurers and explorers in their own wild kingdom. They swim and fish in the rivers and make huts and gardens where they grow pineapples, peanuts and bananas. They chase huge emerald and blue butterflies. They run barefoot and free, and imagine themselves as Tarzan and Jane, swinging on vines through the jungle.

But there are hidden dangers lurking: snakes, scorpions, jerry-wars, malaria – and in the sea and rivers are fearsome crocodiles …

Here in the jungles of Papua New Guinea, the readers of *The Barn Chronicles* will meet familiar characters in a different time, a different place. This is where their adventures first began.

**Winner 2021 Christian Indie Award
Children's Category (8 – 12 years)**

**Available from your local Christian bookstore
or online at *www.rosieboom.com***

References

1. Masset, Claire. (2016). *Beatrix Potter's Hill Top.* The History Press.
2. Lincoln, Abraham. (n.d.). https://www.brainyquote.com/quotes/abraham_lincoln_145909
3. Wesley, John. (n.d.). https://www.azquotes.com/quote/1307114
4. Ten Boom, Corrie. (1973). *The Hiding Place.* Hodder and Stoughton and Christian Literature Crusade.
5. Ten Boom, Corrie. (1973). *The Hiding Place.* Hodder and Stoughton and Christian Literature Crusade.
6. Ruffini, Giovanni. (n.d.). https://www.azquotes.com/quote/543781
7. Van Dyke, Henry. (n.d.). https://www.gutenberg.org/files/1139/1139-h/1139-h.htm
8. Carmichael, Amy. (1973). *Gold by Moonlight.* SPCK Publishing.
9. Covey, S. R. (1997). *The 7 habits of highly effective families: building a beautiful family culture in a turbulent world.* Golden Books.
10. Hendrik, Bill. (2010). *Family Dinners Reduce Teen Drug Use.* https://www.webmd.com/parenting/news/20100922/family-dinners-reduce-teen-drug-use
11. Eyre, Linda and Richard. (1993). *Teaching your Children Values.* Simon and Schuster.
12. Boom, Rosie. (2006) *The Gift of Values* – Volume One. HSM Publishing.
13. Shepard, Priscilla. *Fields of Gold.* (1975). The C. R. Gibson Company.
14. Emerson, Ralph. (n.d.). https://www.brainyquote.com/quotes/ralph_waldo_emerson_104538
15. Taylor, Dr and Mrs Howard. (1973). *Biography of James Hudson Taylor.* Hodder and Stoughton.
16. Campbell, Nancy. (2017). *The Power of Motherhood.* Campbell House Publishing.
17. Tibballs, Geoff. (2009). *Just Like Dad Says: A Book of Dad's Wit.* Ebury Press.
18. Watkins, Julian Lewis. (1949). *The 100 Greatest Advertisements 1852–1958: Who Wrote Them and What They Did.* The Moore Publishing Company.
19. Watterson, Bill. (1996). *There's Treasure Everywhere.* Andrews and McMeel.
20. Taylor Scott, Ida. (n.d.). https://www.quotes.net/quote/42536
21. Shakespeare, William. (1908). *The Complete Works of William Shakespeare.* Ward, Lock & Co., Limited.
22. Porter, Katherine Ann. (2013). *The Days Before.* TheClassics.us.

23   Whishaw, Constance M. (1905). *Character and Conduct: A Book of Helpful Thoughts by Great Writers of Past and Present Ages*. Simpkin, Marshall, Hamilton, Kent & Co.

24   Whishaw, Constance M. (1905). *Character and Conduct, A Book of Helpful Thoughts by Great Writers of Past and Present Ages*. Simpkin, Marshall, Hamilton, Kent & Co. Ltd., London.

25   C.N. Douglas (Ed.) (1917). Forty Thousand Quotations: Prose and Poetical. Halcyon House.

26   Ward, William W. (n.d.). https://www.brainyquote.com/quotes/william_arthur_ward_105215

27   Jackson Brown Jr., H. (n.d.). https://www.brainyquote.com/quotes/h_jackson_brown_jr_124501

28   Brault, Robert. (1997). *Book of Positive Quotations*. Fairview Press.

29   Hattersley, Roy. (2000). *Blood and Fire: The Story of William and Catherine Booth and the Salvation Army*. Doubleday.

30   Sunday, Billy. (n.d.). https://www.brainyquote.com/quotes/billy_sunday_183042

31   Milne, A. A. (1992). *The House at Pooh Corner*. Puffin Books.

32   Elliot, Elizabeth. (1978). *The Journals of Jim Elliot: Missionary, Martyr, Man of God*. Revell.

33   Campbell, Nancy. (2017). *The Power of Motherhood*. Campbell House Publishing.

34   Lewis, C. S. (2014). *The Silver Chair*. HarperCollins Publishers.

35   Corbett, James J. (n.d.). https://quotefancy.com/quote/1146097/James-J-Corbet

36   Emerson, Ralph W. (n.d.) https://www.goodreads.com/quotes/20326-adopt-the-pace-of-nature-her-secret-is-patience

37   Davis, Harry. (2000). *Forever Christmas,* Tasha Tudor. Little Brown and Company.

38   Dr. Seuss. (n.d.). https://www.brainyquote.com/quotes/dr_seuss_106026

39   Shepard, Priscilla. (1975). *Fields of Gold*. The C. R. Gibson Company.

40   Rousmaniere, Dana. (2015). *Give People Time and Space to Be More Creative* https://hbr.org/tip/2016/02/give-people-time-and-space-to-be-more-creative.

41   Thorp, Clare. (2020). *How Boredom Can Spark Creativity*. https://www.bbc.com/culture/article/20200522-how-boredom-can-spark-creativity

42   BBC. (1955, 13 Feb.). *Agatha Christie Interview* [TV broadcast]. https://www.bbc.co.uk/archive/agatha-christie-interview/zmwdvk7

References

43	De Witt Talmage, Thomas. (n.d.). https://quotefancy.com/quote/1617136/Thomas-De-Witt-Talmage-A-mother-is-a-bank-where-I-deposit-all-my-worries-and-hurts
44	National Oregon/California Trail Center. (2022). *The History and Significance of Grandma's Apron*. https://oregontrailcenter.org/blog/the-history-and-significance-of-grandmas-apron/
45	Dengler, Sandy. (1987). *Susanna Wesley – Servant of God*. Moddy Publishers.
46	Fairless, Michael. (2015). *The Roadmender*. Leopold Classic Library.
47	Keller, Timothy. (2009). *The Reason for God*. Penguin Books.
48	General Synod of the Anglican Church of Canada. (2001). *Eucharistic Prayers, Services of the Word, and Night Prayer*. ABC Publishing.
49	General Synod of the Anglican Church of Canada. (2001). *Eucharistic Prayers, Services of the Word, and Night Prayer*. ABC Publishing.
50	Wilson, Dorothy Clarke. (1996). *Granny Brand: Her Story*. Paul Brand Pub.
51	Markham, Edwin. (n.d.). https://www.brainyquote.com/quotes/edwin_markham_161556
52	de Montaigne, Michel. (n.d.). https://www.brainyquote.com/quotes/michel_de_montaigne_103821
53	Wilson, Dorothy Clarke. (1996). *Granny Brand: Her Story*. Paul Brand Pub.
54	Fey, Tina. (2022). https://www.brainyquote.com/quotes/tina_fey_429673
55	The Amplified Bible. (2004). Zondervan Publishing House.
56	Debussy, Claude. (n.d.). https://quotepark.com/quotes/1397833-claude-debussy-music-is-the-space-between-the-notes
57	Bartlett, John. (1992) *Bartlett's Familiar Quotations: A Collection of Passages, Phrases, and Proverbs Traced to Their Sources in Ancient and Modern Literature*. Little, Brown.
58	Boom, Rosie. (2006). *The Gift of Values – Volume One*. HSM.
59	Tolkien, J. R. R. (1955). *The Return of the King*, George Allen & Unwin.
60	Churchill, Jill. (n.d.). https://www.azquotes.com/quote/533612
61	Bunyan, John. (2022). https://www.azquotes.com/quote/701580.
62	Dillow, L. (2007). *Calm My Anxious Heart*. Navpress Publishing Group.
63	de Montaigne, Michel. (2022). https://www.brainyquote.com/quotes/michel_de_montaigne_108601.
64	Bunyan, John. (1678). *The Pilgrim's Progress*. Nathaniel Ponde.
65	Wilson, Dorothy Clarke. (1996). *Granny Brand: Her Story*. Paul Brand Pub.
66	Boom, Rosie. (2010). *Where Arrows Fly*. Boom Tree Publishing.

67	Louv, Richard. (2008). *Last Child in the Woods*. Algonquin Books.
68	Louv, Richard. (2008). *Last Child in the Woods*. Algonquin Books.
69	Shepard, Priscilla. (1975). *Fields of Gold*. The C. R. Gibson Company.
70	Conroy, Pat. (2022). https://www.brainyquote.com/quotes/pat_conroy_378941.
71	Tennyson, Alfred. (1851). *Poetical Works of Alfred Lord Tennyson*. Ballantyne, Hanson & Co.
72	Shepard, Priscilla. (1975). *Fields of Gold*. The C. R. Gibson Company.
73	Gosman, Fred G. (n.d.). https://www.brainyquote.com/quotes/fred_g_gosman_400123
74	Barker, Joanne. (2022). *5 Mistakes Parents Make with Teens and Tweens*. https://www.webmd.com/parenting/features/parenting-mistakes-teens
75	Dobson, Dr James. (2018) *Bringing Up Boys*. Tyndale House Publishers.
76	Carlson, R. (1999). *Don't Sweat the Small Stuff at Work: Simple Ways to Minimize Stress and Conflict While Bringing Out the Best in Yourself and Others*. Bantam.
77	Clarkson, Sally (2019). *Ancient Boundaries for Modern Times*. https://sallyclarkson.com/blog/2019/1/31/ancient-boundaries-for-modern-times
78	Dickens, Charles. (1850). *David Copperfield*, Bradbury & Evans.
79	Ford, Henry. (n.d.). https://www.goodreads.com/quotes/978-whether-you-think-you-can-or-you-think-you-can-t--you-re
80	Mather, Victor. (2021, 18 March). *Dick Hoyt, Who Ran Marathons While Pushing His Son, Dies at 80*. https://www.nytimes.com/2021/03/18/sports/dick-hoyt-dead.html
81	Rhema. (n.d.). *The word for today* [Radio broadcast]. Rhema
82	Spurgeon, Charles. (2010). *Lectures to My Students*. Hendrickson Publishers.
83	Dr. Seuss. (2022). https://www.brainyquote.com/quotes/dr_seuss_414097.
84	Graham, Ruth Bell. (2008). *Prodigals and Those Who Love them*. Baker Books.
85	McKay, Brett and Kate. (2013) *Creating a Positive Family Culture: The Importance of Establishing Family Traditions*. The Art of Manliness.
86	Galinsky, Ellen. (1999). *Ask the Children*. William Morrow.
87	Cox, Meg. (2003). *The Book of New Family Traditions*, Running Press.
88	Cox, Meg. (2003). *The Book of New Family Traditions*, Running Press.
89	Carlson, R. (1999). *Don't Sweat the Small Stuff at Work: Simple Ways to Minimize Stress and Conflict While Bringing Out the Best in Yourself and Others*. Bantam.
90	Milne, A. A. (1992). *The House at Pooh Corner*. Puffin Books.

References

91 Comer, J. M. (2019). *The Ruthless Elimination of Hurry*. WaterBrook.
92 Graham, Billy (2004). *The Enduring Classics of Billy Graham*. Thomas Nelson.
93 Childcare Answers. (2022). *Responding to Toddler Behaviour and Emotions*. https://childcareanswers.org/resources/toddler-behaviors/#:~:text=Play%20helps%20build%20a%20warm,ideas%2C%20and%20explore%20their%20imaginations
94 Aha! Parenting (2022). *Peaceful Parenting Your Strong-willed Child*. https://www.ahaparenting.com/read/Parenting-Strong-Willed-Child
95 Lott, L. (2007). *Positive Discipline A–Z*. Harmony.
96 Mencken, H. L. (2022). https://quozio.com/quote/5af4216d/1025/morality-is-doing-whats-right-no-matter-what-youre-told
97 Collins Dictionaries. (2018). *The Collins English Dictionary*. Collins.
98 Dengler, Sandy. (1987). *Susanna Wesley – Servant of God*. Moddy Publishers
99 Cain, S. (2012). *Quiet: the power of introverts in a world that can't stop talking*. Random House.
100 Centre for Autism. (2022). *Social Narratives*. https://life-skills.middletownautism.com/background/teaching-life-skills/social-narratives/
101 Covey, S. R. (1997). *The 7 Habits of Highly Effective Families: Building a Beautiful Family Culture in a Turbulent World*. Golden Books.
102 Twain, Mark. (n.d.). https://www.brainyquote.com/quotes/mark_twain_100358
103 Covey, S. R. (1997). *The 7 Habits of Highly Effective Families: Building a Beautiful Family Culture in a Turbulent World*. Golden Books.
104 Chapman, G. (2010). *The Five Love Languages*. Farmington Hills.
105 Whishaw, Constance M. (1905). *Character and Conduct: A Book of Helpful Thoughts by Great Writers of Past and Present Ages*. Simpkin, Marshall, Hamilton, Kent & Co.
106 Whishaw, Constance M. (1905). *Character and Conduct: A Book of Helpful Thoughts by Great Writers of Past and Present Ages*. Simpkin, Marshall, Hamilton, Kent & Co.
107 Therese of Lisieux (n.d.). https://www.finestquotes.com/author_quotes-author-Therese%20of%20Lisieux-page-0.htm
108 Bailey, Faith Coxe. (1959). *D. L. Moody*. Moody Publishers.
109 Confucius. (n.d.). https://quotefancy.com/quote/2948/Confucius-He-who-knows-all-the-answers-has-not-been-asked-all-the-questions
110 Whishaw, Constance M. (1905). *Character and Conduct: A Book of Helpful Thoughts by Great Writers of Past and Present Ages*. Simpkin, Marshall, Hamilton, Kent & Co.

111	Bunyan, John. (1678). *The Pilgrim's Progress*. Nathaniel Ponder.
112	Cossman, E. Joseph. (n.d.). http://www.quotss.com/quote/The-best-bridge-between-despair-and-hope-is-a-good-night%E2%80%99s-sleep
113	Bonhoeffer, Dietrich. (n.d.). https://www.brainyquote.com/quotes/dietrich_bonhoeffer_164002
114	Hornby, A. (2020). *Oxford Advanced Learners Dictionary*. University Press.
115	Emerson, Ralph Waldo. (n.d.). https://www.brainyquote.com/quotes/ralph_waldo_emerson_106883
116	Saint Francis de Sales. (n.d.). https://www.brainyquote.com/quotes/saint_francis_de_sales_193306
117	Chinese Proverb Quotes. (n.d.). https://allauthor.com/quote/4990
118	Keller, Helen. (n.d.). https://www.brainyquote.com/quotes/helen_keller_385215
119	de Balzac, Honore. (n.d.). https://www.brainyquote.com/quotes/honore_de_balzac_145948
120	Tolkien, J. R. R. (1954). *The Fellowship of the Ring*. George Allen & Unwin.
121	Linnros, Clara (2022). *Sibling Squabbles*. https://www.medscinet.com/bvcelvis/syskonbrak.aspx?lang=2
122	Deatrick, Mary Rae. (1079). *Easing the Pain of Parenthood*. Harvest House Publishers.
123	Shepard, Priscilla. *Fields of Gold*. (1975). The C. R. Gibson Company.
124	Absurdness.com (2005). Donkey lifted by cart. https://www.flickr.com/photos/turtlebird/12224390
125	Drummond, Henry. (2018). *Pax Vobiscum*. Franklin Classics Trade Press.
126	Smith, Gipsy. (2012). *Gipsy Smith: His Life and Work*. Kingsley Press.
127	Carter, William Hodding. (1953). *Where Main Street Meets the River*. Rinehart & Company.
128	Carmichael, Amy. (1973). *Gold by Moonlight*. SPCK Publishing.
129	Dillow, L. (2007). *Calm My Anxious Heart*. Navpress Publishing Group.
130	Johnson, Barbara. (2005). *The Best of Barbara Johnson*. Thomas Nelson.
131	Wikipedia contributors. (2021, October 7). *Second wind*. In Wikipedia, The Free Encyclopedia. https://en.wikipedia.org/w/index.php?title=Second_wind&oldid=1048776722
132	The American Heritage Medical Dictionary. (2004) Houghton Mifflin Company.
133	Second wind. (n.d.) *The American Heritage Dictionary of Idioms* by Christine Ammer. (2003). https://idioms.thefreedictionary.com/second+wind
134	Collins Concise English Dictionary. (2006). HarperCollins Publishers.

References

135	Wikipedia contributors. (2021, October 7). *Second wind*. In Wikipedia, The Free Encyclopedia. https://en.wikipedia.org/w/index.php?title=Second_wind&oldid=1048776722
136	Phillips, Casey. (2012). *Experts say getting your 'second wind' is a real phenomenon.* https://www.timesfreepress.com/news/2012/apr/19/second-wind-101-runner-energy
137	Newspapers.com. (1916, 27 Jan). *Helen Keller is Favourite Here.* https://www.newspapers.com/clip/109894784/january-27-1916-helen-keller-here/
138	Wellman, Sam. (1997). *William Carey: Father of Missions.* Barbour Publishing, Inc.
139	Culross, James. (2019). *William Carey.* Wentworth Press.
140	Einstein, Albert. (n.d.). https://www.brainyquote.com/quotes/albert_einstein_106192
141	Hudson, Hugh (director). (2010). *Chariots of fire.* Warner Home Video.
142	*Oxford Dictionary of English.* (2010). Oxford University Press.
143	*The Collins English Dictionary.* (2018). Collins.
144	Wikipedia contributors. (2022, November 24). *Endurance*. In Wikipedia, The Free Encyclopedia. https://en.wikipedia.org/w/index.php?title=Endurance&oldid=1123495833
145	*The Collins English Dictionary.* (2018). Collins.
146	*Oxford Dictionary of English.* (2010). Oxford University Press.
147	Shepard, Priscilla. *Fields of Gold.* (1975). The C. R. Gibson Company.
148	Buchwald, Emilie. (n.d.). https://www.goodreads.com/quotes/9274-children-are-made-readers-on-the-laps-of-their-parents
149	Bramwell-Booth, Catherine. (1973). *Catherine Booth.* Hodder & Stoughton Ltd.
150	Park, R. (1992). *A Fence Around the Cuckoo.* Viking Books.

Index

A

Accidents:	275
Addiction:	24, 141, 170, 180
Adventure:	24, 41, 90, 145, 148, 204, 311
Affirmation:	237 - 8
Allegory:	139, 140, 263
Allowance:	28, 178
Always child:	232
Anxiety:	36, 161, 203, 212, 234, 242, 297
Approval:	62, 75, 81, 237 - 8
Apron:	97 - 108
Assembly:	248

B

Babies:	7, 10, 17 - 8, 37, 81, 92, 115, 122, 152, 230, 285, 298
Blessing:	7, 10, 16, 18 - 23, 27, 34, 37, 44, 69, 83, 92, 107, 142, 153, 201, 215, 217 - 8, 232, 241 - 2, 244 - 5, 248, 253, 261, 263
Booth, Catherine:	41, 317
Boredom:	94 - 5, 160
Borneo:	5, 28, 40, 196
Brand, Jesse, Evie, Paul:	109 - 10, 117, 145 - 6
Brokenness:	110 - 1, 117, 138
Building:	13, 15 - 6, 26, 42, 44, 50, 67, 80, 148, 292, 319
Bunyan, John:	138 - 140, 262 - 3

C

Caricature:	16 - 7, 165
Carey, William:	305 - 6, 310
Carmichael, Amy:	18, 37, 257, 292, 307
Change:	17, 35, 53, 58, 62 - 3, 65 - 7, 86, 92, 122, 161 - 2, 196, 202, 219, 234 - 5, 267, 282 - 3, 318 - 9
Character training:	29, 34, 80, 87, 170, 312
Chores:	6, 22, 34, 143, 177 - 8, 232
Communication:	26, 50, 59, 66, 167, 222, 237
Comparison:	17, 79 - 80
Compass, moral:	50, 54, 250, 262
Compassionate:	10, 97, 102
Co-operation:	188, 222, 225

Index

Conflict:	67 - 8, 164, 192, 196, 209, 211, 219, 222, 278, 282		
Conscience:	191, 244, 250 - 1, 253, 265		
Consistency:	188, 210, 225, 282,		
Covey, Stephen:	22, 49, 50 - 1, 54 - 5, 84, 92, 235 - 6		
Cracks:	115 - 118		
Criticism:	66, 68, 237 - 8		
Cuckoo:	322		

D

Dates:	20 - 22, 58, 202, 219, 283
Debussy, Claude:	119
Decisions:	116, 224, 253, 256, 262, 265 - 6
Defeat:	107, 114, 131, 134
Devotions, family:	27 - 29, 34, 87
Diastole:	121 - 123
Dinner table:	25 - 6, 198, 232
Disappointment:	65, 168, 269
Discouragement:	46 - 7, 130, 267, 278, 291, 309
Dobson, James:	24, 163, 220
Doubt:	129 - 130, 161, 214
Drugs:	26, 65, 139, 163, 179, 233
Drummond, Henry:	287
Dyslexia:	2, 12, 74, 82, 271 - 2

E

Edelweiss:	18 - 9
Encouragement:	44, 54, 62, 75, 83, 116, 134, 141, 165, 193, 236, 238, 297, 300, 303
Exemption, homeschooling:	36
Extroverts:	67, 233

F

Failure:	6, 28, 45, 47, 53, 73 - 5, 113 - 4, 117, 131, 188, 249, 282, 287, 306 - 7, 320
Faith:	3, 12, 27 -9 31, 43, 60, 85, 116, 169, 170, 196, 201, 243, 263, 270, 305
Fatigue:	47, 67
Fear of God:	104, 243 - 252
Finance:	59, 107, 166
Finishing:	6, 169, 307, 320
Folly:	254 - 257
Forgiveness:	29, 64 - 5, 137 - 8, 189, 192, 226 - 7, 238, 250, 277 - 8, 281 - 2
Fuel :	72 -3, 77 - 87,
Fun:	20, 27, 34, 50 - 55, 181, 183, 200, 206, 218, 280, 283, 316

G

Galileo:	134
Gentleness:	68, 171
Gezellig:	9 - 31, 54, 234, 311, 216
Gift of Values:	29, 34, 94, 130, 170
Giovanni, Fra:	87
Goals:	73 - 5, 84, 201, 273
Grapple:	37, 168, 270, 272
Gratitude:	18, 83, 205
Gray, Carol:	234

H

Habits:	66, 195
Haste:	94, 213, 237, 265
Hearting:	44
Holy Spirit:	84, 87
Home-schooling, journey:	33 - 8, 71 - 6, 120, 134, 169, 186, 275, 308, 318, 320
Hospitality:	23, 54, 75
Hoyt, Rick, Dick:	185 - 6
Humour:	86, 219
Hurry:	94, 213 - 4, 272

I

Impatience:	108, 162, 270 - 2, 274 - 5
Internet:	36, 44, 94, 106, 125, 149, 178 - 9, 244
Interruptions:	212 - 3
Introverts:	233

J

Joy, stealers:	17, 80

K

Keller, Helen:	276, 303 - 4
Keller, Timothy:	102
Kindness:	52, 62 - 3, 189, 213, 241

L

Laughter:	10, 22, 26 -7, 31, 75, 86
Leaders:	217, 227
Lewis, C.S:	84
Life skills:	92 - 3, 161, 172, 177 - 183, 278 - 9
Listen:	26, 52, 68, 93 - 4, 123 - 4, 140, 154 - 5, 159, 163, 167, 171, 183, 190 - 2, 221, 230, 232, 238, 243 - 4, 248, 250, 254 - 9, 280, 297
Lott, Lyn:	223
Love languages:	237

M

Marathon:	6, 123, 185 - 6, 298 - 300
Marriage:	15, 17, 52, 57 - 69
Memories:	20, 204 -5
Memorisation:	35 - 6, 55, 104, 106, 241, 249, 297
Mission statement:	49 - 55
Motherhood:	17 - 9, 42, 45

N

Nature,
deficit disorder: 148
Newton, John: 137 - 8
New Guinea: 5, 20, 148, 311
Noisy children: 6, 46, 83, 158, 232, 273, 319
Nurture: 3, 12, 166, 208

O

Opportunities: 18, 80, 91, 153, 222, 238, 262
Over-react: 226

P

Parenting, permissive: 221
Patience: 85, 108, 175, 269 - 276, 279, 303
Peace: 87, 90, 143, 187, 190, 207 - 215, 219, 276
Perseverance: 186, 224, 272, 303, 309
Physical touch: 20, 166, 219, 237
Pilgrimage: 248
Pilgrim's Progress: 262
Play: 12, 21, 50, 93, 95, 154, 213, 217, 238, 242, 273
Plod: 305 - 310
Power struggle: 220
Prayer: 28, 46, 65, 69, 83 - 4, 99 - 108, 123, 196, 212, 249, 272
Pride: 80, 247
Priorities: 267
Prodigal: 116
Prophetic word: 133

Q

Qualifications: 171 - 2
Quality time: 19, 36, 165, 202, 219, 237
Quarrels: 63 - 4, 277
Questions: 10, 26, 30, 52 - 3, 78, 110, 142, 161 - 2, 166 - 7, 170, 183, 191, 197, 230, 249, 253, 260, 264 - 5, 271 - 2

R

Read aloud books: 27, 34, 197, 257, 311 - 6
Rebellion: 132, 137 - 9, 163, 247
Refreshing: 291 - 8
Relationships: 15, 20, 36, 52, 58, 60, 62, 64, 69, 172, 182, 227, 238 - 9, 257
Remembrance: 84
Repentance: 189, 192, 249
Risks: 148
Routines: 195, 225
Rutherford, Samuel: 58

S

Second wind:	298 - 305
Selah:	119 - 125, 190
Seuss, Dr:	192
Sexual purity:	189
Shadows:	229 - 234
Siblings:	18, 79, 230, 232, 277 - 8, 282 - 3
Silence:	61, 120, 124, 214
Slow down:	17, 64, 213
Stars:	2, 39 - 47
Stone walls:	44
Strong willed, children:	130, 189, 217 - 227, 230
Structure:	33, 35, 89 - 95, 119 - 120
St. Francis of Assisi:	215
Sullivan, Anne:	303

T

Taylor, Hudson:	40 - 1
Tears:	55, 98, 102, 110, 139, 173, 213, 218, 291, 294
Teenagers:	22, 50 - 1, 141, 161 - 175, 218, 230, 244, 263 - 4, 275
Ten Boom, Corrie:	5, 9 -13, 107, 257
Tennyson:	151
Thankfulness:	83
The Hiding Place:	5, 9 - 10, 60
Time:	3, 19, 94 -5, 99, 110, 122 - 5, 249
Tiredness:	17, 87, 210
Tongue:	52, 61 -2, 140, 236, 239, 241, 297
Traditions:	25, 195 - 206
Twain, Mark:	62, 161, 236

U

V

Values:	2, 29, 50, 54, 80, 115, 156, 171, 196, 198, 264, 312
Van Dyke:	18, 31
Vessel, cracked:	109 - 118

W

Weeping:	102, 139
Wesley, Susanna:	97 - 108, 122, 231,
Wisdom:	64, 68, 82, 100, 140, 175, 190, 220, 253 - 268, 271, 320
Working together:	22, 42 -6, 59, 152
Words, power of:	61 - 2, 66, 68, 107, 140, 142, 226, 235 - 240, 282, 302
Worry:	78, 107, 129, 139, 209, 211, 287, 292, 308

X

Y

Yoke:	286 - 8

Z